CONFRONTATION

Confrontation

Norman Garbo AND *Howard Goodkind*

Harper & Row, Publishers

NEW YORK

FIRST EDITION

LIBRARY OF CONGRESS CATALOG CARD NUMBER: 66-10643

C-Q

For Adele and Rhoda
And also, of course, for
Mickey, Bob, Jim and Tom

Statement from the Authors

The authors have chosen for their story a time of fear and accusation, when the United States was tuned to a high emotional pitch, and when even the strongest men searched their pasts for youthful errors in judgment that might, if revealed, ruin them and their families. For dramatic purposes, and to provide verisimilitude, it was necessary to include references to historical figures of the period. The fictional characters with whom the book is concerned lived and worked in Washington, D.C., and inevitably their imaginary lives involved them with the President of the United States, the Secretary of State, and other high government officials. But these incidents were entirely fabricated. In every sense, this book is a work of pure fiction and is not intended to resemble any event or series of events. Neither are the characters intended to resemble any actual persons, living or dead.

CONFRONTATION

Chapter One

1952: New York City

The sound engineer in the control booth adjusted his earphones and leaned comfortably back in his chair. Amid a complex of switches and flashing lights, he appeared relaxed, almost bored. He toyed with a dial and watched Justin Blaine through his glass partition. The commentator at the radio microphone was running a bit behind schedule as he neared the close of his evening newscast. Glancing at the big studio clock, the sound man saw that it was 7:12. He held up three warning fingers and waited for Blaine to notice.

Without breaking the cadence of his delivery, Justin Blaine lifted a hand to acknowledge the signal. He worked in shirt sleeves before a paper-strewn desk, and talked in a rambling, easy style that kept him at the top of the national rating lists. His manner also played havoc with time schedules.

This evening Blaine was decrying the situation in Korea, condemning the tragicomic fact of thousands dying in a war that was being euphemistically referred to as a "police action." His voice was angrier, harsher than usual, and although the studio was cool, beads of moisture stood out on his forehead.

The engineer looked once more at the clock. It said 7:14. He

1

held up one finger to signal the wrap-up. Blaine nodded . . . a solidly built, round-faced man with prematurely gray hair and horn-rimmed glasses. The lenses were thick, and the dark rims tended to give him the look, even in middle age, of an overly studious school-boy. He finished his last thought and ended with his famous clos-ing line, "Have a pleasant tomorrow." The control man twisted a series of dials and tuned in an announcer's voice from another studio.

"Mr. Blaine?"

Justin, who was stuffing papers into a briefcase, glanced up.

"Your wife called," the engineer reported. "She said not to forget to stop at the drugstore on your way home. Your prescrip-tion's ready."

Blaine nodded. He finished gathering his papers, straightened his tie and put on his jacket. Then he picked up his hat and coat from a chair and started toward the door. As he passed the control room, he rapped on the glass and waved good night to the engi-neer, who grinned and waved back.

Blaine pushed through the soundproofed door into the red-carpeted opulence of the tenth-floor corridor. He walked past the offices and studios of the news department, between rows of framed portraits of the network's commentators, all of whom were represented except himself. For a single day his own photograph had been there too, until he'd had it removed, pronouncing the display pretentious, embarrassing and offensive to his ideas of per-sonal privacy. The episode had made him the special peeve of the network's public relations department, as had his continued insist-ence on no personal publicity.

He stopped at a row of elevators and pressed the down button. Then, as he waited, he put on his coat, wrapped a wool scarf about his neck and buttoned up against the gale winds and driving rain outside. Blaine pressed the down button once more, and while he waited stared vacantly at the closed elevator door as his hand probed the inside pocket of his jacket. He felt the stiff, folded document resting there and fingered it carefully. He had done this many times in the past eight hours.

The elevator door slid open. "Down, sir?"

Blaine blinked at the elevator operator. He stood unmoving, apparently lost in thought.

"Down, Mr. Blaine?"

Blaine slowly shook his head. "No," he said. "I don't think so."

The man looked at him curiously. "You all right, Mr. Blaine?"

"What?"

"You all right?"

Blaine came out of it. "Yes," he said briskly. "Yes, of course. Forget it. I'm going up."

The operator seemed unconvinced, but shrugged and closed the elevator door. Blaine hesitated for a moment and then abruptly pressed the up button. The decision made, he paced impatiently. The up car arrived and he got on.

"Executive tower," he told the operator.

On the forty-ninth floor he stepped off into the chrome, marble and polished-wood luxury of the executive foyer. The reception desk was unattended. He peered into the next room and noted that Mannheim's secretary was gone and her typewriter neatly covered for the night. But the door to the President's private office was ajar and Blaine could see Mannheim still at his desk. He knocked.

"Phillip?" he said. "I thought for a moment the barn was empty."

Mannheim lifted his head and smiled.

"Hello, Justin. It's the damned storm. Everyone's run home early." He went on writing. "Sit down. I'll be with you in a minute."

Blaine removed his coat and dropped it onto a ten-foot maroon couch, but did not sit down. He lit a cigarette and slowly circled the huge, high-ceilinged room, with its towering glass walls which overlooked the lights of New York. The vertical blinds were open and sheets of wind-driven rain could be seen whipping fiercely against the tall casements. Mannheim had designed the tower himself, and the office and everything in it clearly reflected the flamboyance of his personality and range of interests. Framed photographs of celebrity friends crowded one walnut-paneled section, along with industry awards and an assortment of golf trophies.

"Come to think of it," Mannheim said, "this is the first time I've seen you around here more than five minutes after your broadcast." He dropped his pen and swiveled around to face Blaine. "I hope you're not going to put in a request for overtime."

Blaine was too abstracted to bother smiling. He was rarely amused by Mannheim's sarcasm. The network President was always careful to keep his remarks pleasantly light, but there was still an undertone of annoyance with Blaine's no-nonsense attitude toward his work. A devoted follower of the after-hours, drink and good-fellowship approach to professional achievement, Mannheim loved to slip in digs at his top commentator's refusal to be part of anything that did not deal directly with his job.

Mannheim laughed. "I envy you, Justin. The rest of us poor slobs are really afraid to walk away from this monster building at night. We're afraid to turn our backs on it as long as there's anyone left here to slip in the knife."

Blaine pulled one of the clubs from a golf bag standing in a corner and absently studied the curved, gleaming head. "Phillip Mannheim?" he said. "Afraid?"

"Phillip Mannheim most of all. It's a big drop for me . . . a long way down." He smiled. "Why do you think I'm the last one out every night and the first one here in the morning?"

Blaine slid the club back into its bag. Talk about fear. He wondered if he'd been smart to come up here at all.

"Let me tell you something," Mannheim said, his pale, sharp eyes serious. "You're lucky. All artists, performers, creative people are lucky. They've got something unique to offer, something special. In your case it's perception, an awareness of the true meaning of events, a sense of perspective, and the rare ability to project ideas with warmth and clarity. This insures your value. It's something no one else can steal or offer in your place. What have *I* got?"

"Three hundred thousand a year," Justin said, "plus stock options."

"I'm an executive," Mannheim said, ignoring the irony. "I'm a reasonably efficient executive, with a reasonably good brain, but I can name three other men at this network now who are just as capable as I and at least one who may be more so, and not a moment goes by that I don't feel their breath warming the back of my neck." He stared broodingly at the storm-lashed facings of his tower, then watched Blaine for a moment. "All right," he said. "What is it? You'd never come up here to make small talk. What's the trouble?"

Blaine removed the familiar, well-fingered document from his pocket, walked to Mannheim's desk and dropped it in front of him. Then he stood at one of the great, glass walls and peered down through the rain at the city. He had an odd sensation of floating in space.

"A subpoena?" Mannheim said.

Blaine did not turn. "A subpoena."

Mannheim frowned as he read aloud: "For 11:00 A.M. tomorrow morning before the House Subversive Activities Committee." There was a short silence. "I suppose they've finally found out you were a Communist."

Blaine turned, his eyes blinking rapidly behind his glasses. He must remember, he thought, never to underestimate this man. It could be fatal. "You knew?"

"Of course I knew. It's my job to know." Mannheim rose from behind his desk, each fold of his custom-tailored suit falling into place. He was a big man, well over six feet, and he knew how to use his height. He towered over Blaine. "Tom Gallagher told me you had been a member of the party when he first brought you into the network."

Blaine grimaced. "Good, old, loyal Tom."

"No, no," Mannheim said. "Tom did the right thing in telling us. We should know these things about our people. It didn't hurt you any here, did it? In less than twelve years you've gone from a minor job in the news department to the top of the heap as a commentator. Though I'm rather surprised it's taken the committee this long to track you down."

Mannheim picked a golf club from his bag and lined up an imaginary putt. "So you see," he said, "I've understood a bit more than you thought about that personal privacy mania of yours."

Blaine did not say anything. Mannheim went to the window and frowned out at the blackness. "It's like the end of the goddamn world up here," he said.

"For me," Blaine said gloomily, "it probably is."

Mannheim put away his club and waved impatiently.

"Don't talk nonsense. There's nothing for you to worry about. You're not a member of the party any more. This is something from years ago when Communism was just a parlor game you damned intellectuals enjoyed playing. The committee knows that. They'll have you down, ask a few questions to make the voters back home happy, and it'll all be over."

"It won't be as simple as that," Blaine said. "You know what the papers can do with something like this in an election year."

Mannheim shrugged. "There may be a bit of a fuss for a while, but it'll die down. Besides, the network'll be behind you. We've got a few drums of our own to beat."

Blaine shook his head. "I appreciate your support, but—"

"Christ!" Mannheim had suddenly noted the time. "It's nearly eight o'clock, and I'm late for another of my wife's stiff-assed dinner parties." He grabbed his coat from a standing rack and put it on."

"Listen," Blaine began but stopped. He wanted to tell Mannheim the rest of it, but was restrained by instinctive, long-practiced caution.

"Stop worrying!" Mannheim ordered. He reached for his hat with one hand and a monogrammed attaché case with the other. "You're a born worrier, Justin. Now just relax. You're no kid. You knew long ago what you were getting into with this Communist bit. So pay for it now with a little public embarrassment. It won't be that bad. I told you the network is behind you, didn't I? What else do you want me to do, fly to Washington with you and hold your hand in front of the committee?"

Blaine breathed deeply. "That won't be necessary."

"Do me a favor, will you?" Mannheim thrust a few final papers into his case and started toward the door. "Call my wife and tell her I'll be home in an hour. Tell her the Merritt Parkway's flooded. Tell her anything. Why the hell I ever let her talk me into a house in Connecticut . . . ! An hour's ride in a damned hurricane." He hurried out shaking his head.

Blaine stood looking after the tall man, wondering how clever he'd been to hold back the rest of the story. He knew what Mannheim was capable of if he thought he'd been played for a fool.

Blaine wandered morosely about the big office. The great CBN tower, he thought ruefully, a public landmark, a monument to power, the apex of a billion-dollar network, the source from which *his* voice reached several million listeners nightly. In nine years of party activity, with all his efforts to change the world, he had never influenced more than a minuscule fraction of the people he could now move in fifteen minutes of air time.

It was a lot to be giving up—the influence, the authority and the other good things that went with it. And give them up he must, for Mannheim's reassurances would mean nothing when the explosion came. Today, the high point; tomorrow, the start of the long downhill slide from eminence and the joy of getting fifty thousand a year for doing what he'd once have been happy to do for nothing. It had been easy to get used to these good things, especially for Alice. How easy would it be to get used to being without them—especially for Alice?

After calling Mannheim's home, he dialed his own home number. His wife answered on the third ring.

"Hi, Hon," he said. "I'll be a little late."

"A little late?" Alice Blaine's voice was sharp with concern. "Why? What's happened? Where are you?"

"In Mannheim's office."

"What on earth are you doing there?"

Blaine hesitated. "I told him," he said. "I hadn't expected to, but I decided to tell him."

"You *what?*"

Blaine pulled the phone away from his ear.

"What do you mean you told him? Are you crazy? How could you ever think of—"

"Take it easy!" Blaine cut her off. "I'll be home in half an hour. We'll talk about it then."

There was a short silence and Blaine had a clear image of his wife struggling to compose herself. "Your pills," she said at last, "don't forget to pick up your pills."

"I won't forget."

He hung up, gathered his things and went out to the elevator.

2

The subway was only half a block east from the CBN building, but Blaine was drenched by the time he started down the stone steps. "I'll look for a cab. Maybe you'll be lucky," the doorman had said. "Tonight I don't feel lucky," Justin had said, and had pushed on. Now he clutched the side rail as he descended, feeling for the steps cautiously. At the bottom, amid smells of urine and wet cloth, he stopped and wiped his glasses. He fumbled with one hand for a coin and then felt in his jacket for the subpoena. He briefly considered the irony of his fear of losing this thing which, of all things in the world, he would most like to be rid of. He pushed through the turnstile and stood waiting on the crowded platform for the Lexington Avenue local. When the train came and he sat swaying in the enclosed dark roar, he saw himself reflected in the grimy window across the aisle, shadowy and unreal, a lumpish middle-aged man. He was forty-six years old, he thought, and looked fifty-six. But when would he start feeling that way? Inside, he felt no different than he had at fifteen. Self-consciously he straightened his shoulders. He must remember not to slouch. And he must also lose twenty pounds. He looked like a fat, aging butcher.

The train lurched, throwing a young woman against him. Blaine wondered at his sudden interest in his own appearance. He usually paid as little attention to his person as he did to the furniture in his office. Was he perhaps considering the impression he'd make on the committee tomorrow? Well, they'd hardly be overwhelmed when he walked in. That would come later.

He came out of the subway at Sixty-eighth Street and walked west into the pelting rain. Then he remembered the prescription and had to go back to Lexington Avenue for it. He always resented the inconvenience of the pills, and especially the trouble with him that made them necessary. The doctor called it high blood pressure, but Justin knew it as a sudden racing of the heart and, if he didn't take a pill at the right time, dizziness leading to unconsciousness. The first attack had been enough to make him careful about the pills, however much he resented them.

The druggist had heard the broadcast about Korea. He fiercely brandished the bottle of pills. "I tell you, Mr. Blaine, we've got to show these lousy Commies the only thing they understand—a bayonet in the guts. We've got to let them know we—"

Justin virtually had to pull the pills from the druggist's hand to get away. Leaning into the wind-driven rain once more, he crossed Park Avenue against the light and was almost hit by a car he did not even see. Near the corner of Madison, he turned into one of a series of handsome, converted town houses. The brass-grilled door was unlocked and he entered the elaborate, marble lobby and shook a small puddle from the brim of his hat. He started toward a flight of graceful, winding stairs, but changed his mind and rode the self-service elevator to the second floor.

Alice Blaine opened the apartment door before Blaine had the key out of his pocket. "My God, you're soaked!" she said. "Couldn't you get a cab?"

"At the first drop of rain," he said, "every taxi in the city of New York instantly disappears from the streets." He took off his wet things and draped them over an antique coat rack in the hall. He kissed his wife's cheek and walked past her into the high-ceilinged library that opened off the foyer. His first glimpse of her face had told him just how bad the explosion was going to be, and he preferred having it take place in as comfortable surroundings as possible.

He did not have long to wait. Alice had picked up a towel from the guest bathroom and followed closely behind him. She handed him the towel and watched him stand before the fireplace, mopping his neck where the rain had run down the back of his collar.

"How could you?" she began quietly. "After all our training in the party—after all our years of living and learning the hard way —how could you just walk in there on *pure impulse* and tell something like this to Mannheim? Have you suddenly lost your mind?" Her voice rose. "Don't you think you should have at least discussed it with *me* first? Or have you forgotten I'm just as much a part of this as you?"

Justin sat down wearily in an armchair close to the fire. His face was drawn and behind his glasses, his eyes watered slightly. Mostly, he knew, she was just hurt at his not having consulted her. "No, I haven't forgotten. But there's—"

"You know there's *always* more than one way to handle things!" Alice Blaine's face showed more dismay than anger. She was a slender, blond, full-bosomed woman of forty-six, who at a quick glance might have passed for Blaine's daughter. Her oval face was almost completely free of lines, and even without makeup her cheeks were firm and highly colored. Now she seemed literally aglow, and in her agitation began pacing before him.

"Just going up and blurting it out to Mannheim," she said, "was probably the most senseless way of all."

"Settle down, will you," Justin said. "You make me nervous walking back and forth like that. Besides, Mannheim knew before I told him."

Alice stopped pacing. She looked at Justin with large, spaniel-like eyes that gave her a curiously gentle quality. "What are you talking about? What did Mannheim know?"

"That I'd been a Communist." Justin smiled ruefully. "He's known it for twelve years, ever since I went to work for CBN."

"But how? I just don't see how. We've been so careful."

"It was simple enough. Tom Gallagher told him when he first brought me in."

"Tom?" It took a moment to sink in, and then astonishment deflated her indignation and dismay. "To do something like that to his closest friend!"

She looked at Justin and saw that his left eye was twitching sporadically. It was a sign she knew well. She would have to watch him even more carefully, she thought. She walked to him and cupped his chin in her hand. "I know it's not easy, Jussie, but try to relax. This is exactly the kind of tension you're supposed to avoid." She kissed him on the lips. "Did you remember to pick up your pills?"

"They're in my coat."

"Don't forget to take one later. You didn't take one all day yesterday." Alice straightened. "You'd better change your wet things while I get dinner on the table. I hope the meat's not dried out."

Justin went into the bedroom and put on a robe and slippers. When he returned, Alice had the dining room candles lit and the wine poured. He sat down opposite her at the large, oval table, failing to take his usual pleasure in the gleaming silver and colorful centerpiece, the graciousness of the setting. Leisurely dining had become a ritual they both looked forward to and enjoyed. After years of hurried, perfunctory meals in squalid surroundings, it had come to have a special meaning. Just as the spacious apartment itself, with its lovingly accumulated furniture, paintings and pieces of sculpture, was visible assurance that their unexpected blessings of prosperity and calm were real. But now all Justin was able to feel was a sense of impending loss.

They began to eat in silence.

"Is the roast all right?" Alice asked.

"Yes. Yes, it's fine." The meat was sticking in Justin's throat and he had to wash it down with wine. He hoped he'd be able to get through the meal.

"You're sure it's not overdone?"

"Quite sure."

"I can add more gravy."

Justin forced down a mouthful. "No. It's perfect as it is."

"I expected you home at the usual time. That's why it's a little dried out." Alice sipped her wine and glanced at him over the rim of the glass. "You should have called me if you expected to see Mannheim."

"I told you before," he said patiently. "I didn't expect to go. It was just something I decided on impulse."

Alice Blaine nodded and Justin could see the effort it took for her not to press it further at that moment. But after serving dessert, she could hold back no longer.

"All right," she said, considering the dinner truce officially over. "Let's talk about it. Were you able to reach Kelly on the phone?"

"Only his secretary. Kelly was out of Washington. He won't be back until just before the hearing tomorrow morning."

"Couldn't she tell you anything?"

"What is there to tell?" Justin said tiredly. "She checked the list of witnesses scheduled for tomorrow and my name was there, as I knew it would be."

"But why the subpoena? Why couldn't Kelly have just called you? Good God! He knows your reputation."

Justin toyed with a mutilated remnant of lemon chiffon pie. "Because they're on to something and they don't want to be bothered with pleasantries." There was a cold, faraway smile on his lips. "Though perhaps part of that subpoena is my own fault. I've purposely operated from an ivory tower. I'm really a stranger to them in Washington. They might have warned me about this thing if I'd been more friendly, more the working, ingratiating correspondent."

Justin took out the subpoena, which he had transferred to the pocket of his robe, and placed it on the table next to his coffee. Alice reached across the table and Justin handed it to her. He had called her from the office when he'd been served that morning, but this was the first she'd seen the paper itself. She studied it in silence for a moment, then dropped it onto the table.

"Let's forget the emotionalism and get down to cold facts. Exactly what does Mannheim know?"

"That I was a member of the Communist Party."

"Is that all?"

"So far as I know."

"And what about your job?" she asked. "Where did he say the network stood in this."

"The Great White-Haired Father gave me his personal assurances that the drums of CBN would be loudly beaten in my behalf."

Alice frowned. "I don't think it's going to be anywhere near as bad as we thought," she said slowly. "We let ourselves be carried away by the shock of the subpoena."

Justin did not say anything.

"We may have an uncomfortable few weeks," Alice went on, "but I can't see any reason for a big explosion. So you were once a member of the Communist Party. All right. So were a lot of other people. In those days it wasn't the god-awful thing it is today. In 1939 you became disenchanted with the whole mess and broke away. Since then you've been pure red, white and blue." She waited for Justin's approval of her summary. "What do you think?"

"I think," Justin said, standing, "that I'm going to have a big fat brandy with my coffee."

"The doctor said you—"

"To hell with the doctor." Justin went to a cabinet and poured a double shot into a snifter. "How about you?"

Alice shook her head and Justin returned to the table with his glass. She waited as he sipped the drink. "You haven't answered my question," she said. "What do you think?"

Justin studied the way the candles caught the blond highlights in his wife's hair, several shades darker now than when he had first met her, but which she still wore in the same cropped style. "I think you sounded exactly like Phillip Mannheim."

"Did he figure it the same way?"

"In the exact same oversimplified way." Justin sighed. "Except that his excuse is ignorance of the true facts. What's yours?"

"I don't know what you mean," Alice said.

"I mean that Mannheim doesn't know the whole story," Justin said dryly. "You do. And when the committee reads the statement I'm going to hand them, telling all the facts, you're going to hear a blast that'll make—"

"*What?*" Alice put down her cup with a clatter that sloshed a small wave of coffee over the rim. "You're actually going to *tell* them?"

Justin sipped his brandy, feeling the stream of warmth move down into his stomach. His wife's reaction came as no surprise. From the moment, earlier that day, when he'd decided on his course of action, he had anticipated it.

Alice was staring at him across the table as though at a lunatic. "You're going to walk in there and in a single moment destroy everything we've worked years to build up? I don't believe it. You must be joking."

"Listen to me," he said, speaking with great care because he wasn't nearly as certain as he pretended to be. "I've been thinking about this for a long time. It's the only way. I can't go on talking to millions of people each night, knowing what I do, yet keeping quiet about it. In a strictly moral sense, this silence is probably the worst thing I've ever done."

"Oh, Jesus!" Alice rose, her face showing her anguish. "Don't hand me that high-flown morality. Jussie, this is me you're talking to—me—not your radio audience. For twelve years you've managed to keep quiet without your conscience bothering you. And if it weren't for this subpoena, you'd go right on managing!"

Justin looked up at her standing there in her bright, fashionable dress. She looked very pretty, slender and soft.

"Don't you think we owe this country something? We know names, places, enemy agents—a former spy in one of the highest government positions. I've never enjoyed deliberately hurting anyone, you know that, but if I can—"

"Jussie! Jussie! Jussie!" Alice dropped limply back into her chair. "Why do you always need the pretense of being a sweet, gentle, harmless soul, caught in the cruel web of circumstance? This is a picture of yourself you've enjoyed since I've known you."

"All right," he said. "If it'll make you feel better, I'm cruel, sadistic and conscienceless."

Alice picked up a napkin and mopped at the place where she had spilled the coffee. "I didn't mean that. You *are* sweet and gentle. I couldn't love you as I do if you weren't. But you're not nearly as gentle as you like to think. You'd never have gotten as far as you did in the apparatus if you were. Remember Peter Wechsen? You managed to turn him over to the OGPU without blinking an eye. And you know very well what that meant."

"Peter Wechsen," Justin said stiffly, "was a threat to our lives and the lives of ten others. He gave me no choice."

"Don't you think I know that? All I'm saying is that you can be as hard and coldly practical as anyone else when the occasion demands. So don't talk morality to me when the whole of our lives is involved. If you're going to turn your testimony into a confession, I want to hear a few sensible, practical reasons why it should be done."

Justin cradled the snifter lightly between his palms. There were times, he thought, when he would have preferred his wife to be a simple, fluttering woman who would regard her husband with uncritical, adoring eyes. He stood up and walked to the arched French doors that opened onto a small balcony overlooking the rain-swept street.

"I see it as a calculated risk that I've *got* to take. I figure it's better to give them the whole thing tomorrow, to admit everything, than to sit there squirming under the Fifth Amendment while they drag it out of me over weeks of testimony. This way I at least have a chance to explain my reasons for doing what I did, to show them my motives weren't bad." He turned back toward the glass doors. "They hope to turn me into a circus that'll last until Election Day.

But I'm going to fool them. I'll get it over with fast. Let them use someone else as a goat. Can't you see how much more sense that makes than trying to hide something they already have in their files anyway?"

"No!" Alice said. "You never can be sure what they know or don't know."

"This time," Justin said wearily, "I can be sure." He drained the rest of his brandy in a single burning gulp and put the glass down on the table. "In any case, that's the way it's going to be."

"You've decided?"

"I've decided."

"And it doesn't matter," she said softly, "that I think you're wrong, that I think you're making one of the biggest mistakes of your life?"

"It matters," he said. "You know it matters."

Her hands made small tortured movements on the tablecloth. "But not enough to change your mind."

"Please," Justin said, watching her fight back tears, "don't make it any harder for me than it is."

Alice wiped her eyes with the back of one hand. She looks like a small girl being cruelly punished without reason, he thought. "Your pills," she said suddenly. "You keep forgetting to take your pills!"

Later she sat pretending to read in the living room, while Justin worked at the typewriter in his study. From time to time she would look across the foyer, through the open door, and see his face, tired and solemn in the yellow light of the desk lamp. Blindly, she turned the pages of her book. Was this really to be the end of everything, of the few good years? After what they had been through, didn't they deserve at least a bit more of the good? A chill passed through her and she shuddered. She hugged herself and curled up in the large overstuffed chair. The words she was trying to read blurred before her eyes.

It was after one o'clock when they finally got to bed and Justin handed her the finished statement to read. It was several pages long. Although he listed very few specifics, he confessed former membership in the Communist Party, and admitted being a key member of the Washington espionage apparatus.

With a cold feeling Alice finished reading the document. She read it again, then for a long time just stared at it. Her husband's career, she knew without doubt, was finished. The network could not possibly continue to employ him after this explosion. She turned to comment on the statement and saw that Justin had drifted into sleep without even waiting for her reaction. A faint flush colored his cheeks and without his glasses his face seemed young, almost cherubic. She hadn't seen him look so at peace in years.

There was heavy fog at the airport early the next morning, and Justin's plane was almost an hour late taking off. When it did finally get off the ground, the air was rough and the signal to unfasten seat belts was long delayed. His stomach a bit queasy from the turbulence, Justin opened his briefcase and prepared to edit his statement for the fourth time that day. He had already gone over it at home, on the way to the airport and in the terminal lounge. But he'd made only a few minor changes, and these more from nervousness than need. The essentials, he knew, were all there.

"Your ticket, please, sir?"

The stewardess smiled down at him, young, pretty and airline perfect. Justin handed her his boarding pass and she checked off his name. "Thank you, Mr. Blaine." She looked at him. "Are you Justin Blaine, the news commentator?"

Justin nodded.

The girl's professional smile widened and became real. "I listen to you whenever I can. I've often wondered what you looked like."

"Now you know," Justin said dryly, "why I'm not on television."

She laughed. "You're really quite distinguished-looking and you *should* be on television."

Justin smiled his thanks and the girl continued down the aisle.

He'd already turned down several attractive television offers. There were too many people who might have recognized him from the underground years. His name had been different then, so there was no need for concern about radio work. Now, of course, there'd no longer be need for concern about anything.

Justin looked over his papers one last time. It was all there . . . the places, the methods, the results and the names of those who served with him when he worked for the Washington espionage apparatus.

Among them was the name of Webster Evers, the present Under Secretary of State.

3

A witness was testifying as he entered the main meeting room, and Justin slipped quietly into an inconspicuous seat near the door. The hall was enormous, with two great banks of spectator seats rising toward the back and separated by a center aisle. There was a platform at the front where the committee members sat, brass name-plates before them, along with individual microphones. Newsreel cameras and floodlights were set up to the right of the witness chair. Other photographers moved about, noisily working their cameras. A circus, Justin thought, the thing was set up like a damned circus, and he was slated for the headline act.

A pale, frightened-looking man sat stiffly in the witness chair, answering questions in a hoarse voice. Justin recognized his interrogator as Morris Kantrowitz, the committee's counsel. The dark-haired young lawyer had kept the committee on the front pages of the nation's newspapers for over a year, as he uncovered chapter after chapter of the Communist "conspiracy." But lately the excitement had died down, and it was generally accepted that with the elections almost within touch the committee members needed something to recapture public attention. Well, they would get it.

The chairman slammed his gavel on the table to quiet a buzz of chatter from the rear of the chamber. Chairman Eustace B. Kelly, Democrat from Massachusetts, was a permanent fixture in the House of Representatives. His tall frame, topped by a thin mat of silky white hair, and his sonorous voice had grown familiar to millions of Americans over thirty years. In the rear of the room, visitors and newsmen still circulated. Again he rapped the gavel. "I must insist," he intoned, "that my friends in the back take notice of me." His huge gray brows frowned over humorous eyes. "My wife has told me to act with more authority."

The other Congressmen laughed, the room settled down and the questioning of the witness continued.

"All right, Mr. Seldin," the committee counsel said, "if you are not now, as you claim, a member of the Communist Party, were you a member at any time in the past?"

The witness shook his head.

"Please answer yes or no."

"No." The single word escaped with great effort.

Kantrowitz looked at the man. "You're under oath, Mr. Seldin. It's not against the law to have been a Communist, but it *is* against the law to perjure yourself before a Congressional committee." He paused. "I repeat. Were you ever a Communist?"

Under the lights, the witness' face shone with sweat. He mopped it with a damp handkerchief. "I don't think so. I belonged . . . I joined up with a lot of things when I was a kid. It's hard to remember exactly."

"You mean you *may* have been a Communist, but you're not sure?"

The man's eyes were lost, hopeless.

"Please answer the question," Kantrowitz said sharply.

"Yes. That's what I mean. I'm not exactly sure."

"Well, perhaps I can *help* you to be sure." The lawyer consulted a typewritten sheet. "According to our records, you joined the American Communist Party on June 17, 1931, and were a member in good standing for at least two years. From then until 1938, you were also a member of three other organizations on the Attorney General's subversive list." Kantrowitz's voice and manner were cold, mocking. "Is your memory becoming a bit better *now*, Mr. Seldin?"

Justin tried not to listen to any more of the man's fumbling, evasive answers. They made his stomach want to turn. This was the sort of performance he was determined to avoid. It still bothered him that Alice should fail to understand this. Until the moment of parting at the airport, she had stubbornly insisted he was doing the wrong thing. "Tell them nothing," she had pleaded hopelessly, even as she kissed him good-bye. "Please. Tell them nothing until you absolutely have to."

Justin's briefcase and hat slid from his lap and fell to the floor. He bent to pick them up and struck his forehead sharply against the edge of the seat in front. When he straightened, the bruise began to ache and he could feel blood coming out on his forehead, sticking to his eyebrow. He fumbled for a handkerchief and discovered, without great surprise, that he had none. The blood trickled down over one eye. He took off his glasses and wiped the eye with the back of his hand. His knuckles came away bright red.

Justin became aware that the pale man had stopped talking and was leaving the witness chair. He motioned to a uniformed attendant. "Will you please tell Congressman Kelly," he said, "that Justin Blaine is here."

"Yes, Mr. Blaine." The man frowned. "Did you know you're bleeding, sir?"

"It's nothing," Justin said. "It'll stop."

The man looked at him. "Yes, sir."

The man walked down the aisle to the platform and spoke to the chairman. Justin saw Kelly glance in his direction, then nod and say something to Morris Kantrowitz. A moment later the young lawyer walked briskly toward him. Justin watched him approach, a short, sharp-faced man, bursting with almost visible nervous energy. Kantrowitz smiled as he drew closer and extended his hand.

"How do you do, Mr. Blaine," he said. "It was good of you to come all the way down here for us. We appreciate it."

Justin took the offered hand, wondering at the kind of twisted humor that would clobber a man with the indignity of a subpoena and then graciously thank him for submitting to it.

Kantrowitz stared at Justin's forehead.

"It's all right," Justin said quickly. He touched the cut and found that the bleeding had stopped. "Just banged my head on the seat. It's nothing at all."

"Are you sure?" the lawyer's voice was anxious. "If you wish, we can have a doctor take—"

"No, no, no. . . ." Justin rose. "If you people are ready for me, I'm ready for you." He was aware of everyone in the big chamber staring at him. His nerves felt taut. He was anxious to get the thing over with.

"Yes, of course," Kantrowitz said. "You can testify immediately. I imagine you're on a tight schedule."

Justin left his hat and coat on the seat. Carrying only his brief-case, he followed the lawyer to the witness chair and sat down. The newsreel lights blinded him and he blinked into the unfriendly white glare. His short fingers worked clumsily at the clasps of his briefcase. Composed, he thought; he must be careful to appear calm and composed. For public executions, impassivity had long ago been proved best. Finally, the three pieces of paper were out of the briefcase. Justin passed them across a wide table to the court stenographer, who in turn passed them up to Morris Kantrowitz on the committee platform.

The chairman banged his gavel. "Gentlemen," he said, "I have an announcement to make before swearing in the next witness."

Kelly's amplified voice reverberated throughout the chamber. The cameras whirred and panned and stenotypists tapped at their little metal containers. Justin had a strange feeling that the Congressman was smiling at him.

"Before we go any further," Kelly went on, "I must offer a public apology to Mr. Justin Blaine, who is one of our foremost interpreters of the current scene, and who has so graciously consented to appear before us today to share with us the benefit of his knowledge and experience."

The chairman paused with studied effect. There had to be a limit, Justin thought, even to the phony graciousness of politicians. He sat very still, waiting for the knife to appear from out of the velvet glove.

"Mr. Blaine is the first of several distinguished special witnesses, who are highly placed in the communications industry and whom we plan to call during the coming weeks. We hope these men will be able to shed light on many aspects of our investigations."

Justin stared at the gaunt speaker. He glanced over at Kantrowitz. The lawyer was reading his statement rapidly, hungrily.

"Mr. Blaine, through an error in my office," the Congressman continued, "your name was placed on a list of witnesses to receive subpoenas instead of a letter of invitation. I hope you will forgive us for this unintentional discourtesy."

The other committee members smiled and nodded. Justin felt sick, numb. The room seemed to be falling away. They had known nothing; they had known absolutely nothing.

Kantrowitz ran his fingers through his hair and looked at Justin incredulously. He approached the chairman. Putting his hand over the microphone, he whispered into Kelly's ear, and then handed him the statement. Kelly motioned to the other committee members to gather round him, and soon they all stood huddled together, reading over the chairman's shoulder.

The reporters at the press tables hunched forward, waiting. Kantrowitz was whispering to the group of Congressmen, gesturing emphatically with a pointed finger. The group of lawmakers seemed stunned. They kept looking from the statement to Justin, then back to the statement. Then Kantrowitz nodded vigorously and they all returned to their seats.

The chairman spoke first, his voice edged with sharpness and suddenly far different from before. "Before the witness reads a prepared statement, Mr. Kantrowitz will have him sworn and conduct the usual preliminary questioning."

During the swearing, Kantrowitz shifted tensely in his seat. He adjusted his papers and tapped a pencil on the table. He was like a finely trained athlete awaiting the crack of the starting gun. Now, as Justin Blaine sat before him, expressionless, drained, the lawyer appeared more taut than any of the press people had ever seen him.

The questioning began.

"Your full name, sir?"

"Justin Blaine."

"When were you born?"

"April 2, 1906."

The answers came automatically, without thought, without emotion. Justin knew that the ordeal would never end. Was this then what he had wanted after all—a final purging of conscience, an insane self-destruction? Like a man lost in an endless expanse of ocean, knowing that rescue was impossible, but swimming mechanically without direction or goal, dully he answered question after question.

"What is your occupation?"

"I am a news analyst for the Continental Broadcasting Network."

"How long have you been so employed?"

"For about twelve years."

"That was twelve years? I'm sorry, Mr. Blaine, but I'm having trouble hearing you. Will you please speak directly into your microphone?"

"Yes. Twelve years."

"Were you born in the United States?"

"I was. In Red Bank, New Jersey."

Chapter Two

1923: Red Bank, N.J.

It had showered earlier, but the rain had done little to relieve the heat. Puddles in the red clay of Red Bank's streets steamed before the town's cluster of stores. A few old men sat dozing in front of the post office and a black dog suffered at their feet. A Model T clanked across the square. Horses hitched nearby flicked flies and did not look up.

Justin Blaine left the grocery store and waddled slowly along the cracked walk. The bundles he carried were bulky, but he would have walked the same way without them, for his feet were flat and the high corrective shoes he wore seemed to exaggerate rather than help the condition. He was only seventeen, but had none of the easy grace of youth. All movement was a necessary struggle to which he was resigned without interest. Nor did there appear to be much else that interested him. His dark eyes peered straight ahead through heavy lenses, ignoring people and traffic.

The town sidewalk ended with the row of stores and Justin continued along a dirt road. There were houses on either side, huddled together on narrow, carelessly tended plots. The houses were small and old, with only the decay and none of the charm of age.

He turned at the next corner and the road stretched steeply uphill. By the time he was halfway up, sweat had soaked through his shirt and he was breathing heavily. He stopped to shift the bundles, the sun behind him now, lengthening in shadow the squat lines of his graceless body.

Noticing his dark ghost on the ground, he squared his shoulders and briefly walked on tiptoe to emphasize the illusion of slender height.

The houses grew farther apart. There were empty lots between them now and sometimes a patch of potatoes. After a while Justin came to a rusted iron gate, kicked it open and pushed through. The house, thirty feet beyond, was larger than those about it, but in an even greater state of disrepair. Its Victorian trim and shutters were peeling and warped and its dark porches hidden by shrubs. In front, a weathered sign hung crazily from one hinge. It read: "THE BLAINE WRITING SCHOOL . . . FREDERICK BLAINE, DIRECTOR."

Justin shuffled along the weed-choked path to the porch steps. Puffing, he climbed the steps and crossed the porch to the front door. He turned the knob and it came off in his hand. He put it back, turned it with care, and the door opened.

His mother was in the kitchen. She was small and slender, her earlier beauty lost in lines of disappointment.

"Did you get everything?" she asked.

Justin dumped the bundles onto a table. His glasses had slipped crookedly to one side of his nose, giving his round face a lopsided look.

"Fix your glasses. Don't you know they're on crooked? How on earth can you see?" Her voice had grown high with constant exasperation. As Justin took small packages from his pockets, Mrs. Blaine examined the bundles. "What about the flour and tea? I hope you didn't forget the tea again. If you . . . thank goodness. Sometimes I don't know where your head is." It did not matter that this time he had remembered the tea; she had a reserve history of default to draw on. "Now you'd better get on into the office. Your father's been up in arms, waiting for you."

Justin dug inside his shirt and pulled out a sheaf of mail. "Why?" he said flatly. "He sent me for the mail, didn't he?"

"Don't ask me," his mother said with impatience. "Just hurry on in there. He's been screaming about some kind of list Bess needed half an hour ago. And for God's sake, don't aggravate him!"

Justin shuffled out of the kitchen and through a dark corridor. His feet padded on threadbare carpeting. At the end of the hall a door stood part way open. He stopped and took a long, deep breath. His father was seated behind the big rolltop desk, staring out the window.

Bess Reardon was struggling with a jammed key on the typewriter. This was the office of the Blaine Writing School: a big, high-ceilinged room, crowded with a haphazard clutter of desks, file cabinets, books and assorted memorabilia. On a flaking wall was a framed, plain dust jacket from Frederick Blaine's one published novel. There were also time-yellowed copies of its reviews, which had hung there for eighteen years. About them were mounted enlargements of blurbs from *True Confessions, College Humor* and *Screenland*. The ads urged hopeful writers to send their manuscripts, along with ten dollars in check or money order, to the Blaine Writing School for a professional analysis. Or, if they wished, they could send no money and be billed later. The ads extolled the literary stature of Frederick Blaine, promised his personal attention to each manuscript, and described the rich rewards achieved by successful clients writing at home in their spare time.

Frederick Blaine turned as his son opened the door. He was a big, slovenly, dark-haired man, with nicotine-stained fingers and bitter, defeated eyes. His face, normally a tired gray, was pink with annoyance and heat. "Well!" he said dryly. "The Red Bank Flash!"

Mrs. Reardon looked up from her typewriter, but did not say anything. Trapped by marriage and religion into producing four children before she was twenty-five, she was plumply pretty in an open, vacuous way. She had a pert pug nose and a voluptuous lower lip. The office was her daily escape. As she watched Justin lumber slowly across the room, her eyes were not unsympathetic, but she regretted the way he moved.

Blaine ground out his cigarette. "Now would you mind telling us what in hell you did with that damned delinquent list? We've turned this place upside down for the past hour."

"Stop that silly swearing," Bess said. "It won't find the list any faster." She fingered the back of her bobbed blond hair. "And why pick on the poor boy? How can you be so sure he's to blame?"

"He's to blame," Justin's father said grimly. "Let me tell you something. If this whole damned house burned to the ground and a dozen of your sacred priests swore my son was five miles away in church, I'd still know that somehow, in some way, he was to blame." He glared at his son. "What did you do with the list?"

Justin dropped the few pieces of mail onto his father's desk. He seemed undisturbed. "There wasn't much," he said. "Just this." He adjusted his glasses and frowned. "Was I the last one to have that list?"

Blaine belligerently picked up the mail and tore open the envelopes. "Great! Three lousy checks. The summer of peace and plenty. Another few weeks like this and I'll burn down the house myself for the insurance."

Justin's hand was in the back pocket of his outgrown knickers. He pulled out a folded sheet of paper, blinked at it in surprise and slowly opened it. "I guess I did have it," he said. "I'd forgotten. I was going over it this morning when Mom called me." Avoiding his father, he handed the missing list to Mrs. Reardon.

"That's my boy!" Blaine mumbled hopelessly. He rose behind his desk and tugged at his elastic sleeve bands. The celluloid collar of his shirt rested on the window sill beside him. He swept a dramatically scornful arm toward his son. "Look at him." He paused for effect. "Just look at him, my dear Bess. You see before you a young man who only a month ago was graduated from Red Bank High School at the very head of his class, a year before his normal time, and acclaimed a near genius, a young man honored by scholastic medals too numerous to count. Impressive? Certainly impressive."

Blaine's face contorted in oratorical mockery. "Then perhaps you can tell me, dear Bess, why, whenever he has to take on the simplest task in this office, does he give the impression of being a total idiot? Why, whenever the chance to help his father is involved, does he carefully place his brilliant mind a thousand miles away in cold storage? Look at him! Do you think I can reach him? Do you think he's heard a single word I've said?"

"Oh, leave the boy alone," Bess said. "Some people are like that. My Danny's a lot the same way and he's thirty-two years old, not seventeen."

Blaine looked at his son. "I want this manuscript sent out tonight." He held up some hand-scrawled papers.

Justin took the sheets from his father and carried them back to his desk, moving in silent obedience.

Blaine said, "Insert Paragraphs 1, 3 and 7. I think those should cover the mess. Christ! The idiots who think they can write."

Frederick Blaine had managed to reduce most of the problems of literary composition to a series of form paragraphs. Now it was simply a matter of judging which criticisms were most applicable to a manuscript, and mailing them. In doing this, Blaine did not consider himself more cynical or less ethical than any other businessman. He was dealing with a mass-produced product. For ten dollars per manuscript, he intended to give away as little of himself as possible.

"I have an idea," he said. "On that delinquent list—" he smiled bleakly—"this time send out the dunning notes on open-faced postcards. Let the bastards' neighbors and postmen know they owe me money. Maybe that'll get us some action."

Bess looked doubtful. "That's not a very nice thing to do."

"Neither is not paying your debts. What the hell am I supposed to live on? Those dead beats have *my* money!"

"Are you sure it's not against the law or anything?"

Blaine shrugged. "I don't give a damn. I'm just sorry I never thought of it before." He shook his head in disgust. "The conscience of the people! Hit the parsimonious hypocrites in the eyes of the neighbors. That's where it *really* hurts."

Bess offered a mock sigh of despair. "You're a lost and unregenerate soul, Mr. Blaine." She rose and placed a cover over her typewriter. "But your devil's work will have to wait for tomorrow. Right now I've got to go home and rescue my mother from the children. Bless that woman. I don't know what I'd do without her."

"You'd stay home with the four squalling kids and go out of your mind." Blaine studied his secretary's body with an abstracted eye. There was something in the way Bess Reardon moved that caused a stirring.

Bess turned to examine the seam of a stocking. "You're right," she said, "and don't think it doesn't worry me. What kind of mother am I to run off for six hours a day and not miss the little darlings in the least?"

"Why don't you ask the good Father McKeehan for his opinion?"

Bess laughed. "I'm afraid of what he might tell me." She took a flowered hat from a cabinet and pinned it to the back of her hair. She bent to examine herself in a wall mirror and was pleased by what she saw.

"Justin," Blaine said, "stop praying over that damned manuscript. I want Bess to drop it at the post office."

"It's ready," Justin said. He sealed the envelope and crossed the room to give it to the secretary.

"Stamps!" his father said tiredly. "I know these minor details must be a great bore to someone with your talents, but I've found our mail does get there faster when we use stamps."

Justin went to the stamp drawer. Bess was in the aisle between desks and his body brushed hers in passing. It felt soft and yielding. He blinked and mumbled a vague apology, his round face faintly flushed. Bess was looking in the mirror and did not appear to notice.

When she had gone, Justin stood uncertainly in the center of the room. He looked at his father. Blaine was staring morosely at nothing. With the late sun edging his face, his tiredness, his long-contained disenchantment stood out in sharp relief.

"Was there anything else you wanted me to do?" Justin said.

His father turned slowly. "You can't wait, can you?" His voice was quiet, softly bitter. "You can't wait to escape up to that god-damned room of yours and just close the door and shut yourself away."

Justin did not say anything. He knew what was eating his father, why he had been at him so hard these past few days. His father had given him the first five chapters of his new novel to read and was still waiting for his opinion. The manuscript hung over them like a great stone, for his father did not wait easily. Yet the manuscript was never mentioned.

"What goes on up there? What goes on in that fine, mysterious mind of yours once you're alone?" Blaine squinted at his son through a curtain of smoke, searching. Then he turned away. "Go on," he said. "Now's your chance. Escape."

Justin did not move. Finally, when his father said nothing more, he left the office.

He moved quietly along the dark corridor that passed the kitchen. He did not want his mother to see or hear him. She would only find some additional chore for him to do. Going up the stairs, he was careful to avoid the creaking step.

His room was close beneath the eaves and stifling with heat, but he did not care. His hand touched the head of a stuffed squirrel and he looked, for a moment, at the soft, bushy tail and button eyes. There were nearly a dozen other small animals and birds mounted about the room, but the squirrel was the first he had done and was still his favorite. Lately he had lost interest in taxidermy. Nor was he especially absorbed any more in the detailed and complex astronomical charts with which he had papered the ceiling. Sometimes he could still briefly enjoy picking out the constellations, but his imagination was stirred by closer, more earthly regions. Now he hungrily read every travel book and pamphlet he could find. His bookshelves were heavy with volumes on the Greek and German philosophers, the Great War and a generous sampling of three centuries of English literature. Here stood the investment of five years of earned and begged pennies, and he had devoured it all. But now it was only travel that seemed to hold him. He wanted to know about places. He wanted to be able to see, feel and smell the way they were. In seventeen years, he had hever been more than fifty miles from Red Bank. He had never known people different from those among whom he had been born, and he did not know many of them well, especially the ones his age.

He lay down on the bed with a large, colored map of the United States and traced an imaginary route West. He picked towns and cities in which he would stop, and determined the name he would use when he got there. It had become a ritual he enjoyed. He did not know why he considered it necessary to change his name, nor did he think of it as particularly strange, but rather the natural thing to do. You went to a different place. You did different things. You met different people. You became different yourself.

But today it did not go well. He left Red Bank and went on to Pittsburgh, Chicago and Denver, but somehow he could not quite lose himself in the journey. An intrusion deep inside gnawed at him when he lay still and became worse if he stirred. His loins tightened with it. He thought of girls he knew and imagined their bodies and their passions. He imagined what they did with other boys. He remembered times when he stood on the porch and they would come by in the summer evenings, in their groups of four or five boys and four or five girls, laughing, heading for a party at Sarah Conroy's house—for another of the *idiotic* parties at Sarah Conroy's house. He had never been to one, but he could guess what went on. And sometimes he had passed by and seen them through the lighted windows, doing damn-fool silly dances, their bodies pressing together, their mouths open with laughter. Stupid. Or other times, when no light came from the windows but the sounds of giggling jabbed at him and he could picture the fumbling and groping in the darkness. Tickling their childish senses. Like some primitive tribal fertility rite. Idiots. None of them, he was sure, had the courage to finish what they started. Disgusting. At least they had the good sense not to have asked him to join them.

He closed his eyes tight.

And the crazy part was, he thought bitterly, that his parents would have liked to see him running along as part of this stupid herd. For as long as he could remember they had been after him about not having friends, as if having friends were the single most important thing in the world. What matter if the friends were a pack of dull fools? You had to have them. Anything, not to be alone. Anything, not to be different. *There* was the awful stigma. Be different and you were marked as a leper. Lose yourself among the thick-headed sheep and you were a swell guy. Well, he had never been a swell guy and he didn't give a damn for any of it. Let them mark him as a leper. In this town it would be a badge of honor.

Again he looked at the map. You went to a different place. You met different people. *You became different.* He tried to see himself as different, with a new name, a new face and body, rugged, slender, graceful, a man. For a moment it worked; he could see the new image—for a moment—and then the image melted back into the fat, foolish face, the myopic eyes, the clumsy body, the crippled, aching feet, the whole silly, twisted joke of a boy that Justin Blaine was and would ever be.

The tightening in his loins was now a persistent ache. He breathed deeply and his shirt gave off a memory of Bess Reardon's cologne. He thought of her softness as he had brushed past her, and this thighs trembled. Had she noticed him? Had she noticed the stirring he had tried to hide before it diminished? Would he be able to look at her tomorrow? And now the stirring was with him again, and the ache was growing, spreading from its center into his legs and shoulders and arms. Justin explored the center, automatically seeking relief.

No! None of that! He pulled his hand away as though burned,

and the ache became a fire. No, he was all through with that. He had sworn to himself after the last time that there would be no more. It was disgusting, and he despised himself afterward. He rolled off the bed and went to the window. A cloud drifted over the sun, softening the glare. Justin studied its silvered edges. The sun broke out and burned his eyes, so that he turned and restlessly paced the room, seeing, avoiding, then finally picking up his father's manuscript.

He leafed through the typewritten pages, but made no attempt to read them. He had finished reading them two days before, and now there was nothing left but to tell his father what he thought. It was the first writing his father had done in fifteen years and he had spent six months on the first five chapters of the novel and it was awful. It was so awful that Justin had been appalled reading it. For two days he had put off discussing it, but knew he could not stall much longer. Well, he would get it over with and there would be a big explosion and that would be that. His father was a great one for explosions. When logic failed, there was always anger to fall back on. Justin often wished he could become as angry as his father. You could get rid of things that way. But somehow he never could. When things went wrong, he felt only emptiness.

The things that could happen to a man. His father had written one good book eighteen years ago, with nothing but a couple of bad attempts since. It had been a wonderful book, and Justin had proudly struggled through it for the first time when he was ten years old and countless times after. There were whole passages he had learned by heart, and once, when he was twelve, he had surprised his father by reciting them aloud for him. It had been his father's birthday and there had been a cake and candles and Justin had stood and recited from the book for ten minutes. His father's face had looked strange, but afterward he had hugged him hard and kissed him and Justin had guessed he loved his father very much.

He put down the manuscript, stared at it for a long moment and then went back to the map on his bed. This time he turned south from Denver and was able to get as far as Phoenix, Arizona, before Bess Reardon's cologne intruded once more. Justin tried to swallow, but his throat was parched and his tongue felt swollen. His mind saw Bess Reardon's body, and his own body throbbed at the vision. His loins craved release. My God, he thought, trying to focus his eyes on the map, it's becoming an addiction. He would be a slave to it and it would destroy him. If he gave in to it once more, he would be lost. He had to make his stand *now*.

He forced his eyes across the desert of Nevada, but the names on the map were blurred. In his gut he knew what was going to happen and the knowledge was both joy and sorrow. Perhaps once more would be all right. Perhaps just this once and never again. He thought of the girls. If he could just hold one, just kiss her, all this would pass away. Just the closeness of a girl would soothe this pressure. But there was no girl, nor would there ever be, and so why be foolish? Why do this to himself? What choice was there? Whatever he did, this thing inside him would kill him. He had lived with it for almost four years and he knew what must happen. The need was too strong.

Yes.

That was it . . . that was fine . . . all right . . . *all—*

"Justin!" His mother's voice from below. "Justin, come down for dinner!"

He sobbed, his hand gripped the bed. He tried to clear his head. He breathed deeply and rose from the bed. His knees felt weak and it was difficult to stand. He saw himself in a mirror. His hair was wildly awry and his face glistened with sweat, but this time he had won. It would never get him again.

2

The ordeal at the table was even worse than that of the evening before. No mention was made of the new novel, but Justin could feel anxiety about the five terrible chapters lurking behind the carping barrage his father directed at him almost without pause.

Several times his mother tried to smooth it over, but his father would not let go. Hurt by Justin's apparent indifference to his manuscript, by his failure to read and report on it promptly, Blaine needed to hurt in return. He struck at his son's appearance. He mocked his secretiveness. He scorned his lack of friends, his distant, abstracted manner. He drew upon every error, every mistake in judgment, every thoughtless remark Justin had made in the past six months, and held them to the light. And through it all, Justin said nothing; he forced food into his mouth and studied the room's heavy, brocaded drapes, its beaded curtains, its dark chairs, with an intense absorption. He would not be drawn in. He would not discuss the novel. He did not want to face the inevitable scene that would follow. If his father asked him directly, he would answer. But he would volunteer nothing.

"Justin, will you bring the dessert in from the kitchen?" His mother sighed. "This heat has me worn out."

Justin stood up, grateful for at least the momentary escape.

"There's some fruit in the icebox," his mother said. "Wash it off well and put it in a bowl."

Justin plodded into the kitchen. He went to the icebox and groped in the cool darkness for the fruit. He was vaguely conscious of his parents' voices in the next room. They were talking about the new novel.

"Another two chapters," his father was saying. "I want to finish another two chapters before I send it to the publisher." He laughed. "I can just picture Mac's face when he reads it. He'll be one surprised boy. He thinks I died on paper eighteen years ago. Wait'll he gets a look at this."

"It's wonderful," Rose Blaine told her husband. "I don't know when I've enjoyed reading anything so much. Now aren't you glad I pushed you into starting again?"

Justin held a bunch of grapes under the sink faucet. He wished his mother had let his father alone. Justin washed the fruit three times. He did not want to go back into the dining room, because when he got there, he would finally have to talk about it.

"Justin!" his mother called. "What on earth are you doing in that kitchen so long?"

Justin brought in the fruit and took his place at the table. He stuffed his mouth with grapes and waited for his father to begin.

"Did you know," Frederick Blaine said, addressing his wife, "that I gave our brilliant son my manuscript to read three days ago, and I've yet to hear one word of comment from him? Do you think it's just too unimportant for him to bother with?"

Rose Blaine frowned. "You know what this novel means to your father. Haven't you read it yet?"

Justin picked the stem from a grape. "I've read it."

"Well?" his mother said. "Didn't you think it was absolutely wonderful?"

Justin took a deep breath. "No." He could feel his parents' eyes, but did not look up.

"What the hell do you mean, no?" Frederick Blaine said harshly.

"No," Justin said. "I didn't think it was wonderful."

Blaine's fingers shook as he lighted a cigarette from the butt of another. He drew on it hard and squinted across the table. "Why not?" He was able to keep his voice low, but had to work at it.

Justin did not say anything.

"Answer me, damn it!" Blaine's fist struck the table and the dishes jumped. "I said, why not?"

Justin shrugged. He had hoped we was not going to be forced into details, but he knew that his father could never leave a fresh wound alone, that he needed to feel the pain.

"Maybe he was tired when he read it," his mother said quickly. "That sometimes happens." She looked appealingly at Justin. "Maybe you were tired when you read it. Maybe you should try reading it again."

Justin fumbled with the grapes. "I wasn't tired."

"But you'll read it again, won't you? You can certainly do that much."

"He doesn't have to do me any goddamned favors!" Blaine said.

"He *wants* to read it again," his wife said. She reached for Justin's hand. "Tell your father you *want* to read it again."

"I want to read it again," Justin mumbled obediently. Perhaps he could stall it that way. He was ready to try anything.

"Like hell you will!" Blaine shouted. "All I want from you is a damned reason. What is wrong with those chapters?"

Justin chewed at his lip. "Everything." He could see now how it was going to be. He wished he were a thousand miles away.

"What? Exactly what?"

"It's too wordy," Justin said. "It's overwritten and pompous."

Blaine's eyes seemed lost in shadow. "What else?"

"The characters are stock and one-dimensional. They are made of paper. They speak and move like puppets."

"What else?"

Justin tried to look at his father but couldn't. He did not want to see what was happening to his face. "It's filled with clichés."

"What else?"

"It breaks every rule in Paragraphs 1, 5 and 7," Justin went on. Once started, he now seemed unable to stop. "It's as if you deliberately set out to give an example of how not to write."

"Anything else?"

"The plot is predictable and obvious." Justin felt the sweat cold in his armpits. "It doesn't go anywhere."

"Go on."

Justin swallowed hard. He shook his head slowly.

"You mean that's all? Everything else about it was fine?"

Justin did not say anything. The silence was hard and heavy. When his father spoke again, his voice was hollow. "I'll bet you enjoyed that," he said. "It must have really given you pleasure to cut me where it hurt most."

Justin shook his head. "No. That's not true. I *wanted* to like it. I *wanted* to tell you it was good."

Blaine looked at him. His anger seemed to have drained. "Then why didn't you?" he said quietly.

Justin frowned. "Because I couldn't."

"Why not?"

"Because I'd have had to lie."

"So?"

Justin stared. His father's mouth seemed to be smiling, but the rest of his face was sad, tiredly reproachful.

"So why didn't you lie?" Blaine said. "You've never in your life lied? You've suddenly become such a paragon of virtue? All at once you've got to stick the shining sword of truth through your old man's guts?"

"You'd have wanted me to lie?" Justin was bewildered. He was used to his father's bluster and abuse, but this was something else. "You'd have wanted me to say I liked it when I didn't?"

Blaine stood up. His eyes were dark with regret. "I think I'd have wanted you at least to try," he said. "I'd have known it soon enough, but I'd have given ten good years to have you at least try." He walked from the room.

Justin gazed after him. Then he looked at his mother and saw, with surprise, that she was crying silently. He opened his mouth to speak, but could think of nothing to say.

Rose Blaine faced down her son. "Seventeen years old," she wept, "seventeen years old and you think you know it all, don't you?"

"No . . . I . . ."

"Shut up!" She blinked her eyes, and tears stained the tablecloth. "Well, let me tell you something. You don't know anything at all. Your father wrote a book before you were born. There are critics' notices pinned to the wall. Read them. They'll tell you what kind of writer, what kind of man, your father is. Just read them."

"I didn't mean—"

"Don't tell me what you didn't mean," Rose Blaine snapped. "Do you think I'm a fool? I know what you mean and what you don't mean. I know when you're being superior. I know when you condescend to your father. I know when you sit in judgment on him. And he knows it too. Why do you think he's always screaming and shouting at you? Do you have any idea why?"

Justin swallowed. He did not trust his voice.

"I'll tell you. He's a man who has suffered. He has known disappointment. But he'd die before he'd let you know what was happening to him inside. Well, *I'm* letting you know."

Rose Blaine stopped for breath and groped in her apron pocket for a handkerchief. Then she leaned across the table. "If you care anything about him, how, when a man hasn't put a word to paper in fifteen years, how could you calmly sit there and cut him to ribbons when he finally *does* try to write again?"

"I didn't *want* to do it," Justin said desperately. "He *made* me. You were here. You saw. He kept after me until he *made* me. Besides, it *was* awful. You must have known it too. His publisher would have told him soon enough."

Rose shook her head tiredly. "His publisher isn't his wife and son. A man needs respect and admiration. He needs it a lot more than the deliberate cruelty some people like to call an 'honest opinion.' "

Justin sat looking at his fingernails. They were picked and bitten halfway to the cuticles. His mother stood up and began to gather the dinner dishes.

"You have a good mind," she said quietly. "Maybe even a brilliant one. You had nothing to do with it. Your father and I gave it to you. I just wish we'd been able to throw in a heart to match."

Justin felt pity for his mother. She always seemed to be trapped somewhere in the middle. He wondered when she had last been able to express an honest opinion. Yet his mother was not a weak woman. From everything Justin had been able to gather through the years, his mother had always been the one who held things together. When his father's ability to write had failed, she had salvaged the idea of the school from the ruins. She had nursed it along against his initial scorn and apathy, insisting it was only temporary, only something to keep them going until he was able to write once more. That had been sixteen years ago, and Justin often wondered what his father would have done without the school. He had never stopped railing against the talentless fools who sent him manuscripts or whipping himself for accepting their money, but Justin knew he would have been lost without them. It would have destroyed him entirely to take a job, and at least this was something to rebel against. Justin supposed his mother was really the stronger of the two, but he wished she hadn't pushed his father into writing again.

Justin watched her carry the dishes into the kitchen. He sat without moving for a long time. Then he went out onto the porch. It was growing dark. Justin leaned against a post, savoring the coolness on his cheek. The light went on in his father's office and threw a yellow band across the lawn. Justin could see his father's shadow move across it, back and forth in a slow, regular rhythm. He turned to look westward, and for a long time watched the orange glow that lingered there.

3

Justin and his mother stood in the great rotunda of Pennsylvania Station. The eleven o'clock train to Chicago had just been announced and the waiting crowd surged toward the platform gates. Justin barely had time to pick up his bag before he was swept along. His mother clung to his arm and turned to glare indignantly at those who were pushing. She stumbled and, had there been room, would have fallen. Justin looked at her anxiously.

"Maybe you'd better say good-bye here," he said.

Mrs. Blaine shook her head. "I'm going down to the train with you. I want to make certain you have a proper seat. People take advantage if you're not careful."

Justin tugged at his bag and shuffled along. He doubted that one seat was better or worse than any other, but did not argue the point. To his mother, the world was arranged as an anonymous conspiracy against her and hers. For the past two weeks, ever since his departure date had been set, she had showered Justin with warnings and advice about areas of possible disaster. He was to board in the home of his aunt, her sister, in a major American city, but this offered his mother little comfort. When a seventeen-year-old boy went twelve hundred miles from home, she was convinced, more bad than good was likely to come of it. Justin sometimes thought she would almost be disappointed if it didn't.

Finding a job in Chicago and staying with his aunt was a compromise, the only way Justin could leave home with the reluctant approval of his mother, although he had been determined to go, if necessary, with or without it. The past four weeks had been a nightmare. His father had barely spoken. Even the bluster and abuse, to which Justin had almost become accustomed, had stopped, replaced by a frigid indifference, which was far worse. Since their argument over the manuscript Justin had found it impossible to look at his father. He told himself he didn't really care, that it had all been destroyed long ago anyway, that nothing his father said or did could matter to him now. But he knew that it mattered and that it hurt. He knew fully what things between them had become and what they would always be when, after days of screwing up his courage, he had returned the manuscript. From his desk his father had watched him enter the office. It was all silent, with Justin aware of his father's eyes scanning him as he approached the desk and set the manuscript down gently, as if it were a fragile thing, and walked out.

The crowd pressed down the stairs to where the train waited beside the platform. There was the rumble of iron-wheeled baggage carts and the hiss of steam that rose in thick, white clouds. He felt his mother's hand tighten on his arm. The day coaches were at the far end of the train and a long way off. Justin sweated as he labored down the platform, the cumbersome bag jarring his leg as he walked. They passed Pullmans and the dining car and then more Pullmans. They finally reached the first of the day coaches, pushed in, and Mrs. Blaine carefully chose her son's seat in the exact center of the car, the safest place in case of accident. Justin fought his bag into the luggage rack. There were still ten minutes before departure time and he went out on the platform with his mother to wait.

"Are you sure you've got your ticket?" she said.

Justin nodded for the fourth time since leaving home.

"Look," his mother insisted. "It might have slipped out of your pocket in the crowd. These things happen. Look."

Justin took the ticket from his pocket, showed it to his mother and put it back.

"Wipe your glasses," Rose Blaine ordered. "They're all fogged from the steam. You'll break your neck if you can't see."

"I can see."

"Wipe them."

Justin removed his glasses and wiped them on his jacket lapel.

"Haven't you a handkerchief in your pocket?" She shook her head in mute despair. "I don't know how you're going to manage. I honestly don't know. Someone has to keep after you for even the simplest things."

"I'll be all right," Justin said. His mother's eyes were wet. He wished it would hurry and be eleven o'clock.

She brushed some dust from his jacket sleeve. "Take care of this suit and keep it well pressed. It's your only good one. Your uncle said appearance is very important in the insurance business."

Justin nodded automatically. He supposed he should be grateful to his uncle for getting him a job with his company. According to his aunt's letters, it had not been easy to arrange. The prospect of sitting at one of a hundred identical desks in an office and poring over tables of figures day after day held little appeal for him. Yet he knew it was better than staying at home.

"Not a night's sleep," she mourned. "I won't have a single night's sleep as long as you're gone."

They stood without speaking. The platform had emptied.

"I'd better get on," Justin said.

His mother did not seem to have heard him. She was studying his legs. "You look taller," she said.

"I feel taller." He was five feet five inches, the shortest boy in his graduating class.

"You're still growing, you know."

"Yes," he said.

"They say you grow until the age of twenty-one."

Justin did not know where to focus his eyes.

"Remember to look for Aunt Mary at the station," Justin's mother said quickly. "She promised to meet your train."

Justin kissed her cheek and tasted salt. Her arms circled his neck, holding him hard.

"Be careful of your feet," she wept. "Don't stand on them too much. The doctor said you shouldn't stand on them too much."

Justin edged toward the train.

"And write," his mother pleaded. "Please . . . please write."

Justin nodded, smiled weakly and boarded the train. His mother was outside the window when he reached his seat. She was blowing her nose into one of her good lace handkerchiefs, one of those she used only on special occasions. Justin suddenly felt very sorry for her. There wasn't going to be much ahead for her that would be good.

The train started with a lurch and moved slowly ahead. Justin's mother walked beside the window. She bent and said something to him, but he could not hear her. He shook his head and pointed to his ears. The train was moving more quickly now. His mother had to hurry to keep up. She said the same thing again and there seemed a great urgency to it. Justin tried to read her lips. He fought to open the window. It was stuck. His mother could no longer keep up with the train. He peered desperately back at her, straining to understand as she shouted her smothered message for the final time. Justin felt a wild, unreasoning sense of its importance. Then she was gone.

His eyes missed nothing, devouring the rolling hills and green farmlands, the miles of city concrete, the huge factories with their gray pennants of smoke. He was free of Red Bank at last, and the clearly visible proof of it stretched to the horizon. It was all there to be seen and smelled and, if he could reach out his hand far enough, touched. At each stop he got off the train, walked along the station platform and breathed deeply as if each place were touched with its own new and wholly individual flavor.

There was only one thing to dampen the thrill of the journey— his destination. He did not object to Chicago. He had read about it a hundred times, and under other conditions he would have been happy to go there. It was the thought of his life there that bothered him. He had met his aunt and uncle only twice, but he remembered them clearly. His aunt was a tall, ascetic-looking woman who had been a schoolteacher and who spoke even to adults as though they were children. Her husband was an insurance actuary. Justin recalled him as wearing somber suits and an air of great importance. He had once told Justin that he was very fortunate to have been born in the twentieth century, that because of it he might well expect to live to be sixty-two years old. Justin had been ten years old at the time and had felt no elation at the news. He had been certain he would live forever.

It was dusk when he passed through Pittsburgh. Justin stared at the great mills, at the furnaces flaring red against the sky, at the chimneys standing like great arms reaching upward. The shifts were changing, and as the train moved slowly through the city he could see thousands of men pouring from the sheds into the busy streets, and he felt that in passing near them in the steel train he had formed a kinship with them, for he too was on the move. Justin had read about Pittsburgh, and he knew about steel, but no amount of reading could have prepared him for the sight of it. The sheer size of everything was overwhelming. The moving masses of strong men, the sounds of work and release, the living flames in the gathering dusk, all became for him an affirmation of power, of creation, of greatness.

And suddenly he realized an awesome thing—he was free to become part of it. To be one with it, that too could be—he thrilled as the word came to him—immortality.

The feeling did not pass with the city. It stayed with him through the darkness of the Ohio Valley and stretched to the distant glow of Youngstown, where it flared anew. Things were *made* here, he thought. Men started with nothing and when they were through, things had been made. He had never made anything. For seventeen years he had lived with his two hands and never had he even helped make anything with them. Now he was on his way to a far-off place, where he would sit in a tall office building and read endless rows of neatly spaced numbers, and that would be called his work, and from that nothing would come nothing.

This idea rode with him, and his bitterness grew. The lights were dimmed in the coach and the other passengers were sleeping, but Justin peered steadily into the night. He could see how it would be living with his aunt and uncle: the carping and nagging of home and not even pleasant memories of his childhood to make it bearable. He had been willing to agree to anything to get away, and now he was away.

Now he had to agree to nothing.

The train passed through the outskirts of a city. It had started to rain, a soft, foglike drizzle that haloed the scattered lights. The lights grew closer together and there was a glow of furnaces and dark forms of mills. The tracks widened to a sprawl of yards and car barns. The train stopped for a signal and waited, then lurched ahead once more. From the next coach, Justin heard the conductor shout the name of a city. It sounded vaguely like Cleveland. The train pulled into the station, and Justin watched a few passengers get off. As steam rose in clouds and mixed with the rain, he pressed his face to the window, trying to see more. A thought was building. It grew as mail and baggage were loaded and unloaded from the train.

The conductor shouted for final boarding. Justin abruptly stood up, pulled his bag from the rack and stepped from the train to the platform. He stood motionless as the train left, and he watched until the red tail lights had faded and disappeared. After a while he slowly tugged his bag into the station. He sent a telegram to his mother, in which he said only, "I changed my mind. Don't worry." He did not send a telegram to his aunt, guessing his mother would call her. Then he went to the ticket window and received a refund of eight dollars and twenty-seven cents on the unused portion of his ticket.

He left the station and wandered slowly along the streets. It was night; there was little traffic and few people were walking. He passed rows of darkened lofts and small factories.

The drizzle had thickened to a slow rain, but Justin barely noticed. He was looking at the buildings and the glistening pavements. He was in a new city, a place where he knew no one and where no one knew him. Less than half an hour ago, he had not even known he would be here; he still did not wholly believe it. It was like being born again. A wave of exhilaration swept over him and he grinned in the darkness.

He shivered with a passing chill. The wetness had begun to soak through. He turned a corner and saw a lighted sign that said, "HOTEL." He went toward it.

An old man dozed behind a desk in the dingy lobby. Justin approached and put down his bag. It made a sharp sound on the uncarpeted floor and the old man opened his eyes.

"I'd like a room," Justin said.

The old man peered at him without interest. There were red whiskey spots on his cheeks and nose, and his bald head shone smoothly. "For how long?"

Justin paused. He had not thought this far.

"Dollar a night," the clerk said. "Five dollars a week. Paid in advance."

Justin considered the weekly saving. He put five dollars on the desk. "Make it a week."

The old man took the money and pushed an ink-stained register toward him. Justin picked up a pen and looked at the big book. Half a page of names stared back at him. He put the pen to the proper line and started to form the letter J. Then abruptly and without further thought, he changed it to a B and scrawled, "Bill Baker . . . New York."

The old man gave him a key. "Room 407. Three flights up and to your right."

The stairs were steep and the flights long, so that Justin had to rest on each landing. Gasping, he dragged his bag heavily behind him. Near the top he stumbled, fell and lay for a moment on the creaking wooden steps. He silently cursed the weakness, the failure of his body. Hearing footsteps below, he hurriedly got up and lurched to his room.

Inside there was a double iron bed, a warped bureau and a rickety table. A rust-stained sink was fixed to one wall. Justin turned on the faucet and washed a family of roaches down the drain. He was thirsty, but there was no glass and he had to cup his hands to get at the water. He went over to the window and tried to open it. It was stuck. He strained against it and hammered the sides with his hands, but it would not budge. He fought a wild desire to kick his foot through it. He heard footsteps and voices in the hall, and then the sound of a door closing. Voices came through the wall behind his bureau. He could not make out their words, but could separate a man's from a woman's. The man's voice sounded loud and happy and the woman laughed a great deal. After a while he did not hear them any more.

Justin undressed and lay down on the bed in his underwear. The mattress sagged in the middle and he rolled to one side where it was firmer. His suitcase lay on the floor, unopened, and he stared at it for a long time. Then he got up, opened it, took out his books and arranged them in a double row on the bureau. He lay down again and the room did not look so bad to him. He thought of his new name and spoke it aloud. Bill Baker. He did not wonder about why he had made the change. It had seemed the natural thing to do . . . a new city, a new name. This was the way it had always been in his thoughts. But he supposed it was stupid of him to have written Bill instead of William. No one ever signed a hotel register with a nickname.

The naked bulb overhead glared into his eyes and he turned it off. He lay in the darkness, listening to a rat scurry between the walls. There were more footsteps and voices down the hall, but they faded and disappeared. Justin thought of the telegram he had sent his mother. He should have addressed it to his father as well, but it had just come out that way. It wouldn't matter to his father anyway, although his mother would cry when she read it. She would imagine all sorts of terrible things happening to him. Justin could see himself as his mother would picture him, dying alone in some distant, forgotten room. He felt a sweet glow of self-pity. In the midst of his funeral, a lovely, wistful affair guiltily attended by all who had ever mocked or neglected him, the weight of the long day finally proved too much, and he fell asleep.

4

The sun streamed through the shadeless window and slashed Justin's eyes. He sat up in bed, bewildered. Then he saw the room and remembered. He went to the window and looked out at gray buildings and chimneys and the far glint of Lake Erie. He tried again to open the window, and this time, with a rasp of regret, it moved. He smiled broadly at the city of Cleveland and hurried to put on his clothes.

He bought a newspaper and found a diner that looked cheap and clean, where he ordered rolls and eggs and previously forbidden coffee. The strong coffee tasted awful, but he finished it. Then he looked through the "Help Wanted" ads of the newspaper. He paid no attention to the sales or clerical jobs. He was going to use his hands, to be part of building something. The McGuire Company, contractors, were hiring workers for a new office building on Fourteenth Avenue. Justin asked a policeman how to get there, and half an hour later he stepped off a trolley at the building site.

Ground had been broken and steam shovels were already at work. They clanged and thundered at the earth, dumping great scoopfuls of dirt and rock into waiting trucks. Justin, fascinated, watched them for a moment, and then approached a long line of men that stretched toward what was evidently the hiring shack.

The men were of varied shapes and sizes, roughly dressed and hard-looking. Many of them had valises, as if they had just come into town looking for work and still had no place to live. Justin got at the end of the line. Moments later there were others behind him. The line was moving, but very slowly. Although it was a hot day, Justin was wearing his tie and jacket, and he realized how foolish he must look. He should have stopped to buy some work clothes. And his glasses. No one else was wearing glasses. He wished he could take them off, but it was impossible; he would fall into the first open hole.

The men waited silently in the sun. Justin took off his tie and jacket, glancing at the man behind him, who towered far above him. The man's sun-bronzed face was marked, broken, almost heroically ugly, and he had a fierce, jagged scar across the throat. But his eyes were bright, young and the clearest blue Justin had ever seen. The man smiled and his face creased into a thousand tiny lines. Justin smiled back. The man was carrying a valise and he wore the faded blue shirt and trousers of some kind of army uniform. The bottoms of his trousers were tucked into a pair of fine, highly polished boots. It was only four years after the war had ended and many men still wore old uniforms for work clothes. Most of them looked as if they had bought theirs as surplus in an army-navy store. This man looked as though he had worn his as a soldier. Justin wondered in which army.

"I guess we've got a long wait," Justin said, and then realized with surprise that for perhaps the first time in his life he was initiating an exchange of small talk. Yet this seemed right. They were to be fellow workers. Justin had never been a fellow worker before, or a fellow anything.

The man nodded pleasantly.

"Do you know how many men they're taking?" Justin asked.

The big man shook his head.

The line shuffled slowly ahead a few feet.

Justin looked at the man's valise. It was as battered and worn as its owner's face. "Just get into town?"

The man nodded.

A silent type, Justin thought. There was nothing unfriendly in the man's manner. Despite his lack of conversation, his eyes were warm and responsive. Justin decided to keep trying. "So did I," he said. "Where are you from?"

The man smiled. He moved his arm in a sweeping arc that embraced most of the horizon.

Justin laughed and the sound was strange to his own ears. "That takes in a lot of territory."

The man's smile broadened.

"Where were you just before you came to Cleveland?" Justin said.

The man groped in his shirt pocket and took out a small pad and the stub of a pencil. He scribbled on the pad and showed it to Justin. It said, "Chicago."

Justin felt his face flush. The man was a mute. It was stupid not to have guessed it before, but he had always thought of mutes as being deaf. He glanced at the scar edging the man's throat.

"I'm from New Jersey," Justin said. "Red Bank."

The man smiled and wrote the word "nice" on his pad.

"Not so nice," Justin said.

The man shrugged and spread his hands. There was an air of easy, relaxed strength about him that Justin found compelling.

The line inched ahead. Men were still arriving and the line grew. Justin's feet began to ache and he sat down on a pile of boards. The big man sat down beside him. Justin looked at his own hands and saw that they were small and white and he began to worry about being hired. There were so many men, all so much more capable-looking and stronger than he. He envied them their wide shoulders and thick necks and gnarled, calloused hands. He picked up a handful of dirt and pretended to examine it. When he put it down, his hands were less white.

The mute touched his shoulder. Justin turned and the man pointed to a latrine shack in the distance, then to his eye, then to his valise.

Justin took the work slip. It was hard for him to believe what had happened: a man who was a complete stranger had just risked a badly needed job to help him. Why? In a few minutes this big man had done for him what no one had ever done in seventeen years.

"What's your name?" the foreman asked.

"Bill Baker." It came out naturally and easily this time.

The foreman scribbled in his big book. "Eight o'clock Monday morning." He looked at Justin and shook his head. "And for Christ's sake, try not to get yourself killed the first day!"

Justin and the mute walked away together. Justin wanted to speak, to tell him something of what he felt, but did not know how. At last he said, "Thank you," and even this seemed to clot in his throat.

"Listen," Justin said abruptly, "do you have a room, a place to stay?"

The mute shook his head.

"I have one. I paid for a whole week. There's a big double bed and there'd be plenty of room for you and we could . . ." His voice ran down. "I mean . . . maybe it would be better than living alone."

The man looked at him. His eyes gleamed against the dark brown of his face.

"I have a dozen books in my room." Justin hurried on insanely. "I mean, if you like to read or anything you . . ." He did not want to lose him. The man nodded solemnly. Justin grinned and led him toward the trolley stop, as though he had taken a great prize.

Justin asked him his name, and the man gravely wrote on his pad "Nikolai Ivanovitch Vdowishkin." He frowned at it for a moment, laughed silently and drew a line through it. Fascinated, Justin watched the emergence of a new name beneath the old— "Nick Vishkin." There it was again: new place, new life, new name, and strong was the temptation to tell Nick about his own new identity. Still, he had made a good start as Bill Baker. He would let it ride.

It was still early in the day, and they stopped to buy Justin denim work clothes and heavy laborer's shoes, which made his transformation complete. Later, they walked through the crowded city streets, an odd pair. Justin's head barely reached to the big man's shoulder. For every one of Nick's steps, Justin needed two. Nick's pace was graceful, setting off the waddling movement of his young friend. And there were stares directed at the round-faced bespectacled youth in his stiff, oversized work clothes and at the scarred giant beside him. Justin was aware of the looks, but he clumped proudly along in the high, round-toed shoes, chattering more than he had ever done in his life.

At first it seemed difficult to communicate with Nick. Never before, Justin found, had he tried so hard to read the meanings in another man's eyes and expression. The pad helped, although Justin was impatient with the slowness of it. Gradually Justin began to make out simple words in the movement of Nick's lips. It would take time, he knew, but steadily, almost imperceptibly, he was becoming attuned to his new friend. As he strived to learn about him, Justin discovered in Nick a source of fascination rivaling any book he had read.

He learned that Nick was a White Russian who had been wounded on the Eastern front during the war and repaired as well as possible in two years of American Red Cross hospitals. Nick had emerged with a fair knowledge of English and a great curiosity about America. So far he had worked in fourteen American cities in four years; Cleveland would be the fifteenth. He dismissed the Bolshevik Revolution in two words: "No God."

5

Monday had dawned gray and damp, and Justin shivered with cold as they arrived at the building site. Groups of men huddled quietly about the hiring shack, waiting for their assignments. They carried lunch pails and buckets under their arms. Justin had one too, filled with sandwiches and fruit and a thermos of hot coffee, which Nick had instructed him to buy at a diner. Now he stood close to Nick and felt the solid reassuring touch of the big man's shoulder.

The foreman arrived, today wearing a shirt beneath the crossed straps of his overalls. He broke the men into crews and gave them their work orders. Justin and Nick were joined with three other men, given picks and shovels, and sent to the far end of the vast building area to dig foundation and drainage ditches where the steam shovels could not be used. The place had been marked for them with stakes and lines of taut string. They piled their lunchboxes together beside a wooden fence. Justin looked at the others in the gang.

One of them, a very black and grave-faced Negro, was already at work swinging a pick with ease and skill, the blade making a soft, chunking sound as it bit into the dirt. Justin heard one of the men call him Randy. Beside him, a short, curly-haired man leaned on his shovel and watched. "My name is Sarkis Aharounian and I'm an Armenian," the man said, as though this were a great and vital piece of information. Justin noted later that he said everything this way. The third member of the crew was a wiry, young man with a sharp beaked nose topping a walrus mustache. He said his name was Joe. Justin guessed he was an Italian. He spoke English without an accent, but with the deliberateness, formality and careful phrasing of one not born to the language. He showed very white teeth when he smiled, which he did often and without apparent reason. He coughed a lot.

Nick showed Justin where to start digging and how to hold his shovel. He broke up and softened the earth with his pick and Justin shoveled it out. The work did not seem very hard to Justin. The shovel felt solid but light in his hands and there was time to rest while the ground was being picked. When the sun came out and burned away the chill, the men took off their shirts. Justin took his off too, but was ashamed of the pale softness of his body. He compared it to the hard-muscled, bronzed look of the other men and hoped the sun would darken him fast.

Sarkis noticed. "Hey, looka Bill! He's whiter than a virgin's tit!"

The other men laughed.

Randy swung his pick. "Want to change, Billy? How about a little black for white? It might do us both good for a while."

Joe coughed and smiled. "It's a sin to waste such skin on a man. My sister Maria is plagued with hair and dark skin. She would be very jealous to see this."

Justin flushed, but there was no vindictiveness in the ribbing. The kind of mockery he was familiar with was not like this.

The sun moved higher and brought the gleam and smell of sweat to their bodies. The shovel no longer felt so light and Justin's back ached when he bent. The foreman examined their work and passed by without comment, and Justin felt that he had passed a major test. Someone cursed and yelled for water and Justin went for a bucket, filled it at the main pump and brought it back with a dipper. He watched the men drink; the way they poured the water into their mouths and over their faces, and let it splash their bodies. When his turn came, he tried to do the same, but the water went down wrong and choked him so that Nick had to slap his back until he caught his breath.

His hands were starting to rub raw at the pressure points. They burned with each stroke, but he bit his lips and tried not to look at them. Each time he bent there was a lightning-like splitting of his back where it joined his hips. He wondered how much longer it was to the twelve o'clock whistle. He had to last at least that long. The sun was almost directly overhead. All he needed was a little rest, he thought. Then a foot slipped in the shifting dirt and he pitched forward onto the handle of his shovel.

His breath stopped at the pain, and tears burned his eyes. He sank slowly, sitting doubled over on the edge of the trench. Nick hurried over and looked down at him anxiously. Baker nodded that he would be all right, but could not speak. He tried to breathe, but the air would not come. Gradually the ache subsided, his taut muscles relaxed, his breath returned.

Rising slowly, he reached for his shovel. Sarkis picked it up for him and saw the boy's hands as he passed the tool.

"Son of a bitch!" the Armenian said. "Lookit the kid's hands!"

The crew stopped work and gathered round. Baker looked at his hands. Raw flesh showed where his palms and fingers were rubbed through the skin.

"You'd better pee on them, boy," Randy said. "They'll infect sure as hell if you don't."

Baker looked at the Negro, thinking he was joking, but Randy's face was solemn. The others nodded in agreement.

"It will heal it quickly," Joe said. "Urine holds nature's salt. It's the best thing."

Baker looked at Nick for final confirmation, and then he walked modestly over to the fence.

"What's a matter, kid?" Sarkis called behind him. "Ashamed of it? It's the best part of you."

At noon the men settled down with their lunch pails. Justin sat against a rock with Nick. The rest of the gang sprawled about them. There was no shade in the hot sun, but a soft, licking breeze made it pleasant. The foreman came up with his lunch and sat close by. He looked at Justin's hands.

"You! . . . Kid!" He threw away the wet stub of a cigar and spat brown. "I got some gloves in the shack. Put them on. You ain't gonna last the day otherwise."

"What about me, boss?" Sarkis' voice was mincing, girlishly high. "Ain't you got a little something for me?"

"I got this for you, Armenian."

The men laughed.

"You could do worse," Sarkis said. "Ask the Turks. They know. For three hundred years they've been after our ass. Sweeter than lamb."

The foreman threw a stone. Sarkis went on eating, his dark eyes and face fluid, mercurial.

"You're always talking about Armenia," Randy said. "How long did you live there?"

Sarkis stuffed his mouth with bread. "Till I was about seven. My old man got us out two steps ahead of a damn Turk knife."

"Hell!" Joe mocked. "You ain't even Armenian. I at least lived in Italy for ten years. But I still don't go around screaming myself Italian."

Sarkis straightened. "That's because you're ahamed of it, you wop! An Armenian is different. An Armenian is always an Armenian. He doesn't have to be born there. He doesn't have to even see the place. It's in the blood. *That's* where Armenia is! If two of us meet in a desert, *that's* Armenia! We're a small people. Not even two million of us left. Shit on by the world for five hundred years and not killed off yet."

The mute grinned and applauded loudly. Sarkis fought down a stubborn piece of crust and looked at him. "What about you, Cossack? How come you didn't hang around to get yours out of the big revolution? Were you one of them grand dukes or something? Did they kick your royal ass out?"

Nick shrugged and spoke without sound.

Justin watched his lips and interpreted. "He said the Bolsheviks couldn't take the place of God."

"How the hell do *you* know what he said?" the foreman asked. "I didn't hear a goddamn thing come out of his mouth."

"The kid can read his lips," Randy explained.

Justin glanced about self-consciously. "Ask Nick something. I'll tell you what he answers."

"Lenin," Joe said. "How about Lenin? Did you ever see him?"

Justin studied the answer on his friend's lips. "Once, at a parade. A small man with a great voice. He looked like nothing, but they listened when he spoke. He made fine speeches."

"Shit!" Sarkis said. "Speeches and parades, that's all the Bolshies are any damn good at. They talk and march and the people are still getting screwed. You were smart to get the hell out, Cossack."

Randy sucked thoughtfully at a chicken bone. "I don't know," he said. "At least they say a colored man's as good as a white. For me they've got that much pulling for them."

"Hell, they ain't *got* no colored men in Russia," the foreman said. "They can say anything they want about that."

Randy did not seem to hear him. "They've got no lynch mobs in Russia."

"Quit gripin'." The foreman bit the end from a fresh cigar. "You been lynched lately?"

"No," Randy said quietly. "But my brother was." No one said anything, and he looked without malice at the circle of white faces. "I'll tell you something. I've been doing a lot of reading about the Bolsheviks. Maybe there's still plenty wrong there, but at least they've made a start. I can't laugh at them."

The foreman spat. "Why the hell don't you go there if you think they're so great?"

Randy smiled slowly. "Maybe I will one day. Meantime there are just four things in this world I care enough about to roll out of bed for and they're not in Russia." He took a worn photograph from his wallet and passed it to the foreman, who passed it along to the other men. Justin saw a pretty Negro woman and three smiling children. They all nodded and returned the picture to Randy.

Justin was surprised. The other men were drifters without permanent homes or family ties; they moved where the jobs were. He had supposed it to be the same with Randy. He was also surprised at the Negro's speech, which was little different from his own and free of Southern mannerisms. And, also unexpected, Randy clearly had more schooling than the other men. Justin had never actually known any Negroes before. He had never spoken to any of those living in Red Bank.

"Hey, boss," Sarkis said, "you got visitors."

Justin saw two men motioning to the foreman, who frowned and stood up. They were just outside the hiring shack and wore expensive-looking clothes with tight, narrow pants and double-

breasted jackets. Justin could not hear their voices when the foreman went to talk to them, but the men seemed very angry. They
waved their arms as they spoke, but the foreman just listened to
the men and did not say anything at all. Finally, the men walked to
a gleaming black car and drove off. The foreman stood looking
after them. When the car had turned a corner and disappeared, he
walked back slowly.

Joe coughed into his mustache. "Trouble, boss?"

The crew had been watching, as had other groups in the area.
The foreman took off his hat and ran an arm across his dripping
forehead.

"Bastards!" he swore softly to himself. "And all because I
didn't tell them I was hiring yesterday. The goddamn notice was in
the paper. It was no damn secret."

"They looked like a couple of Turks," Sarkis said. "Who the
hell were they?"

"Goons from the Workers' Protective Association," the foreman
said dryly.

"They can go to hell," Randy growled. "They're not squeezing
any fifty-cent pieces from me. I've got too many of my own
mouths to feed. I'm not taking from them to feed any damn white
pimps."

The foreman shrugged. "It's your four bits. But let me tell you
something. Four bits a week is cheap. I've had those bastards
around for five years. I've seen them go to work. Four bits is
cheap."

"Why can't we just tell the police?" Justin said.

The foreman looked at him with a mixture of wonder and pity.
"That'll only cost you two bits more." He glanced at his watch,
picked up his lunch pail and blew two long blasts on his whistle.

"What do you think, Cossack?" Joe asked.

Nick closed his lunch bucket and considered the four men in his
crew. His pale eyes were mild, and his lips carefully formed a
reply.

"He said there was the same kind of thing in Chicago," Justin reported. "Also in Boston and New York and Pittsburgh. He said if that's the way it's got to be, we can't change it."

"They sure as hell changed plenty in Russia," Sarkis offered.

Nick smiled and spoke without sound.

"He said he's not interested in any more revolutions," Justin interpreted. "He said he'd rather pay fifty cents a week and be able to go to church on Sunday."

"I can have Jesus without paying four bits for it," Randy grumbled.

The gloves helped Justin's hands, but there was nothing to save his back. Nick did not appear to notice, yet his picking became slower, more deliberate, so that Justin was given greater intervals of rest. Later the other men invented errands for him—water, a change of tools, further instructions from the foreman. The conspiracy was silent and unacknowledged and, if questioned at all, would have been cursed and denied. But it was there and with it Justin was able to push through the afternoon. When the five o'clock whistle sounded the end of his first day's work, he wanted to cry and shout at the same time. He had stood with men and he was one of them. He had worked with his hands.

Chapter Three

1952: Washington, D.C.

Representative Henry Ainsley Pilgrim III, Republican from Illinois, rose at his table and waved to Morris Kantrowitz, counsel from New York. The committee's investigator had just appeared at the entrance to the Representatives' Dining Room on the subground level of the House Office Building. Kantrowitz wound his way around chairs and tables, patting shoulders and nodding to friends as he passed.

"Eating alone, Henry?" he asked. "What's the matter, your constituents neglecting you?"

"Yeah, and it's a pleasure."

Kantrowitz showed mock surprise. "Disenchanted so soon? Take heart. Your career is young."

Pilgrim grinned broadly at Kantrowitz as the lawyer settled into his seat. Kantrowitz noted something predatory in the gleam of Pilgrim's blue eyes. "Well, Mighty Mouse," Pilgrim said with satisfaction, "we dug us up something bigger than the Hiss-Chambers case, and who'd have expected it? You call in a big newsman for color and class, settle back to hear some platitudes on the dangers of international Communism, and next thing you know, you've got an ex-spy leading you through bonanza-land. Hell, Kelly hadn't even talked to him before to find out what he had to say."

"Henry, what Blaine was expected to say he's said often in his broadcasts. Besides, Kelly was busy getting things started for the San Francisco hearings. *That's* where he expected to dig up the rich dirt. Things had just about petered out here, so he wanted to bring in a few stars like Blaine for some flash at the end."

"Which may just blow up in Webster Evers' and you-know-who's faces."

"Maybe yes, maybe no." Kantrowitz was dour, rarely exhibiting optimism, even when riding his highest crest of success. "Let's see what the papers do with it. Maybe the Communist menace is going out of fashion."

"Like hell it is. This Blaine's going to carry us for lots of years. Taking on no less than Evers himself! Can you imagine what's going on at the White House right now?"

Kantrowitz scowled. "Henry, sometimes you forget that in spite of this hunt I'm in, I vote Democratic. You and I are not joyed by the same news."

Pilgrim leaned back and smiled. "I assume the committee can count on your wholehearted cooperation in this. Nor would our chairman bow to pressure from higher up . . . or would he? And, oh, yes, Morrie, call me Hank."

Kantrowitz glanced over the menu at him. The smile was still there, looking natural and pleasant in Pilgrim's sunburned face. But the eyes . . .

"You're really champing at the bit, aren't you? We've just had this package dropped in our laps—only an hour ago—and already you're taking on the President. Hasn't it occurred to you that our friend Blaine may be off his nut, or the biggest liar who ever walked?"

"A liar? Why? Why would he do that?"

"I don't know why, Henry, I don't know anything." Kantrowitz turned back to his menu. Suddenly the items on the list— marinated herring, tomato juice, onion soup, chef's salad (with

French dressing, Roquefort 25¢ extra), roast beef, shrimp curry, steak and kidney pie, fruit delight ice cream and so on—seemed absurd in their triviality. In another room in this same building was a list that could cause an uproar as big as any in the nation's history. And how much extra payment would dressing like Webster Evers be worth to someone like Pilgrim?

He was startled by Pilgrim's voice breaking the silence.

"Tell me, Morrie, where do we go now? Have you been able to talk to Kelly?"

"For a minute, just before I came down here. I agreed there was no point in continuing to question Blaine until we have a chance to catch our breath. Let's hold off any further public testimony for a couple of days, and let's just work him over in executive session. We'd better know what he's got before he spills red ink over the whole town."

"You mean over the whole nation." Pilgrim leaned forward, his eyes tauntingly narrowed. "Are some of *your* friends worried, Morrie? I'm not afraid of getting hurt."

Kantrowitz ignored him. He called a waiter and with a private smile ordered chef's salad. Pilgrim ordered the same. "But with Roquefort dressing," he said. "It's two bits extra, but it's worth it."

Let's try to put this into perspective, Kantrowitz told himself as he stared sightlessly at the diners around him. Absently he ran a finger down his long, aquiline nose. Certainly this was the biggest break since the committee's establishment. Never had they expected actually to turn up Communist espionage in high places. The FBI might, but not his collection of lawyers, accountants and assorted dealers. If it's true, he thought, it's a gold mine, but a fragile one. Many dangers. Evers has been a policy-maker in the State Department since the second Roosevelt administration. He's almost legendary in Washington, a *Wunderkind* of foreign affairs in the thirties become a dynamic, mature statesman in the fifties. Given a Democratic win in November, Evers would be Secretary of State. But even now his influence—my God! (Morrie flushed) the power!—would be like heavy artillery; he could wreck the committee. You couldn't touch him without also touching the White House. Like eggshells, this thing. The committee would have to move as if on eggshells before pointing the finger at this man on the say-so of this confessed spy, or maybe this liar, or this nut.

Yet, if Blaine's stuff were true . . .

Pilgrim was flashing his most charming smile at the House Speaker five tables away. He bobbed and nodded, his blond crew cut bright in the fluorescent lighting.

A gold mine fragile as eggshells, Morrie thought, and greedily stomping into it would be men like Pilgrim. Already during this one session Pilgrim had asked question after question, blundering toward confirmation of his most grisly hopes. The Republicans were searching desperately for election issues. Pleased as he was at the potential advantages in latching onto Justin Blaine, Kantrowitz was sickened by the thought of what the Republicans might do with Evers, guilty or innocent.

The salads arrived; the Roquefort was like a gobby pallor over everything. Morrie looked at it as if it were an outrage. Pilgrim dug right in.

Pushing his plate away, Kantrowitz sighed deeply and tiredly. Just turned thirty but looking older, he still felt like an alien in Washington. Somehow he just could not mesh himself with the machine, with the other committee counsels and the legislators and the agency boys. He thought of a counterpart counsel-investigator in the Senate, a clever smooth lawyer, also from New York, an operator of operators. When he was around, you knew it and looked out, but you could never quite grab on to him, the eyes would never really open to you. Oh, but such a success: never would *he* appear in a wrinkled suit or with an unpopular idea.

Abstractedly, he stared at the flesh that showed through Pilgrim's hair cut. Pilgrim bent over a salad, Morrie thought, a study in intensity. He smiled. *I've* got intensity and I've got that Kantrowitz *sechel,* that special shrewdness. Hadn't his mother said dozens of times, "With my Morrie's *sechel,* he'll be President before he's fifty . . . if they'd let a Jew in the White House"? No, he thought, even if they would, I don't have enough *sechel* to mesh.

Over coffee, Pilgrim launched into a repertory of tasteless jokes and embarrassing gossip. Morrie timed his nods and chuckles carefully and wondered, How could such a man get elected and reelected? The wonderment was rhetorical. Newspaper friends had told him about Pilgrim's amazing ability to rise above his real self when on the stump, how he could present a stern, almost humorless aspect to the voters. With that face it was easy. His only unusual feature was a rather broad, flat nose, but even that seemed to add distinction to his face, a countenance set off by a perennial sunburn, crew-cut blond hair and a sharp, cleft chin—a politically reliable, white, Anglo-Saxon, Protestant image. An image of the serious, straightforward family man, above reproach, but compellingly attractive; from aristocratic stock, but with a feeling for the common folk; democratically earthy, but with an aura of the creative and killing power of money and influence. Sexy. His second term in Congress was ending, and still he had no record of legislation introduced. But then, Morrie thought, did he need one?

Even as Morrie smiled at a repulsive punch line, he concluded, you can't write Pilgrim off as a clown. You've got to watch him carefully.

Reporters were waiting for them as they left the dining room, and they followed the two men down the corridor, firing questions about what the committee would do next. Would they subpoena Evers? What did they think the President's reaction would be? What else did Blaine have to spill?

Pilgrim let himself be cornered and turned to them with a grim smile, his face mirroring the suffering in the statement he gave the newsmen about trusted men in high places selling out their country. Kantrowitz headed up a flight of steps and disappeared into the offices of the committee, where his three assistants were already gathering every piece of information they could suck from their files about the past and present activities of Webster Evers.

2

As Justin Blaine was leaving the hearing room, a delegation from the State Department was arriving at the Washington National Airport to greet a visiting delegation from the Middle East. Leading them were the Chief of Protocol and a tall, elegantly dressed man of slender face: Webster Evers, the Under Secretary of State, representing the Secretary himself. The group stopped inside the waiting room and looked out through great picture windows to where microphones had been set up and where the Marine Band with honor guard were standing in the chill air.

"Considering the cold," the Protocol Chief was saying, "it would seem all right to give the statements inside. The Marines can stand it, but I don't think those Arabs can."

"Nor could we," Evers said with a slight laugh. "If I'm going to welcome them, I'd rather not do it through chattering teeth. Yes, let's move the microphones inside. Have the band play them into the building; they shouldn't feel slighted about that."

He beckoned a young man to his side. "Frank, will you notify the press that we're going to hold the ceremony in here? We've been told that the plane has just entered the traffic pattern, so it should be only about ten minutes or so before things start happening."

"Yes, sir," the young man said, and strode off to where another group of men, photographers and reporters, was waiting.

One reporter, however, did not hear Frank's message; he was in a phone booth being jolted by other news. He had just made a routine call to the bureau chief of his paper, the San Francisco *Post-Courier*.

"That's right," the bureau chief was saying, "Jerry just phoned

it in. Now I don't have to tell you about Evers and the delicacy of
all this, but this was testimony before the committee—it's part of
the public record—and we'd like a statement, preferably as a
scoop. Do you think you can manage it?"

"I'll try," said the reporter, "but it's going to be rough to get to
him. Those Arabs are due any minute, and the other press guys are
very close by."

"What are they doing now?"

"Who?"

"Evers, the press guys, everybody!"

"Evers is with the Protocol Chief, talking. Wait, he's just sent
someone over to tell the press guys something. Some of them are
taking off their coats, so I guess the ceremony is going to take
place inside."

"Any of the press talking to Evers?"

"No. I don't think they've heard yet."

"Okay. It may be rough getting a statement even without a
scoop, so just try for the statement and when you get it—and I
expect you to get it—get right back to me. We can take the ceremony off the wire services."

"Right. Here goes."

He stepped out of the phone booth and walked slowly toward
the State Department group. The Arabs' plane was still not in
sight.

"Oh, Mr. Percy," Frank called, and the reporter stopped. "I
didn't see you with the other reporters so I thought I'd tell you
we're going to have the statements inside because of the cold."

"Oh? When should things be starting?"

"There's been a delay. They're circling in the traffic pattern
because there's an airliner with an engine out coming in first. I
guess it's partly because of the cloudiness."

"I see. Say, I wonder if I might be able to speak with Secretary
Evers for a moment. It's . . . it's kind of important, and since
there's a little time . . ."

"Well, Mr. Evers doesn't usually."

"I'd appreciate it. As a matter of fact, I think Mr. Evers would appreciate it too. It's something he ought to know."

Frank looked at him suspiciously.

"Look, would you just ask him? Tell him it's something he ought to know about."

"Should I alert the other reporters?"

Percy clenched his teeth in exasperation. What was the matter with this kid? Should he approach Evers himself directly? No, play it smart. "No. Just ask Mr. Evers."

"All right, I'll ask him."

Percy nervously watched the young man speak to Evers. He tensed more as he saw Evers turn and look at him, perhaps trying to remember if he was one of the regulars, one of the trusted members of the press corps. Well, thought Percy, I am, almost, but maybe not after this, and yet maybe very much after this. But how do I tell him that he's just been publicly called a traitor?

Evers seemed to ponder for a moment and then walked toward Percy, his face relaxed but his eyes alert. Percy could feel the attention of the other newsmen focusing on him, sensing something unusual in Evers' approaching a solitary newsman not known to be on the inside at State.

"Yes?" Evers was in front of him now, a tall, impressive presence.

"Mr. Secretary, I'm Malcolm Percy of the San Francisco *Post-Courier*." What to say? "Thank you for talking to me, sir."

"I'm pleased to meet you, Mr. Percy. I don't think we've met before, have we?"

"No, sir."

There was another slight pause. Percy could feel the interest of the other newsmen gathering. A phone in one of the booths suddenly was ringing. Think, Percy. *Think!*

Evers' polite smile disappeared.

"Well? What *is* it, Mr. Percy?" The voice was still smooth, yet it hinted impatience.

Percy kept his voice very soft, but an edge was there.

"Sir, I thought you would want to know that the radio commentator, Justin Blaine, has just named you before the House Subversive Activities Committee."

Evers frowned and Percy noticed a slight pallor come into his face. Now Evers' voice was softer, yet harsher.

"*Named* me? What do you mean, 'named' me? Named me as *what?*"

A quick licking of the lips. "As a Communist, sir, as a member of . . . a Communist espionage network. I don't have all the details yet. My office just told me what I've told you. I can imagine what a surprise this must be, sir, but would you like to make a statement?"

Evers' face had regained its color. The expression was unchanged.

"A statement to you?"

Percy could hear the reporters getting up from the waiting room chairs and approaching them. Good-bye scoop.

"To me, or to all of us, sir."

Evers had noticed the other newsmen approaching. He turned his face to them and smiled. "Gentlemen, this is nothing that you'd be interested in. I'm just getting acquainted with Mr. Percy here, strictly casual. Anything newsworthy that I might have to say would be said to all of you, you know that."

They did. The press had long ago learned to accept Evers on his terms, which were scrupulously fair—especially considering what they could have been.

The phone was still ringing in the booth, and one of the State people went to answer it. Percy could see Evers glance anxiously at the booth. The reporters were starting back to their chairs when one of them said, "I think the plane is just landing now." The photographers headed for the door and the reporters moved toward the newly set-up microphones.

Evers turned back to Percy.

"Now you listen. I have no statement to make about this. Your telling me this is off the record, and this, too, is off the record: I'm surprised at your chief. He knows me well enough to know I wouldn't bother to respond to such nonsense as this 'naming' by this fellow Blaine. I don't know what Blaine is talking about. So there will be no statement. Now that is off the record, do you understand?"

"Yes, sir."

Evers glanced again at the phone booth. The State man had put the receiver back on the hook and was looking at Evers significantly.

"And this is off the record too. In just a few moments some important foreign visitors are going to be welcomed to the United States by me representing the Secretary of State. This will be an ordinary welcoming ceremony followed by a short, formal, ordinary press conference with questions directed only to Mr. Shamal, the Foreign Minister. You are not to spread this other thing around. There will be no embarrassing disruption. You're relatively new with the State press corps and we are now very well acquainted. Need I say more?"

Percy's mouth was very dry. "No, sir."

"All right." Suddenly he smiled cordially. "And, Mr. Percy, thank you for taking the trouble to tell me. Good day."

As Evers walked to the door, pausing momentarily by the man who'd handled the phone, and then out to where the plane was taxiing onto the ramp, Percy tried to figure out just what happened. Two things, he decided. First, Evers had come through an impossible situation without a scratch. Second, Evers had somehow awed him into a loyalty that would indeed keep him quiet. He walked toward the other reporters, noticing Evers warmly shaking hands with Foreign Minister Shamal. The reporters glanced at him curiously and then looked back to the ramp where the dignitaries were being serenaded into the building by the Marine Band. The honor guard was rigid in its presentation of arms. So smooth, thought Percy, so *smooth!*

Suddenly his stomach pulled tight as he realized that a third thing had happened. He had most probably just lost his job.

3

No one saw anything significant in Webster Evers' brief talk with the Chief of Protocol as the press conference proceeded, or even in Evers' departure from the building as Mr. Shamal droned on about the need for good Arab-American relations in the face of new imperialist threats to the Middle East.

The Under Secretary strode toward the first inline of parked limousines. "Head back to town," he told his driver. "I'll let you know exactly where in a few moments."

As the car rolled away from the airport, Evers closed the soundproof partition that separated him from the driver, picked up the phone and put through a call to the Affiliated News Services. He asked for Francine Moore and in a moment heard the familiar voice.

"Moore."

"Francine, please give your full name. Moore sounds so damned masculine."

"My God, it's you. Where are you?"

"You sound upset. What's the matter?"

"You must have heard about Blaine."

"Yes, I've heard."

"You don't sound terribly concerned."

He pulled on his cigarette and allowed the smoke to drift from his nostrils. "This isn't the first time my name has been slandered. One gets used to this sort of thing."

"No, dear. This time it's different." Her voice, he noted, was taking on the lady-of-the-press tone he hated. "I'm not a neophyte around Washington, Webster. When do I get the story?"

"There *is* no story. In fact, I'm counting on *you* for the details. I thought you might give me a briefing before I face your brethren in my office."

"Fine. Where and when?"

"Can you meet me at the zoo in about fifteen minutes?"

"Why the zoo, for God's sake? It's freezing."

"No," he said, "it's just cold. Besides, that's why I like the idea of the zoo. No one will be there. Meet me at that round enclosure where they keep the prairie dogs."

There was a short silence. Then she said, "I'll leave now."

The zoo was almost deserted. Only a few people wandered along the walks and through the buildings. The trees were bare and the sooty remains of a snowfall filled the crevices of their gnarled roots.

Webster instructed his chauffeur to drive the limousine back to the Department garage. Then he got out and walked briskly down to the prairie-dog mounds. In a large, circular, fenced-in area, dozens of the animals barked as they darted into holes in the dirt mounds, or sat on their haunches like enormous squirrels. Francine was not in sight, so he kept moving. He plunged his gloved hands into the pockets of his Chesterfield and continued walking with long, quick steps, hunched against the cold.

Outside the reptile house he lighted a cigarette, fastidiously brushing away the ash that settled on the front of his coat. As he completed the circular path, he saw Francine hurrying toward him.

She was almost as tall as he, and walked with a loose athletic gait. Her brown hair, streaked with gray, blew in the wind. Her gloved hands were deep in the pockets of her speckled tweed coat, and she did not remove them to wave. The man and the woman stood there, both of them handless, and kissed lightly. Then they turned and walked slowly around the prairie-dog enclosure.

Francine looked straight at him. Her face was more attractive than pretty, with a bright, youthful freshness. Now, with the tip of her nose and her cheeks pink from the cold, she seemed especially vital.

"Well?" she asked.

"Well?" he repeated.

"Let's not be amusing, Webster. You're in trouble."

Evers returned her gaze. "If I'm in trouble, you know more about it than I. I know this man Blaine only by reputation, not by sight. To the best of my knowledge I've never met him, not even casually. I've heard him broadcast several times, but his voice meant nothing to me. I can't imagine what has possessed the man to do this insane thing."

Francine looked straight ahead, frowning as she walked at his side. "Webster, I know we've gone to great pains to keep our relationship a mutually nonbinding one, but there's something between us that most husbands and wives don't have. A kind of trust, of mutual respect. Right?"

Evers nodded slowly.

"You wouldn't lie to me because you're afraid I'd print it, would you?" She stopped to look at him, her face serious, her anxiety trying to push open the door that blocked him from her.

"I'm telling you the truth, Fran," he said quietly. "I guess if I can't get you to believe me, I'm going to have even more trouble with the President and the Secretary of State."

She seemed relieved. "I believe you, dear. I really do. The story was so utterly fantastic that I thought—I admit—for a very brief moment it might be true." She smiled and shook her head. "You stuffed shirt! That man picked the most unlikely candidate for a Communist in all of Washington. Why, you won't even ride a subway or a bus, because you can't stand crowds! How could you possibly care about the masses? Justin Blaine must be the prince of fanatics."

"And yet you did believe him for a moment," he said consideringly, "even you."

"Yes, I did. I admit it."

"Then I must demand an opportunity to face the committee and clear myself. If this farce goes on for more than a day or two, it may seriously damage the President's chances for re-election."

"They won't give you much chance to decide," she said flatly. "I'm sure they'll call you before them if you don't volunteer."

"Perhaps not. There are, I hope, a few powerful friends of mine in Washington who might object to the Under Secretary of State being called to clear his name of a crackpot's slander. I might even have to persuade the President to permit me to appear. He'll probably advise me to ignore the whole thing."

Francine linked her arm through his, the tension gone. "Perhaps you're right. God, I hope so. Certainly, the boys they send over to interview you will be with you. You have quite a following, you know. They admire you, even if you never do give them a decent story." She paused. "And that goes for me too. Not the admiration, but the part about the story."

He smiled distantly.

"No kidding," she said, nodding her head in exaggerated seriousness, "in all the time I've known you, not a single exclusive interview. I have to make a living too. Your affection doesn't pay my rent."

Suddenly Evers did not seem to be listening to her. He felt none of the confidence his manner indicated. He was badly frightened, and he did not like the feeling. The trouble was that whatever satisfactory answers he might offer the committee or Francine, he still had need of answers for himself. Why, after thirteen years of silence, was Justin Blaine suddenly trying to destroy him? How could he protect himself from something he in no way understood and the reason for which he could not even try to guess?

Francine glanced at him and knew that she had lost him, and she knew better than to intrude when he was like this, so they walked in silence. She had learned to adjust to this shutting out, but had never really accepted it. All her life, she thought tiredly, she seemed to have been adjusting to one person or another, until she had become expert at it. Yet it had never done her much good. It certainly didn't help save her marriage.

A gust of wind cut with sudden force and she clung closely to Webster's arm. She noticed his profile, the classic line of nose and jaw, the set, abstracted look of the stubborn mouth, the frown etching his brow. Well, she was no longer young and confused. This time she knew what she wanted, and if she was careful, she would get it. Yes, and she sensed she was closer to Webster at this moment than any woman had ever been. At the first threat of real trouble, *she* had been the one he had turned to. And despite his carefully controlled calm, she knew how deeply and rightly concerned he was, for Justin Blaine was not a man to be lightly dismissed as a fanatic. There had to be more to it, and if there was, even Webster Evers would have to hold on to someone.

She smiled to herself. Perhaps she wouldn't be shut out much longer. Perhaps she would soon learn what *really* went on inside Webster Evers when he closed that goddamned door.

Chapter Four

1912: Harrisburg, Pa.

Returning from church on Easter morning the Evers family strolled slowly, strung out along the sunlit walk in a procession of their own. Webster walked first, prancing restlessly and holding his sister Miriam's hand. Several paces behind came his brother Arthur, slender and strikingly handsome in his gray, military school uniform, brass buttons ashine in stern, symmetrical rows. Then came their aunt, Laura Evers, gaunt and tall, her shoulders drooping. Half a pace behind was Dr. Angus Evers, their father, Laura's brother, his dark face abstracted, a pipe clenched between his teeth. When greeted by occasional passers-by, he nodded his head silently.

Webster glanced at the small file behind him. "The whole family," he said proudly to his sister.

Miriam turned also, a big, heavy-bodied girl of seventeen, nearly twice the size of her six-year-old brother, with the flattened forehead, slanted eyes and snub nose of the Mongoloid. "Family," she echoed thickly, "family . . . family . . . family . . . family . . ."

Webster laughed and squeezed his sister's hand twice in a special signal of understanding he'd recently taught her. She returned the signal and he nodded, pleased. "Good, Mim," he said. "Very good."

Still basking in her brother's approval, the lumbering girl suddenly stumbled over a rough spot in the walk and almost fell.

"Careful!" Laura Evers spoke sharply from the rear. "For God's sake, Miriam, watch where you're walking."

"Don't worry, Aunt Laura," Webster said. "I'm holding Mim's hand." He recognized the familiar edge of exasperation in that high voice and waited for some of it to spill over onto him.

"Don't worry, Aunt Laura," she mimicked Webster's childish treble. "If you're so concerned about your poor old aunt worrying, why don't you behave a little better yourself? Your conduct in church this morning was a disgrace, an absolute disgrace."

Laura Evers was neither poor nor old, but at thirty-two she had already suffered through six trying years as her brother's housekeeper and mother to his children, a situation that seemed to lead to permanent spinsterhood. While her sister-in-law had been alive, Laura had resented her abundance of looks, charm and ability. When Lillian Evers died at Webster's birth, saddling Laura with her ton-load of obligations, Laura came to consider her original resentment as prophetic and justified.

"Toss Webbie in the guardhouse, Aunt Laura," Arthur said, laughing. He and Webster both had their mother's delicate, finely chiseled features, but nearing his sixteenth birthday, Arthur's jaw and cheekbones had begun to broaden into manhood.

Webster grinned back at his older brother, grateful for even this small attention. As they turned a corner, they could see their house down the block. He liked the way the house looked from here, with the red-brick chimneys standing tall above the trees, and the wide verandas making a dark circle on the lawn. He could see the section, at the side, where his father's office was, filled with the great oak desk, the table of surgical tools, the scales, the eye chart and, beyond the desk and a high wooden partition, the other, the more secret place, where medicines were stored on shelves like bottles of wine and colored jewels. This place gave off a special kind of smell that you could sniff in almost every other part of the downstairs floor and which always frightened him a little because the smell made him think of sick people and sick people died. Although dying was still little more than a word to him, he did know it was something very terrible, something spoken of by grownups in hushed voices. He also knew it was something that had happened to his mother and was why he was never going to see her, and why his father acted funny sometimes and did not seem to hear what he said when he spoke to him, or else got very angry and shouted for no reason. He couldn't really figure out what shouting or not hearing had to do with his mother dying, except that Aunt Laura would sometimes get that funny, melted look on her face and say she wished his father would, for God's sake, stop burying and reburying his wife and just learn to leave the dead where they belonged.

"Webster, are you listening to me?"

"Yes, ma'am," he lied, the careful politeness a hastily erected bulwark against his aunt's anger.

Arthur grinned exquisitely. "I think the kid needs at least twenty lashes on his bare little backside."

"Just never you mind being quite so smart-alecky," Laura said. There was something frustrating about her older nephew's poised aloofness. She felt he was secretly laughing at her. His high academic honors caused her to view him with the same mixture of awe and bitterness with which she had regarded his mother. "You're still not so big that you're above the need to respect your elders."

Without breaking stride, Arthur made a small, mock bow of servility. "Your servant, ma'am."

Yet with all Arthur's apparent control and confidence, there was still a hasty, concerned glance toward his father. But Angus Evers marched on, unaware and unacknowledging, his eyes on the horizon, beyond Maple Street, beyond Harrisburg, beyond contact with the minutiae of family conflict.

Finding no relief in the exchange with Arthur, Laura glared at

Webster. Her voice became hoarse with effort. "Why a seven-year-old boy should find it—"

"I'm only six and a half," Webster said quickly, taking refuge in the precious half-year of excusable immaturity. He suddenly wished, hoplessly, that he was a six-month-old baby, cute, plump and gurgling, as his aunt had often described him, to be fondled and held without fear of scolding or need to behave in controlled, adultly unreasonable ways.

"Why a boy who's almost seven years old," Laura Evers droned on, "should find it so difficult to sit quietly in church for a few minutes when . . ."

Webster shut off the flow of words with a flick of his mind. They were almost to the house and he could see the rolling lawns stretching off in back to the small, wooden bridge that crossed the stream and touching the rim of the woods beyond. There had been a great deal of rain and the stream now ran fast and high, its sound against the rocks rising and falling like secret, distant music. The grass was still dull with winter, but where the sun broke through the trees, it shone a pale bright yellow. Webster looked at the woods across the stream and ached. Suddenly he dashed off toward the grove, still holding his sister's hand and pulling her along.

"We're going to play!" he threw the explanation back over his shoulder.

"Your clothes!" Aunt Laura wailed after them. "Come back and change your good clothes! You'll get them filthy back there."

He did not glance behind him at all, but kept his eyes moving from his sister to the grove of trees ahead, then back once more to sister. He had slowed, after his initial dash, to allow Miriam to keep up more easily. But even so, she ran awkwardly and without coordination, her thick legs moving stiffly from the hips. She laughed all the way, in short, guttural bursts of animal joy. Her large pink picture hat flopped wildly and the loose ends of the bow at her waist stood out like the tail of an erratic comet. Never releasing her hand, careful to guide her around occasional rough

places in the sloping ground, Webster ran with graceful ease beside
her. Their feet rattled the planks of the bridge and then were quiet
in the loam on the far side of the brook. At the edge of the pine
grove Webster stopped.

"We're here!" he announced breathlessly. "We're at the place!"

"The place!" Miriam echoed.

Webster inhaled deeply. The air was heavy with sweet pine and
the ground softly matted with needles. Seeing her brother taking
deep breaths, Miriam did the same. It had become a ritual with
Webster at their arrival here, this conscious, hungry taking in of
the special fragrance. He was afraid to stop now, afraid that if he
did not do it, some sort of magic chain would be broken. He could
barely see the rest of the family, back at the road, disappearing
into the house . . . first Arthur, then Aunt Laura, and then, very
slowly, his father.

Webster dropped to his knees in the thick, brown carpet of the
needles. One of Miriam's shoelaces had come undone in the running. "Sit down," he said. "I have to fix your shoelace."

The big girl plopped down heavily. She wore high orthopedic
shoes to give extra support to her ankles, but lacked the coordination to lace them. Webster bent to his task, working slowly and
gravely, inserting the ends of the laces in the necessary openings
and pulling them taut.

Making the bow at the end was still the hardest part to Webster,
especially having to face it on someone else's foot. But he managed at last. "There!" He gave the lace a final, triumphant pat.
"All done." If his aunt had seen the open shoelace, she would have
become angry and yelled at Mim, as if his sister had done it on
purpose.

Miriam's eyes were off somewhere beyond his right shoulder.
His sister was watching two cedar waxwings perched on a low
branch of a pine tree. One of the birds twisted its head to dig
among its red-tipped wing feathers as Miriam stared open-
mouthed. Webster remembered suddenly what the minister had
said in church that morning, about Jesus coming back to life on

this day after having been dead and buried, and how something of His spirit was in every living thing. Maybe one of these birds was even Jesus Himself. Liking the idea, he tried to imagine which of the birds might be the Lord. He chose the one that had preened itself and addressed it. "Hello, Jesus," he said softly. "Welcome to the place."

Miriam clapped her hands in delight. "Hello, Jesus! Hello, Jesus! Hello, Jesus!"

Her voice rang out in the quiet grove and the birds took off in a flutter of fright.

"Mim!" Webster turned on her furiously for spoiling the spell. "Bad!"

The homely planes of the girl's face clouded over and she cried. "Hello, Jesus," she tried again, more softly, wondering what had all of a sudden gone wrong.

Webster looked at his sister's stricken face. "That's all right, Mim. They were just dopey old birds anyway."

Webster rarely lost patience with his sister. When he did, he was filled with overwhelming remorse. He launched into a series of cartwheels in a great circle about her, round and round, pine needles flying from hands and feet, while the world kaleidoscoped and Miriam sat laughing and clapping in its center. He finally collapsed at her feet, happily breathless and dizzy.

"More! More!" she cried. "More! More!"

Webster rolled over in the needles and shook his head. "No more," he gasped. "Too tired."

"More! More!"

Webster struggled to his knees, then to his feet. "All right. But just this once more."

When the last cartwheel had been spun and they sat quietly piling up great mounds of needles, Webster asked, "Do you like church?"

"Church . . . church . . . church." Miriam was instantly intrigued with the word. "Ch . . . ch . . . ch . . . ch . . ." Now it was the sound of a train, gathering speed.

"I don't like church," Webster said gravely. "I don't like having to sit still for so long."

"Ch . . . ch . . . ch . . . ch . . ." Miriam went on serenely piling her needles as the train chugged on.

"The sun gets in my eyes in church," Webster said. "This morning it came through those high, colored windows and kept getting in my eyes. And every time I tried to turn my head away, Aunt Laura made me turn back to the front."

"Ch . . . ch . . . ch . . ."

"Miriam, I'm talking to you." Webster unconsciously imitated his aunt's carping tone. "I wish you'd listen when I'm talking to you."

The girl smiled. "Ch . . . ch . . . ch . . ." She leaned forward and, with her face inches from Webster's, peered deep into his eyes as if probing for something significant and mysterious. Then she puckered her heavy, distended lips and pressed them to the tip of his nose. It was something he had once taught her to do, a simple act of grace and love. Webster sat very still as the small ceremony was performed. He did not want anything to take away from or spoil the moment. This brief, perfunctory act, executed with instinctive feeling by a clumsy, mindless giant, was the only sort of kiss he knew.

"I wish I didn't have to sit next to Aunt Laura in church." Webster's recital of grievances went on as Miriam plucked restlessly at the hem of her Easter dress. "I wish she'd let me sit between you and Arthur sometimes. If she'd only let me sit there, maybe church wouldn't be so bad."

Miriam's interest had evaporated. She rose and started to wander idly about the grove. Her excited cry suddenly interrupted his monologue.

"Looka hat!" Giggling loudly, Miriam was pointing toward the brook. "Looka hat!"

Webster saw it then, the beautiful, wide, straw hat, bobbing downstream like a round skiff, its long, pink ribbon trailing gracefully behind.

"Mim!" Webster leaped to his feet in panic and dashed in pursuit along the bank of the stream. Aunt Laura would be wild and he'd get the blame for it. It was not easy to catch up with the swiftly moving hat. When he did, it was still four feet from the bank and beyond his reach. He found a piece of dead branch and once actually managed to touch the hat, but then the current spun it away.

"Looka hat! Looka hat!" Miriam came stumbling after Webster, happy with this new and exciting game.

His sister's voice doubled Webster's fear. What if she tripped and fell in the water? "Stay!" he shouted. "Stay!" But the warning was lost. Miriam continued to lumber ahead, her guttural voice resounding among the trees. Not fifty yards downstream, Webster could see the black opening of the culvert where the water disappeared under Maple Street. If he did not catch the hat before it entered the tunnel, it would be lost.

The water gurgled maliciously. Webster, stumbling over unseen rocks, kept running. The tunnel loomed closer, while the hat, as if guided by some fiendishly efficient mechanism of its own, remained constantly in the center of the raceway. Webster cried out. "No!" It was no use. The new hat was lost and all the demons of his aunt's wrath would be let loose. A vision of his sister's face dissolving in tears tore through his brain.

2

That day dinner was served early because of the holiday and because Arthur had to catch a six o'clock train back to school. As part of Webster's punishment for wetting his shoes and stockings, he had been fed in the kitchen with Miriam, an outcast from the family.

Now, with the others lingering at the table, he sat playing cards with Miriam on the living room floor, still cut off. Holding up the cards one at a time, he carefully pronounced their names and described them, letting Miriam repeat after him as much as she could remember. He was up to the pictures.

"Jack." He showed her the card. "This is the jack of diamonds. Say it."

"Jack o' dimuns," Miriam repeated thickly, slurring the words together. The big girl sat cross-legged on the bright Persian rug, facing Webster.

"Very good," he said gravely. "See. This is the diamond, this pointed red thing here. And the jack is a blond-haired man with two heads who looks the same upside down." Webster reversed the card to demonstrate and Miriam screamed with delight.

"Two heads! Two heads!"

In the dining room Webster's aunt heard the girl's voice and shook her head disapprovingly. "Webster, don't get your sister so excited!" She frowned into her coffee, the bones of her long, spare face jutting hard against their coarse cover of skin. "Why do I bother?" she sighed. "Why don't I just save my voice? It's like talking to yourself in this house."

Her hands, outstretched and tense on the table, drummed a nervous tattoo. "Thank heaven I'll be getting away from here in another few weeks. Away from all of you. Another year of this household and I'd be fit to be put away with your daughter."

At the opposite end of the long table, Angus Evers drew deeply on his pipe and did not say anything. His sister's despair rarely required an answer, and even when it did, he avoided offering one. Right now her face was flushed and pained at the harshness of her own reference to Miriam, and Evers felt a stir of pity. He knew what she'd had to put up with for the past six and a half years, and there was surely no blaming her for what she was about to do now.

But she'd not been able to accept it yet herself. She still suffered from the bitter conviction that *she alone* was sending the child away, that *she alone* was having the child committed to a place whose name she still could not even force herself to speak aloud. About to be married, Laura felt her joy in the unexpected event marred by the knowledge that Miriam would no longer be able to remain at home because of it. Who would there be to care for her? Certainly she could hardly be expected to smother her new life and marriage by carrying her Mongoloid niece into it like a hideous dowry.

"We'll all miss you, Aunt Laura," Arthur said, meaning it, but helpless to keep the barbed edge of banter from his tone. Yet Arthur knew how much he'd not like it with her gone. In spite of the anger, the bitterness, the constant carping and the rest, at least she was a voice, a person, someone for him to react to, who would react to him in return. Without her he would have only his father and that was having nothing. Sometimes he had the awful feeling that if he failed to come home from school at all, if he just quietly disappeared from sight without explanation, there would be no perceptible change in his father's life or manner. Dr. Angus Evers would just go serenely on, puffing his pipe, tending his patients, reading his medical journals and gazing distantly off at nothing. Sometimes Arthur had a ghastly, recurrent dream, in which he was sinking into a black, stinking bog, with his father standing less than two feet away, on solid ground, and when he cried out, his father did not seem to see or hear him, but just stood there as his son sank.

Laura folded her arms across the ruffles of her blouse. Arthur's glance always made her feel uncomfortable. The boy's eyes had the same dark, soulful quality as his mother's, and like his mother's eyes they tended to make her feel painfully unattractive and inadequate.

"The roast was good," Evers said. The comment, in the hoarse, stentorian voice, was weighted with effort. The very act of speech was a great and heavy trial, as if each word had to be squeezed past a steadily thickening barrier in his throat. His sense of that growth had become so real, so foreboding, that Evers had actually gone for X-rays the month before. There was nothing. Or at least nothing visible on photographic plates. An insane disappointment had been mixed with the relief. There was nothing to be cut out.

No surgeon's blade could be called upon to slice away neatly what did not allow itself to be seen. But it was there, all right. He was a medical man, and a good one, and he knew that rational diagnoses had to be based on scientific fact; but he also knew, X-rays or not, there was something inside him, a rooted, hard core of malevolence, that had flourished steadily since the day of his wife's death.

He had walked, slept and eaten with the ways of death for twenty years. He knew that when it had to come, it came. But this one need never have come at all. He hadn't wanted children. They'd had and shared more between just the two of them than most families with a dozen kids. He'd told her that, argued bitterly and hard, especially after the first, after Miriam. That one should have been warning enough. For anyone but his Lil, it would have been. But not her. She refused to be cheated of anything. But what about him? Even if she'd been willing to gamble with her own life, what right had she to gamble with *his* future? For a long while afterward, he had tried to ease his grief with anger. It was *her* fault. If she had only listened, how different everything might have been. But the anger had faded, leaving only a futile wailing in the darkness and the dull presence of this growing thing. Even now, in a steady flood of self-pity and fear of further loss, he kept trying to shut his heart to what she had left him: a pathetic ruin whose life span, fortunately, would not stretch beyond a few more years; a boy of shining beauty and brilliance, who needed him desperately but whose eyes he could not even bear to look at because they were hers; and finally Webster, lost, instantly orphaned, condemned to solitary confinement by the accident of his birth.

Still innocent and unaware, Webster was, at the moment, busy exposing his sister to the resounding joys of slapjack. "When a jack is turned up, Mim, whoever slaps his hand down first gets the bundle of cards."

Wild confusion. Cards were turned, hands flew and spoils were grabbed. Miriam was incapable of distinguishing jacks from the other pictures, happily slapping down her hand and grabbing the cards at the appearance of kings and queens as well.

"No, no, Mim. Only the jacks. The jacks. See? This one here is a jack."

"Slapjack! Slapjack!"

Resignedly, Webster went along with it. The big girl shrieked with pleasure.

"Webster, don't get your sister so excited!"

Another picture was turned up, a queen this time. His reflexes infinitely more swift than Miriam's, Webster deliberately slowed his hand. He looked at her face to collect his reward from the gladness there. But laughter had suddenly died into stunned silence. Miriam's narrow eyes widened and her mouth hung open. Webster stared at her, not knowing what had happened.

"What's the matter, Mim?"

The girl's lips moved, but no words came out. She was clutching between her legs with both hands, her body rigid. Then Webster looked down and saw the wetness. Originating somewhere out of sight beneath his sister, a growing stain had passed the outlines of her skirt and was now darkening the brilliance of the Persian rug. It spread slowly but inexorably, a great black circle of disaster. Watching it, fascinated, Webster was immobilized by the feeling that it was going to go on and on and on, across the whole of the rug. He now recalled his aunt's warning not to get his sister excited. He had heard it countless times before, because although Miriam was toilet trained, she did lose control.

Webster bit his lip until he felt pain. What was wrong with him? Why hadn't he remembered? He waited for the lightning to strike, even tensed his body against the impact. When, miraculously, it didn't, he took heart from the reprieve. Perhaps there was still hope. Perhaps something might yet be saved.

Miriam sat, unmoving, in the center of the stain, graced with enough understanding to know she had done something wrong but not with the control to prevent it. Webster was on his feet, a finger pressed to his lips. "Shhh." Miriam's eyes lifted. She repeated the gesture to show she understood. "Shhh." Love, hope and trust were squeezed, side by side, into the tiny sound. Webster stole softly out of the living room and into the hall foyer where the linens were kept. An instant later, he was back with two large towels.

"Move over," he whispered.

Miriam moved, and Webster began to mop at the ooze. He scrubbed with fierce, breathless frenzy, as if trying, by intensity of effort alone, to achieve the needed miracle. "Shhh," Miriam whispered, watching her brother, the conspiracy of silence suddenly transforming the calamity into a new kind of game.

The late-afternoon sun filtered through the lace-curtained windows and touched the rug with a new design. Splinters of orange danced before Webster's eyes. In the confusion of light and color, the great dark blot did seem to be fading. The panic in his chest began to ease. He mopped harder, all fifty-three pounds straining against the towel. If he had a little more time . . . Dear, sweet, Jesus, on this most holy day of your Resurrection, just let them give me a little more time.

"Holy Jesus!"

The two words, spoken aloud, seemed almost an echo of his own silent prayer.

"Arthur! How dare you take the Lord's name in this house!"

His aunt's voice exploded hope. Webster turned. His brother stood staring down at him from between the parted hangings. Arthur whistled softly between his teeth. "Kid," he murmured, "I'm afraid you two are really in for it now."

Laura, risen from the table to investigate the cause of her nephew's cry, appeared behind him now. Always prepared for the worst where Miriam was concerned, she was almost relieved at what she saw. At least there was no blood. In her nightmares there was always blood. Stomach cold with suppressed fright, she silently surveyed the scene. She needed a few seconds. She could not, as yet, trust her voice.

White-faced, Webster rose from his knees. The now useless towel drooped pathetically from one hand. "She couldn't help it. I got her too excited. Mim couldn't help it."

Laura swallowed dryly, eyes torn by the great dumb thing cringing penitently in a corner and her tiny champion battling to hold back the tears. Oh, God. She had only just so much to give. What did they want from her? Unable to face the children, she swung her head toward their father in the dining room.

Angus Evers still sat at the head of the dish-strewn table, eyes scanning a jumble of hand-scrawled notes, oblivious of what was going on in the next room. He doesn't even know, Laura thought, he doesn't know or care. She glared at him, whipping up the anger she needed, and when she had aroused it enough to blot out the ruinous despair and pity, she screamed hoarsely at him, "Look! You're their father! At least get up from that blessed table and look!"

Evers peered wearily at his sister. "What's the matter now?" Damn these holidays, he was thinking. If you could work three hundred and sixty-five days a year, there might just possibly be some sense to living. From Laura's face he saw that this was going to be bad. Pushing himself out of the chair, he joined the family.

"It wasn't Mim's fault!" Webster appealed, without hope, trying desperately not to cry. His chin trembled. "She couldn't help it. I got her too excited." The few sentences had become a litany of despair. Started, they could not be stopped. But Laura no longer heard. She had transferred everything to her brother, who, having finally arrived, still contributed nothing but the bulk of his presence.

"Is that all you're going to do?" she wailed. "Just stand there?"

Angus Evers' eyes were two black holes in their sockets. "Well," he said, "I suppose I *could* get a gun from the rack and shoot them."

A savage reply formed in her chest, but somehow stuck in her throat. The gentle irony and lofty detachment of the remark had only lifted him farther above the battle and made her feel more the heartless inquisitor. It was too much. Didn't he know what having to send that sweet, idiot thing away next week was doing to her? And what of that poor, lost child, trying to protect what he would soon lose anyway? How in God's name would she ever be able to look at him again? "Angus." The name broke from her lips, and she ran from the room so they would not see what was happening to her face.

Webster's father only looked at him. Then he took the bath towel from his son's hand. "Bring in a bucket of water, a scrubbing brush and some soap," he told Arthur. Then turning to Miriam: "Go into your room and change your clothes."

Webster was puzzled. Was there going to be no punishment? Was his sister going to be spared? He relished the instant of hope, but could not really believe it. He had never done anything wrong without being punished.

His father took off his jacket and rolled up his shirt sleeves, exposing huge, darkly haired forearms. When Arthur brought in the necessary materials, his father got down on his knees and went to work on the stain. He scrubbed hard with the brush, and a white circle of suds appeared. It covered and hid the terrible blot. When his father asked for more soap, Webster quickly got down on his knees too, as he handed it to him, although it was not necessary, and felt his father's shoulder warmly against him and began to think that maybe it was not such a terrible thing that had happened after all.

3

Later, Webster sat alone in back of the big, black touring car on the way to the station. Arthur was in front with his father. With the sun fading, it was cool in the open car, but Webster was warm with pleasure. He sat very straight on the edge of the seat so that people would be able to see him. It was most important that he be seen. There were few automobiles in Harrisburg, and his father's Oldsmobile was one of the largest and finest. Yet pride in the car was not the major reason for Webster's desire to be seen. He was still busy building up family credits. Of course, Mim and Aunt

Laura weren't along, but this was made up for by the car. In his mental ledger, being seen in the car counted double being seen walking. He kept a careful eye on both sides of the street, as well as on all passing carriages. When he saw someone he recognized, he waved frantically. If they saw him and waved back, it counted four points. If they saw him and did not wave back, it counted for two. If they did not appear to see him at all, Webster still allowed himself one credit, on the assumption they were just being mean and jealous and pretending not to notice.

A solid wave from Mr. Craven on his front stoop—four credits. A doubtful stare from that old, prune-faced Mrs. Schmidt—two more. Tommy Franklin waving wildly from his tricycle and almost hitting a tree—a real great four. That dopey Agatha Lee, chasing her stupid ball with her fat back toward him—one measly point. The shining car chugged on as Webster reaped his harvest of credits, singly and in clusters; each one counted, each one was added up and hoarded greedily, each one seeming to make his precious sense of family just a little more real, a little more secure.

In the front seat, Angus Evers gripped the wheel of the car's right-hand drive with absorbed intensity, apparently aware of nothing but the dusty road ahead, while beside him Arthur felt smothered by the protracted silence. The boy had been talking steadily since leaving the house, chattering about every inconsequential thing he could imagine, trying desperately, in the few minutes remaining, to break through his father's soundlessness. But how? Humor? He laughed, all lightness and warmth. "You should see this crazy kid in our math class. He's got this red hair and when he talks his voice squeaks and cracks. Well, one day, the instructor was a little late coming in and. . . ."

There wasn't much to the anecdote, but Arthur stretched it, embroidering the facts to make it more amusing. He watched his father's face for some reaction, but his father just sat there, driving and looking dark and sallow and distant, nodding at times to show he was listening and even smiling politely when it was finished. But that was all. His voice dropped abruptly. "It's French I'm really worried about though. There's something about the grammar that . . . ." He wove, he thought, a tale of impending doom designed to melt the most rocklike heart with pity.

"You'll master it."

Three words. Dismissed with three words of flatly stated confidence.

Angus Evers leaned to one side, aiding the wheel with body English as they turned a corner. Almost doltishly awkward at anything physical, he handled the car with cautious, grudging respect, as though it were a huge, trained, but still potentially dangerous beast that he could never entirely trust. Right now, however, he was grateful for the effort involved in just keeping the fearsome animal moving in the right direction. It gave him something to do. Without it there might have been no way to avoid looking at the tragic, velvet eyes of the boy beside him. Another twenty minutes, a half-hour more, and he wouldn't have to look at Arthur for another two months. Without seeing him, it wasn't so bad. He'd have to think of somewhere to send him for the summer vacation this year. It was getting harder and harder to be with him as he grew older, harder to remain detached, or at least to pretend to himself that he did not care. There they were, all three of them, reaching for him, and it was getting harder each day to keep from letting them tear him apart. He'd been torn apart once and that was enough. He refused to be vulnerable again. He'd had about as much of that as he could stand. The thing in his throat seemed to be growing again, pressing, displacing heart and lungs. He wanted to be alone with the pain, to be able to cry out. His own silence became unbearable, and he blasted the car's horn to break it.

An approaching horse reared and almost broke. Evers steered tautly around and past the carriage, heedless of frightened, glaring faces. What was wrong with him? Why couldn't he be like other men? Other men lost their wives and managed to adjust, allowed themselves to *feel* again, to show love, like decent normal fathers, to their children, were able to replace the loss with something more meaningful than ninety hours a week of work. He sought his usual release in anger. Other men! What the hell had other men to do with it? Other men hadn't lost what he'd lost. They couldn't even begin to know what he'd had. Lil: quick, responsive, gentle, warm, like a rare and lovely dream. He was lucky to have had her all that time. He'd never been anything but a big, ugly, clumsy slob, but she'd always made him feel like something special. She'd say there was no other man in the world like him, and he knew there was no other woman like her. He knew it only too damned well. When you had a woman like that and they took her away for no decent reason at all, you couldn't just go on as though nothing had happened. Not when they took away everything inside you at the same time. He was still big, ugly and clumsy, but there was no one around any more to tell him he wasn't.

Arthur rambled on hopelessly. "I may be elected cadet captain next year. Everyone seems to think I have a good chance."

"Uh-huh." Dr. Evers' hands gripped the wheel so hard the knuckles showed white. Webster's head suddenly leaped into the rear-view mirror. "Sit down back there," he ordered. "No jumping in the automobile."

Webster restrained himself with great effort. Twelve credits in one bunch. Jimmy, Ralph and Walter, all standing and waving together, all indelibly stamped with knowledge of him, his father, his heroically uniformed brother, in a majestically gliding, brass-lanterned, leather-seated chariot.

"Cadet captain," Arthur said, "is a pretty important position. I mean, only one kid a year is picked." Modesty fought a losing battle with the frantic need for contact. "It's considered a pretty big honor."

Evers braked heavily to avoid hitting a dawdling carriage in front. He squirmed with impatience and the rising dust coated the roof of his mouth. He swore softly under his breath. His mouth thin with determination, he swung the car out to pass the buggy. He had to reach the station as quickly as possible.

"The cadet captain is the one who leads the inspection parades on Saturdays. He calls out the commands and the whole cadet corps obeys. I wish you could come up some Saturday, Dad, and see it." It was a forlorn hope. His father had never once been up to school, not even to bring him there. "Do you think you could? I mean next year? If I make captain?"

Another carriage suddenly turned the corner ahead and came toward them, the horse pulling a brisk trot. Evers gunned the motor and pulled back in lane with little time to spare. He heard the frightened horse neighing and the driver shouted at him, but he did not glance around. His palms were slippery with sweat.

Arthur had barely noticed. He was too involved inside. "Do you think you could, Dad?"

"Huh? Do I think I could what?"

"Come up to watch a parade next year? If I make captain?" He watched his father's face. "Do you think there's a chance you could?"

"We'll see."

We'll see. If only he'd say *no*. At least *no* was an answer. But there was never even that much. It was always *we'll see*.

"I'll come," Webster said. "I'll come up to see you in the parade."

Arthur did not seem to have heard him. "I'll come up to see you," he said again. The thought was thrilling—the uniforms, the flags, bands playing, and in front, leading all the rest, his brother. Webster began to jump up and down. "I'll come. I'll come."

"Shut up," Arthur said.

"I want to see you in the parade." Now that it had been mentioned, it was suddenly very important. "I want to! I want to!"

Arthur's head swiveled. "I told you to shut up!" he said fiercely, grateful for the release. He waited for the hurt to show in the younger boy's eyes. Damn the kid. Who needed him in the first place? If it wasn't for him, he'd still have his mother. The bitterness pumped through his blood. *Mamma!* . . . Oh, Jesus. He just had to think of her and all the aching sensations came flooding back. Sweet, warm smells as she held him; easy laughing as she told a story or listened to one of his; soft, wet kisses; and the talking, always the talking. How he had loved the talking.

"Please!" Webster's voice had begun to choke. "Why can't I see you in the parade?"

"Because they don't like little kids hanging around up at school." Arthur glanced at his father to see if his misdirected vengeance was having any effect. It wasn't. Angus Evers' eyes were glued to the road ahead.

"I'm not a little kid. I'm . . . I'm seven." Now the additional half-year of maturity was suddenly important.

"Forget it. You can't come." With this parting kick, Arthur turned away to brood over his own wounds, the need to hurt his brother now dissolved. If anyone had to be blamed, it should be his father. If he hadn't done that thing with her . . . Arthur shivered, trying to drive the revolting image of the ugly, lethal act from his mind. Each time he thought of it, the lurid picture of that final indignity sickened him. Ever since he had first been introduced to the details of the sex act by a series of fuzzy, tangled acrobatic men and women pictured on the backs of fifty-two playing cards, he had been haunted by visions of his own parents engaged in similar ghastly exercises. How could she have willingly lent her body to such awful desecration? He had felt betrayed, filled with loathing, and he had also hated his father, as he still did—sometimes.

Forgotten in the back, Webster bit back all further pleas. He couldn't trust his voice. If he opened his mouth even a little, he knew he'd cry. He sank back into the deepest corner of the tufted leather seat, adrift, lost in solitary darkness.

4

With the unpredictability of spring, the weather turned abruptly cold again the following Saturday, and Aunt Laura kept Miriam in the kitchen with her all morning. This was the warmest, most comfortable room in the house, and she gave the girl a simple chore to occupy her. Miriam sat before a great mound of peas, shelling and dropping them into a large pot on the floor. She performed the task slowly, awkwardly, hands fumbling at the pods, the released peas frequently missing the pot and rolling along the floor. Laura picked these up in passing and dropped them with the others, saying nothing. She smiled when Miriam chanced to catch her eye. Sometimes she paused to smooth the girl's hair, adjusting the large, pink bow with which it was tied. Miriam wore her newest and best dress, the pink one with the full, circular skirt she had worn Easter Sunday. It had been freshly laundered since the accidental wetting, and she had put it on earlier with an anxious glance at her aunt.

For the fourth time in two hours, Laura sprinkled cleanser into the already immaculate sink and abstractedly began to scrub it. When she heard the front door slam, she walked quickly into the dining room and peered through the lace-curtained window. She watched Mrs. Delaney make her way mincingly through the gate, her legs confined by a hobble skirt, the latest fashion from New York. That left only one patient still in her brother's office, Mr. Lyons. Laura hoped the old fool wasn't going to sit around talking for half an hour. She glanced nervously down at the watch pinned to her blouse. It was only one o'clock. It should have been at least three. Thank heavens Webster wasn't around. It was bad enough this way. If she'd had to look at that boy's face just once, she would not be able to go through with it.

Tears welled at the thought of Webster's reaction, and she dabbed furiously at her eyes with an already damp handkerchief. Damn! What was wrong with her? Where was her self-control? It was idiotic the way she was carrying on. There was only one logical thing to do and she was doing it. She was right. She had to be right. But, dear God, what if she wasn't?

She hurried back to the kitchen, as if the sight of Miriam, sitting and dumbly shelling peas, were the single thing on earth left to reassure her. When she came into the room, Miriam was on her hands and knees, frantically scrambling about the floor after half a dozen renegade peas. "Fell," she mumbled. "Peas fell."

"That's all right, dear." Laura collected them and dropped them into the pot. "You're doing a fine job. A very fine job. You're a big help to your Aunt Laura."

Miriam beamed.

Laura stroked the coarse, black hair, so like her brother's. Why did it happen? How cruel to trap a three-year-old mind in a woman's body. The minister had said that God's will was not to be questioned. Well, she was questioning it. Maybe the child's mother had been gifted with faith enough to accept so ghastly a jest without pushing for reasons, but not she. She was just faithless enough to think how Miriam was proof that the will of Heaven and the pain of Hell were very much the same thing.

"Miriam make more peas?"

Laura nodded slowly. "More peas." She went back to the sink to attack its gleaming surface once more.

At last the sound of the front door opening and closing. Laura dried her hands and went into the front hall. Through the paned door she checked Mr. Lyon's arthritic progress across the porch and down the steps, and then she hurried across the foyer, along a short corridor, through a leather-chaired waiting room and into her brother's office.

Pipe in mouth, Angus Evers sat at his desk, leafing through a medical journal. He wore a white coat, open in front to reveal a black vest, upon which a heavy, gold watch chain formed a looping arc. He heard his sister come in, but did not glance up. His eyes, behind steel-rimmed reading glasses, looked red and tired as they fought through a jungle of tiny, crawling print.

"Angus, are we doing the right thing?" Even as she spoke, she felt stupid and helpless, but she needed reassurance.

Evers peered at her briefly over his journal. He shrugged. "It's your decision."

"That's not fair!" Laura's voice rose. How easily it slipped into the familiar, worn grooves of angry harshness. It hadn't always been so. "That's not fair, to say it's my decision. It *has* to be my decision. You never make any decisions. You never take any responsibility for anything. And now you put it all on me."

"I'm not putting it all on you." Evers took weary refuge behind the bulwark of his journal. He had expected it wouldn't go easily. Throughout the morning's office hours he had felt the threat of his sister's presence moving about the house. Well, she was entitled to some complaint. The least he could do was bare his back for her. "I didn't mean it that way. I know how you feel about the girl." He breathed deeply. "And in spite of my seeming indifference, I think you know how I feel too."

"What choice do I have? I'm getting married in three weeks. I have my own life to lead. I can't take her to live with me. Even if I tried, Walter wouldn't stand for it. Angus, I never thought *anyone* would take me any more. Angus, *look* at me! I'm thirty-two years old, and I'm a six-foot freak and I look and act like forty. Walter may not be much by your standards, but he's my only—my *last* chance. Do you expect me to give him up to spend the rest of my life taking care of *your* child, *your* responsibility?"

Evers removed his glasses and began to polish them with the edge of his white jacket. "Miriam won't live more than a few years, at most." He said it only as fact, a point of medical prognosis, but Laura took it as a further indictment.

"A few years? A few more years is the rest of my life if I don't marry now. That child . . . all three children are your responsibility, and I'm giving them back to you now." Her voice faded to a whisper. "And God help them, because I know you won't."

Evers kept polishing his glasses, thumb and index finger moving in small rhythmic circles, a refuge of mindless movement in a sudden silence. She was right, he was thinking, she was absolutely, utterly right. He was useless to every one of them. He was useless to himself. He could attempt no argument in his own defense. He could only manage to squeeze a twisted sort of consolation from the silent admission, as if, having confessed his guilt and thrown himself on his own mercy, there was no further effort he need make in his own behalf.

Laura stared at the disorderly collection of bills, pill envelopes, empty phials and prescription pads on her brother's desk. Her anger spent, her position justified, she was able to spare a few drops of pity for him. He was what he was. If he *could* be otherwise, he *would* be. Her brother was a far from happy man, yet it was hard to keep hating him for it.

"I have Webster eating lunch at Paul Schmidt's house," she said. "I thought it would be better if he wasn't around when they came for her."

"Yes." Evers abruptly put on his glasses and looked at his watch. "Well, I'd better be getting down to the hospital." His eyes did not quite meet his sister's. "I've a tonsillectomy scheduled in an hour."

Laura watched as he shrugged out of his white jacket, took his hat and coat from a rack and hastily threw stethoscope, pills and an assortment of small instruments into a worn, black bag. Naturally, she thought, not doubting the existence of the tonsillectomy, but certain that with or without it he would somehow have managed to be out of the house at the crucial moment.

"Don't you want lunch?" Knowing he was almost in a panic to get out, she couldn't resist the small cruelty.

"I'll have something at the hospital." He turned at the door. "I'm sorry." His dark face looked sallow and strained in the clear, midday light. "I'm sorry I can't be here with you when they come," he said awkwardly, aware that she knew he was lying, but compelled to do it anyway. "Where's Miriam now?"

"In the kitchen."

Evers nodded slowly. "I'll . . . stop by and see her." He hesitated, as though reluctant to take the final, irrevocable step through the door, his eyes in that instant offering pleading apology for all he had not done, was not now doing and would never be able to do. Then he went out, the worn instrument bag drooping limply from one hand.

She went upstairs to finish packing Miriam's things. There wasn't much, just a few dresses, some underthings, an extra pair of the ugly black orthopedic shoes. It all fitted into a single suitcase. How pitifully little, Laura thought, to show for seventeen years of living.

Surveying the room to make sure she hadn't forgotten anything, she saw the small, stuffed rabbit on the bed. Once fluffy white, the rabbit had been hugged, rubbed, nuzzled, kissed and washed until it was now a gray, formless thing. Laura had tried to replace it many times with newer stuffed animals, but Miriam would not give it up, tearfully refusing to go to bed at night without it. Indifferent to all other possessions, she clung to her rabbit with a fierce, almost maniacal intensity and joy.

Laura put the toy in the valise. Then, abruptly changing her mind, she took it out, closed the bag and carried both objects downstairs, one in each hand. She placed them in a corner of the foyer, near the front door, and went into the kitchen. Miriam was still shelling peas. Laura sat down beside her and watched her fingers struggling with the sealed pods; each seam required a fresh and separate assault. Neither of them said anything. Totally absorbed, Miriam hummed a formless tune. There were a few stray wisps of hair at the nape of her neck and Laura smoothed them down. Stubbornly, they rose. Laura smoothed them down once more and again they came up, and she kept repeating the motion, over and over, rocking gently in her chair, no longer seeing or caring about the hairs at all.

She started at the sound of the knocker. Already? It did not seem as though it should be time. They must be early. She went to answer the door.

There were two of them: a man, short, red-faced and cherubically plump; and a woman, middle-aged, bosomy and broad in the beam, her face frozen in a perpetual, apologetic half-smile. They were polite and businesslike, and the moment they walked in, Laura's chest turned cold. No. It was impossible. She had thought she could, but it was impossible. To send her off with these two strangers? "Listen . . ." She tried to explain to them. She was sorry. All their trouble in coming. They would, of course, be paid. Please . . . They would simply have to understand. . . . It ran on.

The woman's apologetic smile sweetened further. "Miss Evers, everyone feels this way when the moment finally comes. You're no different. You're only human. But you did the right thing in calling us. Trust your own judgment. You made this important decision when you were thinking clearly. You're not thinking clearly now. You're being blinded by emotion. If you're smart, you'll go into the other room and sit down and not even be here when we take her away."

Smart. Yes. Be smart. That was the only way. Go into the living room. Give them her hat and coat. All right. She sat facing the window, her back to the foyer. She would see nothing. Oh, but she could hear the woman's voice, drifting in from the kitchen, skillful, mechanically gentle.

"Well, hello, dear. What a beautiful job you're doing with those peas. Simply lovely. You're a good girl . . . a good girl. . . . How would you like to come outside with us? We're going to take a little trip. Wouldn't you like to take a little ride in a nice carriage, with a nice horse going giddyap?"

There was a reply, halting, guttural which Laura could not quite make out. But Miriam would go. Of course she would go. She had been carefully trained to obey adults. She would obey these people and go.

Then the footsteps in the foyer. Laura stared blindly toward the window, but saw the lost expression on the sweet, dumb face behind her. She twisted her handkerchief into a tight spiral.

"Aunt Laura?" It came thickly, inquiringly. These people had asked her to go with them and she was going, but when did she ever leave the house without saying good-bye to her aunt?

Laura pressed the handkerchief to her mouth and did not answer.

"Aunt Laura?"

Oh, Lord. Why didn't they get her out? "Yes, dear?"

Laura could not understand the garbled reply, but there was good-bye, she knew, buried somewhere within it. Then, at last, the door had opened and closed and she just sat there, thinking of nothing.

The rabbit! What if they'd forgotten to take it? She hurried into the foyer, to see the stuffed toy still lying in the wall niche where she had placed it earlier. Heart pounding, she grabbed it and ran out after them. They were already in the carriage, Miriam sitting tall in the middle. All she could do, when she reached them, was reach up and thrust the animal into Miriam's lap.

The girl pressed it to her lips. "Bunny! Bunny!" She hugged it, pretending to go to sleep as the carriage drove off. Coatless, Laura shivered in the wind. She walked slowly back to the house. In the kitchen, she looked at the huge pot of shelled peas. What would she do with them? They were enough for a month of eating. What, in God's name, would she do with them? And she wept.

5

She was ironing shirts when Webster came racing into the kitchen an hour later. He was excited and breathless, his cheeks flushed with running. "I won! I won! I won three games of hide-'n'-seek. I won everybody."

"You *beat* everybody," Laura corrected. She did not look up from the board. Well, he was here, and there was this to be gotten through. "Wipe your boots before you track mud over my clean floors."

Webster shuffled his feet on the door mat. "I *really* beat everybody!" He took off his coat, started to drape it over a chair, glanced at his aunt and hung it in its place on the rack.

"Where's Mim?"

Laura sprinkled some water on a shirt and became absorbed in a detail of its collar. She did not answer.

Webster did not ask again. He knew enough not to push his aunt when she was in a bad mood. Looking at the way her mouth was, so thin-like and droopy, it was not hard to tell she was angry about something. He was only too familiar with the expression. He just hoped Mim hadn't peed on the rug again or anything like that. He left the kitchen.

Laura put the iron on the stove for reheating. She could hear Webster wandering from room to room, looking for his sister. Several times he called her name, his voice growing louder, more insistent. Mimi was *always* in the house. Why couldn't he find her?

He returned to the kitchen.

"Where's Mim? I looked everyplace, but I can't find her."

Laura touched a moist finger to the iron and listened to the sizzle. She swung back to the board. "Miriam is out," she said brusquely. "She went away."

Webster looked at her. "Where did she go?"

"She went away with some friends." It was rasped out quickly, the words slurred together to distort meaning. But clarity enough remained.

Webster stood there, not understanding it. "What friends?"

The iron moved fiercely, back and forth, back and forth. Laura felt the moisture break out and run down her back. She mustn't look at him. She must not see his face. That was the key.

"What friends? What friends did she go away with, Aunt Laura?" He smiled insanely. He did not want to anger her further. Maybe if he smiled, she would smile too. If she smiled, it would all turn into a game of hide-'n'-seek and Mim would jump laughing from the secret place where she crouched and everything would be fine. "What friends?"

But instead of smiling, his aunt only seemed to grow angrier. The thin line of her mouth because even thinner. "What friends! What friends!" Laura mimicked the anxious, childish treble. "Can't you see how busy I am? Are you going to just stand there all day, bothering me, chattering like a parrot? Now get out of here."

The order would usually have been enough to send him flying, but not this time. He would remain there, immovable, until released by an answer.

Determined not to look at him, Laura bent beneath the weight of the boy's silence. It was too much. She sighed softly. "Well," she said, "your sister's going to be living someplace else for a while."

"Someplace else?" Webster stared dumbly. "Why? Why is she going to live someplace else?"

"Because she wants to! That's why. She *wants* to!"

Webster fought to understand. "But she was happy here. She was very happy here. How could she go live someplace else?" There was something terribly wrong, and his aunt just went on pushing the iron over the board, her face more terribly threatening than ever before. "How could . . . *She's my sister!* This is where she *lives!* If she's my sister, doesn't she *have* to live here with us?"

"Don't ask so many questions. Miriam wanted to live there, and that's all." Hit him hard, she thought, and get it over with. Though it would be kinder to hit him with a hammer. But how else could she handle him? How else, if she couldn't even bear to look at him?

"But . . ." He was groping now for the words, lips working, eyes blinking with hurt. "But . . . she . . . she was my *friend*. She was my friend."

At last Laura lifted her eyes from the board and saw him. *Look at his face.* "You want your sister to be happy, don't you? Miriam will be happier where she is." The wrong thing. Immediately she saw the hurt deepen.

"Happier than here . . . with me?" The knife twisted in the wound.

"I didn't mean . . . It's not the same thing. Can't you understand, it's not the same thing?" Fine. Tell him next about the solar system, the meaning of the universe. Why shouldn't he understand?

"Will I ever see her again?"

"Maybe." For a terrible instant she fought an impulse to clutch him to her, to bathe the small head in tears, to wrap and smother him in her own ache. No. Worse. It would change nothing and afterward only be worse. The iron returned to swift, skillful movement. Steam rose. The odor of heat and moisture. "Now, look!

Don't ask me so many questions. I've a lot to do. Go. Go play. Go
do *something!*"

Webster stared at his aunt in a final, lingering instant of hope,
but she did not even look at him again. No joke. No game. Mim
was gone. You came in and, just like that, she was gone. Numbly,
he took his coat from the rack. Go play, his aunt had said. He
went out into the quickening wind.

The kitchen door opened behind him. "Button your coat,"
Laura shouted. "Do you want to catch your death?"

Webster groped at the buttons. He walked slowly across the
back lawn, kicking at twigs and clumps of dry grass. High in a
dead pine, some crows made an angry, complaining racket. He
picked up a stone and hurled it at them in a savage arc. He
picked up other, larger stones, ran closer to the tree and fired them
in a fierce volley. The stones rattled through the branches and the
birds flapped away, cawing in fright. Webster threw a final stone
after them as they disappeared into the woods. Then it was very
quiet, with only the soft sound of the wind in the trees.

He crossed the bridge that led to *the place,* and dropped to his
knees on the mat of needles. "The place," he said very softly. He
sat there, unmoving, breathing the familiar fragrance. It was no
good, and after a while he got up and went to the brook. He lay
flat, letting his hand trail in the icy water, welcoming the sharp
sensation of cold. Mim . . . He stared down, almost hoping to see
her in the swirling depths, as in the fairy tale with the prince and
princess. There was only his own distorted image staring back at
him.

Angrily, he chopped at the water. Who wanted to see Mim's old
face anyway? She was mean. She didn't care anything about him.
She went away like that and didn't even say good-bye. Well, let her
go away if she wanted to. Let her go away and never come back.
Why should he even care? He was *glad.* He was *glad* he didn't have
to worry about her and take care of her any more. She was only a
big pain anyway. She peed on rugs and lost things and was always

getting him in all kinds of trouble. He was *glad* he wasn't ever going to see her again.

But why didn't she even say good-bye? He wanted to cry, but somehow couldn't. It was always so easy for him, yet for some reason at this, the most terrible moment of all, no tears would come. Cheated of anguish, he groped for understanding. Why? It was unfair. He was being punished for nothing. He began to see it all. Everything began to grow frighteningly clear. You couldn't trust them. You couldn't trust any of them. They didn't care. They made believe, but they never really cared. Not his father, nor Arthur, nor Aunt Laura. Not even Mim.

No tears. Dry. He longed to run, cry, scream so loud people would cover their ears. But he just lay flat on the winter-dry grass, hand limp in the quick-moving stream, able to feel nothing but the cold rush of water. He thrust his hand farther into the brook, welcoming the instant shock. Something to feel, to make him *know*. Cold. Farther. The ice crawled up his arm, soaking his sleeve, piercing sharply. Good. He stared at his arm, which was strangely distorted beneath the surface. The tan fabric looked black. His new coat. Aunt Laura . . . But no fear at the thought of punishment. Good. Make it better. Up to the shoulder now. The slash of a frigid knife. *All the way!* No. His breath quickened, his eyes closed against the sight. Yes. All at once. One . . . two . . . No. Yes. Two and a half . . . three!

It was deeper than he expected. The water closed over him. Roaring. Fear. But at least he *felt* it. He fought for footing, found it, came up gasping. He stumbled to the bank, blinded, dripping, unable to breathe. On his feet once more. The water streamed, but no tears. The wind cut. His clothes seemed weighted with stone; he was shivering, his legs barely able to move, but he started back toward the house. Just wait till Aunt Laura saw *him!*

Chapter Five

1952: The Taconic Parkway, N.Y.

There was little morning traffic, but Alice Blaine drove carefully in the right-hand lane. Driving was a strain for her, but because she knew Justin enjoyed it even less, she always insisted that it relaxed her.

Justin nervously twisted the radio dial beside her. In fact, the radio had dominated the trip. Even though it was sunny and the wooded New York landscape held a quiet wintry appeal, and even though every newscaster repeated the same things every half-hour, Justin was aware of nothing but the raucous voice of the little machine. From time to time Alice would try to distract him by pointing out something of interest and Justin would look and make suitable comment—only to begin twisting the dial once more. Alice reached over and abruptly turned off the radio.

"That's enough. There's nothing new. Stop driving yourself crazy with it."

Justin sat with his hands folded in his lap. After a while he automatically reached for the knob again, but Alice stopped his hand. "Not for a few hours," she pleaded. "At least wait till we get to the cabin. You promised me you'd try to relax."

Justin smiled and squeezed his wife's hand. "All right. I'll be nice and limp." Then the smile faded. She didn't deserve it, he

Chapter Six

1923: Cleveland, Ohio

Sarkis Aharounian met the crew one morning with explosive joy.

"A house!" he crowed exultantly. "We've got a goddamn house of our own."

They were at the equipment shed, waiting to draw their tools for the day. The sky was wind-swept and threatened rain. The crew huddled together and looked at the Armenian.

Joe coughed and spat through his big mustache. "A shithouse," he declared mildly, "is the only house we will ever call our own."

"A cousin of mine, a rug merchant named Dombalian, has given us a house." He waited for the impact of his statement to take effect, but there seemed to be no visible reaction.

"I already have a house in Niggertown," Randy said. "The roof leaks, the windows are always getting broken and the rats fight us for every lousy crust of bread. I don't need any more houses."

Sarkis loftily waved him aside. "This house," he said, "is not for you. This house is just for bachelors. No married men'll be welcome in this house." He grinned lewdly. "We'll call it Pussy Manor."

Justin frowned. "You mean this Dombalian has *given* us a house? Just like that?" It did not make sense to him.

Sarkis snapped his fingers. "Just like that," he said. "Of course, my cousin is a man of pride. He doesn't want to be thought a fool. To our people, any man who gives away things of value is a fool. Therefore, for the sake of his pride, he will charge us a very small rental for the house."

Nick nudged Justin, smiled and spoke silently.

"Nick wants to know," Justin said, "exactly how much your cousin's pride is going to cost us."

"Nothing. Twenty bucks a month."

"For each of us?" Joe said.

Sarkis glared with dark disdain. "My cousin's an Armenian, not a Turk. Twenty dollars for the whole house. Five dollars for each."

The crew looked at one another, impressed. A single room was costing each of them at least that much per week.

"It sounds too good," Joe said suspiciously. "What's the catch?"

Sarkis spat. "The catch is we've got to live with a dumbbell like you who's coughed out the few brains he ever had."

"I have an extra few chairs," Randy offered. "They're not much but you're welcome to them."

"We've got furniture too," Sarkis said. "My cousin said the house is lousy with furniture."

The foreman appeared and his whistle screamed. "All right," he roared. "Knock it off and pick up your tools!"

"Hey, boss!" Sarkis yelled. "You better be nice or you won't be invited to our new house."

"House my ass!" the foreman called back. "You were born in a cat house and you'll die in one."

Sarkis smacked his lips loudly. "From your mouth to the ears of God," he sighed.

They went to look at the house that evening after work. Randy went along. His advice was considered essential because he lived in a house and knew about these things. The house was a short trolley ride from the job, on a dead-end street that backed on a railroad yard. Its weathered shingles had once been painted yellow, but time and the soot of passing steam engines had turned them gray. The small yard was weed-choked and overgrown, and twisting vines clung stubbornly to the porch.

"Hey!" Joe yelled at sight of the vines. "Grapes. We got grapes. When I was a kid we always had grapes." He ran his hand fondly along a thick, rambling vine. "My old man used to make wine from them."

"Sure." Sarkis said. "We'll bootleg dago red and get rich."

They clumped onto the porch and peered into blackened windows, as Sarkis groped through his pockets for the key. Justin breathed the familiar smell of damp, sunless wood and thought of home. He had written his mother a letter the night before, still giving no return address. He had not said much, just that he was working and felt fine and that she should not worry about him. He had not said what kind of work he was doing, but told her that he had a lot of friends. He guessed his mother would at least be happy about that part of it. At the end of the letter, he sent regards to his father.

There were three rooms on the first floor and three on the second. Everything was covered with dust, but there was furniture in all the rooms and the walls were painted and in good repair. It was decided that Joe and Sarkis would each have a bedroom and that Justin and Nick would share one. Justin was glad there were only three bedrooms. At night in the hotel, he would often waken and listen to the reassuring sound of Nick's breathing close by. He was glad this part of it was not going to change.

"You have a good house here," Randy said, clearly impressed with everything, but especially with the indoor plumbing. He shook his head. "Maybe before I die I'll be able to get a place where we don't have to chase half a mile in the cold to pee."

The Negro wandered out onto the porch while the others inspected the kitchen and living room. A few minutes later Justin heard strange, angry voices from the front of the house. He looked around at the rest of the crew, then hurried toward the porch. Nick, Sarkis and Joe followed close behind him.

"Get off that porch, nigger!"

Half a dozen men were in the front yard, wearing peaked engineers' caps and overalls and carrying lunch pails. Their faces were streaked with coal dust and sweat. It was the largest of them, a bull-necked man with tiny pig eyes, who had snarled at Randy as Justin and the crew came out.

Randy glared at the man and advanced toward him, his hands hanging loosely at his sides. "Nobody calls me nigger, Mister!"

"What the hell's goin' on?" Sarkis yelled. "What the hell's the big idea bustin' into our yard and startin' trouble."

"*Your* yard?" the big man said. "Where the hell you get that *your* yard stuff?" He jerked a dirty thumb at his companions. "We all live down this here block and ain't none of us seen you before."

"Well, you're sure goin' to from now on," Sarkis growled. "We've just rented the place."

The railroad men stared at the gang on the porch. "You mean you're gonna *live* here?" a flat-nosed brakeman asked.

"That's damn well what we mean," Sarkis said.

"*All* of you?" a gaunt, raw-boned trackwalker said. He frowned significantly at Randy, who stood glaring back at him.

Sarkis hawked and spat an oyster at the man's feet. "What the hell business is it of yours?"

"It's our business, all right," a paunchy fourth man put in. "We don't want our kids raised with no niggers for neighbors."

Randy started toward him, but the mute's hand was suddenly tight and hard on his arm. Sarkis glanced at the crew arrayed behind him, then turned toward the men once more. He smiled, but Justin saw his hands tense and his legs bend to a slight crouch. "Is that right?" he said gently. "Well what about their bein' raised with shitheads for fathers?"

The bull-necked man hurled his lunch bucket high and hard. Sarkis ducked and it clanged against a porch post. Then he dove, arms flailing, into the knot of men at the foot of the steps. Justin heard the small wooden sound of a man's fist against bone. He blinked with shock and fright. He had never swung a fist in anger in his life; even the sight of violence sickened his stomach. Randy and Joe leaped after the Armenian, and there was a wild melee in the yard. Nick motioned for Justin to stay on the porch, then walked without haste down the steps. Justin saw him reach for the nearest man, lift him bodily from the ground and toss him onto the sidewalk ten feet away. He repeated the same procedure with the flat-nosed brakeman. He was reaching for a third victim when the raw-boned man caught him in the face with a long-handled wrench. Blood spurted from Nick's cheek and he stumbled, but he did not go down. The man swung again and this time hit the mute hard on the side of the head so that Nick's legs started to buckle. As the man raised the wrench once more, Justin cried out hoarsely and lurched toward the steps. His toe caught on a loose board and he pitched forward awkwardly, but clawed at the man's legs as he went down. It was enough to throw the man off and the wrench missed. Before the man could get set again, Nick grabbed his arm and twisted it and the man screamed, dropping the wrench.

Justin picked up the fallen wrench and struggled to his knees. Bodies swirled about him. Something hit him in the face and he fell back, but he did not let go of the wrench. His glasses had been knocked off and he groped in blind panic for them along the ground. He was sobbing. He found his glasses and put them on. One of the lenses was cracked and everything looked split. As he got to his feet, a heavy body crashed into him. Justin staggered back, still clutching the wrench. It was the bull-necked man. His hat had been knocked off and his bald bare head shone with sweat. Bull-neck came toward Justin, grinning with stained, crooked teeth. Justin saw red whiskey blotches on the man's cheeks and nose and black matted hair pushing through the open shirt collar. He knew the man was going to hit him, but at that instant he felt only a vague surprise. When he saw the big fist go up, his eyes tightly shut, he swung the wrench. He felt the impact shudder through his arm, and when he opened his eyes the man's mouth was a dark hole belching blood. Justin screamed without sound. The man's pig eyes were wide with shock. Hysterically, blindly, Justin swung again, and the bald skull shone red. The man went down and Justin went down onto his knees after him. Something pulled at his arm, knocking the wrench from his grasp. Justin kept swinging his bare hands, fiercely, wildly, feeling something go out of him with each blow. He was screaming aloud now, but did not know it. The hate and horror had changed to exultation. He had never known a feeling like it. Then something exploded white in his brain and he did not feel anything at all.

Justin opened his eyes and saw a blurred image staring anxiously down at him. Nick was sitting beside him in the grass, his cheek clotted with blood. The rest of the crew formed a semicircle behind him. Nick smiled and Justin tried to smile back, but felt it come out all wrong. Then he remembered and sat up in quick panic.

"Take it easy, Bill," Randy said. "You caught a hard one."

Justin's head ached and everything swam. He looked for the bull-necked man's body in the grass, but the yard was empty except for his friends. "I killed him," he groaned, "I think I killed him."

Sarkis laughed. "Nobody can kill one of those thick-headed hunkies. But you were sure tryin'. It took three of them to cart that son of a bitch out of here."

Justin felt the back of his head and winced. There was a large lump on it. "What hit me?"

Joe showed him a short length of lead pipe. "Want to keep it for a souvenir?"

"I've never hit anyone before," Justin mumbled dully. "This was the first time in my life. I don't know what happened to me."

Nick had stopped rubbing Justin's wrists. He took the half-broken glasses from his shirt pocket and placed them gently on the boy's nose. His eyes were warm in the fading light. He spoke silently to Justin. "You did what you had to."

"It was my fault," Randy said quietly. His swollen eye gave his darkly solemn face an oddly lopsided expression. "I'm thirty-six years old. I should be used to being called nigger. A man should learn. It was my fault."

"Balls!" Sarkis said.

"You should have told them I wasn't going to live here," Randy insisted.

"It was none of their damn business," Sarkis growled. "They were just lookin' for trouble and they got it."

With Nick's help, Justin stood up uncertainly. He blinked at Randy through his one good lens. He wanted to say something, but did not know what. "Listen," he said gropingly. "Nick and I—we can probably use another chair in our room. I mean, you said you had a couple of extra ones before."

"Sure." Randy nodded slowly, gravely. "Any time. You can have those chairs any time at all."

They moved into the house the following evening. Each man brought his life's belongings in a single suitcase. They dusted and cleaned until three o'clock in the morning, and Justin, whose mother had long been convinced he would live out his life beneath mountains of refuse, was the most energetic and fastidious of the four. This was *his* house, *his* room. It made a difference.

2

Saturday was payday on the job. Justin did not pause long enough in his work to breathe normally. He was going to receive his first week's wages. The job had become familiar. After hours with a shovel, the first aches were passing. The job was a new awareness that brought the excitement of men and tools and sweat. It was a struggle for a living in which they fought together. And he was now a part of this different world. There was joy in his hands and body.

When the noon whistle blew, they lined up at the paymaster's shack. Spirits were high and the men joked roughly and happily in the sun, making the most of the pause. "Patron saint of the whorehouses," Sarkis bellowed devoutly, "we shall kneel before thee tonight!"

The line moved forward slowly. Justin watched the men come out of the shack with their envelopes. Then he was inside. "William Baker," he said to the man behind the desk, and the man looked at his badge number and checked and marked it in his ledger and handed him a yellow envelope. The foreman stood to one side, chewing on his cigar. He grinned at Justin. "Don't blow it all on one woman, kid." Justin grinned back and walked out with as much of a swagger as his flat feet would allow.

Outside he opened the envelope with trembling fingers and counted twenty-six dollars and change. He had never held that much money in his hand before. The bills were new and crisp and he pressed them impulsively to his nose to smell them. Joe laughed behind him. "They don't taste as good as they look."

The crew gathered about him with their envelopes. Justin saw another line that had formed near the only exit in the fence that had been built around the huge excavation. "What's that line for?" he said.

Sarkis spat. "The Workers' Protective Association. That's where we pay our four bits to stay healthy."

"Maybe that's where *you* pay," Randy said. "Not *me*. I've got better use for that fifty cents."

The crew looked at him.

Nick touched Justin and spoke. "He thinks you're being foolish," Justin said. "He thinks you should pay like everyone else and not look for trouble." He paused. "I agree with Nick."

"I don't have to look for trouble. It finds me by itself." Randy grinned. "Let me tell you something. I've got a kid that's been saving pennies nearly a year for a lousy second-hand bike. I figure he's got a better right to those four bits than those silk-shirted pimps."

No one said anything and they moved slowly toward the line at the entrance. Randy walked slightly ahead. Two men sat behind a small table, taking money and issuing cards. Justin recognized them as the same pair he had seen talking with the foreman the first day on the job. Instead of looking threatening or dangerous, they were laughing and joking with the workers and, in their fine, expensive suits, seemed more like prosperous businessmen than a

menace. When Randy passed the table without stopping, one of them called to him.

"You forgot your protection card, boy." He smiled as he spoke and his dark hair gleamed in the sun.

Randy turned. "I'm not buying."

"Don't you want protection?" The line had quieted. "I can't afford it." Randy walked unhurriedly through the gate.

Justin looked at Nick, but the mute's face was impassive. When their turns came at the table, they paid their dues.

Randy was waiting down the block and they stopped at Charley's Bar for a beer. No one mentioned the Workers' Protective Association. Justin felt a mild twinge of regret. The fifty cents meant nothing to him, he thought. There was more money in his envelope than he knew what to do with. Maybe he should have paid for his friend's card. Then he lifted his glass and forced down the beer and did not think of the fifty cents again.

Later, four of them were dressed in their Saturday night suits. Their hair glistened with pomade and was brushed flat. Their faces shone pink from scrubbing. They had eaten a large dinner in a good restaurant, and now they stood on the sidewalk, leisurely picking its remains from their teeth.

Sarkis patted his hard, flat stomach. "All taken care of here," he said contentedly. "Now we've just got another department to look after. Let's go."

"Where are we going?" Justin said, falling in step as they started to walk.

"To the best whorehouse in town," Sarkis said. "Where else?" He suddenly grinned at Justin. "I'll bet you're still cherry. Eh, kid?"

Justin flushed and tried a mocking laugh that did not come off. For days he had known this moment would finally arrive. There had been talk enough about it. Although he still did not know what he was going to do, he was fiercely determined not to lose the respect of his friends.

"I've got a girl of my own at home, you know," he said quickly. "We're sort of engaged."

"What do you mean, engaged?" Sarkis asked doubtfully.

Justin made a futile gesture with his hand. "You know."

"No," Sarkis said. "I don't know."

"He means engaged to be married," Joe supplied helpfully. "That right, Billy*mio?*"

"That's right."

Sarkis snorted. "You crazy or somethin? What do you want to get married for? There's plenty of tail around without getting married." Nick shoved him hard and Sarkis spun across the sidewalk. "What's the big idea?" he complained.

The mute replied without sound.

"What did that Cossack say?"

"He said there's more to a woman than just tail."

"Yeah," Sarkis said with finality. "A big mouth and an empty head. I'll take the tail. You keep the rest."

They came to a block of narrow tenements and Sarkis stopped halfway along it. "This is the place," he said and entered a dimly lighted vestibule. The others followed him. Justin hung back, examining the child-scribbled walls and rows of letter boxes. His forehead was damp and his mouth was dry.

"Listen . . ." he started weakly. But his friends were climbing a darkened flight of stairs and did not hear him. For an instant he was tempted to run. To hell with them all. But he knew he would not do it, because if he did, all the good of the week would be gone. He trudged slowly, despairingly up the stairs.

A large woman with frizzed hair and painted eyelids showed them into a pink-lighted foyer. The room had tasseled hangings, worn upholstered chairs and a table covered with magazines. The woman and Sarkis chattered away like old friends, speaking English, but Justin did not listen. His mind seemed frozen. He dropped into a chair and mechanically picked up a magazine. The woman came over to him and pinched his cheek. He shrank, repelled, from her touch. She said something which his brain did not record, but which made the others laugh. She spoke again and this time her words broke through.

"What kind do you like, honey?"

Justin swallowed and mumbled thickly, "I've got a girl at home. I don't think it would be right. I mean, if we're engaged and all. I just don't think it would be right."

The woman looked at him strangely, then winked and smiled. "It's all right, honey. You just do whatever you want. We've got some very nice magazines here. You just read any of them you want."

The woman left and Justin took refuge in the magazine he had picked up. Sarkis and Joe both began talking to him at the same time, but he did not hear any of it. The Armenian jumped up and down with excitement. It seemed important to Joe too. Nick finally quieted them by placing a hand hard on each of their shoulders and squeezing.

The woman came in followed by three girls. Two were heavy blondes with full-mouthed smiles. The third was small, slender and dark, with a brooding face set off by heavy makeup. They wore tight dresses that clung to their hips and breasts.

"Here they are," the madam said lovingly. "Here are my little babies." She patted the dark one approvingly. "This is Marie. She's Eyetalian. Very hot-blooded."

"For me," Joe said through his mustache. "*Cara mia!* For me."

The girl gave him a dark, professional smile and said something in Italian. Joe laughed and happily pinched her high, round behind so that she jumped. Sarkis already had his arm around one of the big blondes. "*Vy, vy!*" he cried ecstatically. "This one I'll dance over barefoot."

The third girl eyed the mute with alarm and awe. "Jesus, Joseph and Mary," she whispered softly. "Get a load of what I got."

Nick gravely touched the girl's straw-colored hair. His scarred, broken face was absorbed, without expression.

"What's your name?" the blond girl said.

"His name is Nick," Justin said hurriedly. "He can't talk. He's a mute."

The girl shrugged. "That's all right. We don't need to talk."

"He can hear though," Justin explained. "People think because he can't talk he can't hear. But he can hear."

"That's nice," the blonde said coldly, apparently annoyed at her luck. "What're you, Professor? His keeper or something?"

Justin's face flamed red. "He's got more brains in his fingernails than all the whores in Cleveland put together."

The girl came over to Justin. "Take it easy, Professor. We're not such a bad bunch." Without warning she suddenly bent and grabbed him between the legs. Justin leaped back. She laughed. "You might even get to like us someday." Then she returned to Nick and led him through one of several doors that opened off the foyer.

The others also disappeared and Justin sat alone, clutching his magazine. Anyone who walked in, he thought disgustedly, they'd do it with anyone who walked in. Filled with loathing, his mind conjured up lewd visions of what was taking place behind the surrounding doors. Voices and laughter swelled and died away, then rose once more. Sarkis, Joe, the shrill cries of the girls . . . raw sounds of passion flashed hot through his brain. He buried his eyes in the magazine. "Why a League of Nations?" the lead article demanded. "Reading Time, 13 Minutes." Automatically, he looked at his watch. It was 10:14. He began to read steadily, but with little comprehension. The sounds of love-making kept intruding. When he finished, he checked his watch once more. The article had taken him less than ten minutes. He turned to the next article, entitled "The Limited Future of Air Travel." "Reading Time, 11 Minutes." He was well into it when one of the doors opened and Nick's big, straw-haired blonde burst out.

"Jesus Christ!" she cried. "Jesus H. Christ!"

Her filmy pink wrapper was half off and her hair was in disarray. She flung open one of the other doors, and there were complaining shouts and curses from inside.

"That dummy!" she yelled. "You've got to see that dummy! You'll never believe it!"

She sped back, her wrapper flowing open, followed by the other blonde. Justin glued his eyes to the magazine, trying to ignore Sarkis' hoarse bewailing, the blondes' wild cries of disbelief, the sudden explosion of traffic as the madam and two other girls rushed curiously past him.

"Get a load of that!"

"Oh, my God!"

Justin read stubbornly on. The voices merged and faded into the background, and the laughter seemed a long way off. His eyes began to swim. At the end he sat staring blindly at nothing, seeing only the ludicrous image of himself sitting in a brothel, taking the measure of his manhood from a magazine. What was the use of trying to fool himself? he thought coldly. He was still poor Justin Blaine. Calling himself William Baker or any other name, was not going to change a damn thing.

3

They were at Charley's for their after-work beer later that week. Sarkis was telling a long, frequently interrupted story about a girl with very exotic sex appetites he had once known in San Diego. "I swear to Christ," he said rapturously, "she could pull your damn insides out till you screamed." He leaned back in his chair and threw his arms wide in an ecstasy of remembrance.

Justin laughed on cue with the others. He was still uncomfortable around any talk of sex, yet was proud of at least being able to carry it off now with insouciance. Randy caught his eye across the table and smiled and Justin smiled back. The tall Negro drained the last of the single beer he allowed himself each afternoon and stood up. Sarkis frowned. "Where you going?"

Randy reached under the chair for his cap. "Home," he said.

"The same place I go every night when I've had enough listening to you."

"But I haven't finished the story," Sarkis complained. "You haven't heard the best part."

"I'll save it for tomorrow," Randy said. "It'll give me something to get up for in the morning." He grinned at the others. "Don't you wish there was someplace you could go to get away from him too?"

He dropped a coin on the bar, lifted a hand to the crew and left.

"So when I saw her the next time . . ." Sarkis picked up the thread of his story with the fluent ease of the raconteur. He told it well, eyes, hands and voice all adding mood and loving detail to even the most minor obscenities. Justin listened with growing admiration. How far, he thought, might someone with Sarkis' imagination and energy go under better conditions? Yet he was an unskilled day laborer and would probably never be anything else.

Justin recalled the many times he had passed gangs of laborers working near Red Bank. He had seen their sweating bodies in summer and their bundled, shapeless forms in winter and given them no more thought than he would a herd of cows grazing in a field. They'd all been lumped together in his mind under the general heading of laborers; they'd had no more interest or identification to him than that, without personalities, thoughts, hopes, interests. He smiled to himself. And to the streams of people passing his job, he and the others working in the great ditch were probably the same thing. The world, he thought, put you into a great mold, stamped you into a simple, easily recognizable shape and then stopped thinking about you. Only when you tried to change from one shape to another, were you noticed, like the way he'd been noticed the first day on the job, with the wrong clothes and the wrong kind of hands and even the wrong look to his soft, pale face. The schoolboy trying to become a laborer—easier, perhaps, than the other way around, yet not that easy. But he'd gotten what he wanted, and now he was in the properly accepted animal form, clothes rough and shapeless, hands calloused, face brown from the sun. Only his thick lenses remained as the last, stubborn holdover from his old shape.

Justin thought of his mother and frowned. He had written to her three times, but had still not enclosed his address. She could be sick or dead and there would be no way of his knowing. But he still did not want to hear from her. He still did not trust himself against her inevitable pleas to return. Maybe in another few weeks it would be different. Maybe he'd feel more sure about things then. In the meantime, it was enough that she knew he was all right.

Charley came to the table to collect the empty glasses, then lingered a while to listen to Sarkis.

"And there was this special way she had," The Armenian was saying, "of trying to—"

He never finished the sentence. A man burst into the room shouting wildly. "The nigger!" he yelled. "They've got the nigger! They're beatin' hell outa him!"

Joe was up first. He grabbed the man's shirt. "Randy?"

The man nodded, pop-eyed with fright. The others were on their feet, but Justin could not seem to move.

"Who?" Sarkis yelled. "Where?"

"Some goons. In the alley down the block. They musta been layin' for 'im."

Nick had the man's arm in his hand. He half-lifted, half-dragged him toward the door. "Show us," Joe ordered.

Justin followed behind the others, feeling himself move sluggishly, his arms and legs dreamlike and light. The fifty cents, he should have paid the lousy fifty cents. He was stumbling down the dark street, unable to run quickly because he was frightened. There was a lamp post on the corner, and he saw the others pass beneath it, their shadows shortening, then lengthening before them. Farther on they disappeared into a narrow place between two buildings. Justin reached it in time to see some men run out the other end of the alley and scramble into a dark sedan. Sarkis, Joe and several others ran after them. Nick had stayed behind, bent over something on the ground. Justin stopped running.

It was dark except for the glow of a small bulb over a warehouse door fifty feet away. Justin bent beside Nick and looked where he was looking, but did not know what he saw. He straightened his glasses and looked again. There was still only a white mass before him. There was nothing there that resembled Randy. Nick was doing something with his hands, but there was neither sound nor motion. His fingers came away white and sticky.

Whitewash, Justin thought, weakly, they'd smeared him with whitewash. He took out his handkerchief and tried to clear Randy's eyes and mouth, but the stuff was partly dry and was sticking. He knelt helplessly as Nick pressed an ear to Randy's chest.

"Is . . . is he dead?" he croaked.

Nick shook his head. He tried to wipe Randy's face, then gave it up also. The Negro's head was turned to one side, and Justin saw a thin trickle of blood run darkly from his ear and mix with the whiteness. Justin took off his jacket and carefully placed it under Randy's head. He heard shouts and voices from the far end of the alley and saw the others returning. A policeman was with them.

"The bastards got away," Joe gasped, "but I recognized one of them. I've seen him hanging around the job."

They gathered closer. "Jesus Christ!" someone said. "They made a goddamn white man outa him."

Justin looked up at the policeman, a heavy, fleshy-faced man, bulging against his uniform. "An ambulance," Justin pleaded. "Hurry and call an ambulance."

Randy's eyelids fluttered. He stirred and mumbled something.

"He'll be all right," the officer grunted, annoyed by the whole thing. "He don't need no ambulance. Just get him home and let him sleep it off."

"But his ears," Justin insisted. "He's bleeding from his ears. It might mean a concussion."

The policeman peered at him suspiciously. "What the hell are you, a doctor or something?" With an effort, he bent over the fallen man. Randy was breathing heavily and still mumbling. The policeman straightened. "This man's been drinking alcoholic beverages," he declared with satisfaction.

"One lousy beer," Sarkis growled. "He had one lousy watered-down beer."

"Call an ambulance," Justin begged.

"Alcoholic beverages," the policeman repeated, enjoying the important roll of the phrase from his tongue. "I see ten drunks like him a night. He don't need no ambulance. We got no beds for sick whites at the hospital, let alone drunk niggers." He twirled his night stick with skill and authority. "Now get him to hell out of here before I run him in for drinking and disturbing the peace." He sniffed accusingly at the others. "Don't you guys know this country's got a law against drinking?" He strode briskly away.

Sarkis spat after him. "Flatfooted prick!"

The policeman heard and hesitated at the end of the alley. Nick rose and Sarkis spat again. The policeman shrugged and walked on.

"We'd better get him home," Justin said nervously. He had visions of the policeman coming back with reinforcements. "We'd better get him home and call a doctor."

"He'll be okay," someone said. "These niggers got heads like rocks."

"So have you, ya hunky bastard," Sarkis flashed. He started toward the man, but Joe stopped him.

"What's the matter with him?" the man said, confused and hurt. "All I said was he'd be okay."

"Shut up," Joe said harshly. "Come on. Let's see if we can find a taxi."

Justin stayed with Randy while the others spread through the surrounding streets searching for a cab. Randy started to regain consciousness and mumbled incoherently as Justin once again tried to rub the clownlike whitewash from his face.

Chapter Seven

1952: Washington, D.C.

The committee hearing room was hushed as Webster Evers was summoned to the witness chair and sworn in. Every seat in the vast, high-ceilinged chamber had been filled an hour before meeting time, and an overflow crowd watched the proceedings on television monitors set up in a nearby auditorium.

As he stood to take the oath, the Under Secretary faced the committee of lawmakers, appearing more the accuser than the accused. He allowed his gaze to move coldly down the line, touching and lingering briefly on each man in turn . . . Norton . . . Quennell . . . Kelly . . . Pilgrim . . . Kirby . . . and finally Kantrowitz. The committee counsel, Evers noted, looked troubled, the chairman apologetic, and Pilgrim eager and smugly elated. The others merely seemed uncomfortable. Pilgrim, he thought, was undoubtedly going to be the one to watch.

Kelly cleared his throat behind a crumpled handkerchief. "First of all," he declared, "I must announce that Mr. Evers has not been called before this committee, but is appearing voluntarily. I would like this fact noted." The chairman looked for a moment at Evers, as if pleading for absolution of all blame for anything that might happen. "He has voluntarily come forward to answer, under oath, serious charges made here against him yesterday by Mr. Justin Blaine, charges which came as a shock and a surprise, not only to this committee, but to the entire country. I, for one, am delighted that Mr. Evers has chosen this opportunity to reply to them." The chairman paused portentously. "Mr. Kantrowitz, will you please begin the preliminary questioning."

The committee lawyer spoke from his seat at the table. "What is your full name, sir?"

"Webster Evers."

"What is your present position?"

"Under Secretary of State."

"How long have you worked for the government?"

"Approximately twenty years."

"Were you born in the United States?"

"Yes."

"Where in the United States?"

"Harrisburg, Pennsylvania."

The routine questioning clicked on—question, answer . . . question, answer—all facts already known, all easily, truthfully given. Webster sat erect but relaxed in his chair, staring steadily at Kantrowitz throughout the exchange. The lawyer's face was soon moist beneath the glaring floodlights, but Webster did not appear affected by the heat. Legs casually crossed, hands folded and at ease in his lap, he was the perfect, poised career diplomat.

"Mr. Evers, are you now, or have you ever at any time been, a member of the Communist Party?"

"No."

There it was, Webster thought, the first neat, clean bit of perjury, the first lie leading the avalanche to follow. And it came out with no more difficulty than the truth.

"Are you now," Kantrowitz said, "or have you ever at any time in the past, engaged in espionage activities for a foreign power?"

"No, I have not."

The lawyer paused before his next question and the soft whirring of the cameras could be heard against the silence. Someone coughed nervously and set off a ragged volley of throat noises. Kantrowitz said, "Do you know a man by the name of Justin Blaine, Mr. Secretary?"

"Only by reputation. And I've listened, of course, to his radio commentaries on the news."

"You have never met him in person?"

"Not to my knowledge."

"You have never, at any time in the past, known him?"

"No," Webster said, "I have not."

Pilgrim broke in impatiently. "Perhaps you knew Blaine under a different name." He passed an attendant a clipping and the man handed it to Webster. "That is a photograph of Justin Blaine," Pilgrim said, "taken from this morning's newspaper. Does he appear at all familiar to you?"

Webster looked at the picture. Evidently caught in mid-sentence by the camera, Bill Baker—now Justin Blaine—stared, open-mouthed and accusingly, at him. It was the first likeness of his former friend that Webster had seen in more than a decade and he was shocked at the changes the years had wrought. The once familiar face was lined and much fuller than he remembered it and the black hair was heavily streaked with gray. But the eyes, dark, troubled and reproachfully questioning—the eyes, he thought, were the same.

"No," Webster said. "This man does not look familiar to me. I have never known him."

Pilgrim said, "Mr. Blaine has testified quite differently before this committee. He claims that he knew you intimately in the middle and late thirties, that you were, in fact, members of the same Communist espionage network at that time."

Webster stared coldly at the junior Congressman from Illinois. "I'm well acquainted with the allegations of Mr. Blaine. That is why I'm here."

"And you claim them to be untrue?" Pilgrim glanced at Kantrowitz, from whom he had gracelessly taken over the questioning.

Kantrowitz appeared quite willing, even relieved, to relinquish his role of interrogator.

"I most certainly do."

Pilgrim affected a mocking smile. "I see. In other words, one of our country's most distinguished and respected news commentators, a man who has received awards for his reporting and analysis of world events, has without reason suddenly decided to name *you*—a man whom he does not know, has *never* known and has allegedly never even *met*—as his former comrade in a Communist spy network? Is *this* what you're saying?"

Webster's eyes glinted with a hard light but his insides had gone cold. He knew he was most vulnerable on the question of why he had been accused. He had been right in judging Pilgrim the most dangerous man on the committee, for the junior Congressman could stumble close enough to the truth to create doubts about his testimony. Webster hesitated briefly before answering and was disturbed by it. There must not be the slightest hint of equivocation in his manner. When you had nothing to go on but bluff, decisiveness was everything.

"I am saying I know of no reason," Webster said.

"But *why?*" Pilgrim pressed on. "*Why* would *any* sane man attack a total stranger as Mr. Blaine has attacked you?"

"I haven't the vaguest idea. I'm afraid that particular answer is buried somewhere deep within the convolutions of Mr. Blaine's brilliant reportorial brain. However, the world situation being what it is today, it is not wholly unreasonable for a man forced to analyze it to occasionally become a bit confused about his facts."

There was appreciative laughter from the newsmen in the audience and smiles from all the committee members but Pilgrim. Francine had been right about the press corps, Webster thought. They seemed to be with him solidly. Given no blunder on his part, they'd be more than willing to vindicate him.

"Mr. Secretary," Pilgrim said, "very serious charges have been made against you, and although my sense of humor is as good as most, I can see nothing at all funny about the situation. Not while, at this very moment, there are American boys dying under Communist guns in Korea." The Congressman frowned. "As it happens, Justin Blaine has built a national reputation on his ability *not* to be confused by facts. He claims that he knew you and knew you well during the period in question, and has provided us with details to substantiate this claim. If, as you indicate, Mr. Blaine is lying, how do you account for his knowledge of these facts?"

"I'm a public servant, Mr. Pilgrim. Even my so-called private life has always been rather public. I've no doubt that anyone interested in such things could pick up an unlimited amount of extremely dull information about me."

"But what *reason*," Pilgrim persisted loudly, "what *reason* would Blaine have to do such a thing if he did not know you?"

Webster uncrossed his legs and deliberately recrossed them in the opposite direction. They felt hollow, yet immeasurably heavy. His entire body seemed weighted with lead, alien, somehow apart from him. Like his voice, it did as he commanded, but had nothing at all to do with what was taking place inside. *What reason?* There *had* to be one, of course. Bill Baker had never done anything without a reason, had never launched an act without a proper and logical motive. But where was the logic here? No word, not the slightest contact in thirteen years, then all at once *this*? Had something suddenly snapped, created an imagined hurt and begun a rampage of vengeance?

"What *reason*, Mr. Secretary?"

The question came again and Webster realized he had been staring blankly at the unrelenting Congressman. What the devil was wrong with him? That was the second time he'd let himself drift off. All he needed were a few more uncertain moments or evasive answers, and the thing he was here to accomplish would be destroyed. For the first time in years, he felt the cold sweat of panic on his hands.

"I don't know anything about Mr. Blaine's reasons," he said, "nor do I especially care about them. I have my own reasons for coming before this committee and the American people. I am here to declare under oath that each and every one of his statements concerning me is false, that I have never at any time had anything to do with the Communist Party and that I have not, to the best of my knowledge, even met Mr. Blaine."

"And exactly what does 'to the best of my knowledge' mean, Mr. Evers? Does it perhaps suggest that you *may*, at one time, have known Justin Blaine, but have now forgotten the occasion?"

Representative Kelly, frowning and silent throughout Pilgrim's questioning, spoke now. "I don't consider it necessary to press the point, Mr. Pilgrim. I think Mr. Evers has made his position sufficiently clear. In a long and impressive career of public service his word has never to my knowledge been successfully challenged. And as far as I, personally, am concerned, it *still* hasn't been."

Even the chairman, Webster thought, was determined to make things as easy as possible for him. The entire situation suddenly seemed incongruous. Almost everyone in the room, press, spectators and committee members alike, appeared anxious to vindicate him. Only Pilgrim, wanting to soak in as much publicity as possible, persisted in being sensibly tough. *The fools.* Give them lies, evasions, anything but the truth, and they'd rush to believe it, just as long as the package was attractively wrapped. All right. He had all the necessary trappings of appearance, reputation and position. Since everyone was so set on regarding him as a man of truth, he would make their self-deception as easy as possible for them.

"Mr. Chairman," Webster said, "I would like to make a statement."

"Of course, Mr. Secretary."

Webster began his statement, developing it extemporaneously and with apparent feeling as he spoke. It emerged, at first, as the soft-spoken, sincere plea of a falsely accused public servant, changed subtly to a note of outrage or righteous indignation, and reached its zenith in a harsh, blistering attack on the dangerous, unseen forces seeking to undermine the confidence of the American people in their chosen leaders at a time when this confidence was desperately needed. Finally, it condemned and dismissed Justin Blaine as an admitted ex-Communist agent, whose wild, unsupported allegations had already been dignified with far more attention than they deserved.

When it was through, a loud and spontaneous ovation filled the hearing room and the committee chairman did not even attempt to restrain it.

In the corridor afterward, Webster was surrounded by enthusiastic well-wishers, all seemingly eager to shake his hand and personally assure him of unswerving confidence. Oddly ambivalent about his apparent success, Webster worked his way through the crowd of newsmen and spectators. He was still weirdly angered, as he always was by the sweeping acceptance of one of his fraudulent performances. They'd believe *anything*. The *fools!*

Chapter Eight

1920: En Route to Providence, R.I.

Webster leaned his head against the train window and stared out at the bleak landscape. Even the trees, he thought, looked lost and frightened, as if knowing that once the last of their leaves had fallen they'd have to stand naked and alone through the winter. He felt the same way. And the closer the train moved to Edwards Academy, the stronger, the more insistent the feeling grew. Fourteen years old and he was more scared to be starting this school than he'd been to enter the first grade when he was six.

For reassurance, he glanced across the aisle at his brother. Arthur Evers sat alone, absorbed in the work he had brought along on the trip, his darkly handsome head bent, with its inevitable grace, over the briefcase on his lap. The straw coach seat beside him was covered with papers. Webster felt the same warmth and pride he always felt when he looked at his brother. Had Arthur been this frightened, riding toward Edwards for the first time ten years before? Probably not. Arthur was never frightened of anything. He had no reason to be. You just had to look at him to know that. Confidence glowed in his smile and words. Whatever he tried, he did better than anyone else. He'd been top man in his class at Edwards from the first year on, cadet captain, valedictorian and double sword winner at the end. His record was the best in the school's ninety-four-year history. There was a bronze plaque in the school armory with Arthur Evers' name on it.

Webster wiped his moist palms on his knees. He breathed deeply, hoping to ease the tightness across his chest, but the smell of burning coal only clogged his throat and made it worse. Why couldn't he be more like Arthur?

Webster's eyes rested on the important, official-looking documents his brother was working on. There might even be some papers signed by President Wilson himself. Webster still carried in his wallet a tattered news photo of Arthur with the President and the Secretary of State. The picture had been taken at the Versailles peace conference which Arthur, as one of the State Department's brighter young men, had attended. Webster took out the clipping frequently to look at it and show it to people. His brother and the President of the United States.

Arthur reached for a paper at the far end of the seat and his glance caught Webster's. He looked at his watch and smiled. "Past four o'clock. Getting hungry?"

Webster shook his head. "I don't think so. No."

"Should be a sandwich man coming through soon. We'll have something then. It's another two hours to Providence."

Webster tried to think fast of something to say, to hold his brother's attention for a precious moment, but his mind was a blank. By the time he was able to think of something, it was too late; Arthur was back at work and Webster did not dare disturb him. Funny thing. He could hardly *ever* think of anything to say when he was with his brother, and since they were together only briefly, only two or three times a year, Webster hated the lost time.

Yet when they were apart, his mind pumped ideas, hopes, fears, questions, like a hysterical machine. Sometimes he wrote them down in long letters, which he never mailed. Before writing the letters, he intended to mail them, but when he read them afterward, they always seemed stupid and childish. He didn't think his brother would be interested in that kind of stuff. And he certainly didn't want Arthur to think he was stupid.

Webster peered critically at his reflection in the dirty glass. His tie was twisted to one side and a few stubborn hairs at the back of his head rose in rebellion against the pomade. But the slender, dark-eyed face beneath, did it *really,* as everyone said, resemble that of his brother? More than anything else, he hoped it did, although he couldn't see any likeness at all. His brother was beautiful, handsome; he himself, thin and homely, with a fringe of adolescent eruptions making it even worse.

He straightened the knot of his tie and tried to smooth down the cowlick. He had on his best suit, but the sleeves were already outgrown and he needed to scrunch up his arms to make them seem shorter. He wanted to look his best when they reached the Academy, so that Arthur would not be ashamed of him.

Until a few days ago, Webster had been scheduled to make the trip from Harrisburg to Providence alone. Then Arthur had called his father from Washington, and everything had been miraculously changed. Arthur would meet Webster's train in New York and go the rest of the way to Edwards Academy with him. The mere prospect of his brother's company, unshared and for so many hours, had kept Webster awake for two nights.

Frightened as he was at the thought of starting a new school, Webster was still glad to be getting out of Harrisburg. He had left behind nothing, no real friends or attachments. The housekeeper who had replaced his aunt had been pleasant, but cold and impersonal. His father? Nothing had changed. Nothing had happened. Mim? His sister's death in the institution four years ago, distant and unreal, and described by adults as "really a blessing for all," had cut with cold finality even this tie with home. There was nothing in Harrisburg that he was going to miss. And surely there was no one who would miss *him.*

"Cigars . . . cigarettes . . . candy! All sorts of sandwiches!" A Negro hawker entered the coach, pushing his small cart of merchandise.

Arthur looked up and stretched. "Well. Dinnertime. What kind of sandwich would you like?" He grinned.

About to say he wasn't hungry, Webster changed his mind. It would at least be a chance for them to eat, to do *something* together. "I think I'll try a ham." A shy, hurried afterthought: "Thank you."

They bought two ham sandwiches and two orange drinks and sat eating in their separate seats. Arthur looked across the aisle at his younger brother. It wasn't easy, fourteen-year-old kid heading for a new place, new people. And their father had actually intended to ship him up there alone. Typical. Feed him, put clothes on his back, a roof over his head, pay someone to care for him, someone else to teach him, and that was being a father. Well, he'd had the same thing himself ten years before. He still remembered the choking, solitary fear of that train ride. It was a damned good thing he'd called and made arrangements to meet the kid. And it would be nice to see the Academy again. Big-man-on-the-campus returns. They'd remember him, all right. He could use a little of *that* too. An old despair gripped him, but he brushed it aside.

"Why don't you move over here, Webbie?" Arthur gathered his papers together and made room for his brother beside him on the seat.

Webster needed no further encouragement. He shifted quickly across the aisle, sandwich and drink held with great care. His shoulder touched Arthur's. Say something! *Something. Anything!* All phrases, all carefully rehearsed dialogue intended to demonstrate maturity, perception and brilliance, had fled his brain. His mind was empty, hollow. His eyes glanced about wildly, seeking hints, and fell in desperation on the papers. "These papers!" The words exploded in the coach like firecrackers. "What kind are they?"

"Oh, just papers." The usual shrugging off.

Webster looked at the State Department seals, the emblazoned crest of glory heading each page. "Has anyone important signed them?"

Arthur pointed to an illegible signature. "Would you consider the Secretary of State important enough?" He smiled at the entranced look on his brother's face. Well, at least he'd impressed the kid, which was more than he'd ever been able to accomplish with his father.

Arthur crumpled the remains of his sandwich in its wrappings and dropped it under his seat. "Well, I guess I'd better try to finish this work before we get to Providence."

Dismissed. Without waiting to be told, Webster returned to his exile in the other seat. There had been so many questions to be asked. Where had they fled? The needed moment for them gone, perversely they returned. What was it really like at Edwards? Were they very tough on freshmen? What if he was no good at anything? So much that worried him. So much he wanted to know. Yet why let his brother know he was afraid? Why let anyone know? What good would it do? No one really cared. Except maybe Arthur. Hadn't he interrupted important work in Washington just to take him up to school? Wasn't that proof enough?

Providence had a cavernous, sooty station. Seven o'clock and not a cab in sight. Arthur left Webster with the bags and went to make a call.

Webster stood alone in the chill gloom, more grateful than ever not to have had to come alone. People hurried purposefully past, their faces strange and closed. He sat down on a bench beneath a tall, dust-smothered window flanked by a row of open trash cans emitting the stench of rotting apples. His glance moved to a large spider web, hanging in a corner of the window, its fine strands shining in a small patch of late sun. Webster stared, fascinated, at the geometric pattern. At first he thought the spider was gone, and then he saw it at the top edge of the web. He watched it, waiting for it to move, but it showed no sign of life. Webster leaned closer to it, staring. He became aware of the angry buzz of flies about the trash can; he looked at them, swarming about the garbage, settling, then swarming anew. A single fly separated itself from the swarm and buzzed exploringly about his head. He waved it away and it settled high on the wall.

Webster rose slowly from his seat, eyes on the fly. His movements became taut and stealthy. His lips felt dry and he moistened them with his tongue. The fly had begun to crawl downward on the wall. Webster waited, frozen. It was large, sleek, well fed, and had a shining blue head and multicolored, iridescent wings which seemed to glow and change color. Halfway down the stained wall, the fly stopped and rubbed its head with its front legs. Webster slowly raised his hand, palm cupped. The fly continued to rub its head. The spider remained unmoving in its web. Webster's hand edged closer. Then the fly turned and started to crawl back up the wall. In one fluid motion, Webster's hand swept the surface of the wall and closed into a solid trap. He felt a pleasant tickle against his palm and held his fist to his ear to hear the fly's excited buzzing. When it quieted, he turned and threw the fly into the center of the web.

Instantly the spider became a blur of motion. It swept down on the fly and smothered it in a blanket of sticky fibers. Webster chewed a knuckle, eyes wide with horror. *Murderer!* Webster bent closer, sweating. The fly struggled but could not get out. Webster imagined himself the fly. What did it feel? He shuddered.

The spider began to repair the section of web damaged in the action, while Webster watched, his face twisted with loathing. The fly struggled weakly until, finally, it lay still. The spider finished repairing its web, and then went back to the top corner and settled down to wait once more.

Webster glared at it. He hated the spider and hated himself. Partners in murder. Vile. But a strange excitement pumped through him. Damned spider! Hairy, black, menacing. He rolled a discarded newspaper into a club. One blow tore the trap from its moorings and sent the hunter scurrying across the floor. He swung again and missed. Panic in the hairy legs. Again! Yellow pus oozed. Legs twitched. Again! Again! The bludgeon rose and fell.

"What the devil!"

Weapon raised to strike, Webster turned to see Arthur frowning down at him. Webster pointed dumbly to the tiny smear on the floor.

"What is it? What are you doing down there?"

"A spider." Webster rose, brushed the dirt from his knees. He felt imbecilic. He forced a grin and tried to make a joke of it, casually. "There was this crazy black widow. A real killer. Figured I'd save a few innocent lives while waiting."

Arthur shook his head. Kids were still kids. Even the sensible, serious ones, like Webster. "All right, St. George. You can sheathe your sword now. Our taxi's waiting without."

Webster dropped the rolled newspaper in a waste can and grabbed the suitcases. "Without what?" Gratefully, he collected his reward, a slow half-smile from the lips of the splendid, impeccably groomed god beside him.

2

Edwards Academy, a sprawling quadrangle of weathered brick and ivy, was only a twenty-minute ride from the station. They arrived as the last daylight was fading, the buildings standing dark and ominous against the sky. Arthur directed the taxi to Roosevelt Hall, the freshman dormitory. They dropped the bags inside the entrance. "Hurry up," Arthur urged, and Webster could sense excitement in his voice and manner as Arthur led him back down the worn steps. "I want to show you around while we can still see something."

Webster, moving obediently beside Arthur, shivered with cold and fear, but his brother was too absorbed to notice. He felt Arthur's hand insistent on his arm, and was able for a while to take some comfort from this. Then the knowledge that his brother would be gone tomorrow, that he would soon be alone in this place, engulfed him. Alone, without help from anyone, to be judged by strangers by rules he did not yet know. A hundred carefully guarded inadequacies, real and imagined, nurtured by years of adult neglect, loomed threateningly over him. Well, he wouldn't let them find out. He'd make *sure* they wouldn't. He'd tell them, show them *nothing*. Nothing that mattered. They'd see only what he wanted them to see, only the good things. What good things? Suddenly, he could not think of any. But *everyone* had something good. He'd *find* something. And if he couldn't? Then he'd *make* it up, *make* up something good to show them.

"The parade grounds . . ." Arthur was saying, ". . . Inspections . . . retreat . . . sword ceremonies . . ." Webster tried to concentrate on the words, phrases so important to his brother, strange and frightening to him. Lost, forgotten bugles, marching feet. "And these are the grandstands where the reviewing officers would . . ." Rows of dark planks in the purple dusk, figures walking in the distance, singly and in small groups, all in uniform, all belonging. "Some of these trees are a couple of hundred years old." Great masses of towering shadow, huge, spreading, cutting away the last of the light. A couple of hundred years. Time overwhelmed. Old before the Revolution. "George Washington, Nathan Hale, Thomas Paine . . . This walk, these same bricks . . ." Webster's feet stumbled along the hallowed path. "Jefferson Hall . . ." Lighted, silhouette-shattered windows, exalted upperclassmen moving in certainty and knowledge through familiar rooms. Proven. Accepted. Admired.

"The armory and weapon museum . . ." They went inside. The smell of wax and aging wood. Battle standards, muskets, swords, cannon, the crumbling fabric of pulse-quickening uniforms, borne with consistent gallantry by Edwards men through half a dozen wars. "If it hadn't been for this damned trick knee of mine . . ." An instant's bitter regret over the old riding injury that had kept Arthur from equally heroic service in 1918. "Four classmates dead, nine wounded in action . . ." Then, suddenly, the plaque! There it was, hammered to the wall, emblazoned forever in bronze, the words, "ARTHUR POYNTON EVERS, DOUBLE SWORD WINNER, CLASS OF 1914." Webster stood for a long time in front of the plaque. "Come on," Arthur said, impatient, yet unmistakably pleased. "Let's get over to the office."

Outside, lights glowed along the walks. Webster's feet dragged. His brother was still talking, remembering aloud, explaining; but he barely heard. Tomorrow, was all he could think, tomorrow he'd be left here alone.

A tall, heavy-set man in uniform had come out of the administration building and was walking toward them. Arthur said softly, "Well, If it isn't Colonel Kearny himself."

"The Commandant?" Fear thickened Webster's tongue, almost stopped his feet. Arthur's hand was on his arm once more, unconsciously pulling him ahead.

"A little fatter," Arthur mused, "a little more pompous-looking, but otherwise the old bastard doesn't seem to have changed much."

Irreverence shared with the mighty. Webster blinked and said nothing. The Commandant was a huge man, bigger, even, than his father. This fact alone would have been enough to intimidate him. Combined with Kearny's august position, it was overwhelming. Webster's legs weakened.

At a distance of ten feet, Arthur said, "Hello, Colonel. It's nice to see you again." The greeting was easy, casual, supremely confident, no vestige left at all of the cadet-commandant relationship. There was, perhaps, even a hint of amused condescension lurking somewhere in the tone, in the half-smile with which it was offered.

Kearny stopped, frowned, groping for recognition in the uncertain light, his small eyes scanning the young man who had greeted him so familiarly.

"Arthur Evers, by God!" A great hand reached for and enclosed Arthur's. "You've changed, but I should have known at once. I should have known."

"*You* haven't changed, Colonel. I'd have known you in the dark at fifty feet." Somehow, it did not sound like a compliment. "I've brought you another Evers to browbeat. This is my brother, Webster."

Reluctantly, Kearny released his former cadet's hand and grasped Webster's. "Yes, of course." A toothy smile split his heavy face. "Welcome to Edwards, son."

"Thank you, sir." Webster managed to get it out. It surprised him. He'd half-expected his mouth to open without result.

"We've all been looking forward to meeting the brother of Arthur Evers. You have a lot to live up to. A devil of a lot. Your big brother's made a lasting impression on Edwards Academy and everyone connected with it. A lot to live up to," Kearny echoed. Then with expansive confidence, "but I'm sure you'll be able to do it."

Webster stared with wild, hopeless eyes at the uniformed mountain. No! He wanted to shout it, to let this man know, to let them all know right now, at the beginning, that he *wouldn't* be able to do it. But the great man was no longer looking at him, had not *really* looked at him even before. All of Kearny's attention was centered upon Arthur Evers. He had, of course, seen Arthur's picture in the papers many times and knew of the fantastic progress he'd made in such a brief time. Not surprising. Not at all. Hadn't he shown just such promise even during those early years at the Academy? How he had envied—yes, *envied*—Arthur, to be playing so active a part in these exciting, history-making times. And here he was, trapped at the Academy with not even a part in the war. What had Clemenceau been like at that last meeting? And Lloyd George? Jehoshaphat! Just to be in the same room with such men . . .

They had begun to stroll slowly along the walk, the two men in front, Webster lagging a few steps behind, forgotten.

And Paris? Arthur had to tell him about Paris since the war. The Colonel had been there, of course, but many years ago, with his wife. Had it really changed so much? The sly, knowing wink. Ahh! But to be there so young, so unattached. Was it still as marvelous? And Wilson? Was he as sick as rumored? There was so much that he. . . .

They circled the quadrangle. Arthur answered the questions

with cynical amusement combined with pleasure. How satisfying to have the normally smug old bastard buttering him up. It was even better than he'd expected. From a long way off he wished, without even acknowledging the thought, that his father might have been along to hear.

Webster stumbled along behind them in the dark, grateful to remain obscure and forgotten. It made vocal pretense, for the moment at least, unnecessary. Instead, he wrapped himself in the temporary warmth of fantasy. Maybe he could persuade Arthur to take him back to Washington with him tomorrow. Why not? There were plenty of good schools there. He could live with his brother and just walk back and forth to school each day. That would be great. Just the two of them there. They wouldn't even have to tell his father. Not right away, anyway. Why should it make any difference to his father? As long as he was away, out of the house and not bothering him, he wouldn't care. The dream grew, became clearer, more solid. Maybe he could even learn how to cook and. . . .

"Well, here's the boys' dormitory."

They were back in front of Roosevelt Hall. The two men stopped walking. Lost in thought, Webster bumped clumsily into Kearny's back. He mumbled an apology, feeling his face burn.

"I'm on my way home," Kearny told Arthur, apparently not noticing Webster. "Why don't you come up to the house after you get the boy settled? Mrs. Kearny and I would both be pleased to have you spend the night." Arthur remembered the charming, historically impressive, antique-filled Commandant's house on the hill. Thomas Jefferson was reputed to have once stayed there. Perhaps he would even sleep in the same bed as the great American. The idea amused and appealed to him. "Thank you. You're very kind."

Webster's fantasy collapsed. He suddenly hated this fat colonel who was going to expect the impossible, who thought him all the things he was not, who blared and bleated of hopeless heights to climb, while sneaking in to steal his last few minutes with Arthur.

"You know the bulletin board downstairs," Kearny said. "You'll find Webster's room assignment on it. Take him up and introduce him to his classmates, and I'll meet you back at the house. Mrs. Kearny will be delighted. Simply delighted." He looked down at Webster. "Remember, my boy. We're all expecting a lot of you."

"Yes, sir," Webster mourned.

An insane hope. Perhaps he'd been forgotten. Perhaps all the rooms had been assigned and they'd somehow left him out and now there was absolutely no place for him. Perhaps . . . but clearly, inescapably, the bulletin board delegated him to Room 203.

The stairs rose, craggy, iron-tipped, the last visible obstacle to final abandonment. The sounds of laughter broke from behind closed doors. How *could* they? Happy. Unafraid. All of them. Not like him. Nothing like him. Bags leaden, feet stumbling, Webster trailed his brother up the single tortuous flight.

"Wait!"

Arthur stopped, turned. "Yes?"

"Listen . . ." he tried. "I . . ."

"What *is* it?" The faint note of impatience, turned to concern. "You look pale. Are you all right?"

Webster nodded. Please take me with you. Don't leave me here. I won't be any bother. You won't even know I'm there. I promise. I'll do anything you say. Only please don't leave me here alone. I'm scared. I don't want them to see, but Jesus, I'm scared. . . . He thought it as hard as he could. His brother would *know*. His brother would just have to look at him and *know*.

Arthur frowned. "Are you sure?"

Webster dared not breathe. He felt it that close. Then this tall man whom he loved reached out a hand, eyes suddenly dark with feeling. "Poor kid. You're just exhausted." The hand took a bag from him. That was all. "What you need is a good night's sleep." Arthur turned and continued up the steps.

His brother *didn't* know, and there was no way in this world to tell him. He plodded up the remaining steps.

"Here it is." Arthur dropped the bags before a closed door to the right of the stair well. "Room 203."

There were boys talking inside. Loud, confident, afraid of nothing. He stiffened as Arthur knocked. To hell with them! They were only kids. If his own brother didn't know, they wouldn't know either. He felt a cold facing drop over him. It held him firmly, reassuringly, a tight, well-fitting uniform, back and legs braced, almost rigid. All right. Let them try and break through now. Let them try.

When the door swung open he was ready, easy smile in place, right hand poised for the first self-assured, properly hearty handshake.

Chapter Nine

1952: Upstate New York

It was early afternoon when Alice and Justin reached "the cabin," a small, faded-white, shingled bungalow set on a rocky ledge above a lake. When they had first bought the place, it had stood alone in the heavily wooded area, without electricity, and could be reached only by a narrow dirt trail. Now there was a scattering of other houses beside the lake; power lines had been brought in and the dirt road widened and paved, but it was primarily a summer colony and whenever they came up off-season, the Blaines were still alone.

Justin got out of the car and, stretching, looked up at the window beside the stone chimney from which he had once spent nights watching the road with a gun in his lap. The things, he thought, that a man did in one lifetime.

They carried in two boxes of groceries and Justin started a fire on the oversized living room hearth while Alice straightened things in the kitchen. Afterward, they lunched beside the fire. Justin leaned back in a padded rocker and breathed deeply the smells of coffee and burning pine. The heat of the flames was pleasantly warm against his face and through the window he could see the sun catching the unbroken surface of the lake. He smiled. "Life," he said, "can be beautiful."

Alice studied her coffee. "When they let you live it."

Later, when Alice carried the dishes into the kitchen, Justin turned on a small radio that stood on a pile of books. Turning carefully, he kept the sound low. At length, finding no news program, he left the tuner at an orchestra playing "Musetta's Waltz," closed his eyes and let the warmth of the fire soothe the aching in his eyelids. His glasses lay in his lap; his body relaxed.

He opened his eyes to the sound of a chime and then to a man's voice.

"It's four o'clock and time for the afternoon news roundup. In Washington today, Under Secretary of State Webster Evers appeared before the House Subversive Activities Committee to answer charges that he had been a member of the Communist Party. The Under Secretary, appearing voluntarily before the committee, denied under oath that he had ever been a member of the Communist Party or had ever known Justin Blaine, the radio commentator who made the charge before the committee yesterday. In a blistering statement, Mr. Evers said that he was—quote—confused and angry over Blaine's apparently insane attempt to vilify him—unquote. At the end of the Under Secretary's statement there was applause in the committee room. . . . In the skies over Korea American Sabre jets accounted for three MIG fighters. The action took place near the North Korean capital of Pyongyang. North Korean radio claims that five American planes were shot down, but the Air Force says that only one plane failed to return to its base. . . . In a one-hour conference at the White House the President conferred with Foreign Minister Ibn Shamal about Communist encroachments in the Middle East. The Foreign Minister from . . ."

Justin listened unmoving as the announcer went on. The news all seemed suddenly to have jumbled into a single mass of details: Webster's denial, the applause, the dogfight over Korea, the President and Communist threats in the Middle East.

"Under oath!" Alice had come in from the kitchen and now stood white-faced before her husband, a dish towel hanging from her hand. "The son of a bitch dared to say it under oath."

Justin nodded.

"What I don't understand," she said slowly, "is how he thinks he can get away with it." She sat down, still facing him. "With what he knows you have on him, and with the country watching, how can he expect to bluff his way out of it?"

"I don't know," Justin said quietly. What *did* Webster expect? For that matter, what had *he*, Justin Blaine, the insanely vindictive —what? liar?—what had *he* expected? Of course, the others he named in his statement would disappear or take the Fifth down the line. But Evers could not do that. Evers had to play a different game—one not of his making, but one he might be able to win.

"The burden of proof is on me," Justin said, as if he were informing himself. "Right now, I'm the wild accuser, and the papers will play it that way. I'm sure nobody can reach me here. Thank God for no telephone."

"You mean Webster may just pull it off." There was a touch of contempt in Alice's tone. "And you were ready to weep over hurting your old 'friend' Webster. Well? Do you still feel tender about him?"

"Why are we acting so surprised?" he said. "What choice does he have? An admission to any of my charges would mean the end. Good-bye sometime future Presidency, good-bye secretaryship, good-bye everything he is now. Webster's fighting for his life, Alice. Of course he would use his prestige and position to bluff his way through this mess. In his place, I doubt if I'd have acted differently myself."

"No!" Alice rose and angrily turned off the radio. "I don't believe that. I can't picture you behaving in any way like Webster Evers. The two of you are as different as black and white. Compared to you, Webster's a sleek, predatory, unscrupulous animal."

Justin's face became pink with irritation. "Oh, stop it," he said impatiently. "For some reason, Webster's the one person, the one subject, I've ever known you to be blind and unreasonable about. Remember! He and I were *both* Communists. We were *both* doing what we thought best at the time. There wasn't really that much difference between us."

"Different as black and white," she echoed stubbornly, her lips tightening into a hard line. "You both may have worked for the party, but don't confuse your motives. Don't confuse the reasons why you were both in there. Don't confuse your separate feelings about Communism."

"What are you talking about?"

"Jussie, Jussie," Alice sighed, her eyes looking heavenward. "He was never really one of us. He was never part of our cause. He was fighting his own little war and he played the spy to find his own little sense of accomplishment—and to get back at the people he didn't like in the State Department." She waited for Justin to deny what she had said, but he remained silent. She went on, her voice unusually flat and toneless. "You and I *believed* in Communism as the answer to the injustices and anguish of the world. We cared about tyranny in this country because we *knew* what it was like, we saw it happen. Webster didn't know about these things and he didn't care. He wouldn't have known how to care as we did. Maybe we were all wrong, but our reasons were real and desperate to us then, and they went far beyond Webster's. Webster used us. He used us at least as much as we used him."

"You're being unfair," Justin said, but without force. "He took the same risks we did. You're not giving him credit for—"

"Credit?" Alice cut him off harshly. "Credit for what? Credit for using everything he's ever been part of, everyone he's ever known, to feed his own ego and personal ambitions? *That's* the only kind of credit I'd like to give that man."

Justin stared at his wife. "I haven't heard you talk like this in more than thirteen years." It had happened often then, her temper flaring in righteous anger over some party heretic or dangerous error in judgment. In a practical way, she had been a far better Communist than he. She'd had a clear, sharply analytical mind and the underlying toughness necessary for the making of hard decisions. One of the things to which Justin had never been able to adjust was the need to be utterly ruthless, as when some member had to be sacrificed for the broader good of the party. Alice, he recalled, had not been troubled by such weakness.

She had turned off the radio; now he turned it on.

"Can't you leave it alone?" Alice asked.

"No, I can't. I wish I could." Why am I doing this? he thought. To get the latest developments, or is the pain of it all becoming a pleasure? He twisted the dial to the CBN station. "Phil Allgood's show is on now."

They listened to the end of a commercial and to the station identification. ". . . your CBN station in New York. It's four-thirty, and time for Philip Allgood and the news, brought to you by—"

"Jussie," Alice said anxiously, as the opening commercial chirped in the background, "try not to be hurt by what you hear."

He said, "Don't worry." Stiff upper lip, old boy, he told himself, hide the hurt and spare the wife. Wonderful tradition—if only it worked.

". . . and now, here is Philip Allgood," and Phil's New England nasality filled the room.

"Good afternoon. Here is the top of the day's events. The attention of millions of Americans has been focused today on Capitol Hill, where Under Secretary of State Webster Evers spent less than an hour testifying before the House Subversive Activities Committee. He was there voluntarily to answer charges made yesterday by Justin Blaine, a radio commentator, that he, Evers, was a member of the Communist Party and a member of an espionage network. The hearing room was more crowded than usual, and Evers was the only witness scheduled for the day. Wearing a dark, pin-striped suit, Evers seemed completely at ease, although perturbed. This reporter was in the hearing room when Evers was asked the key questions. He categorically denied having been a member of the Communist Party, much less having been a member of any espionage network. When asked if he knew Justin Blaine, the distinguished Under Secretary said that he had never set eyes upon him and certainly did not know him, although he had heard some of his news broadcasts. He was calm even when Representative Henry Pilgrim, Republican of Illinois, suggested that he might have forgotten Blaine and that he had known him several years before. Evers replied that he knew for certain that Blaine was a stranger to him, and I quote his own words here: 'And whatever effort may be made to suggest a link between Mr. Blaine and me would be based on a falsehood. It is bad enough that this unfortunate episode should have forged even this tarnished connection. I hope this will be the end of the matter, for the business of maintaining a wise and strong foreign policy is immeasurably more important to me than answering absurd charges such as this.'

"When Evers was excused, there was a thunderous ovation in the hearing room—even among usually undemonstrative members of the press—an ovation which Chairman Kelly made no attempt to suppress. From the impression I got of the many people who crowded around Mr. Evers to shake his hand, I would say that the Under Secretary has satisfied any doubts the committee might have had about him. This sensational interlude is probably over. And this reporter would also like to ask if we haven't reached a point where our vigilance against Communist subversion has led us to do damage to ourselves as a nation. As Under Secretary Evers pointed out, we are in danger of weakening our stand against Communism abroad by attacking as Communists dedicated patriots at home. . . . Now, here is a message from the makers of—"

Alice clicked off the radio. "And that was a CBN commentator. Phil Allgood, who has eaten with us and drunk with us and sweated through his divorce with us. Even your own network is slanting it for Evers, and even Phil doesn't mind calling you a liar and an enemy of the people, as long as Mannheim says to do it. . . . So where do we stand with Mannheim now? Or should I tell you?"

"You don't have to tell me." Justin stood and felt his legs suddenly go weak. He leaned against the chair. "I've got to prove that Webster perjured himself or I'll be up on perjury charges myself."

Alice looked at him with sudden concern. "Your color's bad. Are you all right?"

Justin nodded. "Just a bit of a headache. I think I'll lie down for a while."

"Yes, and you'd better take one of your pills. You look awful." She shook her head. "All this excitement. I was afraid of all this excitement."

Justin went into the bedroom and closed the door. His head did not really ache. As much as he loved and needed his wife, there were times when Alice overwhelmed him, when she made it impossible for him to think clearly. He stretched out on the bed, remembered his pills and took one from a small box in his pocket. He swallowed it without water, feeling the twinge of impatient annoyance he felt each time he took one, still not used to being so absorbed with his body and its needs. He tried to lie down again, but found himself shivering in the cold sweat of sudden panic. Evidence, he was going to need clear, detailed and irrefutable evidence. He was going to have to prove, without doubt, that Webster Evers had played an active and important role in the Washington spy apparatus. And he was not sure he would be able to do it.

Justin sat up on the edge of the bed. The nightmare quality of it all was hitting him—Evers' performance, his prestige, the influence he could wield, the ease with which he had turned aside the blade of accusation. And here was Justin Blaine, unbelieved, alone and hiding from the world, way out on a limb of his own carving and no one about to help him down easily. How nightmarish the irony: at last the committee had actually stumbled on a spy network, and they were going to back away from it on the smooth assurances of one of the spies!

He went to a big, old-fashioned desk in a corner of the room and began carefully, methodically, to go through the drawers. He emptied out everything that stemmed from the period when he was active in the party. The pile grew: apartment leases, bills, car registrations, newspaper clippings, check stubs, insurance policies, income tax forms, letters, keys, library cards, mementos and souvenirs of dozens of long-forgotten places and events. Justin smiled to himself. A flagrant violation of party rules. Leon Rosoff, the old apparatus chief, would not have approved. *"Collect nothing, save nothing,"* had been one of the maxims of the underground. Maybe, he thought wryly, he hadn't been so great an apparatchik after all.

A yellowed newspaper clipping fell to the floor. Justin picked it up and glanced at the headline: GIANT MUTE ARRAIGNED IN RAZZIO MURDER. And also on the pile, another clipping: MUTE MURDERER TO DIE IN RAZZIO SLAYING. He started to read the suddenly familiar words, but dropped the clippings onto the desk. Pre-party, his mind labeled them, cause rather than effect.

The door opened quietly and Alice peered in. "I thought you were lying down," she said.

"My headache's better. I wanted to start going through these."

Alice sat down on a corner of the desk and poked through the piles. "Did you find anything?"

"Not so far."

"Well, I did." She handed him a small cylindrical package, the very feel of which was to him like a jolt into the past.

"Alice! This isn't—"

"Open it," she said.

He undid the outer wrapping and took out a small film canister which was enclosed in a slip of paper.

"You actually kept one of these?" he asked in amazement.

She nodded.

"But this wouldn't prove anything—a roll of film from a miniature camera."

"You'd be surprised at what it will prove once it's developed."

"Developed!"

"Jussie, read the note."

He took off the rubber band that kept the note wrapped around the film canister and unrolled the paper. The note said:

August 4, 1937

Roll contains memo this date Evers-Hull re German rearm. Aircraft prod. figs. 1936 & projected '37. Also policy recommendations. Only 3 frames of roll shot—all of Evers' memo. Memo del. this date to Hull.

"I don't understand," he said thickly.

"It's very simple, Jussie. I simply kept it instead of sending it on."

"I didn't even know about this! I can't believe you'd break discipline so blatantly. I certainly can't understand why you did."

"That's not important now. What matters is that we have this."

Justin sat on the bed, holding the canister in his open hand. Alice stood in front of him, watching him think it out.

"Is it signed?" he said at last.

"I think so."

"You *think* so! But that's important."

"But didn't he always sign his memos?"

"No! Not always. Sometimes he just typed his name at the top."

"Even so," Alice said, "the fact that we had a copy of it incriminates him. This was top secret. I remember that it was very important."

"Yes, that means something. But why did you keep it instead of passing it on? And why didn't you tell me about it?"

"That's not important now, I'm telling you. The point is that we have it. It proves you're telling the truth."

"*If* we have it. Who knows if the film's still good after all these years? We've got to get it developed."

"How? Where could we take a thing like this?"

"To our local drugstore," he said acidly, hoping the joke would break the sudden, hard tension he could feel building in her. But she wasn't smiling. "If he signed it, and if it's as important as you say, and if it can still be developed, then we're okay. But that's a lot of ifs. For God's sake, Alice, why didn't you tell me you were doing this?"

She looked at him squarely, almost in warning. "Jussie, just take it for the blessing it can be. Don't worry about it." She saw his refusal to let it drop. "Sometimes your sense of integrity is so great you sound naïve. I just had a feeling it might come in handy one day—don't ask me how I knew—and I wasn't taking any chances of your getting rid of it or blurting it out. Darling, you know you sometimes were a . . . difficult spy—although a lovable one." She leaned down and stroked his ear.

"Quite a team: the dangerous spy and the lovable one, shaking the world. But this might do it, if they'll just believe the truth when it's put before them."

She sat down beside him and took his hand. "You'll make them believe and understand it," she said softly. "You will, Jussie. This is one time Webster's not going to get away with it. But you're also going to have to remember every detail of your life where it touched Webster's, and even before. You've got to make these people understand why you became a Communist. They must see the whole truth."

Justin nodded. Of course, the whole truth. The truth about Webster Evers and especially the truth about what Alice said was on the film. After all, besides Webster, who was then Chief of the German Section, only the Secretary and Under Secretary of State had been permitted access to top-secret materials of that nature, especially when they concerned policy, and both those men were above suspicion. It would all have to focus on Webster—the real Webster.

And then there would have to be the whole truth about Justin Blaine, alias William Baker, lovable spy, rabid idealist, a man hard enough to work in the apparatus and to escape from it, but also a man soft enough to wreck himself on illusions. The whole truth. The reasons and motivations and all the paraphernalia that could drive a man this way and that—to be laid out like a blueprint so that the committee and the nation might read it. Gentlemen, to know how Justin Blaine got from where he started to this—this grotesque, this *insane* situation, you start here at A and follow the twisted path to . . . where?

But where was point A? Red Bank? Cleveland? The delusion-crowded halls of academe? How could you know for sure what was significant?

Was point A—or at least B—that first year in New York?

Chapter Ten

1930: New York City

Justin strolled up Fifth Avenue, a folded copy of the *New York Times* under one arm and his topcoat over the other. He walked slowly and aimlessly, with streams of midday shoppers eddying about him. Store windows sparkled in the October sun, their displays bright with color. Fifth Avenue, Justin thought, all the best things in the world squeezed into a few dazzling blocks—the women aloof and beautiful, the men successful and confident, and no sign anywhere of hunger, bread lines and disaster.

At the Fifty-ninth Street Plaza he sat down on the rim of the fountain. It was the first clear day after a long stretch of rainy weather, and the sun felt reassuringly warm on his face. He let it bake into him and listened to the city's spoiled, overfed pigeons. Then he unfolded his paper and turned to the want ads. He went over the meager list of jobs carefully, but without real hope. There would, he knew, be a small army of applicants for even the most menial of the few openings, and married men with families were being given preference. Although Justin did not question the justice of this, he was growing increasingly discouraged and bitter. He had worked a grand total of thirteen days in the four months since college, and his hopes of ever seeing another pay check were fast fading. Was a man really ready for the scrap heap at twenty-four? By twenty-four, a man should at least be putting some direction into his life. But how did you get direction into your life if you couldn't even get a goddamn job?

Nothing he had done in the past four and a half years had had much direction or meaning. After almost two years of work in Cleveland, Justin had returned home to Red Bank. Except for a brief exchange of letters with Nick, before Nick died, he had lost contact with the crew. Yet those days of working with his hands had *meant* something. After them . . . emptiness, and running home to Mamma, as he had thought bitterly at the time. Later, with his emotions under control, he realized he had not been running away at all. He had simply wanted to go home. His father had suffered a severe heart attack in his absence, and the burden of the illness along with worrying about Justin had weakened his mother.

Frederick Blaine, freed of the necessity of earning a living, threw himself wholeheartedly into being a chronic invalid. The old bluster was gone, along with even the pretense of trying to write. Every table in the house was decorated with a little bottle of nitro pills, placed there for possible emergencies. The emergencies occurred, Justin thought, with too frequent regularity, but they were frighteningly dramatic. Each was ushered in with a violent seizure, a hoarse gasping for breath. His father's face would turn reddish purple. The first few times Justin witnessed it, he was panic-stricken, certain his father was dying. But placing a tiny white nitro pill under his father's tongue was like working a miracle, for the attack would subside and disappear, leaving its victim pale and trembling.

Often, Justin would listen to his father's labored breathing and feel certain that it was an exaggeration meant to express suffering. He's using it, Justin would think coldly, to use us, to get pity. He's given up. At such times he would remember Randy and Nick, who had never given up, who had fought for their dignity in spite of everything, and Justin would vow never to settle for less than independence and pride. Cleveland had taught him that much. Still, looking at his father's lined, wasted face, looking at this ruin of a strong man, Justin could not long support the contempt and bitterness he so often told himself he had a right to feel. In spite of the injuries of the past, bitterness would become regret and reluctant love.

His four years at a small, provincial college on a full scholarship, earned by competitive examinations and maintained by hard work, had been mainly an escape from the grimness of his life at home. He had no interest in the active undergraduate social life and shunned the coeds. His professors had little to offer him; he read constantly and far beyond the assignments; and he was able and eager to argue almost any point they tried to make. His teachers were pleased by his fine showing, but puzzled by his hostility. Justin took their courses and listened to their lectures and performed brilliantly out of habit and necessity. But he scorned these men who had never worked with their hands—particularly those pseudo liberals in the Economics Department, his major, who preached the new theories of John Maynard Keynes but whose hearts were really with Adam Smith. A lot they knew about the hard life of the working man!

Three fat and dirty pigeons fought savagely for a peanut, and Justin glanced up from his paper, swooshing away a particularly aggressive bird with it. And how much longer before men would start competing for the peanuts? Here he sat, he thought, adrift among New York's one and a half million unemployed, going through the motions of job hunting. He had etched himself into a pattern: the automatic purchase of the *New York Times,* the checking off of the few least remote possibilities, the lining up and waiting for interviews which, in most cases, never came, the haphazard wandering of streets when the sun shone, and the stale awesomeness of the Forty-second Street Library when it rained. It was a pattern he knew he shared with countless other men, but this did not help the days pass more quickly or more easily for him. He faced, too, the additional frustration of not really knowing what sort of work he wanted to do, even if he had the chance. Nothing seemed of any real interest to him. Of what possible value was some fumbling clerical routine, when everything seemed to be collapsing? Sometimes he was almost grateful *not* to be able to find a job. How could a man with any social conscience at all focus entirely on himself these days? Yet what more, he thought dully, was he doing now?

"For Christ's sake!" a booming voice cried. "Justin Blaine, the pigeon lover!"

Justin looked up at a tall, lanky, redheaded young man with a wide impudent grin, a splash of freckles across his snub nose and the inevitable *Times* folded under one arm. "Tom!"

"Tom!" the young man mimicked. "You haven't seen your old buddy in months; he drops out of the sky in front of you, and all you can manage is a casual 'Tom!' I'm overwhelmed."

Justin smiled faintly. "If you can remember that far back," he said, "we weren't exactly buddies the last few times we met." He looked at Tom Gallagher more closely, noting the tieless shirt, the unpressed suit, the hair badly in need of cutting. Still the conscientious objector, he thought, the rebel in search of causes, the deliberate nonconformist. For more than three years, Tom had been his one close friend at college, sharing disdain for most of the things that absorbed the rest of the student body. They had had a violent argument a month before graduation. "In fact," Justin said, "the last thing you assured me of, was that I was a thick-headed son of a bitch."

"Absolutely correct," Tom said. "Your memory is flawless. And I'm still convinced of the accuracy of my judgment. However, I find I've mellowed with time. I've realized it's ridiculous to seek my own perfection in others. Therefore, old buddy, I forgive you your stupidity, I forgive you your stubbornness. I accept you for the sentimental and lovable jerk you are." The big hand plunged forward. "Shake!"

Justin grinned and took the offered hand. "It's been a long time."

Tom folded his lank form in two and sat down on the fountain beside him. His blue eyes sparkled. "Miss me?"

"I guess so," Justin said.

"Me too." Tom's bushy red brows narrowed. "What the hell did we fight about anyway? Something about your lousy, archaic sense of integrity, wasn't it?"

"Something like that." Justin remembered what the argument had been about, knowing that Tom remembered too. Justin had completed an economics course the year before and was helping to prepare the examination papers that Gallagher's class would use. He had refused to allow Tom to see them and had resented Tom's pressures about it. They had not even said good-bye at graduation.

Tom peered at him. "You have the look of a man in search of a job."

"Very hopelessly," Justin said. "What about you?"

"Me?" Tom Gallagher spread gangling arms wide, and swiveled to watch a coatless, full-hipped girl go by. "I'm just enjoying the sun, the day, what is perhaps autumn's last glimpse of ungirdled behinds." He nodded earnestly. "I tell you, Justin, there is a particularly nostalgic look to a woman's behind on the last warm day of autumn. In all the world there is no sight quite like it." He leaned forward, studying another specimen.

"I take it," Justin said, "that you're out of a job too."

Tom shook his head. "You take it wrong. You can only be out of a job when you've had one, or are looking for one. Neither situation applies to me."

"You mean you haven't worked at all since graduation?"

"That's exactly what I mean."

"And you haven't even tried to find anything?"

Tom made a sour face. "For God's sake, Justin! Stop sounding like a middle-class conscience. You know my chances of finding a job. Besides, my old man's got more money than he can spend in two lifetimes, even with the market crash. What do you expect me to do, look for something that isn't there just so I can feel virtuous?"

"Not if your father doesn't mind keeping you on a perpetual dole."

"Who said my father doesn't mind? He does mind, but there's nothing he can do about it. He's got my allowance cut as far as he dares go. He's afraid I'll disgrace him in some way if he gives me any less." He laughed coldly. "God bless his reverence for public opinion, which he worships almost as much as the almighty buck and the plaster statue of Jesus he keeps in his bedroom."

Tom paused and stared at a new flock of pigeons. A tall, gaunt woman stood throwing bread as the birds swarmed about her feet. "Look at those goddamned birds," he said reflectively. "I tell you, the little feathered bastards'll inherit the earth. And they're welcome to it. I wish to hell I could grow feathers myself."

As if he had uttered something profound, Gallagher fell silent and seemed not to expect an answer. What was it that really brought us together? Justin asked himself. Was it Tom's rebellion against his Catholic upbringing? His open, proud hatred of authority? Justin had needed such strength—as he saw it—then. It had been a hard transformation, his entering college. Cleveland and his father's condition still dominated his thoughts, filling him with a sense of futility, tormenting him through cruel headaches. Tom's outlook had been refreshing, a way out of hanging upon obligations and the certainty of failure they carried with them. Perhaps Tom would be what he needed now.

"What about you?" Tom nodded at the "Help Wanted" pages. "What sort of a job do you hope you're not going to find today?"

Justin looked at him curiously. "What makes you think I don't want a job?"

"Because I know you." Tom tossed a pebble at a pigeon and watched with satisfaction as the bird pecked at it. "I know you better than you know yourself," he said. "You haven't the temperament to just be a stumble-bum like me. Too damned much conscience. You'd keep looking for jobs even if you found and quit them every few weeks. But you don't really know what you want to do any more than I. We can't get all worked up over the nine-to-five idiocy of adding columns of numbers or peddling colored beads. Not when every time you open your eyes, you see the whole stinking world sliding straight to hell in a basket."

Justin folded and unfolded his newspaper. With the sun on his face and the parade of gaily dressed shoppers passing before him, it was hard to feel as sober and bleak as Tom was asking him to feel.

Tom lit a cigarette, his tapered hands looking almost like a girl's. "We read the newspapers," he said. "We listen to the jerks over the radio, picking apart the League of Nations, working up new hates, scared to death of anything that hints of change, digging their heads into the ground so as not to see, not to smell the stink of what's happening to three-quarters of the earth's population. Just as long as the really important people have shinier automobiles each year, just as long as their houses become bigger and their plumbing more efficient, we're told everything's just great. So forget the millions of slobs out of work starving to death each year. Don't waste your time thinking about the five hundred million illiterates. Don't think about them and maybe they'll go away."

Tom crushed out his cigarette and took the newspaper from Justin's hands. He stared thoughtfully at the want ads, as though the rows of small type symbolized futility. Then he carefully and deliberately ripped it in two. "I've just liberated you." He grinned, his eyes bright and mischievous and not at all the way they had looked while he was talking. "For today, at least, I've liberated you from your fruitless search."

"Now I'm just a bum like you."

"You were a bum before," Tom said. "But now you're an honest bum. The world needs all the honest bums it can get. We're its last hope of salvation." He stood up and stretched. "Come on.

Let's get away from these goddamned pigeons. They're making me feel inferior."

Without warning he swooped down on the great flock of birds that swarmed about the tall woman who was feeding them. "Yaaaah!" he yelled, stamping his feet and clapping his hands. "Yaaaah! Yaaaah!"

The frightened pigeons rose in a flapping cloud. The woman stared wide-eyed at Tom.

"Yaaaah!" he growled, advancing threateningly toward her. "Yaaaah! Yaaaah!"

With a small, startled cry, the woman dropped her bag of bread and fled. Tom stood looking after her with satisfaction. Then he picked up the bag and held it out to Justin. "Have some bread."

They spent most of the afternoon drifting aimlessly about the city. Later they took the subway downtown and rode the Staten Island Ferry back and forth across New York harbor. They stood in the breeze of the upper deck for more than two hours, watching the many ships that passed through the greatest port of what was still, even with the depression, the richest country on earth. Despite themselves, they were awed at the sight. And the Statue of Liberty and the New York skyline aglow in the late sun were things they pretended not to notice at all, yet did freshly notice each time the ferry made a crossing.

"Look at them," Tom jibed, when they had left the boat at last and were almost overrun by hordes of homeward-bound commuters and job seekers. "They're like a pack of lemmings swarming happily toward the edge of a cliff."

"At least they're going *someplace,*" Justin said flatly. "At least they're in motion. Where are we going? Back and forth to where?"

Tom looked at Justin with wry amusement. "If you're so damned anxious to tie some kind of rocket to your tail, perhaps you ought to come along on my date with me tonight. You might enjoy watching at least one proposed solution to the world's ills in action."

"I've seen your dates in action. They propose the same horizontal solution to everything."

"Not this one." Tom smiled with wistful regret. "This one regards me, and all other men, purely as potential recruits for the party."

Justin looked at him doubtfully. "You mean you've got a date with a Communist?" He was familiar with Tom Gallagher's opinion of the Communist movement in America, as "a pack of unwashed chronic dissidents." It seemed unlikely that he would be seriously involved with them now.

"Frankly, I find it hard," Tom declared, "to think of Alice Harte as a Communist. This kid grew up three houses away from me on Riverside Drive. Her local fame rested solely on the fact that she had the cutest face, best legs and biggest tits on the block. This Communist frenzy is a recent thing. I ran into her a few times and she kept badgering me about coming to a meeting." He laughed. "She has a wide-eyed way of looking at you when she talks that makes you forget what the hell she's saying. Anyway, I finally agreed to let her take me down tonight. Why don't you come along? You might find it amusing."

They came out of the ferry terminal into the confusion of rush-hour traffic. Justin doubted he'd find a Communist meeting amusing. He'd never been impressed by any of the confused Marxist theories and dialectics gushed by campus intellectuals. But then he didn't feel like going to his room. "Are you sure your friend wouldn't mind your bringing me?"

"Mind?" Tom laughed. "She'll be tickled to see another potential convert. I might even be awarded the Red Star for finding you. Just be sure of one thing. Alice may not look the type, but she's damned serious about this business. Don't kid her about it. She may take it from me, but not from anyone else. She's convinced she's working for the world's sole chance of survival. It's the only thing in which she shows the slightest interest." Tom sighed with elaborate and tragic regret. "It's such a pathetic waste I could weep. Never in all your life have you seen such tits."

2

Tom was to meet Alice Harte at the corner of Second Avenue and Tenth Street at eight o'clock. She was not there when they arrived. They stood beneath the yellow glow of a street light and waited. There was little traffic moving and most of the lofts in the area were dark. Justin looked around uncertainly.

"Are you sure you had the instructions right?" he said.

Tom nodded. He glanced at his watch. "It's only three minutes to eight. She'll be here at eight. You'll see. Not a minute before or after. It's a big thing with her, being very punctual and efficient." He grinned. "Freud calls it sublimation of the female image. But with her it's a losing fight. One look at her and everything comes busting out, unsublimated."

The bells of a nearby church were just tolling the hour when Justin saw a small, slender girl approaching and knew at once it was Alice Harte. She walked quickly, looking straight ahead, and her heels clacked on the pavement with a sharp, military sound. As she drew closer under the street light, he saw blond, mannishly bobbed hair, framing a pretty, but serious face completely without makeup. She wore a severe, formless dress of nondescript color that tried hard, but failed, to hide the superb promise beneath. With almost visible embarrassment, Justin found himself staring at her breasts.

"*Quel dommage,*" mumbled Tom. "*Quel* waste."

She came up to them, frowned at Justin, then looked questioningly at Tom Gallagher.

Tom grinned. "It's all right, Comrade. This is Justin Blaine, an old college chum—intelligent, properly dissolute and sorely in need of a dedicated cause. I figured he might be a likely candidate for you and the other comrades to sink your teeth into. I've been softening him up for you all afternoon. Haven't I, old buddy?"

Justin felt uncomfortable under the girl's close scrutiny. She had wide, intelligent eyes that regarded him gravely, unblinkingly. He was suddenly unsure about the whole thing. "I hope I'm not in the way," he said. "Tom thought it would be all right if I came along."

She continued to study him for a moment, then abruptly extended her hand. "How do you do. I'm Alice Harte."

"Yes," Justin said, feeling very dull. He shook her hand and felt it small and firm against his own.

She smiled a little grimly. "I don't know what Tom's been telling you, Mr. Blaine, but I can make a pretty fair guess. He probably started with a detailed description of my extraordinary physical development, and ended with an amusing little gambit about coming down to watch the comical comrades rant and rave about saving the world. Tell me, Mr. Blaine, did he also promise we'd throw in a few homemade bombs to spice up the show?"

Justin flushed. "No," he said. "I—"

"Hey!" Tom broke in, laughing. "Down, girl! What do you want from poor Justin? He's an innocent bystander. If you're in the mood to let off steam, pick on me. At least I'm used to you."

"And I'm used to you," Alice Harte said. "I don't know why I should be surprised at your bringing along a guest for the show. It's really quite in character. For some reason you seem to enjoy playing the role of a child."

Justin looked quickly from one to the other. "Listen," he said. "Let's forget the whole thing. You two go along without me."

"No," she said. "You're welcome to come. I just didn't want you having any false notions of fun and frolic."

"Alice, baby!" Tom draped a proprietary arm about the girl's shoulders. It was promptly shaken off. "Look at Justin! Have you ever in your life seen a less fun and frolicsome type of individual?"

Alice looked at Justin's sober face and smiled. "Come on," she said. "Let's go."

They walked downtown, deeper into the Bowery and then turned west on Seventh Street.

They were in a neighborhood of run-down tenements, garages and small factories, noisy and teeming with activity during the day, but almost ominously quiet at night. A scattering of derelicts hugged the shadows. As they crossed Third Avenue, an elevated train roared by overhead with a flash of blue sparks.

Justin glanced at the slender blond girl beside him. She seemed at home in the area and he had visions of her striding grimly to meetings through the threatening shadows . . . the Marxist Maid of Riverside Drive.

Tom suddenly laughed. "Hey!" he said. "Get a load of this." Two men dressed in rags stood swaying under the light of a corner lamp post. One was tall and thin and the other was short and they were both very drunk. The tall one clutched the top of his falling trousers with desperate modesty, while his companion struggled to thread a length of rope through the empty belt loops.

"Wait a minute," Tom said, halting to watch. Alice Harte started to walk impatiently on, but he held out a restraining hand. "This is too good to miss."

The men were too absorbed to notice that they had an audience. The short one dropped to his knees, trying to steady himself for the threading process, but each time he managed to push the rope through one or two loops, his friend stumbled and pulled it loose. The tall man released his grip to help with the rope and his trousers plummeted downward, revealing torn, dingy shorts.

"There they go!" Tom roared. "Grab 'em!"

The tall man caught the trousers at his knees and pulled them up with the grave, exaggerated dignity of the blindly drunk. Tom whooped with laughter. It reminded Justin of a vaudeville act he had once seen as a child. "Easy with the rope." Tom laughed. "Take it slow and easy. Come on, buddy," he called encouragingly, "you can do it."

The deliberate threading process began once more. Justin felt Alice Harte stir beside him. He turned to look at her and his smile froze. The girl was watching the two men with such deep pity that he felt as if he'd been caught laughing at a funeral. Puzzled, he watched the hopeless charade repeat itself like a broken film strip, listening to Tom's laughter and jibes, but somehow no longer amused himself. For the first time, he looked closely at the men's faces. The tall one was gaunt and hollow-cheeked, with sunken eyes and the red-splotched skin of the chronic alcoholic. He was hatless and his matted hair clung moistly to his forehead in a fringe of spit curls. The shorter man's face had the flattened, broken look of a prize fighter, his eyes almost closed by layers of ancient scar tissue. He worked his tongue in a corner of his mouth as he struggled with the rope. He kept making soft, reassuring sounds to his friend.

Alice Harte suddenly turned and walked away. She walked quickly, without looking back, and when Tom called after her, she did not stop. Justin and Tom ran to catch up.

"Hey," Tom called. "What's the idea?"

She stopped walking and glared at him. "Look," she said. "Why don't you go home? Why don't you just take your little playmate here and go home?"

Tom laughed. "Baby, you're crazy. You've been trying for weeks to get me to one of your hot little meetings. Now when I'm finally going, you don't want me. Why?"

"Because I think you're hopeless," she said coldly. "Because if you could stand there and laugh at those two pathetic creatures, if you could be so devoid of human feeling as to think that pitiful spectacle was actually *funny* . . ." She shook her head. "I made a mistake. I thought if you came down and saw what we were trying to do, if you saw people working and giving of themselves—not for what's in it for them, but just because they cared what happened to others—I thought if you saw these things, there was a chance it might reach something in you. But I made a mistake. There's nothing in you to reach."

She turned to go, then stopped once more and regarded the two young men consideringly. "No," she decided. "On second thought, I'm not letting you off that easily. People like you *need* an occasional lesson in humanity." She grabbed their sleeves with brisk authority. "And even if you don't learn anything, you're going to at least be exposed to it."

One block farther on, she led them into a low, narrow building and up a dark flight of stairs. On the second floor they entered a huge, barnlike room, once a factory loft, but now converted to what was evidently an artist's studio. The place smelled of turpentine and paint and the accumulated odors of many bodies. The whitewashed walls were crowded with paintings of factory workers and peasants, with oversized hands and feet and broad, empty faces. Justin guessed there were perhaps thirty to forty men and women in the room, sitting or standing about in small groups. Everyone seemed to be talking at once. It was hard to pick out specific voices, but he was aware of a variety of foreign accents.

Alice nodded to several men watching the door and Justin felt their eyes appraising Tom and himself. They apparently passed muster, because Alice herded them across the room and began pointing out and identifying comrades in a low, conspiratorial voice, mentioning names that meant nothing to Justin, but which clearly held a certain stature among the members of the group. They included a short, dark Russian who, Alice said, had survived ten years of Czarist imprisonment, a Greek who was a famous union organizer, and an elderly woman with iron-gray hair who had been the first female member of the American Communist Party. Justin was unimpressed, for they looked more like small-town grocery clerks than the elite corps of a new and enlightened political movement.

Alice glanced at her watch. "The meeting should start in about ten minutes." She turned to say something to Tom, but he was gone.

Justin smiled. "He's over there," he said, nodding toward a corner of the room where Tom Gallagher was talking earnestly to a dark-haired, voluptuous and unwashed-looking girl, "getting a lesson in humanity."

Alice was unamused. "Unfortunately," she said, "the Communist Party has its share of those more interested in bed than world revolution. Sometimes it makes it a damned nuisance to be a woman." She looked at Justin confidingly. "You try to do your work and have to waste precious time and energy convincing people you're not just a cute, easy lay."

Justin nodded sympathetically as a sturdy, thick-shouldered man came over and looped an arm about Alice Harte's waist. "Who's your friend, Comrade?" he said.

Alice removed the man's arm with a patient hand and introduced them. The man's name was Simmons. He regarded Justin with a look of amused superiority.

"How long have you been interested in Communism, Blaine?" he said. "Since you met Alice?"

Justin reacted to the man with instant belligerence. "I'm not really interested at all," he said, "just curious."

Simmons' dark brows arched. "Really?" He smiled gently. "You mean you see a diseased world around you and you're just *curious* about the cure?"

"Communism's no cure," Justin said with more certainty than he felt. "It's more of a fungus feeding on the disease."

"Oh? And what have you got to offer in its place?"

The inevitable Communist rebuttal, Justin thought tiredly. He began, "Terror and dictatorship . . ."

Simmons cut him off. "What have you to offer in its place?" he repeated, and when Justin did not answer immediately, he laughed. "It's easy to criticize our cure, but it's the only one there is. The world isn't just sick, it's dying. We can give it life, and if the medicine doesn't always smell so good, the stink of death's a hell of a lot worse."

He looked at Justin with suddenly cold eyes. "You prissy intellectuals give me a pain in the ass. All you do is sit around playing with words and ideas. You wail about wars, poverty, human misery and injustice, but won't dirty your precious hands to get rid of them. Well, Blaine, we're not afraid of a little dirt. And twenty years from now you'll be damned glad there were a few of us around who weren't."

Simmons turned away and melted into a loudly arguing group close by. "He just got back from China," Alice said. "He was the Comintern agent there for two years. He saw some terrible things. Human life means nothing there. He was almost killed, twice."

"I'm impressed," Justin said dryly. "But why do you people

always rant as though the whole damned world's salvation rested on your shoulders?"

"That's our greatest strength," she said. We're still a small, motley force with plenty of rotten eggs in the box. If we didn't believe strongly, we'd be nothing."

Justin felt himself being studied from all sides. Other people came over and Alice introduced them. Each spoke briefly and left. Justin avoided making any more belligerent statements. It was pointless, he thought, to argue with Communists. They were all fiercely indoctrinated, trained debaters who not only didn't care what you had to say, but in most cases didn't even listen. Several times Justin caught glimpses of Tom Gallagher, still in deep conversation with the dark-haired girl Alice Harte did not seem to notice. She was concentrating on Justin, evidently considering him a more likely recruit. When the meeting was called to order, she carefully chose two seats for them up front.

The meeting was run by two hard-faced men in plaid work shirts, who sat at a wooden table and scribbled voluminous notes on long sheets of yellow paper. Their voices were loud and harsh and they spoke angrily. The earliest to speak were obviously more anxious to participate than to contribute. Their speeches were incantations on behalf of "The Workers of the World" against "Wall Street Moneylenders" and "Imperialist Aggression." These catch phrases, strung together in various patterns, seemed more important than the ideas they expressed. But as the discussion continued, Justin found his air of amused superiority being replaced by genuine interest. The nature of the speakers changed; the specific problems became clearer as the analyses became more lucid. Rant was replaced by sobriety, and intelligent humor began to take the place of vicious sarcasm. As they spoke, Justin began to see anew what that vague thing, "social injustice," was. He learned not only about the growing bread lines in New York but about the spread of pellagra among the Tennessee sharecroppers, the countless deaths from floods and disease in India, the mounting unemployment figures and the hopelessness of good men seeking dignity. And he found himself sickened by the recurrent examples of callousness among the powerful, indecision and hypocrisy in governments, and brutality on the part of interests who benefited from widespread misery. Almost without his realizing it, vaguely directed sympathy was transformed into deeply felt anger, and when Alice Harte offered a strong plea for more government work projects, he felt a stirring of pride.

At one point a shabbily dressed little man with a swollen, freshly bruised face and a bandaged ear stood up and asked for the floor.

"What have you done, Charley," someone called, "given up the red flag for a black and blue one?"

Everyone laughed and Charley grinned, showing a gaping hole where his front teeth had been. "I guess they did give us a pretty rough time," he lisped. "I got away easy. Frank and Ed are in the hospital with fractures. We only had ten men and they hit us with twenty company goons, pick handles and all."

"What were they doing?" Justin whispered.

"Picketing," Alice said. "A Brooklyn factory is laying off men without notice or severance pay because of union activity."

"Were these men fired too?"

Alice shook her head. "They didn't even work there."

Justin gazed curiously and with sudden respect at the man. There was something about his broken face that reminded him of Sarkis. The little Armenian had been noisier and more belligerent, but the undefeated eyes and the stubborn look of resistance were alike.

"We've got to be back there tomorrow," Charley was saying. "We've got to be back there tomorrow and the next day and the day after that. We've got to be back at the lousy plant until they *know* we can't be scared off."

"Who says we can't be scared off?" a bald, pink-faced man with glasses shouted. "Have you taken a good look at yourself?"

Justin laughed with the others.

"Good-bye, Charley!"

"The Republican Party was never like this!"

"Where do I resign? I'm behind in my dues anyway!"

"Win with Hoover."

But when volunteers were called for the next day's picket line, Charley had twenty men, the bald, pink-faced man, Justin noted, among them. Feeling strangely left out, Justin fought a compulsion to rush out to Brooklyn and have his head gloriously bashed in with the others. What idiocy, he thought. He was going to have to be very careful. Tom may have been right. He was probably just sorely enough in need of a cause, *any* cause, to be ripe for nonsensical heroics. Smothering temptation with logic, he compromised by contributing two dollars, when a hat was passed, to the pickets' medical fund.

Afterward, coffee was served. They stood drinking beneath a painting of green-faced factory workers being ground between the wheels of monstrous machines. Justin looked for Tom, but saw neither his friend nor the dark-haired girl.

"He left ten minutes ago," Alice said, "with Gonorrhea Gertie." She laughed. "And for God's sake! Stop looking so damned shocked every time I say something."

Justin flushed and grinned. "I didn't think it showed."

"It shows," she said. "My personal advice to you is, never play poker. You'll be picked clean in an hour." As Alice sipped her coffee, her eyes flicked back and forth, looking over the room and the people in it. "Want me to tell you exactly how you reacted to our meeting?"

"All right," Justin said, flattered by all this attention from so pretty a girl. "How did I react?"

"You started off smug, superior and skeptical, became intellectually absorbed, and at the end were emotionally enough caught up to contribute two dollars which you could not afford." Alice looked at him. "Well? Accurate enough?"

Justin tried to keep his face noncommittal. It was true that he had been held for a moment at the end, but still did not know exactly where the appeal had been. He needed time to let it soak in, to think about it.

Alice did not wait for an answer. "I'm pleased," she said, "that you were able to see more than just the surface. Many people can't. All they see is a slogan-screaming, ragtaggle little crowd. What they don't see is what's beneath it. They don't see the kind of fanatical faith that can make almost every one of these people ready, if necessary, to die for it. *This* is what gives them tremendous power."

Justin drank his coffee reluctantly and in silence. It was bad coffee and the room in which he was drinking it was hot, smoky and full of loud voices. He wondered what he was doing there, listening to this intense, voluptuous girl talk passionately of fanatical faith, power and dying. He knew nothing of such things and did not care about them. But there was that broken-faced little man who had stood up a while ago and—

"Listen," Alice intruded, "no intelligent American can live with his head in the ground any longer. Our system is rotting and must be changed. I hear them over the radio from Washington, telling us things will be better, that this is just a temporary period of adjustment, and I could tear my hair and scream because their lies are so arrogant and disdainful. They sit there on the Hill, hands folded on fat, well-fed bellies, and tell us things even an idiot wouldn't believe. We look around at the bread lines, see millions of strong men unable to feed their children, more factories closing every day, more homes lost, more old people pushed out onto the sidewalks, while a privileged few live in mansions and drive around in limousines. We see all these things, and what do they tell us?" Alice laughed harshly. "They tell us prosperity is just around the corner. They won't admit there's no future, no future at all without change."

Justin smiled. "You seem determined to make a one-night convert out of me."

"No. Not in one night. I wouldn't let you jump into something like this right away even if you asked to. I only wanted you to see that we exist as people. That we're alive and breathing and have convictions. I wanted you to hear some of our theories firsthand, and to learn that they really *are* working in Russia, that they are not simply words in a manifesto, that they represent the *new* society for the twentieth century, just as capitalism was the new society for the nineteenth century. And I wanted you to know," Alice said in her intense, even voice, "that there are people around like Charley, who can go out and have their heads broken fighting for men they don't even know."

"Charley's crazy!" Justin spoke with such vehemence that he surprised even himself. Ideas, theories, he could understand and deal with. He had heard most of them before and, although they had a fine ring, they were only words and did not impress him. But Charley was something else. Charley puzzled and disturbed him. "He's some kind of nut . . . a misfit." Justin waved an accusing hand about the room. "Just as most of these other heroic, high-sounding comrades are probably misfits and failures of some kind too. New movements, revolutions are always created by their breed. They're got nothing to lose themselves, so what the hell. Let's share the wealth. Just give each of them ten thousand dollars and a shiny new car and see how many come to your next meeting. No sane person does anything in this world without a selfish motive. Every professional do-gooder I've ever known had his little quirk—call it guilt, original sin or whatever—that he was trying to shake off by the noble deed."

"Maybe. But if that's so, then I'm a misfit, and so are you." Slowly she extended her hand.

Justin frowned and hestitated. When he finally took the hand, it felt disquietingly warm in his. "You're that confident?"

"With you," she said, "yes."

"Why me? You don't even know me."

"Don't I?" Alice gazed quizzically at him once more, in frank appraisal. "You're forgetting your magnificently revealing face." She laughed. "Now you can stop suffering with that awful coffee and take me home."

3

They came out of the subway at Broadway and Ninety-sixth Street and crossed over to Riverside Drive. They walked along the tree-lined avenue that ran high above the Hudson, with the Palisades looming darkly across the quiet water. Justin looked at the expensive apartment buildings that faced the river, at the uniformed doormen alert at each elegant entrance.

"You live *here?*" he said.

"Two blocks down," she said. "Near Ninety-third Street."

"In one of these buildings?"

Alice looked at him. "Surprised, aren't you?"

Justin did not say anything.

"I know," she said. "You expected a suitably proletarian tenement."

Justin heard a horn blow out on the misty river, the sound mournful and trembling in the night air. "I guess I did."

"And you're also wondering," Alice said, "why I should be a Communist if money seems to be no problem. It upsets one of your theories."

Justin frowned, growing tired of having all his reactions so smugly gauged in advance. "No," he said flatly. "I'm not wondering that at all. I'm sure you just became bored with frittering away your life on luxuries. I'm sure you woke up one day and decided it was time to do something *really* worthwhile for the world, something for the poor, downtrodden masses."

Alice laughed. "All right. I deserved that."

They walked for half a block in silence, side by side but not touching. Their footsteps echoed, and occasionally a car rushed by, its tires whining on the pavement.

Alice stopped in front of a canopied entrance. The doorman touched his cap respectfully, then stood a short distance off, staring at nothing. "This is where I live," she said.

"Doormen," Justin said softly, "have too much dignity. They intimidate me."

"Me too."

"You?" Justin said. "Lenin himself, in full uniform, couldn't intimidate you." He looked at her standing there, composed and level-eyed, and found himself suddenly, unaccountably resentful. No one had the right to be that certain, so convinced that what he was doing was the only thing to do. "You're so damned sure of yourself. It's disgusting."

Alice returned his gaze. "Is that what you really think I'm like?"

"Well, aren't you?" he said, wondering at his own anger. "Aren't you pretty smug and self-righteous and opinionated?"

"Of course I have opinions, but—"

"Taking all the comfort and solid ease that money brings, while you play at storming the barricades a few hours a week." He laughed. "You can't lose, Comrade. You've got it made both ways."

She stared at him for a moment in silence. "It's the idea of the money," she said slowly. "That's what bothers you. You think if there's money, everything else has to be great. You think if I live in a house like this, with a doorman to salute me, what right have I to complain? Isn't that it?"

Justin did not say anything.

Alice took his arm. "Come on up with me," she said abruptly. "I want you to see something."

"Now?" He looked doubtfully at his watch. "It's eleven-thirty."

"Fine," she said. "That's almost the right time."

She drew Justin past the bowing doorman and into the marble-floored lobby.

"Almost the right time for what?"

"You'll see."

Another uniformed attendant was waiting in a wood-paneled elevator.

"Good evening, Miss Harte."

"Hello, Charles. Has my uncle come home yet?"

"No, Miss." He pulled a heavy brass watch from his pocket. "It's still a little early for him."

They got off at the seventeenth floor, and Alice unlocked one of two doors leading from a small vestibule. The foyer inside was long and thickly carpeted and smelled faintly of furniture polish.

"Is that you, Alice?" It was a woman's voice, throaty and harsh.

Alice took Justin's coat and hung it in a guest closet." "Yes, Mother."

"I was getting worried," the voice said. "It's almost time for Uncle Jerry to be home."

Alice led Justin through the foyer into a large, high-ceilinged living room. A slender blond woman sat on a couch doing her nails. Across the room, a bald, heavy-jowled man was reading a newpaper.

"This is Justin Blaine," the girl announced.

The man and woman looked at Justin with neither surprise nor interest.

"This is my mother and father."

"How do you do?" Justin said, wondering uncomfortably what he was expected to observe.

Mr. Harte rose wearily, extending a limp hand, which Justin took and released immediately. Mrs. Harte offered a curt nod and returned to her nails. "Have you forgotten it's Friday night?" she asked her daughter.

"Have I ever?" Alice said. "Justin lives out in New Jersey. He missed the last train, so I asked him to spend the night."

She sat down in a love seat beside the fireplace and motioned Justin to sit beside her. No one said anything and the room was still except for the rustling of Mr. Harte's newspaper. Justin looked at Mrs. Harte. She was a pretty woman, with the same delicately shaped face as her daughter, but she was too heavily made up and marked by a pinched, sharply calculating expression about the mouth. Her hair was obviously bleached, and even Justin, with little knowledge of these things, could see that her clothes were fashionable and very expensive. So naturally, he thought, her daughter wore no makeup at all and a dress like a sack.

Mr. Harte's baggy eyes met his over the top of his paper, then retreated downward. The paper trembled between his fingers.

"What do you do, Mr. Blaine?" Mrs. Harte said, extending one hand and critically examining her nails, which were long and crimson and exquisitely tended. She spoke lazily, barely moving her lips, and Justin wasn't sure he had heard correctly.

"Justin's a writer," Alice said quickly. "He writes articles for magazines."

"Oh," Mrs. Harte said, and went to work on her cuticles.

Justin glanced at the girl sitting stiffly beside him. Her manner was more cautious. She had lied twice in five minutes, which meant that her parents probably knew nothing of her Communist ties.

He removed his glasses and sat nervously polishing them. No one said anything and he felt the silence. He tried to think of something to say, but his mind was blank. Two minutes, he thought, looking anxiously about the room, three minutes, of just sitting here in the rich living room of a strange house with three people he did not know, and not talking. There was a prohibitive intimacy about the silence.

"Listen. . . ." he began.

But at that moment the foyer door opened and a lusty male voice boomed, "Uncle Jerry's home!"

Mrs. Harte dropped her manicuring tools and tensed on the couch. Her husband let his paper fall to the floor and seemed to shrivel still farther into his chair. Alice slowly stood up and remained standing, her hands working at her sides. Justin leaned forward, watching the door.

A big, fleshy-faced man entered, strode to the center of the room and stood there, grinning. Justin saw gold teeth, a wide, flaccid mouth, small puffy eyes and a veined, bulbous nose. No one spoke. The big man swept the room with a single glance, which passed over Justin as if he were part of the decor. He wore a blue suit and matching fedora, the brim of which swept downward on one side.

"Ready?" he said.

"Ready!" came the answering chorus, like part of an old, familiar and carefully rehearsed ritual.

Uncle Jerry dug both hands deep into his trouser pockets. He held them there, while he looked teasingly, suggestively at the faces of Alice and her mother. They stared back at him, waiting. Alice's expression was flat, inscrutable, but Justin saw her mother's eyes widen and her lips part as though she were having difficulty breathing.

Uncle Jerry laughed hoarsely. "Here it comes!"

Both hands left his pockets and shot upward. Justin gaped disbelievingly. The air was suddenly filled with flying money. Bills of every denomination cascaded onto the carpet, the furniture, the people in the room. A twenty and a ten settled in Justin's lap, but he did not notice. He was watching Uncle Jerry. The big man's hands were back in his trouser pockets. He took them out and more money flew, this time to the far corners of the room. He laughed wildly, the sound bubbling out along with the bills. When the trouser pockets were finally empty, he started on his jacket. There seemed no end to the flow. Then Justin saw Alice and her mother and he stopped watching the man.

The two women were scrambling about the carpet on their hands and knees, collecting the money like two gleaners. They probed beneath chairs and tables and lay flat to reach odd strays behind the couch, unmindful of modesty as skirts rose and bodices dropped. Uncle Jerry's puffy eyes followed them hungrily. "Come on, baby!" he chortled. "Come on, you sweeties, you. Get it . . . get it . . . get it . . . for Uncle Jerry!" By now all his pockets were empty and he followed the two women about the floor, panting encouragement, his hands fondling and petting, his face gleaming with sweat.

Justin saw Alice's face, pale and masklike as she moved through the strange rite. Her mother was flushed, trembling and near to frenzy. She clutched frantically at the scattered bills and thrust great handfuls into her already bulging bosom. Alice, too, was stuffing her collection down into the front of her dress, which was apparently the required receptacle. Once, as she crawled toward Justin, her eyes met his with a glance of such bitter, mocking irony that he looked away. And as he did, he saw her father and remembered that this man also was in the room. Mr. Harte sat slumped in his chair, his eyes glazed. He seemed to see and hear nothing. He breathed deeply and slowly, like a man under anesthesia and the fingers of one hand drummed evenly and without stopping on the arm of his chair. A five-dollar bill lay crumpled across his right shoulder and remained there until his wife finally saw it and snatched it away.

"Come to Jerry! Come to Jerry!"

With all the money recovered at last, Uncle Jerry sagged heavily into a carved, wooden chair. His mouth hung loosely and he kept moistening his lips with his tongue. He beckoned to the two women and they settled obediently into his lap, one on each knee. Then they began removing the bills from their bosoms, smoothing, counting and sorting them into neat piles on an Oriental coffee table. Uncle Jerry prattled a senseless, torrent of baby talk and endearments. His eyes rolled and a tiny trickle of saliva slid down his chin. His big hands shuddered like a spastic's as they groped, uncontrollable and unaware, across the women's bodies.

"Oh, you sweets," he wheezed. "Oh, you dolls. Count it for Jerry. Oh, you cuddle-babies. More . . . more . . . more. Keep it coming for Uncle Jerry. That's the way. Oh, yeah . . . yeah . . . yeah. Jerry loves ya. He'll take good care of his babies. He'll treat his babies fine. Oh . . . Oh . . . Oh . . ." The hoarse voice rose and gasped a final spasm of the litany.

"Three thousand, four hundred and thirty-five!" Mrs. Harte cried as the counting was finished. Her formerly well-groomed hair hung in disarray and her skirt was twisted halfway up her thighs. "The best week of the year!"

"Good. Good." Uncle Jerry grinned and gathered up the stacks of bills. His voice had quieted and he seemed, to Justin, to have reached a state of spent blessedness. He peeled off a few bills from one of the rolls and pressed them into the bosoms of the two women. "There, my little blond dolls," he simpered. "Buy yourselves some pretties."

Then, with a final pinch, he rose and waddled from the room, one bearlike arm draped across the shoulders of Mrs. Harte. Alice slowly sat down on the couch. After a moment, Mr. Harte got up and started to leave. At the door, he turned and bowed with his head to Justin. "Good night, Mr. Blaine. I hope you sleep well."

Justin stared after him as he disappeared through the thickly carpeted foyer. It was, he thought hazily, like something out of *Alice in Wonderland*. Any moment now the Mad Hatter would come bouncing in. Except that this Alice had neither long curls nor satin ribbons in her hair. All she had was money in her bosom. He looked at her where she sat on the couch, her face still composed, but her knuckles showing white on clenched fists.

"Pretty, wasn't it? In seven years we haven't missed a Friday night performance. I think that's quite a record. Don't you?"

Justin was puzzled and a little sick. "Why do you do it?"

She shrugged. "Like they say, it's a living."

"That?" he said. "A living?"

Alice brought forth half a dozen more crumpled bills. When she smoothed them out, they added up to a hundred and ten dollars. She had clearly kept far more than the man had given her.

"How much do *you* make a week?" she said harshly. When Justin did not answer, she went on, her voice low and toneless. "I was less than fifteen years old when it started. It seemed like just a game then. By the time I found out it was more, we needed the money too badly to give up."

"Your father . . ." Justin began, then stopped, not knowing how to put it.

"My father is a sick, weak man," she said. "My mother despises him and treats him like dirt and I . . ." Alice hesitated. "I love him more than anyone alive."

She was silent. From somewhere at the far end of the apartment, Justin heard a woman's laugh, high and mocking.

"I would like you to understand." She was talking now in her patient, teacher-like, Communist Party voice. "Money is the corruptor. My father had it once and my mother liked it. When it was gone, Uncle Jerry moved in with his. We give him his little pleasures and everything remains lovely." She shook her head. "That's some Uncle Jerry. Three thousand a week from bathtub gin and he's king of the hill. A living testimonial to capitalism. Millions of men out of work, children going hungry, and bootleggers live like Roman emperors. A nation of moral bankrupts. But not for too much longer. You'll see. It'll change. We'll *make* it change."

She stood up. "All right," she said. "So you've seen the source of my luxurious living. Not that it was Uncle Jerry who ripened me for Communism, though I suppose he did leave his own unique little marks on me." She smiled. "Perhaps he made me one of your misfits. Anyway, you've had enough education for one night."

Justin stood up too. "You may be disappointed. I'm not as susceptible as you may think. If you've sold me anything, it's that you at least know where you want to go. I don't."

Alice led him through the foyer and took his coat from the closet. "Lenin said that the role of the Bolshevik is patiently to explain. I've started that much. Now you can go home to New Jersey."

Justin stood there.

"What's the matter?" Alice said.

"I missed the last ferry."

She looked at him.

"It left at midnight," he said. "I forgot. And you said before that I was sleeping over. I thought—"

"I said that for my parents' benefit." Alice eyed him coldly. "Listen, I don't know what your friend Tom told you about me, but—"

"Oh, no! I didn't mean . . ." Justin flushed purple. "You mustn't think. . . ."

She stared at him for a moment, then laughed. "I guess I've been fighting off wolves too long." She hung up his coat once more. "There's really plenty of room here."

Alice settled him into an elaborate guest room at the far end of the apartment, turning back the bedspread and fussing with window shades and curtains. She brought out a pair of paisley-patterned pajamas and tossed them on the bed. "Pure silk," she said. "Courtesy of Uncle Jerry, who permits none but the finest fabrics to touch his sensitive skin." She smiled grimly. "And whose title of 'Uncle,' incidentally, is purely honorary. Or did you figure that much out for yourself?"

"That much," Justin said, "I did manage to guess."

She said good night and started to leave, but turned at the door. "What about tomorrow?" she said. "Do you have any special plans?"

Justin shook his head. "No. I haven't."

"I was just thinking. Perhaps I should take you out to Brooklyn in the morning, let you see Charley and some of our other crazy misfits in action. You may learn something from watching." She peered at him searchingly. "Are you bothered by violence?"

"I thrive on it," Justin said dourly. "If I can't start off my day with a little bloody brawl, I—"

She cut him off. "I'll wake you at eight." The door closed behind her.

Justin stood staring at the door. Then he undressed and put on the paisley pajamas. The silk felt smooth and cool against his skin. Later he put out the lights and lay sleepless for a long time in the darkness, the sounds of the river muffled and mournful in the distance. Decisive, he thought resentfully, the girl was just too damned decisive, and peremptory. Who the devil wanted to go to Brooklyn?

But by the time Justin fell asleep the idea of going to Brooklyn, or any place, with Alice Harte was beginning to seem less and less unpleasant.

4

The factory was a sprawling, dirty brick building, with a high, wire fence around it and a fifty-foot sign on top that said HORGAN'S TOOL AND DIE WORKS. It stood in the shadow of the Brooklyn

Bridge, backed against the East River, its smoking chimneys further darkening an overcast sky. Before the main gate was a long line of pickets, along with scattered groups of workers and a squad of mounted police.

It was raining, and huddled beneath a leaking umbrella, Alice and Justin stood watching from the edge of a cobbled gutter. They had been there for more than an hour and Justin was beginning to shiver in the chill wetness. He pressed closer to the girl for warmth, judging this due payment for the discomfort and pointlessness of his being there. He saw little sense in the entire display. What did these men hope to accomplish? If they marched back and forth for the next twenty years, the fired men would not be rehired, they would not be granted a cent of severance pay, nor would the men still working go out on strike in their behalf. With millions desperate for work under *any* conditions, strike threats meant nothing. All that would happen, Justin thought bleakly, was that a few more heads would be smashed.

So far, however, there had been no threat of violence. Chanting slogans and singing songs, about fifty pickets paraded slowly, in single file, before the factory entrance. Many of them carried placards which read, "IN UNION THERE IS STRENGTH" and "SOLIDARITY FOREVER!" and "TWO WEEKS' PAY OR TWO WEEKS' NOTICE" and "WE MADE HORGAN RICH, NOW WE'RE IN THE DITCH." Other signs, by this time rain-soaked and bedraggled, could no longer be read. Charley, Justin saw, carried one of these, its cardboard limp and drooping, yet somehow borne like a regimental standard. Justin recognized the other men from the meeting, all of whom greeted him and spoke to Alice as they passed. He felt a little guilty standing there, not so much because he was not among the marchers, as because he was an impostor, whom they seemed to have already accepted as one of them. Yet, futile or not, there was a pleasant feeling of warmth, he grudgingly admitted, in being considered part of something once more. He had not felt it since he left Cleveland.

Most of the men were former employees of Horgan's Tool and Die Works, but mingling with them were other jobless and a scattering of union organizers. Those not on the picket line stood about in wet, silent groups, their faces grim, a look Justin had come to know well during the long months of his own pavement-pounding. It was a terrible thing to see the confidence and fight leak out of a man like water from a cracked jar. "How do I go home?" a tall, neatly dressed man, a stranger, had once wept to him. They had been waiting six hours, along with a hundred others, for an interview that never came. "How do I go home and look at my wife? I'm not even a man any more. I haven't touched her in six months. Jesus, if you can't look at a woman, how in hell can you touch her?"

Twelve o'clock whistles blew and moments later hordes of workers streamed out of Horgan's and surrounding plants. The crowd of watchers swelled, spilled off the sidewalks and into the gutters. Traffic slowed to a crawl, and the mounted police clattered up and down the line, trying to keep the cars and trucks moving.

"Here's where the trouble starts," Alice said.

Justin looked at her. She stood tensely beside him, her eyes scanning the crowd. "How do you know?"

"This is how the companies always work. They wait for the lunch hour crowds, then bring in their goons to turn a peaceful demonstration into a riot. After that, the police have to step in and break it up." Alice pointed to several clusters of hard-looking men, edging their way into the crowd. "There are some of them now. See those bulges under their coats?"

Justin nodded uneasily.

"Pick handles and lead pipe," she said. "Standard tools of the trade. Long live the Republic!"

"Listen," Justin said, "you can hardly blame those hoodlums on our system of government. Blame Horgan. Isn't he the one who's paying them?"

"Maybe. But with the unofficial sanction of the City of New York. Those cops see them and know exactly what's going to happen. But do you think they'll do anything to prevent it? Oh, no. They have detailed orders about picket lines. Get rid of them, they're told. They damage the prosperous, trouble-free reputation of our great city. And if a few dozen heads are broken in the process?" Alice shrugged. "Well, they're probably only a bunch of dirty Commie heads anyway."

Justin was feeling more and more uncomfortable. Alerted, he noticed more men with bulging coats arriving, along with another squad of mounted police. Rain dripped down the back of his neck and he shivered, but not because he was cold and wet. He was scared. "Do you want to go?" he asked without hope.

Absorbed in her estimate of the situation, Alice did not seem to have heard him. Someone in the picket line started another song and the others picked it up.

> The union is behind us, we shall not be moved,
> The union is behind us, we shall not be moved,
> Just like a tree that's standing by the war-r-rtah,
> *We shall not be moved.*

The voices soared above the honking of truck and automobile horns, the clatter of horses' hooves. Justin remembered singing the same song in church as a boy. Except that instead of the union it was Jesus who had been behind them. The signs of the times, he thought; a brand-new Messiah being hailed. And what station of the cross would they number that which was about to take place here today?

A policeman came up on a steaming horse. "You'd better get out of here, lady," he told Alice. "There's going to be trouble."

Alice glared up at him from under the umbrella. "Then why the hell don't you lice do something to stop it?"

Huge in rain cape and helmet, the officer gripped the reins with one hand and soothingly patted his mount's neck with the other. He was a blue-eyed Irishman, with a weather-reddened, impassive face. "One of the comrades, eh?" He grinned. "You people just never get enough, do yuh?"

Justin watched him ride off, wondering if a man became a policeman because of a natural affinity for violence, or whether his work developed a love for it. In either case, he found he had rarely come across a cop he liked, although the job admittedly had to be done by somebody. "I think we'd better go," he said.

"If you want to leave," Alice said without looking at him, "go ahead. Don't stay on my account."

"Of course," Justin said flatly. "I'll just walk away and leave you here."

Alice looked at him then, her face wet and shining beneath the dark umbrella "I can take care of myself. You don't have to worry about me."

Justin was suddenly furious at the position in which she had placed him. He did not want to stay, he *feared* staying, yet obviously he could not leave without her. Who the hell was she to commit him and his safety to a cause in which he was not even convinced he believed? And what if he *did* believe in it? Would he want to stay then? Would his insides stop quaking *then?*

"Don't talk like a fool," he said. "You're the only woman in this whole damn crowd. What are you trying to prove?"

"We shall not be moved!" Alice sang with the others using the lyric as her answer. She smiled at the expression on Justin's face. "And stop looking so angry. It doesn't become you. Listen," she said, solemn once more, "what happens here at Horgan's is important. Unions are being smashed all over the country. If we can keep a picket line going here, if we can show a strong, solid front, maybe even squeeze out one or two small concessions, it will help us gain confidence and recruits in a hundred other places. What I want you to—"

Alice's last words were lost in a fusillade of hoarse, angry shouts.

"Go back to Roo-sha, ya Commie bastards!"

"Lousy Reds!"

"We don't want no damn unions here!"

A few rocks sailed over the pickets' heads and one hit a placard, but the line kept moving. Justin tried to draw his head farther into his collar. More men were pressing into the crowd around them and he saw several lengths of pipe. For the moment, the singing had stopped. Then Charley started the marchers off on the Internationale, and the chant, belted by a hundred husky voices, started to drown out the yelling.

Arise, ye prisoners of starvation. . . .

My God, he thought, with an opening line like that, how could they miss?

His throat dry, Justin gripped the umbrella in a trembling fist. Everyone around him was shouting or singing and the sounds assaulted his brain. He looked at the excited faces of the chanting pickets, eager converts to the new international religion.

But it was becoming increasingly difficult to remain detached and mocking. A picket was hit in the face by a rock and his features became covered with blood. As he fell, two men dragged him away and another picked up his fallen placard and took his place in line.

Arise, ye wretched of the earth. . . .

Pick handles and lengths of lead pipe appeared in larger numbers and the crowd began to mill and surge. Justin unknowingly gripped Alice's arm with his free hand and stood as though dazed. I've got to get her out of here, he was thinking, but did not move.

The world has found a new salvation,
A better land's in birth. . . .

More of the singing pickets were struck by rocks and Justin saw a horde of club-swinging goons attack the rear of the line, which broke, reformed, then broke again. Individual scuffles had erupted all around him, accompanied by shouts and screams, and men were on the ground, crawling brokenly, like squashed bugs. But the chanting plea for brotherhood, its words hope-filled and immutable, soared on.

It is the final conflict,
Let each rise in his place. . . .

All that remained of the picket line were a dozen swaying placards, dipping and rising above the crowd. Then the police drove
their mounts out of the gutter and onto the sidewalk, swinging
night sticks with indiscriminate relish, and the last visible pleas for
solidarity and justice disappeared.

The international party shall be the human race.

Alice had yanked the umbrella from Justin and was flailing
wildly with it at every club-swinging goon within reach. Her face
was grim, but she still gasped snatches of the Internationale with
each blow. Feeling weak and ineffectual, Justin tried to pull her
out of the spreading free-for-all. Something hit him across the back
of the head, but he hardly felt it. A man fell against him, screaming wildly, blood spurting from his head. Justin tried to hold him
up, but the man slipped from his grasp and disappeared.

In that instant Alice was swept away and Justin struggled
toward her. When he reached her, she was pressed up against the
wire fence that surrounded the factory. She had lost her umbrella,
and her raincoat was ripped, but she was still swinging her fists.

"Damn it!" he yelled, furious at his helplessness. "Damn it, let's
get out of here!" But Justin saw that he could not have gotten her
out now even if she had been willing. They would die there, he
thought coldly.

Then police sirens sounded in the distance, and the crush eased
as groups started to pull away. Charley suddenly appeared beside
them with his toothless grin. He was still carrying the remnants of
his sign, a pole surmounted by a fragment of cardboard.

"The paddy wagons," he announced. "Come on. There's no
point in getting booked."

Using the pole to clear a path, he led them free of the police and
the brawlers. Justin counted more than a dozen bodies stretched
out on the pavement, some moving, some still. They were half a

block from the factory now, with men running and scattering in all directions. At a corner, they stopped for a moment to get their bearings. Breathing heavily, Justin waited beside Alice while Charley peered down the street to see from which direction the police vans would be coming.

Justin noticed a man trotting toward them. He was carrying a pick handle in one hand and what looked like a small bottle in the other. Suddenly he speeded up and dashed straight at Alice. "Commie bitch!" he yelled. "Dirty Commie whore!"

Justin felt himself start to move sluggishly, slowly, although he knew that if he did not move faster and somehow stop the man, Alice was going to be hurt. The man lifted the bottle and Justin heard the quick scraping of shoes behind him. Charley leaped in front of Alice and swung his pole just as the man threw what was in the bottle. Charley dropped his pole and clutched at his face, moaning in pain, and the man fled.

With Justin's help Alice managed to pull Charley's hands away from his face, revealing a glaring red acid burn on one cheek and part of his forehead. Justin felt as though he were going to be sick.

"How are your eyes?" Alice held Charley's hands to keep them from extending the damage. "Can you see?"

Clearly in terrible pain, Charley blinked and managed a feeble nod. "One eye's all right. The other's kind of blurred. I guess I was lucky."

There were ambulances following the police vans, but Charley refused to go near one and they took him to a nearby hospital in a cab. The doctor who treated him said he thought there was only minor eye damage, but that his face would be permanently scarred. Charley grinned beneath swaths of bandages. "A raving beauty I never was anyway."

Justin groped for something to say, but his tongue felt thick and unwieldy in his mouth and all he could think of was his own failure to act in time. He touched the injured man's hand, where it lay on the coarse hospital bed sheet, then turned away.

Later, while riding beneath the East River in the subway, Justin and Alice sat squeezed together in a crowded car that smelled of damp clothing and unwashed bodies.

"Oh, those bastards," Alice swore softly. "Oh, those dirty, miserable bastards."

There was a great tiredness in her voice. Her face was drawn and streaked with dirt; her wet hair was plastered to her head; her clothing was ripped. But her eyes were dry and hard.

"And what," she whispered, "was he trying to do that was so terrible? Was he trying to *hurt* anyone? Was he committing some kind of awful crime by trying to save a few men's jobs?"

Justin stared at the row of strange, solitary faces across the swaying car. He had no answer for her questions. He did not even have an answer for his own. Why couldn't he ever *act?* Why was he never anything more than a spectator? It was disgusting, he thought heavily, disgusting. There was no reason to his life, no purpose. He was like a piece of dead driftwood. *Charley* had to be the one to leap forward and save Alice. *He acted,* automatically. Justin had been right there beside her, but he'd been too slow, too fat, too uncertain, to move even three feet in an instant of danger. He shuddered. If the girl had depended on him, she would be lying in the hospital now, blinded.

He was twenty-four years old and this was 1930, a year of national crisis, and what was he contributing to anyone's life? It was time to change, to do something with purpose, to *act.* And if it would be hard for him at first—Justin glanced for reassurance at the tired, but still pretty, still supremely determined face of the girl beside him—well, then, he had at least found himself the right teacher.

5

There was still a little daylight along Thirty-fourth Street, but as Alice turned north on Third Avenue, it was lost beneath the elevated tracks. The street lights were not yet on, and with few stores in the area still in business, the shadowy loft and tenement doorways were dark caves. Alice strode purposefully uptown, ignoring the glances and comments aimed at her by the groups of rough-looking men loitering along the way.

It did not show in her face or manner, but she was nervous about the evening ahead. Although she had been seeing Justin for almost two months, and felt that she knew him as well as she had ever known anyone, she was still not that sure about certain of his reactions. Tractable and open to reason in most things, he could be unpredictably stubborn where his emotions or sense of morality were concerned. If he was convinced something was wrong, nothing and no one could persuade him to do it. And she had that kind of feeling about her plan. However, she brooded, there was little point in trying to judge it in advance. She would know soon enough what he thought.

After passing the corner of Thirty-sixth Street, Alice entered the doorway of a grimy tenement. A naked bulb hung in the tiny vestibule, illuminating peeling plaster and scrawled obscenities, several of which had been altered by some prim, unseen hand (probably Justin's, she thought, smiling) to make their letters form "BOOK." She pushed through a cracked-glass door and started up the stairs rising steeply beyond it. Between the third and fourth floors, a paunchy man squeezed past her on his way down, eying her breasts and making an obvious effort to brush them with his arm. Alice looked at him with disgust. On the fifth floor she approached the first door on the right and entered without knocking.

"Ready?" she said briskly, not at all winded from the climb.

Justin looked up from his work. He was seated at a littered table, indexing a pharmaceutical manuscript for a technical publishing house. For this he received fifty cents an hour. He smiled slowly, letting himself enjoy the sight of her. Each new meeting produced the same instant of wonder. "Yes, I guess so." He glanced at his watch and saw that it was nearly five o'clock. That gave him a full eight hours of work today. Four dollars. If you survived the boredom, you could live on it. Anyway, it was a job, the only one he had been able to find, and he was not complaining.

He went over to Alice and kissed her awkwardly and a little self-consciously, still half-expecting her to push him away and surprised, as always, when she didn't. This, a light, unimpassioned kiss on the lips, represented the total extent of their love-making to date. Emboldened by the apparent ease of his success near the beginning, he had once touched her breast. The violence of her reaction had discouraged him from ever trying again. Actually, he was quite content to let things go as they were—even relieved not to have to venture further advances, for then he need not make a fool of himself. Alice offered him so much now, he felt, in sharing her confidence and vitality, her ideas and plans, her bursting awareness of life, that he saw no reason to jeopardize all this by seeking something he might have liked but did not especially crave, and which she obviously did not want at all.

"Where are we going?" he said, having long ago fallen into the comfortable pattern of letting Alice make all plans.

"What's the difference?" She spoke expansively to hide her tenseness. Because tonight was so important, she had deliberately made no special arrangements, preferring to see how things went. "Don't worry so much about details. Have a little sense of adventure." She studied him. "Know what your *big* trouble is?"

Justin grinned, delighting in her unequivocal certainty, just as he delighted in everything else about her. "No," he said. "Tell me. What's my *big* trouble?"

"You're too stodgy. You're not adventurous enough. Must you know exactly where you're going every minute? Come on. Let's go. Take a big chance. You never can tell. You might like living that way."

"All right. I'll live dangerously. But in my coat, if you don't mind." He put on a mackinaw, made a note of his day's output and ventured a final, loving glance about the shabbily furnished room. He had taken the tiny apartment three weeks before, the income from his new job making these slightly larger quarters possible. This, too, had been accomplished under Alice's prodding. He was too big a boy, she'd insisted, to go on living on small handouts from his parents.

Justin followed Alice down the stairs, his steps careful and plodding in contrast to her swift, impatient descent. She reached the street a full flight ahead of him and waited.

The street lights were on, but Third Avenue still retained its own special, threatening gloom. Justin finally reached the sidewalk and they started slowly uptown. A train rolled by overhead and they turned toward Lexington to escape the roar. At the corner they stopped at a lunch counter for a stand-up dinner of hot dogs and orangeade. Then they walked without apparent destination, drifting west and north, passing the inevitable clusters of idle men.

On Fifth Avenue Alice halted in front of an elaborate display of gowns and women's accessories in a shop window. "Look at it," she said with disgust. "Will you *look* at it!"

Justin looked.

Alice shook her head. "A bread line could be kept stocked for a year on what one lousy window of baubles costs. The time, money and energy that some women waste on themselves! Doesn't it *revolt* you? I mean, in days like these there are a dozen major industries just *making* the stuff women pile on their faces and backs. Besides being a criminal waste, it's such a fraud. They're all such fakes, such phonies." She grabbed Justin's arm in agitation. "If people can't accept one another for what they are, without all this sham and make-believe, then they shouldn't be together at all. If a woman has to use that sort of garbage to lure a man—change the shape of her body, the color of her hair, the tone of her skin, and God only knows what else—what's the point? Even if she does fool the man, she hasn't *really* got him. The poor guy doesn't even know what she *looks* like."

They were walking west on Forty-second Street, the great bulk of the library looming beside them. "Of course," Alice continued, "everyone has to work out his own values." She grasped Justin once more. "I've found out what's important to *me,* what's of real meaning and interest to *me,* just as I know you're learning what's important to you."

Justin smiled. "I may as well dedicate my life to indexing pharmaceutical manuals. You won't let me join the party. You won't take me to any more meetings or demonstrations. In fact, since I told you I *wanted* to do something, you've actually gone to great pains to keep me *away* from everything. Then when I press you for reasons, you get mysterious and tell me to just wait. All right. So I've been waiting now almost two months. How much longer do I wait?"

"I can't tell you that."

"Why not?"

"Because I don't know."

"Then who does know?" Justin said.

"I've told you. Someone I've gotten interested in you. Someone very high up in party circles."

They moved through the tangle of Sixth Avenue traffic, ignoring angry horns and glaring drivers.

"What's his name?" Justin said.

"You'll never learn not to ask questions, will you?"

"Oh, come on." Justin had to laugh at the gravity of her expression. "You take yourself and these things much too seriously. Why do you always have to be so *secretive* about them?

"You'll find out why," she said. "As soon as you become actively involved yourself, you'll find out. When there's no reason to reveal a name, you just don't mention it. Please. You've been patient a long time. Just be patient a little longer. You know the party needs everyone it can reach. Only . . ." Alice's voice automatically dropped. "Only they're beginning to get the feeling that it may be better to have certain qualified, better-educated people working for them outside the *official* party."

"What is that supposed to mean?"

"Well," Alice said, "an active party member has only limited usefulness. They're planning to keep you in the background for a while. Out of things. When the time comes that you can be of some *real* value, they will let you know."

Justin did not say anything and they walked for a while in silence. It was becoming increasingly difficult for him to remain inactive. In the weeks since the violence in Brooklyn, when he had first thought seriously of committing himself to a definite course of action, his sleep had been torn by recurrent nightmares of bleeding heads. And even awake he was never wholly free of the fearful visions. He kept imagining the streets of New York five, ten, fifteen years from now. Terror and violence everywhere. Ten-year-old children using knives to steal bread. Old women roaming the avenues in rags and dropping dead of hunger. No factories working because no one would have the money to buy what they'd sell. Half of all able-bodied men in the police force, and having to club the other half to keep them from rioting. He kept seeing these things and Alice told him to be patient. The cancer-stricken man, Justin thought sourly, being patient while the tumor grows in his belly.

They crossed Broadway and entered the honky-tonk noise and glare of the West Side; the bars, store-front freak shows, clip joints and burlesque houses. "And this," Alice said, "is what people see first when they visit New York. It's a disgrace to the city."

A crowd, gathered before one of the burlesques, blocked the sidewalk as a barker harshly cried the promise of lust fulfilled. "Here y'are! Here y'are! See the physical won-der of the a-ges, Gloria Greene . . . of out-*standing* proportions . . . of fab-u-lous . . . mus-cu-lar . . . dex-ter-i-ty. Watch them go round and round until you are dizzy. You will not be-lieve your own eyes . . . a con-tin-u-ous per-for-mance go-ing on right now. . . ."

Alice tried to push past the cluster on the sidewalk, but the press was too heavy. The men stood there, hungry eyes devouring the seductive, life-size posters under the marquee. "Disgusting," Alice said.

Justin was busy looking at the posters of Gloria Greene. The photos, he decided, had been skillfully retouched. Nature could never have created anything with such proportions. "What did you say?"

"I was talking about the twisted values people have. Just watch how these men rush in there, wasting hard-earned money to look at that trash." A man accidentally jostled her in the crowd, and Alice shoved him so hard he almost fell. She looked at Justin, who was still staring at the posters. "Don't tell me *you're* interested in this kind of slop too?"

Justin shrugged. "I've never even *seen* a burlesque show."

"So what? Neither have I. But that doesn't mean I can't judge the tripe they're peddling inside. That doesn't mean—" She broke off. "Wait a minute. Let's go in *now*. Let's go in right now and you'll see for yourself the high type of entertainment people look for."

"You're crazy," Justin said in alarm. "You can't go in there. They'd never let a woman in there."

"Of course they would. For money you can get in anywhere." She pushed through to a ticket seller in a barred booth. "Do you let women in?" she asked.

The man leered at her with three and a half teeth. "You *bet* we let women in, baby."

"Go ahead," Alice told Justin. "Buy the tickets."

Justin looked at her. "You mean you *actually* want to go in?"

"Of course. And stop looking so worried. You'll be a lot more shocked than I will."

Justin had to agree. Alice's worldliness was a constant source of amazement to him. Next to her, he felt naïve, almost childlike. He fished through his pockets for change. Certain that everyone's eyes were on them, and that his face must be a flaming red, he followed Alice through the lobby and into the darkened theater.

They had to grope their way down the aisle until they found a pair of empty seats off to the right. A spangled chorus was prancing across the stage to the heavy beat of a piano, drum and a few pieces of brass. Justin squirmed on a broken spring and tried to focus his eyes on the stage. It was hot and stuffy in the theater and his glasses began to fog. He took them off, wiped them and saw, with distinct shock, a dozen bare breasts bouncing in front of him. Adding to the sense of unreality, each nipple was rouged a flaming red, like the bull's-eye of some white, gelatinous target.

Alice nudged him with an elbow. "Move over," she whispered.

His eyes were nailed to the bouncing circles. "What's the matter?"

Alice nudged him again and Justin looked over and saw a man's head lolling, in drunken sleep, against her shoulder. He moved over to the next empty seat and Alice followed him. The chorus jiggled and pranced off the stage to scattered applause, and a blue spotlight hit the faded curtain. "La-dies and gen-tul-men," a hoarse voice announced, "the cur-va-ceous star of our show, the o-rig-in-al Tex-as tor-na-do, Miss Glo-ri-a Greene!"

Whistles, howls and catcalls. The drum in the pit went ba-ba-*boom,* ba-ba-*boom,* ba-ba-*boom* . . . slowly, deeply, each *boom* sending an invisible shudder through the darkened theater.

"Primitives," Alice whispered. "The call of the jungle. Not the slightest change in ten thousand years."

Justin took each boom squarely in the pit of the stomach. He was staring at the circle of blue light, into the center of which Gloria Greene had moved, satin-gowned, wide-hipped and with a glorious bosom. More howls and whistles. Ba-ba-*boom,* ba-ba-*boom* . . . ba-ba-*boom* . . . She started slowly across the stage, hips grinding on the "ba-ba," and bumping, with a violent trembling quake, on the *"boom."* A glove was slowly peeled from each hand, then tossed, with elaborate abandon, offstage. She had long, shoulder-length red hair, which seemed to swing to the motion of her hips. Justin licked suddenly dry lips. Her bosom, beneath its tight, satin casing, still defied reasonable acceptance. It *couldn't* be.

"Ba-ba-*boom* . . . ba-ba-*boom* . . . ba-ba-*boom* . . ." A chorus of men in the audience added the weight of their voices to the drum.

Alice laughed. "A real high-class talent." She glanced at Justin to share her amusement and found that he had not even heard her. Nor was the expression on his face nearly the one she had anticipated. Instead of mocking superiority, there was total absorption. This was hardly the reason she had brought him in here. Or was it? She frowned in the darkness. Had she subconsciously lured Justin to this awful place for quite a different purpose? The thought disturbed her. She decided abruptly to stop this ridiculous stalling and get it over with once and for all.

"Listen," she whispered, "I want to talk to you about something."

Gloria Greene was unsnapping the side of her gown. Ba-ba-*boom* . . . ba-ba-*boom* . . . With not a beat missed, her hips and hair swung, perfectly united.

"I said—" Alice squeezed Justin's arm for attention—"I want to talk to you about something." The words were louder, slower, evenly spaced.

"Yes?" Justin blinked as the top of the gown followed the gloves into the wings. A fringed and beaded bra strained, but somehow held.

"I've been thinking," Alice said, "that since you've finally gotten yourself settled in your own apartment, it might not be a bad idea if I moved in with you. We could share the rent and other living expenses, you'd have someone to cook and clean for you, and I'd be able to get away from that ghastly mess at home. We see each other all the time anyway and I think it would work out well for both of us."

"What?" Justin thought he had heard correctly, but his attention was split, torn between Alice and Gloria Greene, and it was hard to be sure. Besides, it *couldn't* mean how it sounded.

Ba-ba-*boom* . . . ba-ba-*boom* . . .

Alice watched Justin and felt a sudden rush of doubts. What was she getting herself into? Was she *sure* it was what she wanted? Did she know him as well as she thought she did, or would she just be replacing old problems with new? But as she whispered the proposition once more, her earlier certainty returned. Of course it was right. She had thought it over long and carefully and Justin was perfect for her needs, everything she wanted—a fine mind she could respect, compassion, a social conscience that was growing stronger all the time, a future in the party that she could help develop and share, and he was neither obsessed with sex nor narcissistic about his person, as were most of the other strutting, posturing males she had known. Thank God, she thought, he wasn't that much to look at. How often the really important things in a man were subjugated or destroyed entirely by his absorption with self, by pure, pompous vanity.

"Well?" she said. "What do you think? Does the idea sound reasonable to you?"

Gloria casually stepped out of the lower half of her dress. Ba-ba-*boom* . . . ba-ba-*boom* . . . Powdered thighs quivered, breasts and buttocks bounced, all the world seemed part of the joyous movement.

"Yes. It sounds *very* reasonable." Justin could feel his pulse pounding, but managed to keep his voice calm, even light. He must take this very casually, he thought, as casually as she had stated it. Any display of emotion, any gushing mention of the forbidden word love, of what he felt just being near her, would surely ruin everything. He didn't understand her. All he had done was touch her breast that once and she had exploded. Now she matter-of-factly proposed living together as they sat watching a strip-teaser in a burlesque house.

On the stage, the bra was about to be unhooked. Skillful, tantalizing hands reached back for the hook. Ba-ba-*boom* . . . ba-ba-*boom* . . . shake . . . bump . . . *grind*. Justin was bent forward in his seat, almost in physical pain. "When would you like to move in?" Still dazed by the entire prospect, he was suddenly nervous. Sexual demands, he assumed, would be made upon him. What if he failed?

"In a few days," Alice said. "Whenever it's convenient." Surprised at the ease and casualness with which her idea had been accepted, she began to worry again. She had expected shock, bourgeois arguments of morality, stubborn insistence upon marriage. She had even prepared herself, if all else failed, to agree to go through the meaningless rituals of legality. Because Justin's calm acceptance seemed so totally out of character, she began to wonder if she knew him as well as she had thought. Oh, God. Don't let it be just sex that he wants. Please. Not with him too. She couldn't bear it if *he* turned out to be like that too.

The bra had come off to the sound of explosive cheers. Justin sat blinking. It was incredible. Absolutely incredible. Sounds of inner torment rose from the audience. Ba-ba-*boom!*

"What about your parents?" he said.

"What about them?"

The drumbeat had quickened . . . ba-ba-*boom* . . . ba-ba-*boom* . . . ba-ba-*boom* . . . but Justin no longer even heard it. There was a much louder drum sounding in his brain . . . *Alice . . . Alice . . . Alice . . .* He wanted to jump up and down, yell it out. Yet he merely whispered softly, "What will you tell them?"

"I'm over twenty-one," she shrugged. "I can either tell them nothing or the truth—that I'm moving in with you. It's none of their damn business anyway. They probably won't even notice I'm gone. The only one who'll miss me is *dear* Uncle Jerry." She made a sour face and shuddered. And how many years of decent, normal living would it take to erase *that* little blemish? Or would some of the dirt be left and carried inside always?

Justin's hand found and held hers in the darkness. It was real, he thought. He could feel the soft convincing warmth in his, she was still talking about it, and he had not simply imagined the whole crazy, wondrous thing.

Ba-ba-*boom* . . . ba-ba-*boom* . . . Red hair, breasts, hips! Gloria Greene climaxed with a series of final hysterical bumps and disappeared behind a curtain.

Alice and Justin sat without talking, suddenly neither of them able to think of a single thing to say. On the stage, a comic with a broom handle in his pants was chasing a blonde around in circles, while his partner cheered him on. Shouts of encouragement came from the audience.

"Let's get out of this rat trap," Alice said abruptly. "God, what a pack of low-grade morons."

They groped their way back along the aisle. Outside, the barker was still extolling Gloria Greene's "fab-u-lous . . . mus-cu-lar . . . dex-ter-i-ty." They worked their way out of the crowd and drifted along Forty-second Street, still silent and newly self-conscious with one another.

"I hope," Alice said after a while, "you haven't let me talk you into something you don't want." She laughed nervously. "I mean, I suddenly dumped this thing into your lap in there and—"

"No, no, no. It's a fine idea. I'm sorry I didn't think of it myself." His words stumbled over themselves in their haste to reassure her. Think of it himself? That was a laugh. And if he had, would he ever have dared say anything about it?

"You're *sure?*"

"Very sure." This was the first time, he thought, curiously, that he had ever seen her confidence, her certainty, slip even this slight bit. A new fear struck him. Had she changed her mind? Was she just trying to get out of it now?

But Alice gripped his arm and said nothing more as they walked past stores, theaters, people, the vibrant incandescence of night-time New York. They stopped at an arcade for popcorn and Alice wandered about the amusement area, looking at the exhibits. Justin studied the way the lights touched her hair. Some men turned to stare admiringly and Justin tasted the unaccustomed sweetness of possession. God, she was lovely. And this woman, he thought, wanted *him!* The idea was incomprehensible. What of value could she possibly see in him?

He caught a glimpse of himself in one of a series of comic mirrors. A puffed-up, distended clown. He moved to the next glass and became a different kind of freak. On top of the third mirror, an accusing legend read, *"As You Really Are."* Justin stared at himself. Was he supposed to laugh at this too? A brain anchored in a homely lump of clay? *What did she see in him?*

"Jussie!"

He turned. Alice was motioning him to join her at an exhibit. He started toward her through the crowd. All right, he thought, so he didn't understand it. What difference did it make? She *wanted* him. He'd be more than happy to settle for this.

Later, they went back to his apartment. They sat side by side on the worn couch, looking out at the tenement roofs, dark against the sky with the winter stars blooming above the chimneys. Everything seemed very far off—the picket lines, the violence, the nightmares and visions of disaster. Even the elevated roaring by, rattling cups and dishes and windows, could not disturb the sudden, warm peacefulness.

His eyes closed, Justin carefully kissed her, feeling her hold the kiss like a caress. The kiss ended, but he dared not open his eyes. Again he touched his lips to hers, gently, delicately, feeling a sense of joy and tenderness well up in him, a sense unlike anything he had expected in his most voluptuous dreamings. His hands held her shoulders softly, but now he embraced her tightly and their mouths became more fervent. She held herself to him, trembling slightly, her mouth opening, demanding him, and he answered, not thinking now, but glorying in this knowledge of her wanting more of him and still more.

He had been afraid of being afraid at such a moment. He had feared being ludicrous, of blundering into contemptuous laughter, but now there was no fear. There was not even a sense of himself, except of his wanting her and her responding so beautifully, so warmly and beautifully.

Somehow, in his daze, he helped her undress and got off his things, and the touch of her against him was more delicious than he could have imagined. For an instant he was afraid of his inexperience, of ruining this wonderful thing that was happening, but at the crucial moment, as he faltered, Alice was there, *with* him, to help, and later he would wonder why he had been afraid at all.

Her voice was in his ear, so different from what it had always been, whispering *"Jussie, Jussie,"* and he knew her joy too.

And in the final moment, he knew what they, together, would always be.

They lay close afterward, restrained and overcome, and Justin was afraid that now that it was over she would hate him for it, and every moment of her silence made it seem worse. And she thought, not once, not once, at any time, did he say he loved me. Not even once.

Then she said, "Jussie?"

"Mmmmm?"

"You'd be uncomfortable, wouldn't you? You'd never really feel right living with a woman unless you were married to her, would you?"

About to protest, something stopped him.

"Never," she said. "It's that old moral backbone. You could *never* make it bend."

"I didn't say that." He saw now how it was going to be and played it accordingly. With all her sharp, crackling, no-bourgeois-nonsense talk, he thought elatedly, three hundred years of Puritan background were still not that easily overcome.

"You don't have to say it. Don't you think I know you by now?" Her arms clutched him more tightly in the darkness. "All right," she declared in a tone of fresh decision. "So we'll get married. Yes. Why not? What's the difference? If it'll make you happier, more comfortable, we'll just get married. The whole thing's meaningless anyway. A few mumbled words, a piece of paper—presto! We're married. Everything's nice and legal and respectable. And you, my moral, bourgeois friend, can be supremely happy."

Justin was kissing the back of her neck. "Well," he said, "now that you've found out that much about me, I've got something even more shocking, archaic and unforgivably bourgeois to confess."

"What?"

His lips drew fresh inspiration from her throat, the lobe of her ear: "More than it's decent and respectable," he said, "more than it's normal, sensible or logical, more than I ever thought possible . . ." His voice dropped to a barely audible whisper. "I love you."

Chapter Eleven

1952: Washington, D.C.

On the day following Webster Evers' testimony, a bright late-winter morning, Chairman Eustace B. Kelly gathered his committee for informal session in the gloom of their oak-paneled conference room. The men spoke loudly and there was even some laughter, but Hank Pilgrim, seated at the end of the long table, could feel the nervousness behind the noise. To him it was like an over-extended wake at which they were anxious to bury a body that was exasperatingly not yet dead, that was, in fact, growing steadily livelier.

And that was capable of killing them.

The junior Congressman from Illinois doodled some ranks of five-pointed stars on the legal pad before him and censored out the intruding noises, a skill he had learned in school and developed in his social life, so that now he could pretend attention while filtering through only what he needed to hear. This afternoon he had heard enough. A dozen times, in a dozen ways, the same thing had been said—the unacknowledged acknowledgment that the members were scared white and wanted out as fast as possible.

From the moment of Evers' denial the committee had expected trouble, but nothing like the multitude of telegrams and phone calls—and soon, they knew, the letters—condemning the members and threatening their replacement in November. Newspapers which had blandly reported the investigations, thereby providing free the committee's lifeblood of publicity, now made hard, threatening statements about certainty of facts and evidence. Commentators spoke solemnly of Star Chambers and witchhunts. In one day the easy road to power had become a swamp and, thought Congressman Pilgrim, in the sanctuary of their conference room these Congressmen could only try to brace themselves through the comforts of oratory.

Suddenly no one seemed to be speaking and Pilgrim glanced up. He grinned at the four other men, who sat like pallbearers paralyzed by embarrassment.

"Gentlemen," he said, "I think I detect an air of panic in this room. Our constituents would not be proud of us."

Representative John Norton, Democratic Congressman from North Carolina, swore softly under his breath. "I'd like to make a suggestion," he drawled, "as to what my constituents can do if they are so inclined." He picked up a fistful of correspondence and shook it angrily. "Yesterday they were namin' their first-born after me. Today I'm some kind of monster."

Norton stared gloomily at Pilgrim, resenting his youth, his looks and the bright political future his wife's money guaranteed. Although Pilgrim was the lowest-ranking member of the committee, his father-in-law's reputed half-billion dollars allowed him confidence far beyond his years and experience. That the other committeemen took a condescending view of his opinions did not appear to disturb him. It seemed, rather, to goad him into irreverence for seniority and established position.

"And I don't know what *you're* lookin' so damned smug about, Henry," Norton grumbled. "You're gettin' boiled in the same oil as the rest of us. Or do you have some secret resource we don't know about?"

"Nothing secret," Pilgrim said. "But I sure as hell don't think wailing and moaning is going to help us." He swept aside a stack of telegrams. "I say damn the torpedoes, full speed ahead."

Chairman Kelly smiled ruefully. "A dramatic solution, Henry, but not very practical. Go full speed ahead now and we just smash harder against the rocks. I'm afraid this calls for reverse engines."

Pilgrim's expression was derisive, almost insolent. "What's the matter, Mr. Chairman? Has the Big Man been putting on the squeeze? Is he afraid of possible embarrassment for the administration?"

"That's not the question facing us," Kelly said coldly. "Right now we—"

"I say it *is* the question facing us!" Pilgrim looked hard at the men seated about the big table: Democrats Kelly, Norton, and Alfred P. Quennell of Pennsylvania; and Harry Kirby, of Montana, the only other Republican. Whenever procedural disputes arose, they were usually settled in favor of the majority party, but predictable defeat had never muzzled Pilgrim despite the lack of support from Kirby, a perennially ailing ulcer patient who favored his condition with a therapeutic silence in all things controversial. "I say," Pilgrim insisted, "that if we back down now under administration pressure, we may just as well disband. The committee will never be taken seriously again."

"What do you mean, *administration* pressure?" Quennell argued, pointing at a stack of telegrams. "Does *this* look like *administration* pressure?" He picked up one he had set aside. *"This* happens to be from the head of Blaine's own network, Phillip Mannheim, a Republican from four generations back."

Quennell adjusted his glasses and squinted at Mannheim's telegram.

" 'Gentlemen,' " he read, " 'Our nation faces challenging and dangerous years. This is no time for us to be split and weakened by conscienceless partisan witchhunts. You are responsible men. I sincerely hope you will not press this investigation further and thereby risk destroying the confidence of our people in the integrity of their leaders. Phillip Mannheim, President, Continental Broadcasting Network.' "

"I'm touched," Pilgrim said.

"A man's patriotism," Norton intoned, "should never be cause for ridicule."

Pilgrim grunted and went back to his doodling. Kelly took the telegram from Quennell and studied it, his pale eyes anxious. Pilgrim's remark about White House pressure had not been far from the truth. Word had already filtered down to let the affair die discreetly. And Kelly had no intention of jeopardizing his remaining years in office by spearheading a senseless and unpopular crusade.

"I think," he said with professional deliberateness, "that we would be wise not to take Mr. Mannheim's opinions lightly."

"Why?" Pilgrim said belligerently. "Because they happen to agree with your own? Who the hell is Mannheim?"

Kelly controlled his temper with effort. "He's a man with his finger on the pulse of the nation, and if he takes a stand like this, you can be damned sure he's certain of his ground. Also, and perhaps most important of all, Justin Blaine happens to be his top commentator. If he's decided not to back up the statements and integrity of his own man, there's got to be a pretty good reason."

Pilgrim lit a cigarette and drew deeply. Everything that Kelly, as well as the other committeemen, had said was true, but he was still reluctant to let die what had seemed like a sure way to national prominence and acclaim. There was also the nagging and still unanswered question of why a man of Justin Blaine's stature would create so wild a fantasy if there were not some element of truth to it.

Norton cleared his throat and nervously tapped the table with a pencil. "I would like to go on record," he said, "as advisin' a policy of restraint and caution. If we ruin the reputation of our Under Secretary of State, and then find there isn't sufficient evidence to back it up, we may just as well dig us a large hole and bury ourselves."

"And what if there *is* sufficient evidence?" Pilgrim asked. "What if there *is* sufficient evidence to prove that our Under Secretary of

State was a Communist spy, and we do nothing about it because we've been frightened off?" He leaned contemptuously back in his chair, knowing he had made these four nervous men more nervous. He felt neither loyalty for them nor respect.

He smiled maliciously at Norton. "Would you also like to go on record as advising that we shirk the performance of a vital duty because it happens to be a momentarily unpopular one?"

The Congressman from North Carolina glared at Pilgrim, but did not reply, being reluctant to commit himself far in any direction and, like Kirby and Quennell, hoping that Chairman Kelly would press their position strongly enough himself to decide for him. But Kelly was too seasoned a campaigner to charge into danger. As the committee's chairman, the member most exposed to adverse criticism, he intended to keep his flanks well protected.

"Gentlemen," he declared, "haggling among ourselves is not only demeaning, it is fruitless." He took a long drink of water from the glass in front of him. "There is only one thing we must consider in deciding on our course of action, and that is the welfare of the United States."

Kelly paused and looked imperiously about him. Oh God, Pilgrim thought, now he's going to wrap himself in the Stars and Stripes and screw a hundred and fifty million Americans. He watched Kirby's cheeks puff out as he smothered a belch.

"We're in an admittedly difficult position," Kelly went on, "as well as a responsible one. We must be careful not to do anything impulsively. Irreparable damage might be done, not only to the possibly innocent men involved, but also to the faith of the people in their appointed and elected officials." He spoke with a clipped, nasal Boston twang. "I believe that we should give ourselves sufficient time to think about this, to meditate upon the implications, to delve more deeply into the pertinent facts. Then, when we're more certain of where we stand, we can act with confidence and authority and without fear of making a public spectacle of ourselves and our government."

The room was quiet and Pilgrim could almost hear the smothered sighs of relief of the other committeemen. This was precisely what they had wanted to hear, for it lifted them painlessly from the hook. Kelly's words had seemed oddly familiar, as he spoke, and Pilgrim suddenly remembered having read almost the exact phrasing that morning in the Washington *Post*'s outspokenly Democratic editorial.

"Approximately how long a period of meditation," he said quietly, "did the chairman have in mind."

"Seven, perhaps eight months." Kelly shrugged.

Pilgrim nodded slowly. "Just time enough to spare the administration any possibility of embarrassment before election day."

"Oh, come off it, Hank," Quennell said. "We all know it's the only sensible thing to do. There's not one of us wouldn't be eaten alive if Blaine couldn't make his charge stick. And I for one don't intend to take the risk of being shipped back to Pennsylvania on a rail."

Norton nodded vigorous agreement, while Kirby fumbled for his afternoon pill and looked miserable.

"At this moment," Pilgrim said, "I am fighting a strong compulsion to vomit. What about Blaine?" he prodded. "If he's lying, he should at least be indicted for perjury. Every one of his accusations against Evers and the others was made under oath. Are we just going to forget about him?"

"If we indict Justin Blaine," Norton said hurriedly, "we'd be in just as much trouble as we would investigating Evers. The same witnesses would have to be called and the same testimony heard. Either way, we'd be nailed to the wall for smearing top officials." The Southerner bit off the end of a cigar and spat fiercely at the floor. "Lousy Commie bastard! Who the hell asked him to spill his guts out all over the place? Nobody wanted his damned confession."

"As a matter of policy," Kelly said, "I think we should avoid giving out statements on the subject." He looked pointedly at Pilgrim. "The official committee line will be something to the effect that the matter is being investigated in closed session, with a full report to be issued at the proper moment sometime—"

"After the Presidential election," Pilgrim finished mildly.

Kelly ignored him. "—sometime in the not too distant future. Meanwhile we can put Blaine on ice by accepting whatever bits of evidence he chooses to submit and telling him they are being studied."

"And what if he chooses not to be put on ice?" Pilgrim asked. "What if he chooses to make a great big stink instead? Do we have the FBI quietly polish him off in the national interest?"

Kelly leaned toward him. "You can save your jokes for radio and television."

"I wasn't joking," Pilgrim said. "It isn't inconceivable that Blaine won't sit still for your lovely plan. He might be—may God and the President forgive me—a truly dedicated patriot."

"A truly dedicated patriot," Kelly said flatly, "does not sit on his vital evidence for twelve years and then gush it forth only after a Congressional subpoena." He shook his head. "You don't have to worry about Justin Blaine pressing the matter. I had a good look at his face on that witness stand. He'll be only too happy to let it die. And when he finds out where Mannheim stands on the matter, he'll be ready to kiss our hands for letting him off the hot seat."

"Phillip Mannheim," Pilgrim said, "will fire him anyway. Regardless of what happens now, Blaine is a marked man. He couldn't get a job for the next ten years selling newspapers on street corners."

Kirby sighed. "If I didn't have ulcers when I joined this committee, I'd have them now."

Pilgrim crumpled three pages of five-pointed stars into a tight ball and tossed them into a waste basket. He had known what the results of the meeting would be, but this did not help make it easier to accept. The door had been closed on a spectacular, once-in-a-lifetime opportunity. Yet one could not actually blame Kelly or the others for their decision. It was the only way out of an impossible situation. To press it further could be political suicide. Then why, he wondered irritably, this unaccountable feeling of guilt, as though he had just defected from some significant but nameless obligation?

He stood up. "Gentlemen, we should be congratulated. Our achievements here this afternoon are without historical precedence. In less than two hours we've driven back the course of American political justice two hundred years."

2

In the late afternoon traffic, it took Pilgrim more than half an hour to drive the short distance to his Georgetown home. The house was one hundred and sixty-two years old and pure Federalist. Pilgrim's wife had fallen in love with it despite the bad plumbing and creaking floors. Pilgrim himself was indifferent to its aged charm, as he was indifferent to most of the material things his wife's money was able to provide. The money itself was important, being the major reason he had married her, but he was far more interested in the type of life and career it promised him than in the specific physical trappings it could buy.

Henry Pilgrim's life plan had begun at sixteen with the happy discovery of his attractiveness to women, and been brought to predetermined fruition with his marriage to William Garland's only daughter. Pilgrim had executed this undertaking with efficiency and meticulous attention to detail. While a sophomore at Northwestern University, he had carefully listed more than a dozen of the most financially eligible coeds at the school, had rated them according to money, looks, personality and intelligence, and had made his decision without the distraction of sentiment. Elizabeth Garland had been one of the least physically attractive of the candidates, but her intelligence and wealth placed her far ahead of the field. It had been a good decision, opening to even better prospects.

He parked the car in a large garage behind the house, which

he entered through the rear. A cook was at work in the kitchen. "Good evening, Mr. Pilgrim. You're home early tonight."

"Don't tell the voters, Mary. They'll want a rebate on my salary."

The woman laughed. "You work hard enough for them. You work too hard. Some nights I see the light on in your study till all hours."

Pilgrim took a crisp roll from a basket. "Don't be taken in by the light," he said. "I leave that on to impress the neighbors."

He left Mary chuckling among her pots and climbed the circular foyer stairs to the second floor. He stopped for a moment to fondle his son, who was being prepared for bed by a maid. The child was just learning to put a few words together, and Pilgrim was beginning to feel his first sincere interest in him, although he still looked somewhat disbelievingly at this blond, blue-eyed bundle, whose pink fingers were bowed in curiously exact replicas of his own, and whose ear lobes, too, were of the odd design shared by numberless generations of Pilgrim males. A conspiracy, he would sometimes think, a conspiracy of nature to lull us into illusions of immortality.

The door to the master bedroom suite was closed and he entered without knocking. He heard the shower running in the bathroom and stretched out on the bed without calling to his wife. He had been unaware of it before, but now he could feel tiredness and strain drawing his muscles. The sound of the shower stopped and a moment later Elizabeth Pilgrim came into the room, drying herself in a huge, green bath towel. She was a tall, slender woman, with long legs, small pointed breasts and surprisingly full hips, which Pilgrim teasingly described as the only part of her really built for service. Her dark hair framed a rather plain face, but there was an intensity in her eyes as she searched for a comb on the cluttered dresser. She did not see her husband. Watching her, Pilgrim thought she would probably still have the body of a sixteen-year-old when she was sixty.

She found the comb and saw him on the bed as she turned. She started and the towel slipped from her grasp and fell to the floor. "My God! You scared hell out of me." She approached the bed without picking up the towel. "You're home early. Is anything wrong?"

"Wrong? I can't see a thing wrong." He reached for her hand and drew her down beside him.

She frowned as she studied his face. Her fingers touched the dark places under his eyes, the deep lines edging his nose. "The meeting went badly, didn't it?"

"To hell with the meeting." He pulled her to him, holding her loosely, gently touching her back, which was still damp from the shower, and breathing her sweet cleanness. He felt her response, strong and spontaneous as when they had first come together more than eight years before. It had surprised him then too, this rich, wild vein beneath the sometimes painfully awkward exterior.

"Wait." Elizabeth got up to lock the door, but was back in an instant. She kissed his lips, eyes, neck and the special place beneath his ear that made him see blue sparks.

Afterward he lay holding her in spent, half-drugged possession, knowing it had been as good as such a thing could possibly be, better than with any other woman he had ever known, better than with the buxom virgins of his youth, better than with the practiced whores of Chicago, better certainly than the long succession of dull, predictable, easily managed adulteries in the nation's capital. Then why, he wondered, the constant search? If the best and the most was here, why the others? It was a question that had badgered him frequently since his marriage, but still remained unanswered. He knew it was more than simply a matter of sexual need. That part was amply taken care of at home. The insatiable male ego then? A hungering for reassurance? A constantly required variety? The answers were all too pat, glibly Freudian, oversimplified. They meant nothing, told him nothing. And when he occasionally considered the possible consequences of being found out and weighed them against the limited rewards, the whole idea made even less sense. There was a desperate need in the world today, he thought, for an adulterer's handbook, with questions, answers and proper codes of behavior all carefully cross-indexed. It would be an instant best-seller.

Elizabeth stirred beside him, nuzzling his neck. "Want to talk about it now?" she asked quietly.

"Talk about what?" he said, startled for the moment.

"Whatever is bothering you. It *was* the committee meeting, wasn't it?"

Pilgrim grunted, annoyed because she suddenly made him feel like a child given a pacifier.

"What happened?"

"What I expected to happen. They're putting the whole deal in cold storage until after the election. It'll die there, of course."

Elizabeth propped herself on an elbow to look at him. "That's too bad," she said slowly. "I have a feeling about this man Blaine. He doesn't strike me as someone who'd make wild accusations."

"Maybe not. But we couldn't chance his not being able to make them stick. If Evers beat him down, we'd be dead."

She ran her hand absently over his chest, her dark eyes thoughtful. "I was speaking to Dad on the phone before. He seemed to feel the same way about Blaine."

Pilgrim's face showed interest. William Garland was one of the few people in the world with whom he was genuinely impressed. From the first moment he had met the industrialist, Pilgrim had been aware of the man's tremendous personal presence and had been awed, even frightened, by it. There was no doubt in his mind that Garland had known why he was marrying his daughter and had agreed only because it was what Elizabeth wanted. The implication was also unspoken that Pilgrim had better make damned certain he did nothing to endanger Elizabeth's happiness. So far, Pilgrim judged himself lucky. The two men got along well, and it was Garland's money, more than any single factor, that had assured his son-in-law's seat in Congress. And Pilgrim had few illusions about what would happen if he were ever caught in the wrong bed. Which made his long history of dalliances, when he coldly considered them, seem even more insane.

"What did he have to say about it?" he asked.

"Mmmmm?" Elizabeth was kissing his cheek and neck.

"Your father," Pilgrim said a little impatiently. "Exactly what did he say about Blaine?"

"Just what I told you. He felt there had to be some truth in his statements. He said an investigation, if handled right, could probably blow this town sky-high." She laughed. "But you know Dad. He'd be happy to use an atomic bomb if it would help get a Republican back in the White House."

Pilgrim lay staring at the pale blue ceiling. "Where was he when you spoke to him? At home or the office?"

"At home. He's flying to London tonight for a few days. I think he just called to hear Hankie gurgle his five big words. I never thought I'd live to see *him* acting the doting grandfather."

Pilgrim reached for the phone beside the bed, dialed the operator and gave her William Garland's private number in Chicago. He covered the receiver with his hand. "I'm curious about his reaction when he hears we're dropping the case."

The phone rang at the other end, but Pilgrim still had to get past a butler and a private secretary before he heard his father-in-law answer. He wasted only a moment on the amenities before he said, "We had a rump session on the Blaine-Evers affair today. I thought you might like to know the whole thing is being buried."

"Buried?" William Garland's voice, deep and imperious, exploded. Pilgrim smiled and moved the receiver from his ear to share the response with Elizabeth. "How the hell can you bury something like this? It's like trying to hide Boulder Dam."

"For nine or ten months," Pilgrim said, "it will be meditated upon and investigated in a proper and conscientious manner. By that time it will have died a natural death."

"You mean by that time," Garland growled, "another Democratic President will be stinking up the White House. How did you ever let Kelly railroad this thing? I assume it was his idea, with a big goose from the administration."

"It wasn't that simple. You know the kind of public reaction we've been getting. All of us felt it would be political suicide to push it under these conditions. And I for one frankly doubt that Blaine could face down a man like Webster Evers, regardless of what evidence he managed to come up with. Otherwise, I would have taken a stronger stand."

"Well, you're wrong!" Garland said loudly. "You're dead wrong, every last one of you. I say Justin Blaine *can* face down Evers. I say he's speaking the *truth!* You have a chance here to expose the biggest cesspool of treason since Benedict Arnold!"

Pilgrim looked at his wife lying naked beside him, nodding as her father spoke. This was the remarkable thing about successful men like Garland, he thought. Regardless of how few cold facts they actually had, they would still venture an authoritative opinion on any subject. Pilgrim felt a stir of excitement.

"Let me tell you something," the firm voice pressed on. "If you handle this thing right, you can be a national hero." There was a pause. "Are you listening to me, Hank?"

"I'm listening," Pilgrim said, knowing now that this was exactly what he had called his father-in-law to hear.

"Where's Blaine now?" Garland asked. "I've noticed he hasn't been doing his regular broadcasts."

"Supposedly trying to collect evidence to document his charges. We haven't heard from him since he appeared before the committee."

"What are Kelly's plans? What sort of statement is he giving out? When is he giving it?" Pilgrim had a clear mental image of his father-in-law's lean, angular face frowning. The dark, heavy brows would be drawn low over deep eye sockets. Garland was no more than average in height and build, but when he spoke there was a controlled intensity to his voice that could make even the most innocuous declaration seem of deep significance.

"A statement will be issued tomorrow," Pilgrim said. "It will be to the effect that things must be looked into more fully before any further public hearings are held. We'll claim the committee was taken by surprise by Justin Blaine's testimony, and in order not to be accused of impetuous and irresponsible name-blackening, we intend to have our private investigators carefully research and check out the evidence. This, of course, will take time."

Garland grunted sourly. "A masterpiece of political double-talk. If private industry were run with the speed and efficiency of government, there'd be a major bankruptcy every week." Real disdain showed in his voice. "I don't know why the hell you want to waste your time chasing your tail in Washington. If you came to work for me, you'd at least see some results for your efforts."

Pilgrim nodded grimly at the prospect of working for Garland. I wouldn't last a month, he thought, before taking off for some Pacific island. Elizabeth smiled at her husband's expression and cuddled closer on the bed. Her hand idly explored his flat stomach. From down the hall came the faint sound of a child's high-pitched squeal as Hank, Jr. was lowered into his tub.

"But as long as you're there," the voice grudgingly conceded, "you may as well shoot for the top. And you've got as good an opportunity to do it now as you'll probably ever have. That is, if you've got the guts to gamble."

"You mean on Blaine?"

"Let Kelly make his announcement tomorrow, then get hold of Blaine. Speak to him alone. Find out exactly what he's got. If the evidence looks strong and conclusive enough, you're in business— and I mean for yourself, without partners. The rest of the committee can go to hell."

"Just like that?"

"Just like that. Once you've decided Blaine can produce, you'll call your own press conference. You'll claim disagreement with the committee's majority decision to delay further action. You'll say that your own investigation has produced conclusive proof that the nation's security would be endangered by such a delay. You'll be St. George on a white horse. Public opinion will force the committee to take action. Then when Blaine proves Evers a perjurer and traitor to his country, they'll be booming you for Vice President."

"Sure," Pilgrim said flatly, "and if Evers does the same to Blaine, they'll be booming me for a public hanging." But his voice could not convey his quickening pulse beat, or the sudden resurgence of hope he was feeling as he listened. Garland's laugh came through coldly. "As I said, it's a gamble. But I think you'll agree the stakes are big enough to make it worthwhile." The industrialist laughed again. "Besides, if worse comes to worse, you've always got a job here with me."

"I'll take the public hanging," Pilgrim said, then was a little surprised at his own audacity in speaking so to the Great Man, who seemed to take Pilgrim's refusal to work for him as a personal affront.

Elizabeth looked at Pilgrim reprovingly. "I think you're right, Daddy," she said into the phone, knowing exactly how and when to salve her father's sensitive vanity. "This could be a wonderful opportunity for Henry. How marvelous that you thought of it."

Pilgrim grimaced and she pinched him impishly.

"Well, Henry?" Garland said. "Are you going to shoot for the top or run scared with the pack? The decision's all yours."

Pilgrim laughed. "I guess the decision was made when I picked up the phone to call you. I just wanted to hear you say it."

"Good," William Garland said briskly. "You won't regret it. I know men. I've been listening to Justin Blaine's commentaries for years. He's neither a fool nor a fanatic. I'm willing to accept everything he's said at face value. In my time, I've gambled more on a lot less. Just make sure he can back up his accusations with hard proof. And don't waste time. Act fast. I'll be at the London office for the next two days, then Paris and Rome for several days after that should you need me." There was a short silence. "If this goes right, we'll not only get a Republican in the White House next year, but you may even be living there yourself one day. Good luck."

There was a click and the connection was cut off. Pilgrim looked at the phone, then slowly returned it to the night table. "There is nothing better to have in this world," he said, "than confidence, and your old man has cornered the market on it."

"You have your share," Elizabeth said.

Pilgrim shook his head. "What I've got is vitality. It's often mistaken for confidence, but there's a difference."

Elizabeth leaned over and eyed him with an expression of exaggerated disdain. "What vitality?" she teased.

But Henry Pilgrim's mind was elsewhere. As he stood up and walked toward the bathroom, the cheers of the nominating convention drowned out the voice of his wife.

3

The press conference began at eleven o'clock the next morning in the committee room, with Chairman Kelly standing before a large American flag and reading a three-page statement. The other committee members were seated informally on either side of him, facing a barrage of lights, cameras and reporters. Pilgrim was at the far right, with a clear view of Kelly's bony profile and jiggling Adam's apple. He looks, Pilgrim decided, like an unsuccessful undertaker apologizing to the relatives of a poorly embalmed client. The statement was a transparent and obvious subterfuge. All the clichés were there, he thought, all the worn evasions.

"We do not intend to lend the stature and dignity of this committee," Kelly intoned, "to the publicizing of irresponsible accusations. We must make very certain—very certain indeed—of all evidence before we proceed with the unpleasant task of destroying the precious good names of men. . . ."

Pilgrim stared coldly at Representatives Quennell, Norton and Kirby, sitting uncomfortably in their straight, wooden chairs, a patina of moisture giving their faces an odd gleam under the lights. Kirby, he saw, was struggling desperately not to belch before the cameras.

"We have an enormous responsibility," Kelly declared, as if he were addressing a joint session of Congress, "to maintain the same high standards of integrity and fair play for which we, as the elected representatives of the people . . ."

Pilgrim saw Norton glance toward him. Norton's face held a stiff, impatient expression of controlled embarrassment. He had shaved too closely, and there were little flecks of dried blood on his face that showed through a thick layer of talcum powder. Quennell sat looking off at the cameras with the forced half-smile of a man who has waited too long to have his picture taken. He was addicted to heavy, tweedy suits, which he believed gave him the air of a country squire, but which only caused him to perspire the year round, and especially heavily now under the warmth of the floodlights.

"Therefore it is the avowed intention of this committee," Kelly recited, rocking a little, "to withdraw this affair from public scrutiny until such time as we are convinced that *all* the pertinent facts have been carefully sifted and appraised. Then and only then, will the American people be given them. . . ."

At the completion of the statement, there was a fusillade of questions from the floor. Their answers were shared, with equal evasiveness, by all members of the committee but Pilgrim, who was careful to keep himself silent and apart from the rest.

In his office afterward, Pilgrim waited for his secretary to go out to lunch, then put in a call to Justin Blaine's home in New York. When there was no answer, he tried the CBN Building. The switchboard operator connected him with the news department.

"I'd like to speak with Mr. Blaine," he said.

"Just one moment, please," a soft, properly schooled female voice told him. There was a short silence, then the voice returned. "I'm sorry, but Mr. Blaine is not in."

"Do you have any idea when he *will* be in?" Pilgrim asked a little impatiently.

"I don't have that information."

"Well, will you please connect me with someone who *does*," he he said coldly. "It's important that I speak with him. This is a Washington call."

This time there was a longer silence, and Pilgrim drummed nervously at his desk top with a pencil.

"I'm sorry to keep you waiting," the girl apologized, "but no one seems to have that information. Mr. Blaine's home number is listed in the directory. You might try to reach him there."

"I already have; there's no answer." Pilgrim frowned. "Look," he said, "this is Representative Henry Pilgrim of the Subversive Activities Committee calling. There must be *someone* in your organization who knows where to reach Mr. Blaine."

"Yes, sir," the girl offered submissively. "I'll connect you with the Public Relations Department. Perhaps they'll be able to help you."

The call was shunted to two more people without result. Mr. Blaine, Pilgrim was told, was on a temporary leave of absence and had not reported in for several days. There was some vague mention of a country place upstate where he sometimes spent weekends and vacations, but no one seemed to know anything more definite than that.

"What about close friends?" Pilgrim said, starting to sweat. "He must have some close friends who would know where the place was. Do you know of anyone who might have at one time been invited there?"

The director of CBN public relations was himself now on the phone. "Mr. Blaine," the director said slowly, "was not a man given to close associations. I don't know of anyone who could honestly be described as a close friend." There was a pause. "Of course," he went on, "the man who headed this office before me was an old friend of Mr. Blaine's but Tom Gallagher hasn't been here for years."

Pilgrim straightened in his chair. "Is that the Tom Gallagher who writes for IP?"

"Yes. As a matter of fact he's with their Washington Bureau. Do you know him?"

"I've only met him at press conferences," Pilgrim said. "But if he's the only lead you can throw me, I'll try him. Thanks."

He immediately called the International Press office in Washington. Expecting further difficulty, he was relieved to be put through to Gallagher at once. He was becoming worried. His plans called for quick action, and he could do nothing without first speaking with Blaine. He felt a surge of sharp, unreasonable anger at the commentator for disappearing at a time like this. He identified himself rather brusquely, then said, "I understand that you're an old friend of Justin Blaine's, Mr. Gallagher."

Gallagher did not answer at once and Pilgrim realized how the statement must have sounded. He laughed. "That statement," he said, "is not meant as an accusation. It's more of a question. And this call is unofficial and off the record."

"Well, that's a relief." Gallagher's voice was dry, almost terse, and Pilgrim remembered him from press meetings as a tall, spare, redheaded man with a sharp wit and a way of asking uncomfortably probing questions. His syndicated column was widely read and, although liberal in political tone, was never distinctly partisan. "I was just getting ready to swear life-long fealty and devotion to the Republican Party."

"You could do worse things," Pilgrim said.

"Name *one.*"

Pilgrim laughed. "What I'm calling for," he said, "is to find out if you know where I can reach Blaine. He's not at home or at CBN. A country place was mentioned, but no one seemed to know exactly where it was. That's when your name was brought up."

"Naturally," Gallagher said. "It's the family curse. For two thousand years the name of Gallagher has been brought up at the most conspicuously inauspicious moments in history. Why should it change now?" There was a pause, and Pilgrim could hear the faint sound of typewriters going in the background. "What do you want with Blaine? Your committee's putting this thing on ice."

"My wanting to see Blaine has nothing to do with the committee." Pilgrim hesitated, not wanting to reveal too much, but still anxious to convince Gallagher of his sympathetic position in relation to his friend. "I'm digging into this thing a bit further on my own. I don't believe Justin Blaine is being treated fairly."

"Why, Representative Pilgrim," Gallagher asked sardonically, "isn't the role of crusader a new one for you?"

"Your sarcasm is wasted on me, Gallagher. Do you know where Blaine's country place is or don't you? You'll just have to take my word that it'll be to his benefit for me to find him."

He stared dourly out the window as he waited for Gallagher to decide whether or not to trust him. The lawn of the House Office Building was soft with melted snow, and a pair of stray dogs dug deep, circular trails as they sniffed inquiringly at one another. How much simpler and more sensible, Pilgrim thought, watching, to leave all truly important judgments to the nose, and with how much less risk of serious error.

"I know where it is," Gallagher said slowly. "It's in upstate New York. But there's no phone. I don't know how you can reach him without going up there."

"Then I'll go up there," Pilgrim said without hesitation. "Just give me the exact address."

"It's that important?"

"It's that important."

"But you're not even sure he's there," Gallagher said, apparently interested now. "You may be traveling five hundred miles for nothing."

"Then I'll travel five hundred miles for nothing," Pilgrim said. "Unless, of course, you have some other suggestion."

"Maybe I do," Gallagher said. "There's a country store and gas station just a few miles from the place. Justin usually stocks up on food and things when he's there. They've got a phone. Let me call and find out if he's been by."

"I'd appreciate that."

"Give me your number," Gallagher said. "I'll call you back in a few minutes."

Pilgrim gave him the information, then hung up and paced the large, wood-paneled office as he waited. He tried to plan his next move if Blaine wasn't there, but could think of nothing. Had Blaine heard about the committee's statement, and if he had, what was his reaction? Probably relief, anger and disgust. He would, of course, be spared the ordeal of further testimony, but without a chance to prove his accusations, he would also find himself condemned as a traitorous perjurer. If only he didn't take it into his head to disappear.

The phone rang.

"He's there all right," Gallagher reported. "He and his wife stopped by two days ago for a load of groceries."

Pilgrim breathed deeply. "Good. Just tell me how to get there and I'll be on my way in less than an hour."

"Not so fast, Congressman," Gallagher said evenly. "There's a deal to be made first."

"What do you mean?"

"I mean I go with you." Gallagher allowed an instant for the statment to sink in. "Is that agreeable?"

Pilgrim frowned. "What's your angle?"

"Nothing personal, Congressman," Gallagher drawled, "but I just want to go along to make sure friend Justin gets a fair shake." He laughed. "Also, if there's a story in this, I intend to write it, not read about it. Agreed?"

"Do I have any choice?"

"No."

"Then it's agreed." Pilgrim glanced at his watch. "It's twelve-thirty. Can you meet me at the airport in an hour? I want to be on the two-o'clock flight to New York. We can rent a car and drive the rest of the way."

"I'll be there," Gallagher said, his voice remote and mechanized over the wire. "And, Congressman? Let me be the first to congratulate you."

"On what?"

"On going into business for yourself."

There was a distant click and Pilgrim hung up. This was a man, he thought, about whom he was going to have to be very careful.

Chapter Twelve

1952: Upstate New York

It was near dusk when Tom Gallagher swung the rented convertible off the Taconic Parkway onto a winding secondary road. The road climbed as it turned and they narrowly missed an approaching car as they crested a hill. Gallagher grinned, but did not slow up. Seated beside him, Pilgrim relaxed his foot on an imaginary brake. The columnist's driving seemed desperate. "Take it easy," he cautioned. "My agreement didn't include dying with you."

Gallagher laughed. "Everybody dies, Congressman."

"Never mind your homespun philosophy," Pilgrim said. "I'd still prefer to delay it a while." He drew on a cigarette and peered at his companion's lean, snub-nosed face through the smoke, envying the illusion of youth that Gallagher's freckles and thick red hair conveyed. Pilgrim's own hair was beginning to thin alarmingly at the crown and temples, and he made nightly inspections in the mirror to gauge the damage. A man's strength, he felt, might not be affected by a loss of hair, but his confidence sure as hell was. Evidently, this was something Tom Gallagher was never going to have to worry about. He'd be buried with his damned hairline intact. "How long," he said, "before I can start breathing again?"

"Another ten, fifteen minutes. We're almost there."

Pilgrim turned down the window a few inches and tossed out his cigarette. In the purple twilight, the countryside looked bare and depressing. Even the trees seemed desolate, as if they would never reach spring and grow leaves again. Pilgrim closed his eyes, annoyed at the irrepressible movement of his thoughts. He wanted to be confident when he spoke with Justin Blaine, to convey to Blaine and to be sure within himself that in Henry Pilgrim rested a special authority, a rightness that would justify the irregularity of what he was doing. He needed to feel within himself the magnetism of certainty and strength that draws to it trust. He knew that here would be the first crucial test that would determine if he really did possess that rare force that generates power in and of itself. And yet, at this moment, he felt weak and frightened. The feeling had been with him even as he had called Gallagher, and it had remained with him through the flight, a faint numbness in his limbs. He had subdued it through sheer activity, but now it would not be denied. At last, Pilgrim knew, he had reached the one remaining point at which he could turn back to the safety of conformity. The immensity of what he was doing confronted him. He was opposing a powerful committee of the Congress, and he was opposing it alone. He was opposing the leadership of his own party, which had, in its wisdom, decided that the pressures of the situation were too great to keep the Blaine affair alive. And he was opposing the President of the United States and all the power gathered in him. Suddenly he saw that his courage might only be audacity, and he saw himself not as the dynamic young fighter but as the presumptuous young pup making trouble and asking for trouble.

If his audacity was enormous, so could be his punishment. He envisaged the process that would effect his destruction. The press would be indifferent to his charges and then would turn on him. The administration would retaliate by setting the reliable, fatal wheels into motion. Those wheels would spin threads of pressure, advantage and obligation that would quickly reach leaders of Pilgrim's party, who, only too glad to get clear of the mess, would lend their power to the quiet work of erasing Henry Pilgrim. And Henry Pilgrim would find himself labeled indiscreet or controversial or irresponsible or blundering or, at last resort, dangerous, and he would find himself alone, pushed further and further to the periphery of things, until his situation would be impossible. He would become a man who was asked nothing, was told nothing, could do nothing, would be nothing, whose days among his colleagues would be an agony of humiliation and regret.

Suddenly he was jarred by a swift swaying of the car as it narrowly passed another vehicle. He looked at Gallagher and saw the newsman sitting calmly behind the wheel, leaning slightly forward, looking purposefully ahead.

Pilgrim realized that he could not turn back, for he had already compromised himself with Gallagher. He could feel his jaw sag as he recognized that his moment of free decision had already passed, that he had already committed himself.

All right, then, he thought, settling back into a new freedom that came with acceptance, if the game was on he would have to play it hard all the way. When you're in the valley of the shadow, he told himself, you stay alert and keep yourself certain. You take a man like Blaine and make him the first milestone on the way to triumph, and you do it by being persuasive and strong. And having Gallagher along could be an asset now that the course was set. The man was shrewd, tough and sharply calculating, and he was reasonable. Convinced that gain was to be had from pressing the case further, Gallagher had subtly become an ally, whose syndicated column would be a welcome bulwark in the face of an unfavorable press.

"There's the place I called," Gallagher said as they tore past a country store fronted by a single, old-fashioned gas pump. "Blaine's shack is up in those hills to the right. It's bleak and lonesome as hell up here in the winter, but to old Justin—" he grinned crookedly—"it offers the rare and mystical strength of spiritual renewal. He once hid out here for months after he broke with the party and the OGPU was hunting his head. Personally, I'd rather take my chances on getting shot than be buried for even a week in this hole."

Pilgrim winced as the car swayed dangerously close to a guard rail that bordered a sheer drop. "I hadn't realized you'd known Blaine quite so long," he said. "You were close to him during that entire period then, weren't you?"

"What entire period?"

"While he was a Communist."

Gallagher glanced over at him, his eyes suddenly cold and wary. "Look," he said. "I went to college with Blaine. I knew him before the party and after. I lost touch with him entirely for the nine years while he was in. Afterward I got him a job at CBN when he was starving and on the run. That's the whole story about me and his Communist period. Is that understood, Congressman?"

"Understood," Pilgrim said hastily.

Gallagher stared ahead. "Guilt by association," he said flatly. "The proud and shining hallmark of our times. Screen all friends and companions for communicable social diseases and unpopular political notions. Bar your doors to all controversial issues. Offend no one. Lead a properly antiseptic life and be safe. Commandments for success in the year of our Lord nineteen hundred and fifty-two."

Pilgrim smiled. "They haven't been *your* commandments," he said, "and *you're* a success. Your column runs in over three hundred papers and I can't remember having ever read one in which you didn't offend *somebody* or blast *something*. How were you able to manage it?"

"By being sneaky," Gallagher said easily. "By offending only unpopular people."

Gallagher made a screeching turn onto a climbing, rutted road. There were patches of snow showing between the trees on either side, and Pilgrim glimpsed a deer disappearing behind some brush. They bounced through a grove of pine and it was suddenly dark as the branches thickened overhead. Gallagher switched on the headlights, reluctantly forced to slow up by the steepness of the hill. Then a lake gleamed darkly off to the right and they passed several boarded-up summer cabins.

"That's it ahead," Gallagher said. He nodded toward a small bungalow perched high on a shelf overlooking the water. Lights shone from the windows and spilled out onto a wide front lawn. They followed a graveled driveway upward from the road and parked beside a crumbling garage. Gallagher got out and stretched. "You'd better wait here," he told Pilgrim. "Let me at least warn them."

Pilgrim lit a cigarette and watched Gallagher walk toward the house. The front door opened and a woman came out, squinting into the fading light. She was small and slender and wore a man's heavy sweater thrown over her shoulders. She came forward onto the lawn as Gallagher approached.

"Hello, Alice," Pilgrim heard him say lightly. "I just happened to be passing by and thought I'd—"

"What the hell are *you* doing here?" Alice Blaine's voice crackled sharply.

"Is that any way to greet an old friend?" Gallagher said. He tried to embrace her, but Alice swept aside his arms.

"Don't 'old friend' me, you lousy bastard!"

"Alice!" Gallagher sounded genuinely shocked and hurt.

Alice stood glaring at him, legs apart, fists planted belligerently on hips. "The first day!" she raged. "The first day he went to work, you had to tell them. You couldn't wait."

"What the hell are you talking about?"

"I'm talking about you ratting to CBN that Justin had been a Communist. I'm talking about a supposed friend with as much loyalty as a cobra."

"For Christ's sake, Alice!" Gallagher shouted disbelievingly. "That was twelve years ago! Anyway, I had to protect myself and it never really hurt him."

"Keep your voice down," Alice hissed. "I've finally gotten Justin to nap, and I don't want your damned bellowing to waken him. It's the first decent sleep he's had in days." She looked up at the columnist consideringly. "What are you doing here?" she said more calmly.

Gallagher sighed deeply and this time managed to kiss her. "That's more like it. That's my sweet, gentle, ever-loving doll."

"What happened? Did you smell a story in Jussie? Now that those bastards on the committee have dropped him, you suddenly decide your old buddy might make good copy for a few columns?"

Gallagher grinned. "Not exactly. I just thought you and Justin might enjoy meeting one of those 'bastards on the committee' in the flesh, so I've brought Representative Pilgrim up for a little informal chat." He turned toward the car. "Congressman, would you mind coming up here, please? I'd like you to meet one of your more ardent admirers."

Alice stared open-mouthed as Pilgrim climbed out of the car and walked toward them. "I'll be damned. It *is* him."

"Big as life," Gallagher crooned, enjoying himself, "and twice as handsome. The Republican Party's manly gift to the housewives of America."

Pilgrim brought forth his best boyish, winningly sincere smile. "Please ignore him, Mrs. Blaine. He has the typical Washington newsman's sense of humor—perverted." He made a small, formal bow with his head. "I'm very pleased to meet you."

Alice looked at him coldly. This one, Pilgrim thought, was not going to be easy. He had been unprepared for anything like Alice Blaine. Heard from the car, she had sounded like a tigress protecting her young. And now, seen close up, her appearance proved even more of a surprise than her vocabulary. Under any circumstances, Alice Blaine's face and figure would have drawn a second glance. When contrasted with the harshness of her speech, her delicate good looks were astounding.

"I'm sorry to have to intrude unannounced like this," Pilgrim said, "but it was important that I speak with your husband. Since you had no phone, I talked Tom into bringing me here."

Alice's eyes had not left his face. "What do you want with my husband?"

Pilgrim hesitated, wondering if he were going to be kept standing out on the lawn during his entire visit. "Well, I—"

"According to the radio," she broke in, "you people have decided to bury him like some piece of garbage you dug up by mistake. What's the matter? Was the smell getting too strong for your sensitive noses?"

"Alice!" Tom Gallagher said, obviously delighting in Pilgrim's discomfiture. "You are talking to a United States Congressman."

"To hell with the United States Congressman!" she said bitterly. "Let me tell you something, *Mister* Congressman. My husband is a sick man, a very sick man, and I have no intention of letting you or any other Washington cutthroat get close to him. If you want to talk to him, you'd better run back to your barnyard and scratch up another of your subpoenas, because that's the only way you're ever going to get him again."

Pilgrim stood helplessly. "Look, Mrs. Blaine," he said, "I understand how you must feel after the way we—"

"Who's that out there?"

Justin Blaine was peering from the open doorway. "Is that you, Tom?" He came toward them.

"You'll get pneumonia!" Alice wailed, as Justin approached in his shirt sleeves. "It's freezing out here."

Justin, his hair rumpled, his face still creased with sleep, frowned. He looked in surprise at Pilgrim, then at Gallagher, then once again at Pilgrim. He did not say anything.

"Don't speak to him," Alice pleaded. "You don't have to. He's only here to make more trouble."

Still staring at Pilgrim, Justin did not appear to have heard her. "Why is everyone standing out here in the dark?" he said quietly. "Come inside."

"Justin," Alice began, then stopped as he looked at her sharply and turned back toward the house. The others followed in silence.

Inside, a fire was going on the hearth, throwing a restless orange glow over the plank walls. Pilgrim shivered slightly as he went to warm his hands before the fire. Gallagher took off his coat and sprawled on a couch, appearing to be amused by the situation.

"Alice," Justin said, "would you put up some coffee, please? I think we'd all welcome something hot."

Pilgrim watched with relief as she left the room. "Let me tell you why I'm here, Mr. Blaine," he said too hurriedly. "I believed your testimony. I'm firmly convinced you were speaking the truth. I don't want to let this case be quietly shelved."

Justin's glasses glinted in the firelight. "That's not what I heard on the radio this afternoon."

"Never mind what you heard on the radio," Pilgrim said. "That was the committee's statement. I'm not here representing the committee."

"Then whom *are* you representing?"

"The Congressman," Gallagher said dryly, "has decided to live by the spirit of free enterprise. He's representing Henry Pilgrim, Incorporated."

Pilgrim lit a fresh cigarette and tossed the match into the fireplace. "I'm representing our country's need to hear the truth," he said. "Too many elected officials bow to public opinion even though they know it's wrong. I can't live that way. I can't serve my country that way. I've got to follow my own conscience. I've got to do what I know deep inside is right."

There was a mocking laugh from the doorway. Alice stood with a coffee pot in her hand. "Congressman," she said, "you're tearing at my heart."

"Go make your coffee," Gallagher ordered mildly, "and leave politics to the menfolks."

Alice disappeared, obviously intending to miss nothing from her position in the kitchen.

Pilgrim kept his eyes steadily on Justin's face, knowing he had the commentator's guarded interest. He would have to watch the way he spoke to these people. It was too easy to fall into the manner of the politician. "What I'm trying to say," he went on, "is that I want to know, to *see,* the actual evidence you've got of Webster Evers' guilt. If it's as conclusive as I hope, as I feel it *must* be, then I'll see that public opinion *forces* an exposure."

Justin removed his glasses and rubbed his eyes. The strain of the past few days was evident in the deepening circles. "Why should I push it?" he said tiredly. "I've already given them the important facts. I've named the names. If they won't accept them, that's their problem. Why should I rake myself over the coals trying to convince them it's the truth?"

"Because as I see it," Pilgrim said carefully, "you have no choice. Surely you must realize your only chance now is to vindicate yourself. Even your own boss, Mannheim, has cut out on you, which means you're out of a job, without hope of finding another at any network in the country. You should have seen the telegram he sent the committee." Pilgrim peered at Justin, his eyes narrow and searching. "But you have the chance now to become a national hero."

"And yourself, too, of course!" Alice shouted from the kitchen.

Gallagher laughed, his head thrown back on the arm of the couch. "You're going to have to stop looking for purity of motive, Alice," he called back. Then he spoke directly to Justin. "The important thing here is that the Congressman has given us a pretty accurate estimate of the situation." He straightened and spoke directly to Justin. "He's right, you know. If you don't prove Evers was lying and you were speaking the truth, you'll be living on handouts the rest of your life. And this time even *I* won't be able to get you another job."

Justin did not seem to be listening. He sat stiffly, hands folded in his lap, a curious, half-abstracted frown across his brow. Pilgrim felt a dim flicker of pity for the man. Any doubt that may have remained in his mind concerning the truth of the testimony was gone. The only question that now remained, he thought, was the actual proof. Despite Alice Blaine's fierce protectiveness, her husband was clearly a man who made his own decisions, and he was certainly not a fool. Self-preservation alone would force him to take a stand.

Alice came in carrying a tray of coffee, cheese and crackers. She set it down on a low table before the fire and began to pour. No one said anything. When the last cup had been poured, she put down the pot and looked at Justin. "I say no!" she declared quietly. "I say to hell with them all. Let them bury it and be damned."

Gallagher sipped his coffee. "Just like that?"

"Just like that," Alice said. "I don't *care* what a hundred million fools think. I don't *care* if Justin never broadcasts again. We'll manage. We'll manage even if we have to leave the country to do it. All I care about is not having my husband's insides torn out just for a good name. And that's exactly what's going to happen if we try to push this thing any further."

Pilgrim shook his head, wishing there were some way to get this woman out of the room. "Can't you see that it's no longer that simple? It's gone far beyond the two men involved. Whether he likes it or not, your husband is faced with an enormous moral obligation to his country. He's faced with—"

"Stop it!" Alice's fist struck the frail table. "Don't you *dare* use words like moral obligation to us. Do you think we're fools? Do you think we have to be lectured on morality by the likes of you? Do you think we don't know what you are and why you're here?" Alice sat with both fists clenched on her lap, her face flushed, her eyes pale and angry. "I saw what one session on that witness stand did to this man. If he doesn't have to, he's not going back for more. He's not going to sit there and be picked apart just so a conscienceless vulture like you can build a career on his bones." She stared at her husband across the table, but Justin's eyes and thoughts seemed to be elsewhere. "Aaah," she said wearily, "what's the use? I talk. I make loud sounds. But it's like whistling into the wind. I know what he's going to do. I guess I knew what he was going to do the moment you two walked in here."

A log exploded in the fireplace, sending a shower of sparks

against the protective screen. Alice started, then slumped in her chair. She smoothed imaginary wrinkles from her lap and suddenly seemed like a tired, aging housewife.

Justin blinked apologetically through his lenses. "I'm sorry," he said, "but you know I've got to do it."

"Why?" Alice asked bitterly, "because of your *enormous* moral obligation to your country?"

"No," Justin said, "to myself." He turned to Pilgrim. "We might as well start at the beginning. What do you want to know?"

"I'd like to *see* your documentary evidence, Mr. Blaine. What you can *tell* me to prove you knew Evers and were a spy with him will be valuable, but he could find ways to refute or get around it. Evidence in black and white is what we really need."

Justin thought of the pathetic pile of clippings and scraps that made up his "evidence," that and the little canister of film that might contain anything from irrefutable incrimination to nothing at all. No, he couldn't risk an opening impression of zero. His story would have to be his most powerful ammunition, and with all that the story contained, shouldn't it be enough?

"I'm sorry, Mr. Pilgrim, but I'd rather talk first. I want to give you the background, to let you know the whole truth about Webster Evers."

Barely disguising his disappointment, Pilgrim sighed in resignation. "All right," he said. "I want to hear as much as you can remember about your relationship with him. And I mean *everything*. No fact will be too small."

He grinned at Blaine, finding himself beginning to like this cherub-faced ex-spy who could make him a national celebrity. "Even if I have to camp here in your living room, I intend to hear everything."

1934: Washington, D.C.

Great wet flakes of snow clung to the Chevrolet's windshield, then melted and ran like tears. Webster Evers peered through the moisture as he drove slowly down the snow-covered street. He was beginning to regret having come out at all on such a night, particularly since the party to which he was going did not excite his interest. But the prospect of spending still another evening alone in his apartment had seemed even less appealing than the snow.

A short distance ahead, a string of cars was parked before a large, brightly lighted house. Webster pulled in at the far end of the line, and then plodded through the snow to the entrance. As he waited at the door, a great drone of voices could be heard, which seemed to envelop him as the door opened and a white-jacketed houseman led him into a large vestibule cluttered with rubbers, galoshes and dripping umbrellas. Webster gave him his hat and coat and cautiously pushed through the crowded foyer into the more crowded living room. A drink was put into his hand and another was spilled on his sleeve by a small, pink-faced man.

People greeted him and he nodded in return, but he knew few of them by name and was still surprised at how many people seemed to know him and even to defer to him. That a good reputation had preceded him from Rome and Berlin he knew, but its potency was still hard to comprehend. More than once the words "boy wonder" had been uttered about him, supposedly out of his hearing, and that was even more surprising considering his treatment at the State Department, where his reputation was respected much more than his opinions.

It was hard to keep up with the steady influx of new faces as the Roosevelt administration grew in power and personnel. Webster himself had come to Washington on the orders of FDR's Secretary of State, Cordell Hull, and Webster, too, had been regarded as a curiosity by the pre-New Deal Washingtonians who had managed to hang on. Now, after a year of Washington, he was beginning to see himself more ironically, as he regarded the confusion, indecision and pettiness of the departmental machinery. The "boy wonder," he thought ruefully, is beginning to wonder a lot more about government service. Had it been like this in Arthur's day?

"Webster, darling!"

The shrill voice floated above the chatter as Webster saw his hostess waving to him from across the room. He smiled and waved back, hoping that Henrietta wasn't going to try to reach him.

He moved carefully in the opposite direction, thinking that half his time in Washington was spent avoiding the very people he had originally spent an even greater part of his time trying to meet. "Posterity," a blond, double-chinned woman was declaring, "will forget everything about the Seventy-third Congress except the repeal of prohibition." Those about her nodded and glasses were raised in gratitude. "God bless them." Webster moved beside a passing tray of hors d'oeuvres, skillfully removing a wedge of caviar-coated toast.

A small group stood talking intensely beneath a cubist painting of a chartreuse woman with three breasts and a double navel. "Fifteen years late," a tall man in a tan Norfolk jacket said. "We recognized the Soviet Union exactly fifteen years too late. Precious time has been wasted. It has hurt both our countries, both our economies." He frowned at Webster. "And if it was up to some of the Fascist reactionaries in our State Department, we'd probably have waited twenty years more."

Webster made a small bow of acceptance, amused at *this* ironic turn his reputation had taken. There were so many people now in Washington who were quick to label others, he thought. To them, a man who had served in the American Embassy in Fascist Rome and then in the American Embassy in Nazi Berlin had to be a Fascist himself. It was as if living two years in each place had caused the vileness of the Black Shirts and the SA to seep into him so that he exuded their smell. That he had quietly but firmly pressed for recognition of Russia seemed to go unnoticed by the majority of the newcomers, such as the man in the

Norfolk jacket, himself a newcomer in the Agricultural Adjustment Administration. Maybe I have a reactionary-looking bearing,
Webster mused.

"Apples are being sold on the street corners of America," the
AAA man expounded loudly, "and we still refuse to face facts. We
still think we can legislate life back into the corpse of a dead
economy. In Washington everybody is huddled against everybody
else for comfort while the rest of the country starves. It's like a
nest of snakes hibernating for the winter." The AAA man downed
a canapé, washed it down with half a glass of champagne, and then
reached for more caviar.

Feeling the man's stare upon him, Webster said, "You sound
like a very ungrateful type of snake. You should either stop complaining about our happy little nest or get out on those street
corners with your apples."

The other man and the two women in the group turned to look
at him. "And I also think," Webster continued mildly, "that it
doesn't make sense to wail about social justice while your mouth is
stuffed with caviar."

The other man laughed. "Greed," he said, "is probably the
soundest and most universal basis for human action. Don't make it
sound like anything to be ashamed of, or we'll all be lost." He was
squat and sturdily built with heavy steel-rimmed glasses. Webster
remembered seeing him from time to time, but they had never been
introduced. Flanking him was a fierce-eyed dark girl with fleshy
hips, and a red-haired girl with the flat, pretty face and predatory
air of a professional model. The short man waved a stubby hand to
indicate the crowded room. "Greed," he said. "Everyone you see
in this place is here because he wants something, even if only the
free food and drink."

Webster looked curiously at the man, ignoring the fact that the
redhead was favoring him with an inviting stare. "What are *you*
here for?" he asked.

"For the sound of human voices," the man said. "For the simple
sight of a large group of living, breathing, actively conscious

people." He smiled. "These days, most of my life seems to be buried in the Library of Congress. My wife is sure I'll go stir-crazy unless she takes me out at least one night a week for crowd therapy."

Webster wondered which of the two women beside him was the wife, then decided it was neither. They did not seem to fit the intelligence apparent in his eyes.

"What about you?" the man said. "What's your excuse for indulging yourself while our countrymen go hungry in the streets?"

"He doesn't need an excuse for anything," the AAA man grunted dourly. "You're talking to Cordell Hull's wonder boy. All he has to do is walk around the State Department looking distinguished and making profound judgments."

Webster sipped his bourbon and turned slightly to one side as he saw Henrietta Crowley working her way in their direction. "It's not always that easy," he said, "to make profound judgments. Especially today when anyone with the price of the *Daily Worker* can become an expert on foreign affairs."

The dark girl glared at him. "And exactly what," she said, "is that clever remark supposed to mean?"

"It means, dear lady," Webster said, smiling politely, "anything your pure and blessed little heart would like it to mean." He felt a brief instant of reprieve as Henrietta stopped to gush over a slim, dark, bespectacled young man who, Webster knew, worked for the NRA's planning division. Since she'd been widowed, he thought, no man under forty was safe in the same room with her.

"Never mind my pure and blessed little heart," the girl said in a clear, cold voice. "I'm getting sick and tired of listening to snide cracks by you bright-faced reactionaries in the striped-pants set. Maybe if more of you people *did* read the *Daily Worker,* the country wouldn't be in the howling mess it's in right now."

Webster's finely drawn brows lifted. He nodded slowly, noting that the redhead was offering him an openly provocative smile. "Perhaps you're right," he said. "I'll speak to Mr. Hull about it in the morning."

"You think you're being funny," the girl said, flushing, "but you could do a lot worse. God, when I *think* of what's going on under our noses at this very moment and we sit and do nothing about it."

"What," Webster said, "is going on under our noses at this very moment?"

"Ethiopia," she declared with deep portent. "The Kingdom of Ethiopia is about to be gobbled by the Fascists and our State Department stands around at cocktail parties."

Webster assumed a mildly offended expression. "I hadn't really thought anyone had noticed." He looked at the girl's dark face, noting the same tense exaltation that seemed to have become standard for those personally bent on the world's salvation. "But since you brought up the subject of Ethiopia," he said gravely, "I happen to believe that the best thing that could possibly happen to that miserable patch of wilderness would be to be taken over by the Italians. That is, if the Italians should be foolish enough to want it."

The girl's eyes widened. "What?"

Webster nodded firmly. "Why those poor savages have made absolutely no progress in the last three thousand years. There they sit, scratching fleas in the same filthy mud huts in which they sat a thousand years before the birth of Christ. At least the Italians would be able to bring them some of the benefits of their growth and culture." He drank deeply and gazed at the girl over his glass. "Don't you agree?"

"Agree?" The girl's face was a deep purple. "You think those Fascist butchers can—"

"The Italian people," Webster broke in serenely, "have a heritage of culture that cannot be dismissed by simple name-calling. We tend to forget that the Roman Empire once embraced two-thirds of the known civilized world, and that the masterpieces of the Renaissance are yet to be surpassed. I think we should do all in our power to encourage Italy to take over Ethiopia and—"

"My God!" The words came out as a strangled sound. "And this is what runs our State Department!"

The AAA man took her arm. "Come on, let's get some more champagne." He led her off mumbling, followed by the redheaded girl.

The man with the glasses stayed behind, smiling. "You've sold *me* anyway," he said. *"Viva Italia.* Let the Roman Legions take over their share of the white man's burden. It's about time they relieved the overworked British and French anyway."

Webster laughed. "A good argument. I'm sorry I didn't think of it myself." He looked at the squat, sturdily built man and decided he liked him. "I'm Webster Evers," he said extending a hand, "and don't quote me in the Library of Congress. I'll deny every word."

The man took his hand and shook it. "Bill Baker," he said. "Have no fear. I make it a point never to betray official State Department confidences." He grinned broadly. "Though I don't know what you had against that poor girl."

"I had nothing against her," Webster said. "In fact, I never saw her before. But I'm becoming so damned tired of listening to the pious pronouncements of our parlor liberals that I find myself arguing even when I agree with them."

"Amateur liberalism," Baker said mildly. "The special spirit of Washington these days. Though I suppose it could be worse."

"How?" Webster grimaced as he saw Henrietta bearing down on him once more. "They're utter bores and I can put up with just about anything in this world but chronic dullness."

Henrietta came up, beaming. "Webster, darling, I have the awful feeling you've been avoiding me."

"You're wrong, darling," Webster said smoothly. "I look forward to our every meeting."

Henrietta smiled at Baker. "And the appalling part is that I know he doesn't mean it."

"Why do you put up with him?" Baker asked.

"Because he's without doubt the handsomest, cleverest and

most amusing man in Washington. And, on the rare occasions when he wants to be, the most charming." She kissed Webster behind the ear and sighed deeply. "Also," she said, "since he'll probably be President someday, I've got to keep trying to be nice to him."

Bill Baker smiled at Webster. "If I wasn't impressed before," he said, "I am now, Mr. President."

"You needn't be," Webster said flatly. "Henrietta picks her Presidential candidates the same way as the rest of America's female voters—by some mysterious singing in the sex glands."

"Never mind," Henrietta said, "I think we did very well with FDR. And you certainly can't blame sex for Hoover." She surveyed the room. "Where's Alice? I haven't seen her since you two came in. Though God only knows how I could miss her. She looks as though she's carrying triplets."

"Bite your tongue," Baker said. He waved vaguely. "She's probably brooding in some corner. She's getting a little impatient with the waiting."

"Well, this is one thing," Henrietta said, "that even the redoubtable Alice Baker can't rush." She brushed sensually at Webster's lapel with an exquisite hand tipped with long red fingernails. "Be nice to Bill," she said as she left them. "He's almost a father."

"What does it feel like," Webster asked, "to be almost a father?"

Baker smiled. "A little confusing," he said, "a little awesome and a little frightening. I'm still not sure about being responsible for my own life, let alone taking on another."

Webster finished his drink, lifted two glasses of champagne from a nearby tray and handed one to Baker. "I'd be happy to drink to your first-born."

Baker accepted the toast with a nod and they stood for a moment, drinking in silence.

Then a tall, dour-faced man appeared and whisked Baker away to meet someone and Webster was alone. His glance drifted idly about the crowded room, shifting, without particular interest, from one group to the next. Suddenly his eyes met those of the nameless, dark girl he'd been baiting a few moments before. She was standing alone near the bar and staring at him with such obvious distaste that Webster was, for the moment, startled. He offered her a small bow of appeasement, but her gaze cut coldly into him. Then feeling uniquely helplessly like a fish being reeled in, he walked toward her.

"I surrender," he said gently. "Before you fire even one more shot, I surrender completely. I was just teasing you before. Actually, I have the most profound sympathy and respect for the Ethiopian people." He nodded with deep solemnity. "The most profound sympathy and respect."

"You're a goddamned liar," the girl said and started to turn away.

Webster caught and held her arm, feeling it unpleasantly heavy and lumpish between his fingers. "No. Really. I'm sorry about that. It was stupid of me." He released the girl's arm and although her face was still coldly shut against him, he did not walk away. "I guess I still respond to attractive women," he said in rueful tones, "like an adolescent."

She sniffed suspiciously, but there was an air of preening. "And what is *that* supposed to mean?"

"Simply that instead of throwing snowballs at a pretty girl to make her notice me, or pulling her pigtails, I deliberately say things to antagonize her. Rather ridiculous for a grown man, don't you think?"

"Very ridiculous." She looked at him in sullen appraisal. "You don't really have to go to all that trouble, you know."

"I think," Webster said, "that you have just said something nice." He took her empty glass from her hand.

"Scotch and soda," the girl said, and Webster ordered a fresh drink from the barman. He watched as she lifted the glass. "And it probably doesn't bother you at all," he said with charming reproach, "doesn't disturb you in the slightest, that I don't even know your name."

"Not in the slightest."

"Pity will soften you," he said. "Anyone whose heart can embrace the oppressed of the earth will surely find room enough in it even for one so undeserving as myself."

The girl regarded him with a mixture of distrust and dislike. "Look," she said. "I'm sure that in some circles this approach would be considered charming, even irresistible. But, please, save us both a lot of trouble and don't waste it where it won't do any good. I haven't the patience for you bright, clever boys. You bore me."

This time she did walk away. Webster stood frowning after her, his face suddenly red with frustration and annoyance. Stupid, fat-assed bitch, he brooded. Yet compulsively, as he made this considered judgment, part of his mind was already planning to find out who she was. He knew he would call her the following night, and the night after that and even the night after that, if necessary. In two weeks he'd have her crawling after him. The *bitch!*

He saw Baker waddling toward him and welcomed the squat, sturdily built man gratefully like an old friend. It was getting harder and harder, he thought, to find anyone with sense to talk to in this town. They stood comfortably together, while the party eddied about them. Webster listened to a seventy-two-year-old Senator assure a group of listeners that Adolf Hitler was nothing but a brash upstart who would vanish from the world scene within six months.

"Which way do you suppose it happens?" Webster said. "Does a man enter public life because he's a fool or does he become a fool because he's entered public life."

"I don't know," Baker said, "but either way the results do seem to be depressingly alike." He smiled, his eyes bright behind the heavy glasses. "Though if you're with the State Department, you should have the chance to see at least a few good brains in action. Anthony Burdick seems to have done a tremendous job on the Philippine independence compromise, at least according to the newspapers. And what about Tom Harper? You've got to admire the way he helped ease that Manchurian affair."

"You're right. I *should* have an opportunity to see good minds in action at State, and on occasion I do, but only on occasion. As for Burdick and Harper, only a succession of minor miracles kept them from messing up both crises."

"Should you be telling me tales out of school?" Baker warned.

"They're not betrayed confidences, but open secrets, which only the press keeps hidden. What's holding up the Department's reputation is a hard-working public relations staff and the reflected brilliance off Cordell Hull's white hair."

Baker laughed. "You certainly don't talk like a State Department career man."

"Perhaps it's because I really do care about the Department and what it's supposed to be doing that I talk this way."

"May I ask what you do in the Department?"

"I'm on the German desk, which is without doubt the most frustrating section."

"How long have you been on it?" Baker asked, as they withdrew to a wall where there was a pocket of quiet.

"I arrived here only last year. I started with State in twenty-eight at the embassy in Rome, and in thirty they sent me to Berlin. It's been quite an education, watching Mussolini and Hitler operate."

"You mean those brash upstarts who are going to disappear in six months?"

"The same. I've seen Mussolini transform a peace-loving, civilized people into a machine bent on a dream of imperial Roman glory and it frightens me. And I've seen Hitler hypnotize Germany into a regression to something that defies description. And that terrifies me."

"Oh, well, the Italian trains are running on time."

"And the Italian people are marching in time. They aren't cut out for conquest and empire, but before they learn that, they are going to wreck the peace."

"Well, Mussolini has been in power a long time, but surely

Hitler is too wild to be able to govern Germany for more than a couple of years. If you've read *Mein Kampf,* you know what I mean."

"Mr. Baker, I've seen the Nazis live *Mein Kampf* and I believe that Hitler will be in power for a long, long time. What no one seems to realize is that Hitler has a world vision, which means that he has a source of strength that no one else in the world but the Communists have, and he understands the weaknesses of the democracies, which means that if he can strengthen Germany, he can perhaps go farther toward domination of Europe than Bismarck or the Kaiser ever could."

"But the Versailles Treaty! Surely that—"

"The Versailles Treaty has already been broken enough by Germany to make it useless. It's no longer a matter of a broken treaty. It's a matter of stopping Hitler now, any way we can, by sanction, by threats, by conspiracy, by invasion, any way, before he has the army and air force that he intends to create."

"That's quite a foreign policy you've got there," Baker said with a slight laugh.

"That's the nicest thing that's been said to me since coming to Washington. But, I must add, these are my personal views, not official ones."

Webster noticed a pregnant woman working her way toward them from the foyer. She had short blond hair and a delicately pretty face. She was clearly in a state of extreme distress.

Baker saw her and frowned. "What's wrong?" he said anxiously. "Is something wrong?"

Alice Baker shook her head, but beads of moisture stood out on her forehead and her cheeks were drawn and pale. She drew her husband slightly to one side and spoke to him in a voice that Webster was unable to hear.

"We'd better go," Baker said. "I'll call a cab." He took his wife's arm, then remembered Webster and turned. "I'm sorry. An emergency."

"Can I help?" Webster asked on impulse. "I've got a car outside. It won't be easy to get a cab in this snow."

Baker looked at his wife, then nodded quickly. "We'd both be grateful. It's not supposed to be time, but she thinks . . ." he shrugged helplessly.

"My car is parked down the block," Webster said. "I'll get it and meet you in front."

The snow was still coming down heavily and it took a few moments to clear the car's windshield and warm the balky motor. When Webster backed up to the lighted entranceway, the Bakers were just coming out, two bundled figures huddled darkly against the snow. Alice stumbled and almost fell and Webster got out of the car quickly and helped her into the back seat. The pain had evidently become more severe, and she was biting her lip to keep from crying out. Her husband climbed in the back and held her awkwardly. "The General Hospital," he told Webster. "It's on Connecticut Avenue."

"I know where it is," Webster said. He shifted into gear and felt the wheels spin wildly before they took hold. There was almost no traffic and only a few tracks marred the smooth surface of the snow. "There's a blanket folded somewhere in back," he said over his shoulder. "Have you got it?"

"Yes," Baker said after a moment. "I called the doctor before we left. He's going to meet us at the hospital. He thinks it may only be false labor." He seemed to be speaking more for his own comfort than anything else. "His name is Corbett, Dr. Franklin Corbett. He's supposed to be a very fine obstetrician."

Webster drove as quickly as he dared, braking carefully on the turns. The hospital was several miles away, on the far side of the city, and the roads grew more slippery as they entered the heavily trafficked areas. The voices from in back became soft and private and Webster tried not to listen, but they kept intruding anyway, with Baker asking his wife how she felt at regular sixty-second intervals and she steadily assuring him that she was fine, absolutely fine. The things, Webster thought, that could happen to a man at a cocktail party.

Baker chuckled nervously. "I don't even think," he said, "that you two have been officially introduced. Alice, I'd like you to meet our benefactor, Webster Evers."

"Of the State Department?" Alice Baker asked.

"There's no escaping it," Webster said, though somewhat flattered.

"Is this some sort of new service," Alice said, "being offered by Cordell Hull to make up for his ineptitude in foreign affairs?"

Webster laughed. "Precisely. We've got to build up goodwill in whatever way we can."

"It won't work," Alice said, speaking with an effort. "I'm grateful, but it won't work."

Webster smiled to himself. "I can't really blame you," he said. "Though I refuse to accept personal blame for all our mistakes. As a matter of fact, I like to think of myself as the one small, flickering light of hope in all of our great, black bureaucratic muddle."

"Very poetic," Alice sighed painfully.

Webster swerved to avoid a car speeding through an intersection and they skidded in a half-circle. There was a soft moan behind him. "I'm sorry," he said, straining to see through the dripping windshield.

They rode in silence for a while and there was only the muted hum of the engine until Webster heard the soft voices behind him.

"There's no reason to worry," Alice assured her husband. "A lot of women go through this in the sixth or seventh month. It's just a warning to take things easy. You mustn't worry."

"I'm not at all worried," Baker said.

"A little bleeding and a few pains," she said. "It's nothing. I'm sure I can hold onto it. I'm absolutely sure."

"I know you will."

"We've waited too long for him for anything to happen now." She laughed faintly. "Him. I like the way I keep calling it him."

"Shhh," Baker said. "You shouldn't talk so much."

"I can talk, I told you it's—" A smothered cry of pain cut her off. "Don't look at me," she whispered. "When that happens, I don't want you to look at me."

Baker did not say anything and Webster glimpsed him in the rear-view mirror as he bent to kiss his wife's cheek.

"We're going so slow," Alice sobbed. "It's taking so long to get there."

"It's the snow. We can't go any faster."

"I know. I know."

"Please don't talk," he pleaded.

"I'm such a nuisance," Alice sighed. "Oh, God, how I hate being such a nuisance."

"Shh. Shh."

"Don't look at me. Please, Jussie. Don't look at me."

Webster's knuckles showed white as his hands tightened on the wheel. Jussie, he thought dimly, an odd nickname for a man called Bill.

Alice moaned softly. "Oh, I wish we were there. I wish . . . I wish . . ." Her voice was smothered in a new spasm of pain.

The road ahead was straight and empty, yet although Webster cautiously fed the car more speed, the speedometer still read under thirty-five. He pressed the accelerator harder, feeling the wheels take hold, slip, then hold once more. Driving in snow made him nervous, just as doing anything without full control made him nervous. He wished he had chains on, but he didn't even own a set.

"Look out!" Baker yelled.

The cry came the same instant Webster saw the car, a taxi, as it sped across their path from a side street. Webster pumped the brakes and nothing happened, and he hit the horn and swung the wheel wildly to the right. The car swung around, skidding in a complete circle and missing the rear of the taxi by inches. Webster frantically fought the wheel, but it whirled loosely in his hands. "Hold—" he shouted, but never completed the warning, for the car leaped the curb and slammed into a lamp post, loosening the globe and exploding it, in an icy shower of glass, onto the roof. Webster felt the steering wheel press against his chest. Trembling, he snapped off the ignition.

He squeezed from behind the wheel and looked in back. Alice and Bill lay on the floor of the car. "Oh, Lord." He reached over to help Baker, who was struggling to right himself, and together they managed to ease Alice back onto the seat. The pregnant woman's face was contorted with pain and she was making small, anguished sounds to herself.

"I'm sorry," Webster said miserably. "Christ, I'm sorry." Angrily he noted that the taxi had disappeared. He stared at Alice Baker's face. If anything happened because of . . .

"Please." Baker's anxious plea intruded. "The hospital. Let's just get to the hospital."

Grimly expecting the worst, Webster got out to inspect the car. The right front fender and part of the hood were pushed in, but no water seemed to be leaking from the radiator. He got back in and tried to start the motor. It coughed twice, then caught. Holding his breath, Webster shifted into reverse. The car backed away from the pole, wheels spinning and whining in the snow, but getting enough traction, finally, to carry them back into the road. He took a deep breath and was vaguely conscious of the ache in his chest where the steering wheel had hit him. His hands still trembling, he drove the car toward the hospital once more, hearing the right front tire bang rhythmically against the dented fender.

2

They were standing in the hospital corridor when Dr. Corbett, a plump, soft-faced man with a neatly trimmed mustache and a self-absorbed professional manner, came out of Alice's room and walked quickly toward them. He had examined her for twenty minutes while Webster waited with Baker outside.

"I'm taking your wife to the delivery room, Mr. Baker," he said. "I'm afraid she can't hold the child any longer."

Baker's eyes blinked rapidly behind his lenses. He moistened his lips with his tongue, but did not say anything.

A muffled scream broke from behind the closed door and reverberated down the empty corridor. Baker started toward the door, but the doctor stopped him.

"The nurse gave her some morphine," he said. "She'll feel better in a moment."

Baker looked at the fine line of the doctor's mustache. "What are the baby's chances?"

Corbett shook his head. "I'm not going to try to fool you, Mr. Baker. This is hardly the beginning of the seventh month. Of course there have been cases of survival, but the odds are small. Also, your wife is bleeding pretty badly now. I don't like it."

Baker nodded slowly, accepting the logic of the doctor's prognosis without question. His eyes were off somewhere and his hands worked spasmodically at his sides. An elevator door opened and an attendant appeared pushing a rolling stretcher. He was followed by an intern, his stethoscope swinging around his neck. They went into Alice Baker's room.

"I have to get ready," Dr. Corbett said, "I'll let you know as soon as it's over."

"May I see my wife?" Baker said.

"They'll bring her out in a few moments," Corbett said as he walked into the elevator. "You can see her for a second or two then."

Webster stood leaning against a white wall, smelling the hospital odors and aching for a cigarette. There was a small waiting room farther down the corridor where smoking was permitted, but he did not want to leave Baker alone. As he looked at the chunky, graceless figure of this man whom he had not even known three hours earlier, he felt annoyance at having been drawn into his life and problems.

There was another scream from inside the room and Baker said, "Jesus Christ," very softly.

A moment later the stretcher was rolled out. Alice Baker was wrapped in blankets and only her pallid face could be seen. Her eyes were tightly closed against the pain and she was unaware of her husband until he bent and touched her hair. Then she opened her eyes and looked at him.

"Jussie . . ." she whispered, starting to cry. "Jussie."

Baker's face seemed frozen. "It's all right," he said insanely. "It's all right."

"I couldn't do it," she wept. "I couldn't hold onto it. I had only one thing to do and I couldn't even do that."

"You mustn't talk like that," he begged.

"I tried. I swear I did. But I just couldn't do it. You wanted him so much and now . . ." Tears ran down her cheek into the blanket. "I'm no good."

"You're wonderful," he said thickly. "You're the only thing in this whole damn world I care about."

"I'm no good. I'm no good. I'm no good." The pains came and Alice turned her face away and arched in agony under the blankets. Until the elevator doors opened and the intern, the attendant and a nurse wheeled the stretcher in, Webster did not know where to look. The elevator doors closed and Webster and Baker were alone in the corridor.

"There's a waiting room down the hall," Webster said. "We can smoke there."

Baker looked at him as though aware of his presence for the first time. "I appreciate all you've done," he said, "but there's no point in killing your whole night. Why don't you go on back to the party?"

Webster shuddered. "If you don't mind, I'd prefer the hospital."

Baker smiled faintly. He did not say anything, but his dark eyes were grateful.

They sat smoking in the waiting room for a long time, talking little. The night sounds of the hospital were soft and foreboding. Occasionally they would hear the elevator stop on the floor and the doors open, and they would stare along the severe perspectives of the corridor until they saw who it was. A nurse sat behind a desk at the far end, making notations on charts, while a panel of red and white lights blinked on and off above her head.

Sometimes Baker would stare long and distantly out at the city of Washington, its buildings dark and strange beneath the snow. He seemed remarkably calm and controlled. Webster felt he knew Baker's thoughts, yet even now he sensed no sympathy for the man so much as resentment, as though he himself were in some way more deserving of the pity he should be offering. He knew it was illogical, but the resentment was there, unmistakably. It was there for the feeling and closeness Baker shared with his wife, and for the unborn child they had waited for together and were now about to lose, and even for the pain of the loss itself, which would only increase the depth and intensity of everything else they had. In short, he thought wryly, he resented all the very things he had deliberately and steadfastly denied himself and which he still tried to believe he did not want.

The elevator doors opened and Dr. Corbett walked quickly toward them. He wore a rumpled white, surgical cap and gown, and a mask hung from his neck. Baker rose slowly from his chair and stood there, looking like a man about to be sentenced for some terrible crime. Webster rose automatically with him, knowing immediately from the doctor's face that the news was bad.

"I'm sorry," Corbett said soberly. "The child lived only a few minutes. We put him into an incubator at once, but he was very small. Very small."

"My wife," Baker said. "How is my wife?"

"She came through," Corbett said. He rubbed a hand tiredly across his face and removed the white skullcap, leaving a few moist strands of hair standing on end. "However, I'm afraid there are complications."

Oh, Christ, Webster thought. But Baker's face did not change expression. He just stood looking at the doctor.

"There's a growth," Corbett went on, "which we couldn't see before because of the child, but it's definitely in an advanced stage. I want to operate immediately."

"You want to operate immediately?" Baker echoed dumbly.

Corbett nodded regretfully. Webster did not like the gesture. It was too smooth and studied, like the manner of a performer who has learned his role well but does not really feel it. Yet how long could a doctor survive if he were foolishly humane enough to take the deep, personal anguish of every patient as his own? It was, of course, too much to expect. But still, somehow, he expected it.

"There's a form you must sign, giving your permission," Corbett said. "I have it here."

Baker took the pen and paper that the doctor handed him. He held the pen still for a moment. "You're very sure?" he asked. "There's no doubt in your mind that it must be done at once?"

"No doubt at all," the doctor said. "Not in this case. We have absolutely no choice." He hesitated. "Of course you have the right to another opinion. If you'd like to call in a consultant, I can arrange it. But speed *is* essential."

Baker looked at Dr. Corbett; then he signed the form and gave it back to him. "I take your word for it. I trust you."

The statement was intended to be reassuring, but Webster sensed, with some surprise, a cold, almost threatening undertone. There was evidently a hard core of something in William Baker that existed in direct contradiction to the warm, gentle surface manner. The discovery impressed Webster. Warmth and gentleness alone, he had found, were often a cover for an underlying weakness, but not here. He was suddenly sure, not here.

"This may take a few hours," Corbett said. "If you'd rather wait at home I can get word to you there."

"I'll be here," Baker said.

When the doctor had disappeared into the elevator, they sat down once more. Baker smoked in silence and Webster did not intrude on his thoughts. At the far end of the corridor, the nurse got up from her desk and came toward them. "Would either of you gentlemen care for something to drink?" she asked. "Tea or coffee?"

"Thank you," Baker said. "Nothing for me."

Webster shook his head.

"Well, if you change your mind," she said, "just let me know."

Webster watched her walk back to her desk, the starched uniform rustling crisply down the corridor. He considered all the things this lovely young girl had undoubtedly seen in the small hours of the night, the pain and anxiety, the hideous torment of helpless waiting. Thoughts of the marvelous resiliency of the human spirit briefly separated Webster from the Bakers and their problems.

"It was a boy after all," Baker said quietly. "My wife was sure it was going to be a boy all along, and it was."

Brought abruptly back to the present, Webster tried to think of something to say that would not sound inane, but couldn't. Nor did Baker seem to expect any comment. He stared broodingly at the tip of his cigarette and sighed. "The childs lucky to be out of it. So he had his few minutes. Maybe it was enough. Maybe I was wrong to have started him off in the first place. What would he really have had to look forward to?"

"Not too much, I suppose," Webster offered consolingly. "Not if you read the papers."

"I don't need the papers to tell me anything," Baker said, his voice cold and flat and losing itself quickly against the high walls of the waiting room. When he spoke, it was as if he were forcing the words. "I have my own nightmares about where we'll be in twenty years. With my eyes open or closed, I see it. Kids fighting with knives over a crust of bread . . ." He smiled crookedly to himself. "At least my son died comfortably in a nice warm hospital, and not old enough to regret any damn part of it."

Webster looked at Baker's deceptively ruddy cheeks, thinking his vision of the future did not sound like that of a man isolated among the stacks of the Library of Congress. "The way you picture it," he said, "you make me almost envy your son."

"There'll be a lot of us, if we're still around, who will envy him," Baker said. Then he shook his head and smiled strangely. "I'm sorry. I don't want to damage any of your illusions. You are, after all, in the State Department. Illusions are very necessary in your line of work. If you lost them, you'd be like a soldier going into battle unarmed. And the rest of us are depending on you and your valiant little top-hatted brigade. You're our last hope of salvation."

"Now you're making fun of me," Webster said.

"No. Only of what you do." Baker crushed out the butt of his cigarette between nicotine-stained fingers. He looked with a sudden and fierce intensity at Webster. "Or can I afford to make fun of you, *or* your venerable Cordell Hull, *or* your bumbling State Department? After all, you're all we've got and at least you're in there *trying*."

"Thanks," Webster said dryly.

A flicker of humor showed through the anguish in Baker's eyes. "Seriously, since meeting you tonight, I don't know how or why a man with your intelligence ever wandered into government service."

The sharpness of his sorrow broke through once more and he turned away toward the window and the snowy sky.

It was nearly three A.M. when Dr. Corbett came off the elevator toward them. This time he had his street clothes on and looked scrubbed and efficient and surprisingly fresh. Baker and Webster rose again, almost ritually now, to meet him.

"Well?" Baker said with hoarse impatience.

The doctor looked at Baker gravely for a moment and Webster felt a sudden coldness in his stomach. Then he said, "Your wife came through the operation fairly well. She was terribly worn out by the birth, but I'd say she came through fairly well."

"What in Christ's name is that supposed to mean?" Baker said harshly.

Corbett's plump face showed polite reproval, as though there were a particular and carefully thought-out way in which patients' relatives were to be informed of their condition, and he was one man who had no intention of being hurried through it. "I had to perform a hysterectomy." he went on. "There's still no guarantee of the future, of course, but I'd definitely say you can be thankful we went in when we did."

"Thankful?" Baker said coldly. His eyes did not leave the doctor's face. "What about now? How is she now?"

Corbett considered the question carefully. "The next twenty-four hours," he said, "are the crucial ones. But I'm hopeful. I'm definitely hopeful."

"May I see her?"

The doctor shook his head. "Not until tomorrow. She'll be under heavy sedation till then anyway." He started to inch his way toward the elevator. "I suggest you go home and get yourself some sleep right now."

Baker did not say anything. He was still looking directly at Corbett, but seemed to have forgotten him entirely.

"I have to go now," Corbett said with a hint of impatience, sounding as if he had an important appointment from which he was being unjustly detained. "I've arranged round-the-clock nurses for Mrs. Baker and I'll be by to see her myself at about ten o'clock." He frowned for a moment at Baker, then turned and walked back to the waiting elevator.

Webster reached for his hat and coat where they lay on the couch. When he straightened, he saw that Baker had walked to the window and was staring out once more. "Come on," he said. "I'll take you home."

"It has just occurred to me," Baker said in a steady, matter-of-fact voice, "that my wife may very well die." Then he picked up his things and followed Webster out of the waiting room.

Chapter Thirteen

1952: Upstate New York

Justin paused in his story and pulled out a handkerchief. His face was dripping. Except for the crackling of the fire, the room was still. Pilgrim sat staring at him, totally absorbed. Then the Congressman nodded, silently expressing satisfaction with what he had heard. He had already evaluated the effect these words would have when heard over nationwide television. He glanced up at Gallagher, but the newsman seemed lost in thought.

Justin had edited the facts carefully as he spoke. To spare Alice the agony of reliving that night, he had mentioned nothing of the wild ride to the hospital, or the operation that followed the delivery of his dead son. Alice, in turn, had left the room almost as soon as Justin had started the narrative, hoping to find a place where his voice would not penetrate. But the soft, persistent monologue had found its way through the thin walls and, willing or not, she was forced to hear it all. Now, from behind her closed door, she heard Pilgrim's voice break the silence. "This is *exactly* the kind of verification we need," he was saying. "Of course, the details will have to be checked out, but I don't want to tip our hand by doing it before I make Evers face you in public. He might rig up a plausible explanation if we don't catch him by surprise." There was a brief pause. "What happened next, Mr. Blaine?"

Alice heard a chair move as Justin shifted his position at the table. Then his voice again: "Well, one thing led to another, and we became quite close with Webster. Of course, he never knew why, but I was careful to avoid meeting his other friends."

Once more Alice tried to shut out the words, but they kept breaking through. Slowly, inexorably, they recreated those tense months in Washington, seventeen years ago. . . .

The man who called himself William Baker stood at his living room window and looked at the tenement courtyard below. He was watching a streak of late sun bleach a row of underwear and striped pajamas. The sun broke through an opening between two buildings, hung there and then was cut off by a distant steeple. It slowly disappeared, leaving only the dreary purple of dusk.

Baker glanced at his watch. "Fifty-two seconds less than yesterday," he announced. "Today we have enjoyed the energy-giving rays of the sun for a total of eight minutes and thirty-four seconds."

"That's enough," Alice said from the kitchen. "Any more energy and I wouldn't be able to contain myself." She came in carrying dishes and silverware, which she placed on a cloth-draped bridge table set up in the center of the living room. Ordinarily, they took their meals in the kitchen, but there was space for only two at the table there and a guest was expected that evening. "Besides," she said, "I think the benefits of the sun have been exaggerated. Every tropical country I know is at least a thousand years behind the rest of the world. I'm sure it has something to do with the sun."

Baker turned away from the window. "Never mind your theories," he said. "I'm beginning to feel like the Prisoner of Zenda in this dungeon."

"All right. The moment we become rich, we'll take a front apartment." Alice walked back into the kitchen. "In the meantime, you can stop brooding about the sun and set the table. And the next time you invite Webster for dinner without telling me, I'll make you cook for him too."

Baker lit a cigarette and frowned through the smoke. "I wanted to talk to you about Webster," he said. "I asked him over tonight for a special reason."

"I'm sure you did," Alice said from the kitchen. "And I'm sure it's the same special reason you've been asking him over at least twice a week for the past three months. To keep me chained to the stove." They entertained very few guests in the tiny apartment, and Webster Evers' regular visits had taken on the form of a ritual. She had grown to dislike Evers, but for no rational reason. She couldn't even communicate her feeling to Justin. "What's so special about tonight?"

"I've got clearance from Rosoff to approach him."

"Approach him about what?"

Baker walked to the table and picked up a handful of silverware. "About us," he said. "Rosoff has been checking him out for weeks. He thinks Webster may be a risk, but worth a feeler."

Alice stood looking at him, her face serious. She had regained much of her looks and figure in the months since her illness, but now there were shadows rimming her eyes. "I can't say I'm surprised," she said. "I expected something like this eventually. I just didn't think it would be this soon."

"And?"

"And what?"

"What do you think of the idea?" Baker said patiently.

Alice disappeared once more into the kitchen. "You don't really care what I think. You and Rosoff have already made up your minds to tell him. You just want me to tell you what a great idea it is."

Baker began to lay out the silver into three neat place settings. He understood his wife's peevishness and accepted it with the same unruffled calm with which he had been accepting it ever since she had come home from the hospital. He found it more hopeful, at least, than the periods of deep depression through which she had gone at first, and which still recurred, though at less frequent intervals.

"Is that what you believe?" he said. "That it's a great idea?"

"No," she said reluctantly. "I think it's a foolish and possibly even dangerous idea. You can never be sure about a man's reaction to something like this. He might even be horrified and go screaming for the FBI."

Baker had to smile at the thought of Webster Evers being actively horrified by *anything*. If any characteristic had impressed him about his friend, it was his ability to accept all things with equanimity. "I doubt it," he said. "I have a strong feeling that what we're doing will appeal to him. Maybe not for all the same reasons, but I don't think that matters. The important point is that with his new position as chief of the State Department's German Section he can be of tremendous value to us."

Alice brought in a small basket of rolls and some glasses. "That is, if he wants to," she said doubtfully.

"He'll want to," Baker said. "I've been watching him carefully these past few months. Everything he says and does points to it." He stared thoughtfully at a bent spoon. "You've heard him on the subject of Fascism and his colleagues at the State Department. His experience in Rome and Berlin during the past four or five years is as perfect as his new position. Besides, he has no ties with anyone that we know of, emotional or otherwise. I'm the only one he's even partially close to."

"I hope you two will be very happy together."

Baker put the spoon in its proper place and looked at his wife. "You don't especially like Webster, do you?"

"Not especially."

"Why? He's certainly gone out of his way to be pleasant to you. He's been more than gracious, particularly during the time we needed him most."

"All right," Alice said. "I'll kiss his feet the moment he walks in." She crossed to the window and stared gloomily out at the hanging wash. "Oh, don't pay any attention to me. I sound like an idiot these days. I can't even stand *myself* any more."

Baker saw, without surprise, that she was crying. She wept quietly and the tears ran down her cheeks, staining the front of her blouse. He went to her and held her, feeling her cheek warm and moist against his own.

"What's wrong with me, Jussie?" she wept. "Tell me. What's wrong with me?"

"Nothing," he whispered. "Absolutely nothing is wrong with you. You're fine."

"I'm not fine. Stop telling me I'm fine." Her arms constricted fiercely about him. "I'm a mess. I look like hell, I feel like hell, and I act like hell. I don't know how you put up with me."

"It's easy," he said softly. "I love you."

"You shouldn't. There's nothing left to love. They took all the good out of me. I'm not even a woman any more."

Baker stepped back angrily. "I've told you to stop talking like that. I don't give a damn *what* they took out. I don't give a damn about kids. All I care about is what they left me. I've still got *you.* I don't care about anything else."

Then he held her once more, feeling her nails dig hard into his back. After a while it seemed to pass and she wiped her eyes with a corner of her apron.

Baker peered anxiously at his wife, deeply moved by her tears. It was hard to believe she was the same tough-minded whip of a girl who had introduced him to the party five years before, who had strictly guided his progress from the beginning, and who had not let up until he finally headed his own Washington apparatus. Convinced that his future in the party was better than hers, she had been happy to transfer her hopes and effort to his advancement. Now, he thought, she had to force even a token show of interest. "But how do I tell him?" he said slowly. "It's an odd sort of thing to tell someone." He laughed. "What do I say, 'Webster, old pal, I'm a spy'?"

Alice went back into the kitchen. "Take a look through *What Is to Be Done?*" she called. "I'm sure Lenin must have a chapter on how to tell your best friend you're a spy."

"I think I'd rather improvise."

Webster came directly from his office, briefcase under his arm, wearing a Homburg, his starched white collar still neat and fresh despite the June heat. He waved to Alice in the kitchen and followed Baker into the living room. "A double bourbon," he said, "and don't let me hear a word out of anyone until it's down."

Baker poured him the drink and a smaller one for himself, then watched as he tossed it off, shuddering as it went down. Webster sat down and closed his eyes. "Those idiots," he breathed. "Those miserable idiots. Another month of their stupidity and I'll be ready for commitment."

"Bad day?" Baker said sympathetically.

Webster opened his eyes. He held out his glass and Baker poured once more. "Each time I think I've witnessed the height of ineptitude, a new pinnacle is reached. Today was unbelievable. A nightmare."

Alice appeared in the doorway with a tray, but Baker caught her eye and she retreated silently into the kitchen, kicking the swinging door shut behind her.

Webster stared broodingly at the amber liquid in his glass. "I walk around that office all day like a madman," he said. "I try to do a decent, intelligent job, but I honestly don't know which way to turn first. I feel like the kid with his thumb in the dike. I can't leave it in much longer and I'm afraid to take it out. Any minute I expect the whole stupid mess to collapse on my head." He sipped his drink slowly. "Remember that Berlin episode I told you about last week?"

Baker remembered the incident clearly enough. It involved a poorly worded State Department dispatch that was so ambiguous that it might have been interpreted three different ways and eventually was. But he frowned, pretending uncertainty. "There were several different situations you mentioned. I'm not too sure exactly—"

"There was only one like this," Webster said disgustedly. "It was that monumental communiqué Paul Conklin sent out."

Baker nodded slowly. "Oh, yes."

"Well, another on the same subject went out today that made Conklin's seem brilliant by comparison. And when I tried, very delicately, to point out the dangers, all I got for my trouble was an idiotic lecture on protocol. I was also told I was negative and argumentative." Webster put down his drink and abruptly reached for the briefcase beside his chair. "This one," he said, "you've got to see with your own eyes to believe."

Baker watched him open the leather case, search inside and finally remove a long, official-looking document.

"Read this," Webster said, "and tell me if you think I'm crazy."

Baker looked at the sheet of paper in the extended hand, but made no move to take it. "Wait a minute," he said. "You shouldn't be showing me things like this."

"Why not?"

Baker laughed, "These things are marked 'Secret' for a reason, aren't they?"

Webster stared at him for a moment. "That's all right," he said. "My responsibility. Who's to say an intelligent layman like yourself isn't better equipped to cope with some of these purely common-sense problems than our career diplomats?"

His eyes on the paper, Baker said, "Isn't the Department pretty fussy about keeping classified material out of the wrong hands?"

"Oh, for God's sake, Bill! You sound like the department security officer, but he's *paid* to talk that way. Of course we have to be careful, but it gets ridiculous. There are more important things at stake right now than security. Germany is becoming a power that no nation in Europe will be able to stop, and we do nothing. It's going to end up in our laps again, and we can't see it."

"Aren't you exaggerating?"

"No one who has seen the Germans in action as I have would say I was exaggerating. But your reaction is just what I get every day. They refuse to believe it could be so bad, or to accept the fact that we've got to stop playing at foreign relations as though it were a polite game, and maybe even adopt some of the ferocity of the Nazis if we're going to stop them. Bill, let me give you one small example of how those people work. It isn't unique; in fact, most Germans see it every day and don't care. You know about the Nazi attitude toward the Jews. Well, it's the same toward anyone politically suspect. One morning a distinguished German scientist came to the embassy in Berlin. He'd heard rumors that he was under suspicion and about to be arrested. He had supported the Socialists during the last years of the Weimar Republic, he told us, and recently he had refused to join the Nazi Party. The Nazis try to get people of distinction to join the party. It adds prestige. They may have suspected him of being a Communist, although as a Socialist he was anti-Communist. Anyway, this man wanted political asylum; he wanted to come to America. He was convinced that if he didn't get out he would be arrested and sent to a concentration camp—those things really exist, you know; people disappear in them for months or years, without a trial. People go through hell in them.

"All right. The point is we *could* have helped him. He wasn't all that important to the Nazis, and they haven't wanted to endanger their relations with us. He sat in the lobby, with his suitcase beside him. He hadn't slept in days, he said, and he looked it. I looked out the window and, sure enough, there was a sedan parked across the street with two men in it. It's easy to spot the Gestapo. It was obvious what would happen as soon as he stepped onto the sidewalk. He stayed with us for hours; the Ambassador was too busy to see him. The final decision was no—for the sake of maintaining good relations! So he thanked us and started to leave. Someone stopped him and tried to hand him his bag, but he said that we should dispose of it, since he probably wouldn't be needing it. I remember he said, 'It doesn't have any clothes in it; it has my writings. I can't do anything for them any more.' He walked outside and the two men got out of the car—you can imagine the rest. Not long after, someone from the Wilhelmstrasse mentioned the matter to me and ended up by saying, 'It would have been all right to let him go. We would catch him eventually, when we conquer France or England or any other country he ran to.'

"That's the way they think, right down to the average 'decent' German. Already they scream, 'Today Germany, Tomorrow the World.' And just as we didn't have the guts to help one poor man at our embassy, we won't have the courage to stop Hitler before it's too late."

"All right, what do you recommend? Bomb Berlin?"

"This isn't a joking matter, but a show of strength should be made. We could start with pressure—and I mean real, determined, clear pressure to stop German rearmament. Without rearmament, which is an open secret in Europe, Hitler has no real leverage. It wouldn't destroy him, but it would be a beginning."

"Have you suggested this?"

"Of course I have—so have one or two others—and as a result I'm considered a troublemaker, a warmonger. There are a lot of tired old men influencing foreign policy in this country, and in France and England too. Many of them are too scared to take a firm stand on anything for fear of another war. Let the League of Nations handle it, they say! And many of our own people say, Europe's not our concern—you've heard them in Congress and read them in editorials—let France and England worry about Europe; we tried and failed in 1917 and to hell with it! And of course this group is supported by the China hands, the Asia-Firsters, who say Japan is the big threat. There are a few who believe that Communism and Fascism will knock each other off, but Stalin won't be strong enough to threaten Hitler for twenty years."

"You're not afraid of Russia?"

"I don't know. The power there is considerable, and there is plenty for the democracies to be concerned about, but anyone who has read *Mein Kampf,* let alone what's being written in Germany now and what intelligence is getting out to us, must see that there is no threat anywhere in the world as serious right now as Hitler. In fact, I'm damn glad that Russia is there."

"What do you mean?" To Bill the turn of the conversation was almost intoxicating.

"Whatever Hitler tries to do in the West—grab Austria or the

Rhineland—I'm convinced his real target is the East, as far as he can go. That's where the raw materials that he needs are, that's where his future lies."

"With all those answers, Webster, it's a wonder you're not Secretary of State." Goad him, Bill thought, and he'll fall into our laps, but be careful. "All right, it sounds logical, but is there any evidence, hard evidence, that Hitler is preparing to move east?"

Webster looked pained. "We can't afford to operate on logic alone, though I'm not claiming my colleagues have an oversupply of it. Of course there's evidence. Hitler's been working up the Sudeten Germans in Czechoslovakia about their heritage. There have been inflammatory statements about the Polish Corridor and Danzig. Nazis are already active in Austria. I'm *sure* Hitler will head east."

"And then what?"

"Let me ask you a question. Do you think Russia can stand by if Hitler goes into Poland? It's inevitable that they'll tangle."

"Wait a minute, Webster, you're going awfully fast. Hitler hasn't a prayer for seizing Czechoslovakia. Austria, maybe, but—"

"All right, Bill, I admit we're guessing, but we're guessing on the basis of unmistakable evidence. That's what my business is. The trouble is—the tragedy is—there aren't enough people in my business with the intelligence or the willingness or the guts to see it. In my opinion it is just this combination of Hitler's audacity and our blindness—and weakness—that could make it all possible."

"But England, France—"

"Yes, I know. Staunch England. France, the most powerful military power in Europe. The Maginot Line, and so on and so on. Listen, Bill, France and England were bled white by the war, and they still haven't recovered. Physically, emotionally, morally, they're dead. I wouldn't count on them. I wouldn't count on anybody."

Webster paused, his grim face reflecting his frustration and disillusionment. Keep it going, Bill thought, keep it going.

"Then Russia's the key?"

Webster rose and walked to the window. With his back to the room he said, "Someday she's going to have to fight for her life against Germany. So will we." He turned, a faint smile on his lips. "That's an odd thought, isn't it? We may be allies."

There it was. Bill took a breath and could feel his heart beating. "Okay, Webster." His voice was surprisingly calm. "If you're right —and I must say you're very convincing—if it's going to come down to Russia and ourselves, then we should start cooperating with Russia now."

Webster snorted. "How, for God's sake, Bill? Do you think we would make a military alliance with the Reds now? And even if we wanted one and they wanted one, who in his right mind would trust them to keep it? I've seen the Communists in operation—they were all over Germany—and I'll say one thing for them: they do things. They were the only effective opposition Hitler had. They give him fits. They've got guts, and they don't play by Marquis of Queensberry rules!" He walked over and picked up his glass. Then he grinned at Bill. "That's why they're so effective."

"Webster, how strongly do you feel about this?"

Webster drank off the rest of his whiskey quickly. "You know how strongly I feel."

"Do you feel strongly enough to take a real chance, to risk everything to do something about Hitler?"

Webster picked up the bottle again, but set it down without pouring. "What are you driving at?"

"Answer my question, Webster."

"What do you mean by risk everything? Career? Life? Virtue?"

"I'm serious, Webster. If you believe that we and Russia are the last hope against Hitler, are you willing to strengthen that hope even at the risk of your career? That's what I'm talking about. Are you willing to help Russia, our eventual ally, now?" There. It was out.

Webster stood stock-still in the center of the room, his eyes looking straight into Bill's. He said slowly, "Go on."

Bill took a deep breath. He could feel the wetness in his armpits

and the trickle of sweat on his forehead. It was too late to turn
back. "Webster," Bill said quietly, "I have something to tell you.
Sit down." Webster hesitated. "For God's sake, Webster, sit down!
What I've got to say isn't easy. I'm about to put our lives—Alice's
and mine—into your hands."

Webster sat down, and Bill could hear Alice open the kitchen
door to hear. He glanced at her. Was it fear he saw in her face or
loathing?

"Alice and I are Communists. We've been so for years."

Webster laughed. "Well, who isn't? My God, you had me worried for a minute. I have an old maid schoolteacher who—"

"Please, Webster, *listen*. We aren't just parlor Communists,
we've been extremely *active* . . . dedicated members of the party.
This is because we feel as you do. Webster, you really know very
little about me. I know I look like the bookish type—fat, thick
glasses and so on—but I've been a laborer on a picket line when
the company goons came to smash heads and get scabs into the
factory to take away our jobs. I've seen men work themselves to
death for slave wages, and I've seen this wonderful system of ours
degrade not only the poor but the rich. When the depression came
and no one—neither business nor the government—tried to do
anything about it, but just kept up their old pretenses about the
American Dream, we knew that we had to do something. We feel
as you do, not only about Fascism in Germany and other countries, but here, in America. You're afraid of Hitler. So are we, but
there are potential Hitlers here too. We also had to do *something,*
just like you. So we became Communists. *But we don't carry party
cards.* Do you understand? The party wouldn't acknowledge us
even if we said we were Communists. You must know what that
means."

Webster stared at Bill, then glanced at Alice for verification.
Her cold, impassive expression was more eloquent than a nod.
This is the first time, Bill thought, that I've ever seen Webster at a
loss for words.

Webster stood up. "There are Communist agents all over Europe," he said slowly, "but I never thought I'd have to come home to meet them." He walked to the window again, then turned to face them. When he spoke, it was with a new bitterness. "You must have enjoyed playing me for a fool. All your talk about security, pumping me for information. I could understand your working this on someone else, but I thought we had become genuine friends. For my part, you were my best friends in Washington. Congratulations on a masterful job."

"Wait a second," Bill broke in. This was worse than he expected. Alice was right, Webster Evers could not be trusted. It had gone wrong, and fat, stupid Justin Blaine had not listened and had blundered into the fire. "If we were playing you for a fool, would I have just put our lives in your hands? Friendship doesn't have a damn thing to do with my job, Webster, though I will tell you I have considered you a good friend from the first night we met, and still do. But it can't interfere with my work. I had to pump you to find out how you felt about things. When I discovered you felt as I do about the biggest threat facing the world today, I leveled with you. You could finish Alice and me now."

"Is that all you've got to say?" Webster's tone was cool, but the bitterness was gone.

"No, it isn't." Bill stood up and began pacing in front of Webster. "We live in a world of lousy decisions. If Russia and the United States are the only two hopes against the Fascist danger, and the United States government will do nothing to cooperate in opposing it, then it's got to be done this way by those few people who have the intelligence to realize it is the only solution."

"What are you suggesting I do?"

"Help us."

"How?"

"You are in the perfect position to do so. We need all the information we can get about German plans, activities, rearmament, and the plans and policies of other countries toward Germany. Without this information the Communist forces fighting Fascism will be operating with one hand tied behind their backs."

Bill stopped pacing and turned to face Webster. There was a long, awkward silence.

"Aren't you afraid I'll report you?" Webster asked finally.

"Yes," Alice said.

"Bill?"

"I don't know what to think. But I don't believe you don't really mean all those things you've been saying—about the Fascist danger, about Russia's key role in stopping it, about the need to be ruthless, about the idiots who work with you."

Webster returned to his chair and sat down heavily. "You're asking me to risk everything, do you know that? Of course you do. You've been risking everything yourselves for some time."

Bill stared hard at Webster and said quietly, "If we succeed, wouldn't it be worth it? For that matter, considering the cause, wouldn't history more than justify it?"

"Look, Bill, I didn't join the State Department to tell its secrets. However you twist the motives, that's what it is. I've come a long way there. I'd say I have an excellent future. Why the hell should I throw it all away—or even jeopardize it?"

"Okay, Webster, forget it. Forget personalities too—our friendship. I agree, this is one hell of a thing to put to you, and I shouldn't have done it. I got carried away with what you said, with your vehemence and ideas, and I agree with you so wholeheartedly I thought you might agree with me, might see the tremendous opportunity to do something really useful, regardless of the risk. But—"

"Wait a minute, Bill, I haven't said no—yet. You can't expect an answer now, this minute, for God's sake! For your information, I did mean what I said, every word of it. But you've hit me with a sledge hammer. I've got to have time to think. And I'm entitled to know a little more before I put my career and possibly even my life on the line."

There was the faintest trace of a smile on Webster's face, Bill noticed. Perhaps there was a chance.

"You can tell me more?" Webster asked.

"It depends. What?"

"Just what am I expected to do? How many people will know—about me? And I would insist on a few conditions. I quit when *I* want to. And no information about any country other than Germany."

"I can't answer any of your questions until you answer one for me."

"Go ahead."

"If you decide no, are you going to report us?"

"No."

"Why?"

"I'm not in the habit of being indiscreet with classified information, nor of ratting on my friends." There was a touch of irony in his voice.

"Not to mention," Alice added acidly, "that you're not in the habit of endangering your career by admitting you are on intimate terms with two Communist agents."

"Stop it, Alice," Bill cut in. He turned to Webster. All right; it was time to let him have it with both barrels. "Alice is right in one respect, Webster. As I said before, there are no such things as friends—or prima donnas—in the party. You take orders; you don't give them. Once you're in, you're in till the party is through with you."

"Then my answer is no."

"Wait a minute, let me finish. You can't dabble at this job any more than you can dabble with Hitler. If you follow instructions and do your job, you'll be left alone. And as for just supplying information on Germany, I'm sure we'd be delighted to settle for that. After all, Hitler is really our common enemy, as you have pointed out. The job calls for total discretion. We cannot function without it, so we are not about to expose ourselves by exposing you. You will have only one contact: me—and of course Alice. You bring your information to us, here. What we do with it is not your concern. You need know no more, or do no more.

"Finally, we demand complete discipline from you. We play for keeps, Webster, but it takes two to play the game—you and us—and each one can hurt the other. I have leveled with you now completely. We are fighting an enormous evil in the only way it can be fought, under the circumstances, and with your help we will win."

Webster stood up and collected his hat. "I don't want to talk any more," he said, "or hear any more. I appreciate your not pulling any punches. You can understand," he smiled ruefully, "that I'm somewhat in a state of shock, and my appetite seems to have disappeared. I'm sorry. I admire your guts—both of you. Beyond this, all I can say is that I'll let you know."

Bill stood in the doorway, watching Webster disappear down the stairs. It was still a question, perhaps, but the danger was almost gone. He stepped back into the apartment, the sound of his wife angrily slamming pots around in the kitchen echoing in his ears, and immediately saw Webster's briefcase half hidden under his chair.

"Alice," he called. "Get the camera. If we work fast, we won't have to wait to see which way Webster will turn."

Chapter Fourteen

1952: Upstate New York

Pilgrim stared at Justin in wonderment, trying to fit the two men—Justin Blaine and Bill Baker—into the same mold. The hard shrewdness of Baker couldn't be part of the makeup of this unassuming, gentle man, he thought, or was that part of the reason for Baker's success? Or, for that matter, was Henry Pilgrim being played upon as Webster Evers had been?

Pilgrim pointed his finger at Justin. "Do you mean to tell me that it was that simple? That you could manipulate a man like Webster Evers so easily? I find it a little hard to believe, Mr. Blaine."

"I can understand that," Justin answered, keeping his gaze leveled at Pilgrim. "And I'm sure you'll find what followed hard to believe too. I assure you, I was surprised as it was happening. But don't sell Evers short. He was caught up in a belief, just as I was, and once a man gets hooked on a faith surprising things can happen to him."

"What did happen next?" Tom Gallagher said.

"We followed through. I was still scared of what Evers might do, but somehow I knew it was going to go the way I wanted. And

282

I didn't have to wait long. He came back to the apartment the same day, as soon as he missed the briefcase. That was part of the surprise—that it took him an hour to remember it. See what I mean by being caught up? By that time we had managed to photograph all the stuff we needed. He walked in and saw the briefcase on the table. He said, 'Thank God it's here. I was afraid I'd lost it.' It was hard to keep a straight face. And then he said that he didn't need to think much longer, but that he still wanted to look into a few things before making his decision. That worried me, so I sprang it on him then and there. I told him about the photographing, and I added that the film was already on its way to the Soviet Embassy."

"Wait a minute, Justin," Gallagher said. "You aren't going to say he believed that!"

"It wasn't that farfetched a thing to tell him, Tom. The film was still in the apartment, but I could have had it on its way to the embassy if I'd wanted. And he believed it. And he hit the ceiling. I was a blackmailer and a louse and—well, it was quite a show he put on for someone supposedly so smooth. But we had him and he knew it, and after he calmed down he settled for it without much trouble. After all, his reasons for joining the apparatus really hadn't changed, and he could appreciate our need for insurance. . . ."

"God *damn!*" Pilgrim shouted, standing up and beginning to pace. "I can't believe it and yet I know it's true. This is great stuff. We're in!"

Watching Pilgrim, Gallagher frowned doubtfully from the wicker chair where he sprawled, his feet propped toward the dying fire. "Hank," he warned, "stay objective. The story is good, but so much will depend on Justin's delivery and ability to stand up under cross examination that it's anything but a cut-and-dried deal." He turned apologetically to Justin. "Don't misunderstand, old friend. I believe you. You're too naïve to lie." Justin smiled thinly. "But the nonespionage facts could easily have been assembled by someone out to damage Evers for some reason of his own. After all, Hank, Evers' activities during those years were no mystery. Many people knew of his comings and goings."

Pilgrim, in no mood for caution, flicked his hand impatiently. "You're wrong, Tom, way off. Evers has denied even *knowing* Blaine. He swears he never met him before. How can he possibly explain away Blaine's intimate knowledge of his daily life?"

Gallagher shook his head skeptically. "Maybe yes and maybe no. People are going to wonder why Justin waited so long. Why, after all these years, he decided to talk. As a matter of fact, why *did* you wait, Justin? Don't you think we ought to know?"

Justin was bent forward over the table, staring at the palms of his hands. "It was a case of mistaken judgment," he said softly. "When they subpoenaed me, I thought—"

"Crap!" Gallagher cut in sharply. "You'll have to do better than that. Do you really expect the public to treat you like a child? After your experience with the network? With your background?"

"What are you trying to do to him?" Pilgrim flared. "What's wrong with you? Are you trying to make him say he's *sorry* for exposing a spy ring that threatened the very existence of this country?"

Gallagher nodded solemnly. "Very impressive, Hank. A beautiful show of righteous indignation. But don't waste it on me. Just remember that the spy ring probably stopped being a threat over a decade ago."

"How the hell do *you* know?" Pilgrim snapped back. "Does the Communist Party send you bulletins telling you who's in and who's out? How was Blaine supposed to know that Evers wasn't still an active agent?"

Justin seemed forgotten by the two men. "I haven't really figured it out yet," he mumbled. "The truth is," he hesitated, "the truth is, I can't say with any conviction why I did do it."

The words were lost as Justin went on with his account. In the next room, behind a carefully closed door, Alice sat at a window, staring out at the blackness. The more she had tried not to listen, to read, to force her mind to wander, the clearer, the more sharply Justin's story had forced entry, until at last, she found herself filling in the gaps, calling forth details, bits of conversation, buried emotions . . . also, finally, things Justin could never have included in his story because he did not know they existed. . . .

1937: Washington, D.C.

Alice had been in the tub less than a minute when the phone rang. She lay back in the soothing warmth and tried to shut out the sound. The extended noon-hour bath had become the high point of her day, the only time she felt at all relaxed, at all free. Four rings. Oh, hell! Justin had left Washington that morning for New York. What if it were some sort of emergency? She got out, dripping, grabbed a towel and reached for the phone.

"I was just about to hang up." Webster Evers' voice was sharp and impatient. "Listen, I'm calling from an outside booth and I haven't much time. I have an important memo that I'm stopping off to let you copy. It's pretty hot. I'll be there in ten minutes."

Alice barely had time to reply before he hung up. She slammed the receiver down. God, how that man irritated her. Everything about him, his officiousness, affected speech, foppish dress, almost feminine handsomeness. She'd argued with Justin about bringing him into the apparatus in the first place, and she still didn't want him in. The information he'd been passing along was of a high caliber, but she mistrusted his conviction about their work and his motives. How could you put faith in a man who did not have the vaguest pretense of belief in the hopes, the real meaning, of the Cause, the good it would finally bring to others? His reasons were all wrong. Alice padded into the bedroom, leaving a trail of wet footprints on the bare wood floor. She rubbed herself dry, trying to avoid the sight of the long, rough scar that ran downward from her navel, but unable to look anywhere else. Two and a half years, she thought, and still this almost morbid fascination. The fingers of one hand explored the high, welted edges of the incision. End as a woman and "X" marked the spot where the dead thing lay. With clothes on, you'd never know, but they'd taken out the works and left you with nothing but a phony clock face and a pair of useless hands. Of course you still had a certain amount of usable equipment, even if it *was* for amusement purposes only. *Great fun. No more worries,* was how the doctor had tried to console her. Of course the doctor had put it far more delicately. "Normal relations might still be enjoyed with certain unmistakable advantages."

Advantages!

Alice flung the damp towel into a corner and stood naked in the middle of the floor. The doctor had been very earnest, very sincere, very *stupid*. How in hell could he even begin to know how you felt inside? She looked down with loathing at what she could see of her body. For fun only. Except that there really wasn't even this. Oh, she pretended all right, went through all the motions, made all the proper sounds—she owed that much to Justin. But it was a performance. And what else did she have to give him?

She was going to cry. In a panic, she reached for her underthings and tried to lose herself in the simple act of dressing, but the tears came anyway. She sat down on the edge of the bed, eyes wide and desolate, and stared wetly at a piece of crumbling plaster on the far wall. At least if she had been left the boy. At least if she had this much, but she had nothing.

It passed, as always, in just a few minutes, and Alice went on dressing. She waited for the inevitable hollow feeling to come and, when it did, welcomed it like an old friend.

Her head was stuck half in, half out of her dress when the doorbell rang. A final yank brought her head through and she stood there, breathing heavily from the exertion. Her hair stood wildly on end, but she made only a few perfunctory passes at it with her hand. She han't bothered with a comb in days.

The bell rasped once more, longer, more angrily this time. Alice straightened her dress. Let the bastard wait. With deliberate slowness she walked toward the door, waited for one final, insistent ring, and then opened it.

Webster's face was, as always, impassive, but his eyes showed pure ice. He nodded coldly and walked in without a word.

"I'm sorry if I kept you waiting," Alice said, not sounding sorry at all. She stared with clear, carefully considered insolence at his impeccable grooming. Not a hair on his head was out of place, not a line of his fashionable suit that did not fall with proper grace. "You *did* say on the phone that you hadn't much time, didn't you?"

Webster refused to be baited. Efficient, business like, he dropped his hat on a chair and took an envelope from an inside pocket. From it he removed a three-page document. "As I said, this is rather important. We've just received new intelligence from Berlin—amazing stuff—and we're reconsidering policy. This contains my recommendations and the new information, and the Secretary has to have it this evening for a high-level discussion at the White House."

"Have you ever been involved with anything that wasn't 'rather important'?"

"What the devil is *that* supposed to mean?" Despite his efforts to mask it, Webster's irritation showed.

She shrugged. "Simply that I think you tend to be overimpressed with your importance in the government."

"Well, judging from the way I was drafted into your service, your husband must have been overimpressed with my importance too. And I haven't heard any complaints from *him* so far." He glanced about the small apartment. "Incidentally, where *is* Bill?" It was Saturday. Bill rarely worked on weekends.

"He's away."

"Away? Away where?"

"You ought to know better than to ask questions like that. Bill's away. That's all you have to know about it." She held out her hand for the folded paper. "Now if you'll just give me that world-shaking document, I'll copy it and you can get back to running the government."

He handed the paper to her, and she went into the bedroom, closing the door behind her and locking it. The snap of the lock angered Webster further. He fit a cigarette into a long holder, lit it and began to pace nervously, glaring at the locked door. *The bitch!* No trust in him yet, and after all he'd given them. He brushed aside the worn excuse of apparatus discipline. He had little patience with it, with *all* the mumbo-jumbo that seemed to clutter up everything you tried to do. He wasn't meant for this cloak-and-dagger nonsense. His irritation with the insultingly locked door grew.

Inside the bedroom, Alice had arranged the document, brought her special camera out of its hiding place and set up the lamp that would throw an intense light on the paper. Remembering that she needed a new roll of film, she quickly got one and slipped it into the camera. She then leaned over the table, focused the lens on the paper and clicked the shutter. She turned to the second page and repeated the process, and then to the third page. Replacing the camera in its hiding place and turning off the lamp, she started back for the door, but stopped as her eyes scanned the first page of the paper. Much of what she read was foreign to her, but other things were clear. German aircraft production had risen sharply over the year; German scientists were conducting research on a new kind of plane, one that flew by means of a propellerless engine, something like a rocket, which could produce tremendous speeds. She also noted Webster's recommendation that the United States press England and France to join her in economic sanctions on critical materials against Germany in the event Hitler made specific moves against Austria or Czechoslovakia. She refolded the document and left the bedroom.

"Tell me," Webster said, "do you really feel it necessary not only to close but to lock the door? Isn't that a bit too melodramatic?"

"Not at all," she said, handing him the document. "You're to know only about the things you're specifically involved with, nothing else. And there wasn't a reason in the world for you to see what goes on in the next room. You know the rules. Or do you consider yourself above discipline?"

"You simply don't trust me."

Alice started edging toward the door, hoping he would get the hint. "That's right," she said, "that's what the rules are all about. We trust only so far, and you're no exception."

They faced each other silently, as if they had reached a level of tension beyond which they dared not go. She picked up his hat and pushed it at him. The brim turned up sharply as it struck his hand.

"Couldn't you have done that gently?" he asked angrily. "What the hell's the *matter* with you?"

She just wanted him to go away. She turned away, hoping he would walk out so she could get back into the tub, so that she could put more away of this awful day.

"I don't know what you're talking about," she said.

"I think you do," he said. "I'm talking about your entire attitude toward me—the sniping, the constant antagonism. Why? It's been going on for months. I don't remember ever having done anything to hurt or insult you or Bill. If I have, I'd like to know about it."

Alice did not answer. With irritation she watched him set down his hat and put a cigarette in a holder and light it.

"Have I?" he insisted at last. "Have I ever said anything?"

"No."

"Then is there something about me personally that bothers you?"

Alice bit back the ready reply to that one. She mustn't get involved, she thought. They had to work with this man. He *was* producing valuable information. Justin would be furious if she alienated him. She dug her heels against the floor and said nothing.

"Then in that case," he went on, mistaking her silence for a negative, "I'd like you to know that I resent the kind of treatment you've been handing me. I resent being treated like an addle-pated child. Despite what you might think, I *am* a person of some responsibility in the government. Since we have to work together, at least treat me with simple civility and respect." The hard line of his mouth eased. "I'm not totally blind. I realize you've been going through a rough period, and you have my sympathy. But I still see no reason for you to take it out on *me*."

Alice felt herself turn cold. The trembling spread to her legs. She wanted to sit down, but didn't trust herself to cross the room to a chair. "*You know what you can do with your goddamned sympathy?*" All good intentions, concern for Justin, the apparatus, the Cause, everything went up in the sudden pyre of anger. She laughed wildly. "Look at what's offering me sympathy. *Just look!*"

Webster frowned, but said nothing.

Alice pointed at him as if at some sort of sideshow freak. "The great sympathizer." Her voice became barely audible. "You asked if there was something about you that bothered me. Would you *really* like me to answer that?"

Webster saw how it was going to be. He nodded slowly.

"All right. Your clothes, the way you dress." Eyes shooting small sparks, she walked slowly about him, taking contemptuous inventory. "It annoys hell out of me. Why can't you dress like a man instead of like a goddamned fairy?" She saw his face flush. Evidently she'd hit a vulnerable area. "Maybe it's the people you run around with in the State Department. The United States Government probably has a hell of a lot more to worry about from fairies in high places than it does from Communists."

Webster ejected the half-smoked remains of his cigarette from the holder and fumbled for another. He was stalling for control. When he felt he could trust his voice, he asked, "What are you trying to say, that I'm a homosexual?"

Alice shrugged with elaborate contempt. "I don't think *anything* about what you are. You're not important enough for me to puzzle over. You and your superior airs, your preening self-importance. I don't give a damn whether you prefer men, women, dogs, cats or monkeys. You asked me what I didn't like about you, so I told you." Her face was rigid, drawn with contained emotion. "I just happen to think men should act and speak like *real* men."

Webster had given up looking for the cigarette. He laughed unpleasantly. "*Real* men?" he said. "You mean like Bill?"

The cool sarcasm was too much. "Yes, like Bill! Who happens to be more of a man than you'll ever dream of being. Now get out of here. If I have to look at you another minute, I'll throw up."

Webster kept smiling because he didn't know what else to do to fight an urge to hit her. He regarded her mockingly. "You know," he said, "for someone as critical of appearances as you seem to be, you're hardly an example of shining femininity yourself. Have you taken a good look in the mirror lately?"

"You son of a bitch," she said softly. Drawn by an old, almost forgotten reflex, one hand flew to the back of her matted hair.

Webster pressed his unexpected advantage. "I don't know what you do to yourself. Don't you care at all about being a woman? You act as though you were ashamed of it."

"Get out of here!" Her voice came out high with anger. "Get out of here you . . . you . . . you fairy bastard!"

"Lovely," he said. "You swear beautifully. It must have been your feminine graciousness that attracted Bill to you."

Alice no longer saw his face. He was only a voice she was trying to shut out but couldn't.

"Or maybe," he pressed on, "it was your exquisite coiffure that swept him off his feet." He studied her hair. "You must have arranged that disaster deliberately. Neglect alone could never have created such a tangled mess." His glance moved searchingly downward, as the attack gathered momentum. Never had he needed so badly to hurt anyone. "And that dress! Where in hell did you find that dress? Not only does it *look* like potato sacking; it *fits* that way too." Carried away by his performance, Webster reached forward to demonstrate the point. "Just look at that." His hand grasped at the overly large, shapeless bodice of the dress. "You can get two other people in there with you." His fingers closed over the rough material. "Look at—"

He never finished the sentence, for Alice leaped back as though he had touched an exposed nerve.

"Listen." He suddenly wanted to explain. He'd had enough of this gut-tearing game. He hadn't wanted to hurt her, but what choice had she given him? "Listen," he began again. Then he looked at her and stopped.

Alice was staring back at him, surprise congealed on her face like an opaque mask. One hand clutched the offended area high on her bosom, where his fingers had brushed, as if it were a new and painful wound. They stood that way, neither of them moving, in astonishment.

Webster began to understand. How could she have so misconstrued? "You don't think that I . . ." He laughed. It was too ridiculous. He'd accidentally touched her breast and now she stood there like a priestess of virtue deflowered. "Oh, come on," he said. "Stop looking so damned horrified. You've been touched before."

"Not by you," she spat. "Never by a fairy bastard like you." She used the offending word like a club now, somehow its earlier effectiveness seemed gone.

"Don't flatter yourself. You're hardly the most seductive sight in town." But her sudden vulnerability was tempting. She was still shaken. He smiled. "All I was trying to do was show you how badly that awful dress fit." He stepped toward her, one hand teasingly extended, as if to repeat the demonstration. "Like this."

"Keep away!" She backed off. Webster followed, enjoying her apprehension. His smile broadened as awareness grew. What he now saw on her face, he thought, might be many things, but it sure as hell wasn't revulsion.

"Keep your goddamned hands *away* from me!"

But Alice had suddenly backed into a footstool. She stumbled, arms flailing as she fought for balance. Webster lunged forward to help. Alice clutched at his jacket and held on, but she tumbled backward, pulling Webster with her. They landed on the floor.

Webster's long hair had drooped forward over his eyes. Tossing it back, he found himself looking into Alice's face directly below his own. She stared dumbly up at him, her eyes weirdly out of focus at that distance. His hair tickled his nose, and he fought back a sneeze.

"Get off me," Alice gasped, breathless beneath his weight.

Webster sneezed. "Pardon me." The apology was as much a reflex as the sneeze. Then, suddenly struck by the ridiculousness of the situation, he began to laugh.

Alice squirmed beneath him. "I said, get off me!" His laughter was the final humiliation, directed at her, at all that she was.

Webster was helpless to stop. The angrier Alice became, the funnier the thing seemed. And he was sublimely comfortable. The sensuous softness beneath him was abstractly erotic. Dreams were often like this—a warm yielding below, a strange, anonymous breath against your face. Despite the attempted movement under him, his body lay absolutely still, unyielding in its enjoyment.

"Get off, damn you!"

Her strangled, furious words intruded. Webster managed to stop laughing, but a teasing smile still lingered. "Why?" His position of physical ascendancy gave him a pleasant feeling of control. In all the months he had known this woman, been subjected to her coarse, angry tongue, this was the first time he had not felt himself in some way on the defensive. "I'm rather comfortable," he said. "Aren't you?"

Alice glared up at him. "Get *off!*" Her voice had softened, even more venomous with loathing. Christ, how she despised him. Never had she felt capable of such hate. She fought back tears of helplessness. Webster's weight full on her made it almost impossible to move, even to breathe. But it was his coldly abusive scorn that did the most damage. She felt a nonentity now, an ugly, sexless cipher. Had she a gun in her hand, she would have put a bullet through his head. She pulled a hand free and went at his eyes. She tore at his face.

"Animal!" Webster found her hand and twisted the wrist back, hurting it. Her other hand was pinned beneath her, but she freed it and scratched him twice more before he caught this one too. "Animal!" He was bleeding. All hint of humor had fled his face.

"Fairy bastard! I'll kill you!"

Webster grasped both her wrists in one hand, then deliberately drew back the other and hit her across the mouth. His hair hung down over his eyes and he was breathing heavily. "Don't call me that again. *Don't ever call me that again.*"

Alice tasted blood but didn't care. She'd gotten to him. "Fairy bastard!"

Webster hit her again, backhanded, the knuckles hurting.

"Fairy bastard!" Let him hit her, knock her senseless. It was the only way he'd stop her.

Webster drew back his hand. He stared at her. It was no use. He could see that much in her eyes. Why did she hate him so? He felt sick with it. He dropped his hand. But if she called him that once more . . . He saw her mouth start to open, the mocking smile. How could he stop her?

"Fai—mmmmm."

His mouth closed over hers, cutting off her words. No sound. He pressed hard with his lips.

Alice squirmed, trying to pull free. Webster's mouth remained, gagging her. She bit his lip and felt him flinch, but he was still there. She rolled her head and shoulders, she tried to move her legs, until breathless, sapped of strength, she closed her eyes and lay still.

Webster relaxed and eased back, but he still held her hands.

Alice opened her eyes. Reddening gashes on Webster's cheeks marked where her nails had ripped. His lower lip was swollen. There was no satisfaction in what she saw. What had she proved? That *his* flesh, too, bled when broken? So what? It made *her* no different. Everything he'd said hurt just as much, was just as true. She was *still* a mess, *still* more a scarecrow than a woman. Worthless. A tear glinted in the corner of her eye.

Webster saw and watched it. Anger drained, he felt only remorse. He had *actually hit her*. How could he have lost control like that? "I'm sorry." There was not enough voice. It came out a whisper. "I'm very sorry." Alice did not say anything. Webster released her hands and slid to one side. He looked at her mouth. His knuckles had split the skin and a trickle of blood oozed.

He groaned softly. "I didn't want . . ." He touched the place with his fingers, tried to wipe it away. But all he did was draw a red smear across her chin. He looked at her eyes, which were moist and dark with despair. "Those things I said—I was angry. I just wanted to hurt you."

Alice turned her face away. "You were right. I *am* a mess. Everything you said. Everything . . ." She wept silently.

"No. That's not true."

She shook her head. "I'm nothing."

"Listen to me." He touched her hair, tried to smooth the hopeless mat into some kind of order. "If you would only try to—" She had turned away again, wasn't even listening to him. He hadn't wanted to do this. "Please . . ." He turned her face so that she looked at him. "You've *got* to believe me." It was suddenly very important. Why couldn't she understand and accept what he was saying? "Any man would want you! Any man," he whispered, and found, with surprise, that he meant it. Despite the clothes, make-up, hair, she was still an attractive woman. His glance touched the length of her body stretched so close, broken of all resistance, all defense. During the struggle, her dress had been pulled far above her knees. He breathed deeply. "Any man," he echoed thickly.

Alice labored to accept. She lay very still, without strength or will for movement. Webster touched her cheek. It was warm. Once more, in silent repentance, he touched her face, Alice said nothing and did not move. He let his hand slide softly to her throat. He sensed now what she wanted, but needed to be sure. There must be no mistake in this.

Knowing himself at the edge of something, he touched the flesh of her thigh. There was a slight shudder, nothing more. No revulsion. No denial. Exultant, certain now that he could have this woman, this once so bitter, once so mocking threat, Webster leaned over and kissed the bruised, suppliant and now unmistakably waiting lips.

He was gone. She had hardly noticed him as he set himself in order—impeccably neat, even after what had happened—and walked out. She was lying on the bed where he had taken her and where a chilling breeze now seemed to move across her naked thighs. There was silence and her own breathing. And there was her knowing that she had become something different, something for which she could not think of a name. No four- or five-letter word would do. It wasn't as simple as that, and it was dirtier than that. What had happened between them had been the final falling away for her. Justin would see it that way, and it would destroy him. He must never know.

Webster must have seen what he was really doing to her—and he didn't care! She wished him dead. She wished him to feel the death he had left within her.

After scrubbing herself in a scaldingly hot tub, she walked into the bedroom. Suddenly, not stopping to ask herself why she was doing it, but sure of the rightness of it, sure of the need to have incriminating evidence against Webster, she went to the hiding place, wound the rest of the new roll of film through the camera and removed it. Quickly she jotted a note sketching the contents of the memorandum, attached the note to the roll with a rubber band, and placed it in another hiding place, one that Justin knew nothing about. That done, she went to the mirror, allowed herself but a glance, and headed again for the clean, white tub.

Chapter Fifteen

1952: Upstate New York

A silence in the living room brought her back to the present. Justin's droning voice had ceased, and he sat leaning forward on his elbows, exhausted, his story concluded. Pilgrim walked to the fire and stared into it, while Gallagher lighted a cigarette.

"It's quite a story," Gallagher said, "quite a story. It may even stick."

"But we need something more," Pilgrim said, staring into the flames. "We can no doubt make a good case for your having known Evers, but I want more. I want proof of his espionage. I want to make your whole story good." He turned to Justin. "What about documentary evidence, Mr. Blaine?"

Justin hesitated. "I hope you're not expecting too much, Mr. Pilgrim. You know, it was part of our work not to keep records."

Pilgrim looked at Gallagher, who was looking quizzically at Blaine. The numb feeling was returning to him. "I am expecting something that will decisively incriminate him," he said. "That's crucial."

Justin pushed himself to his feet and slowly lumbered into the bedroom. "What do you think?" Pilgrim asked Gallagher. Gallagher shrugged.

Justin returned with a small pile of papers and the distorted envelope which contained the roll of film. His face was pale and he did not let his eyes meet Pilgrim's as he gave him the papers. He kept the envelope in his hand. Gallagher moved to a table where Pilgrim set the papers down. Justin sat apart from them as they picked up a clipping, read it and set it down silently. One by one the clippings and notes were picked up, read and set down. Not a word was spoken. When the pile had been gone through, Pilgrim looked up angrily.

"This is worthless," he said. "This means nothing. Notes, newspaper clippings, trash. It doesn't say a thing. For God's sake, Blaine, what the hell do you think these are good for?"

Pilgrim glared at Justin, and Gallagher looked at his old friend with a puzzled expression. Justin stared uncomfortably at his own feet and did not answer.

"What about it, Blaine?" Pilgrim went on. "Don't you see how stupid we'd look going ahead with just this story and nothing to back it up? Look at this." He picked up the clippings about the Razzio murder and Nick's arrest and execution. "What in the name of Christ are *these* all about? This is crazy."

Justin looked up. "I'm sorry. I didn't mean to include those clippings. They must have been mixed in."

"Hell! They're half of what you've got!" Pilgrim said.

"There's something else," Justin said tentatively. He stood up and walked to the table. Out of the envelope he took the film, which was again wrapped in the notepaper. He undid the note and handed it to Pilgrim, while setting the roll on the table.

Pilgrim read the note twice. "You'd better explain this," he said.

"This was one of the secret documents Evers brought to us to transmit to the apparatus. It was drawn up that very day and was available only to Evers, Hull and the Under Secretary. It's about German air strength and recommended changes in American policy. I didn't turn it over to the party. I've kept it all these years."

Pilgrim picked up the tiny object, holding it gingerly by the spool. "Why did you keep it?"

Justin turned in confusion and looked at Alice. "Why? I just thought it—well, that it might come in handy."

"Wait a minute, Justin," Gallagher said. "That doesn't figure. You must have known you would use it someday. Let's keep things candid, right?"

"You shut up," Alice said hotly, walking toward him from the door. "He knows his reasons, and you believe what he tells you."

Justin looked at Gallagher and then at Pilgrim, who was beginning to look skeptical. "It's true, Mr. Pilgrim. Look, those were chaotic times, people did strange things."

"Like keep films of top-secret documents in their closets?" Gallagher asked.

"Mr. Blaine, did you keep this because you planned to expose Webster Evers someday?"

"No!" He was standing in front of Pilgrim now, knowing what Pilgrim was getting at. "No! I can't tell you why I kept it. I can't even tell you that the film's still good, that there's anything on it."

"*What?*" Pilgrim shouted.

"Jesus Christ, Justin," Gallagher said.

Justin spoke quickly, aware of the damage he may have done. "We've got to get it developed to see. It's probably all right, but we should make sure."

"Yes, I suppose we should," Gallagher said snidely.

Pilgrim had sat down, suddenly feeling very tired. His voice when he spoke was almost languid. "About this document that you think you have on the film—is it in Evers' handwriting?"

"No, it's typed," Justin said.

"Then we'll have to rely on his signature as the identification. Well, that will be enough. It *is* signed, isn't it?" he added with sarcasm.

Justin looked at Alice and saw that she couldn't answer.

Pilgrim was on his feet again, his face red with growing anger, "Isn't it *signed?*"

Justin raised his hands slightly in a gesture of helplessness. "I don't know."

Drop it, Pilgrim told himself as he walked to the window. Drop this crazy thing. The fears that had struck him in the car coming up returned. He needn't fear Gallagher now, for Gallagher also would know the problem. Let it go, he thought. Something else, another cause, will turn up later.

Gallagher walked over to him. "We'd better get the roll developed right away."

"Forget it," Pilgrim said quietly. "The memo probably isn't signed. I thought we'd have more to go on. I'm dropping it right here."

Gallagher grabbed his arm and squeezed it. "Don't be crazy. If the roll is good and the memo is signed, you've got all you need. To hell with that other junk. Blaine's story and the memo will do the job."

"If."

Squeezing Pilgrim's arm harder, Gallagher went on more urgently "That's right, but you don't know. Don't chicken out now, Pilgrim. What's the matter with you? We have a bureau in Poughkeepsie where we can get the roll developed without anyone knowing about it. If it turns out bad, you can pull out then."

"It'll be too late."

"Goddamn you, don't panic. What are you made of? If a little thing like this can throw you, what gives you the right to think you could ever go farther than you are now?" Gallagher turned from him in disgust.

Pilgrim stood there, aware that Alice and Justin were looking at him. He did not think about anything, but he said, "Tom says he can get the roll developed on the quiet. We'll take it and see what it contains."

"Like hell you will," Alice said angrily. "That roll doesn't leave this cabin unless we go with you."

Tom stepped between them. "That's all right. Yes, you and Justin had better come too. No one will know where you are. Let's get started." He went to Justin and said very quietly, "Justin, I hope for your sake you've got something good on that film."

2

The tiny room glowed red. Alice and Justin sat on narrow chairs, pressed against a photo-covered wall, while Pilgrim and Gallagher stood beside Charlie Fisher, the International Press photographer who was doing Tom the favor of discreetly developing the film. Only the sound of an air blower and occasional gentle sloshings of liquids broke the silence. Beyond the door was the bureau's news room, in which the night-desk man sat half-awake, made drowsy by the rhythms of a lone teletype machine working this midnight hour. Outside, Poughkeepsie, New York, settled further into its night pace of darkening lights and emptying streets.

The drive to Poughkeepsie had been quiet and brooding. Pilgrim had sat in the front seat beside Gallagher, feeling more and more afraid as he assessed the damage he had done himself by panicking in Gallagher's presence, and as he calculated the further damage if the film turned out to be blank. He was sure now that he had blundered by trusting to Gallagher's discretion. Sometime, to some wrong person, Gallagher would tell about the pursuit of Blaine, about Pilgrim's lapse into overt fear, and—if the film was inconclusive—about Pilgrim's foolish, lone endeavor to defy the committee.

Now, in this violet darkness Justin looked about him at the walls of photographs accumulated over the years through many moods to form a marriage of mundanity, beauty and smut. Women with melon-like breasts leered beside lovely still-life compositions and smiling babies. In one corner, two horses stood caught forever in unconcerned copulation. On another wall, between the Nagasaki mushroom cloud and a dappled composition of shadows, an off-guard expression of stupidity marked the face of the senior Senator of the State of New York.

The three men standing before the table loomed as huge shadows in the dim light, as Charlie moved the film from the developer to the fixative solution and finally to a tray of water. With a gentle motion he rocked each tray back and forth. At last the group broke as the photographer hung the strip of tiny frames from a wire. They dangled there, glistening with moisture, their minuscule images still lost.

Gallagher fished around in a drawer and brought out a magnifying glass.

"Look at number three," Pilgrim said, his voice tense. "That should have the signature."

As Gallagher approached the strip, Justin and Alice rose. The four people gathered around the film. Charlie remained apart.

"Out of the light! I can't see a damn thing," Gallagher said.

Alice and Justin stepped back, but Pilgrim remained, leaning forward anxiously.

Gallagher squinted through the glass.

There was only the sound of the air blower.

"I can't see a damned thing. It's too small. Let's get this into the enlarger, Charlie."

"Just a minute," Pilgrim said, grabbing the glass. "Let me look."

"I'm telling you you can't see anything," Gallagher said.

Pilgrim squinted into the glass. He blinked, shook his head and looked again.

"All right, it's no good. Use the enlarger."

"Shoulda done that in the first place," Charlie said as he unclipped the negatives from the wire and inserted all three frames into the enlarger. Now the group gathered around the large wooden base as Charlie laid a sheet of paper across it. "We'll print later. Let's just see what's here," Charlie said.

A pyramid of light flashed onto the paper, revealing a wild pattern of great fuzzy objects sprawling over a field of stippled white. Carefully Charlie focused the enlarger. Slowly the three frames became more distinct. Slowly, slowly, the fuzz diminished. Lines melded into clearer lines. Carefully Charlie worked and adjusted.

In the other room the teletype rang three bells.

Suddenly it was there.

Clear, distinct, surprisingly elegant, the name of Webster Evers was there, set down in a meticulous, slightly Italianate hand.

"There it is," Gallagher breathed. "There . . . it . . . *is!*"

"That's his writing," Justin said simply.

Pilgrim stared at it. "Wonderful."

Charlie continued to work and the focus became even sharper. Again the room was silent.

Gallagher noticed the date marked at the top of the memorandum—1937—and was aware of a presence in the room, called forth by Justin's account of ideals and betrayal, of deceptions and dangers, of destructive currents cutting at the foundations of national security.

How to explain Evers' place in all this? Or Justin's, for that matter? What bridge of logic could connect humane principles with actions such as this. Evers! Everything in his background should have counseled against such an involvement. *Could* righteous anger and idealism account for it? Gallagher decided not, and remained at a loss for what could have led Evers to such an alien vision of himself. He stepped back from the table thinking, You don't always have to understand something in order to use it. The job will be to prove it happened; let Evers tell us why.

3

During the return drive to the cabin, Pilgrim could not restrain his elation. "We've got him," he said again and again, as his mind raced over the details and possibilities of the confrontation that he could now force into being. Blaine would have to keep to himself, the committee must believe the matter was still closed until the right moment, every detail must be handled right. He looked at the back seat, where Justin and Alice sat silent as before. Justin looked tired and relieved, but on the woman's face was an unmistakable expression of worry and regret.

Tom Gallagher was concentrating on the road ahead.

"What are you thinking about, Tom?" Pilgrim asked. "You look gloomy for a guy about to score a juicy scoop."

"I was just thinking that Evers will say the paper in the film is a forged document. After all, you don't have the original. Who's to say that Justin didn't draw up a document, forge Evers' signature on it, photograph it and then destroy the paper? It would be a pretty good way of explaining the whole thing, and it makes sense."

"You son of a bitch!" Alice exclaimed. "You think Justin would do such a thing?"

"Wait a minute," Pilgrim said, turning back to her and then again to Gallagher. "Are you really serious about this?"

"I'm *not* saying Justin did it, but I *am* saying that Evers could make a good case for it. Just what do you have to prove he didn't?"

Pilgrim sat in silence. Again the gloom of impending failure was settling.

Gallagher eased the car around a close curve and then said, "But what if there were some way of proving the film couldn't have been taken this year? Or even recently? After all, unless Justin knew he was going to be exposed by the committee, why would he want to frame Evers? If we can prove that the film was manufactured in 1937, our case will be a lot better."

"There might still be some holes in it," a now very cautious Pilgrim said.

"Sure there might, but the burden would be on Evers' shoulders. He'd have to be able to explain away an awful lot, and Justin will be able to prove him a liar on the point of their knowing each other. I'll get in touch with the manufacturer. It might just happen that we can date that film—you know, determine when it was manufactured and if that was before Justin would have been expected to forge evidence."

"I don't like the odds," Pilgrim said.

"I think the odds are pretty good. There were a lot of improvements made in film during the war, which means that this film might have been discontinued. You just sit tight until I find out."

"I don't like it," Pilgrim said, "but if anyone is going to call the manufacturer, I'll do it."

They dropped Alice and Justin off at the cabin, watching the couple walk slowly, wearily into what had once been the protection of their hideaway. Just before they said good-bye, Justin had looked squarely into Pilgrim's eyes and said, "This is the second time I've put our lives into someone else's hands. Mr. Pilgrim, we are counting on you." Pilgrim had reflexively stepped back, suddenly afraid of what he saw in Justin's look. At last, he was able only to smile his "sincere" campaign smile and to say, with his sincere campaign tone, "You can rely on me, Mr. Blaine." And he had noticed the flicker of disappointment in Justin's expression.

With Gallagher, Pilgrim drove back to New York where they boarded a plane for Washington. They settled into the soft seats and fastened their safety belts. The plane seemed reassuringly real beside the still lingering presence of the cabin, the darkroom, the car and, above all, the strange 1930's world in which Justin and Alice Blaine had moved. Gratefully, Pilgrim closed his eyes, hoping for sleep.

"It's been a big day, Mr. Congressman," Gallagher said.

Pilgrim opened his eyes and glanced sidelong at Gallagher. "Yes, it has."

"Seeing as how I made this big day possible, I assume I'll have the exclusive inside stuff about your other big days to follow—in advance. Am I right?"

Pilgrim turned in his seat to see Gallagher's face. "I think that can be arranged, along with your clearing with me before you let anything out. Am *I* right?"

"Sure, Hank. After all, if one thing can be arranged, anything can be arranged."

When the lights of Washington appeared, it was Gallagher who was sleeping.

Chapter Sixteen

1952: Washington, D.C.

The press conference had been called for ten A.M. sharp, but when Francine Moore breathlessly reached Representative Pilgrim's office a few minutes past the hour, it hadn't as yet started, and the anteroom was noisy with waiting reporters. Francine found an empty chair beside some bookshelves and settled into it with a sigh. She closed her eyes for a moment, feeling the lids burn. I must get out of this circus, she thought, and get married and have three kids and go to PTA meetings and school concerts and live in a neat house in the country, where it's quiet and you can see a few stars at night and where you can go to sleep at nine o'clock if you feel like it.

"What do you suppose Hank's going announce?" someone said loudly. "His father-in-law's candidacy for President?"

Francine did not laugh with the others. There was little about Henry Pilgrim that she found amusing. She had never liked or trusted him and failed to regard his pronouncements with the same wry tolerance as most of the others in the Washington press corps. She saw in Pilgrim's ambition, looks and charm the force and instruments that might carry him far enough to be dangerous.

The Hearst man said, "Maybe he's going to apologize personally to Webster Evers. Maybe he feels the committee wasn't humble enough."

Francine dug a pad and pencil from her purse, ignoring some glances directed at her at the mention of the Under Secretary's name. She caught a glimpse of herself in the small hand mirror in her purse and frowned in disgust at the deepening shadows about her eyes. She would have to get more sleep, she thought. She was thirty-two years old and it was beginning to show. And less drinking. Bourbon, martinis, have another. The misery in your head made you useless in the morning, and you weren't worth a damn until noon, and by that time you were out to lunch and there would be a martini in your hand again.

She snapped her bag shut with an angry click and stared at the bald head of the reporter in front. One bad night, she thought, and age and disaster threatened on all sides. One evening of Webster's abstracted coolness and all hope turned to ashes. Take hold. *Take hold.* Last night was bad. So what? Why this constant need for reassurance? No one gets inside a man like Webster. He gives you only what he chooses. If you want to keep him, you should have adjusted by now.

She had, in fact, thought she had.

Then there had been that troubled moment when he had called her because he needed her, and she had seen, if only briefly, how it might be. So that now she was back with the futile demanding, for once the threat had passed, once the committee had retreated, the door had been shut again as tightly as before. She was still very much on the outside.

Most of the newsmen were standing or leaning against tables and straight wooden chairs. Reporters, Francine noted, always hated to sit down, as though fearful of losing mobility. It seemed to be an occupational peculiarity, like the heavy, horn-rimmed glasses so many of them wore in the season's intellectual style. She wondered if next year would mark a return to normal sight.

A door at the far end of the room opened and Henry Pilgrim made a brisk entrance followed by his secretary. Pilgrim took his place behind a polished desk and, nervously fingering some mimeographed pages, stood waiting for the room to quiet. The hum of conversation died.

Pilgrim bent and spoke softly to his secretary, a dark, pinch-faced woman, and then he straightened and said, "Ladies"—indicating Francine and another woman reporter at the opposite end of the room—"and gentlemen." His face became solemn. "I've called you here this morning because I have something of importance to report to the American people." He paused and his eyes scanned the assembled reporters with studied deliberation. "I recently spent the better part of a day with Justin Blaine. I cannot reveal the meeting place, because Blaine is trying to get away from the public eye at the moment." Pilgrim squinted at one of his mimeographed pages. "This statement will, I believe, come as a surprise, following, as it does, the statement made only two weeks ago by the committee of which I am a member. Although I did not agree with the decision of the committee, I did not feel at the time that I had sufficient evidence to make a statement of my own. I had argued my point of view when the committee was in closed session. Now I do have a statement to make."

He's nervous, Francine thought. The discovery was pleasant. Suddenly she noticed Tom Gallagher sitting in a corner, serious, relaxed and the only one among the newsmen taking no notes.

Pilgrim went on reading. "During my meeting a few days ago with Justin Blaine and his wife, I discovered important evidence which I believe will throw an entirely new light on the Blaine-Evers controversy. I have heard point after point of detailed and persuasive evidence from the lips of Justin Blaine, evidence which has convinced me, beyond any remaining doubt, that he has been speaking the truth."

Pilgrim paused once more and the room was quiet, except for the sounds of the photographers working.

Beneath her anger, Francine felt her doubts stir anew. What if Pilgrim weren't lying?

"The results of this meeting," Pilgrim declared, "are on file in this office and are available at any time to the chairman of the

Subversive Activities Committee, the President of the United States, the Federal Bureau of Investigation and any other qualified person in the government who wants to see them." His voice became softer, almost apologetic. "I realize that what I'm doing as a junior member of the committee is irregular, but I'm afraid I have no other choice under the circumstances."

Francine had stopped writing halfway through the statement. It was taking all of her effort to sit quietly in her chair.

"Is that all?" the bald man in front of her asked. "Is that your complete statement?"

"Yes," said Pilgrim. "It is."

The statement had clearly made a strong impact on Pilgrim's audience. The atmosphere in the room had changed from one of easy, almost condescending good humor to that of a charged and carefully attentive silence.

"What do you plan to do about it?" the Scripps-Howard representative asked.

Pilgrim shrugged. "That's for the public to decide." His initial nervousness appeared to have left him as he gauged the effect of his words. "The major importance of my job, I feel, is to keep bringing any information I may have to the country's attention. Since I'm unable to move the committee to further action myself, the public must do it for me. A public clamor for action will not be ignored." He smiled.

Francine was aware that some of those in the room were looking at her, but she looked only at Henry Pilgrim. I must keep my mouth shut, she told herself, I must sit here like everyone else and, even when they ask questions, I must keep my mouth shut. They'll get the information. For Webster's sake, *I must keep my mouth shut*. But as the questions were asked she knew she could not. Behind the questions was the assumption that Blaine and Pilgrim were telling the truth. No one was challenging Blaine's word. And each answer that Pilgrim gave was an added point for the press and the public and the committee to use against Webster. She stood up.

"I hope you'll pardon me, Congressman, if I ask you to repeat some of the points in your statement. There are a few things that puzzle me."

Pilgrim smiled condescendingly. "And what are they, Miss Moore?"

"Well," she said slowly, "you claimed that you argued your point when the committee was in executive session. Is that correct?"

"That's correct."

"Well, didn't anyone suggest," she went on evenly, "that you get hold of Justin Blaine and talk with him? Do you mean to say that this important and high-level decision to delay the investigation was made without interviewing Blaine and finding out in detail about any evidence he might have?"

Pilgrim's smile went away. "I didn't say that. I'm afraid you misunderstood what I was saying. What I—"

"Do you mean to say," Francine said more loudly, breaking in over his voice, "that a responsible group of men, who represent hundreds of thousands of voters in the United States, would meet secretly in a room and irresponsibly decide to drop an investigation such as this?"

Feeling her hands tremble, she gripped the back of the chair in front of her.

"If Webster Evers is what that man says he is," she went on, her voice thickening, "he should be put to every test. And do *mature* men independently call press conferences whenever something new comes up, especially if the development affects the work of an entire committee of the Congress? Do they broadcast unproven and damaging opinions, as you are doing? Is this the—"

"Hold on a minute, Miss Moore," Pilgrim said, flushing but trying to sound amused, "I haven't created the evidence. Justin Blaine has stated that—"

"Justin Blaine has stated! But Justin Blaine is a self-confessed spy, a liar and Communist. How can you believe the word of such a man, who may even be a psychopath—"

"Miss Moore—" Pilgrim's voice was peremptory—"are you

asking questions or making a speech? You seem to be making some accusations yourself. As I said, this is not an easy thing for me to do, for I know my position in the committee—"

"I just want to—"

"Please, Miss Moore, I'd like to answer what I think is your question. Justin Blaine has not been proved a liar, and there is no reason why a man would *lyingly* confess that he was a spy. I am not trying to convict Mr. Evers, I am only trying to resume the—"

"But you *are* convicting him!" Francine's voice wavered. Someone touched her arm and whispered something she did not hear. Some reporters discreetly tried to motion her down; others merely looked embarrassed.

Pilgrim looked at the reporters as if in despair. "I repeat. I am not convicting Mr. Evers, nor would I want to. I don't consider myself a judge, but, as a servant not only of my immediate Congressional constituents but of the nation as well, I do consider myself obligated to pursue the truth in this matter. Now does *that* answer your question?"

Francine looked helplessly about the room, realizing with horror that she was crying. "I . . ." Her voice died away as she sat down. "I was just trying to make a point."

She sat staring at her hands. Never had a reporter so made a spectacle of himself at a press conference. There were a few more questions, obviously offered to cushion the incident in the conference ritual. At last Pilgrim said, "If there are no further questions, that will be all. My secretary will provide copies of my statement as you leave." And then he left the room.

Francine heard the scraping of chairs as the newsmen rushed for telephones. She continued to sit until the last of them had gone. Pilgrim's secretary came over. "Would you like a copy of the Congressman's statement, Miss Moore?"

Francine took the paper automatically, wondering now just how much of what was written there was true. But true or not, Pilgrim had planned his attack well. With the public clamor this news would raise, the committee would have no choice but to press the case further. She stared reproachfully at the mimeographed paper. Everything, she thought, everything always turned out to be a lot dirtier than you expected.

She left the room, feeling the impersonal gaze of Pilgrim's secretary against her back. Starting slowly along the corridor, she quickened her steps as she neared the street. She would have to call Webster right away; he would need her. My God, she thought, now he *would* need her.

2

Tom Gallagher strained to adjust his eyes to the half-light. The cocktail lounge had more gloom than atmosphere, with most of the light coming from behind the bar where rows of bottles faced their doubles through a huge mirror. The place was silent and cool and empty, like the night outside.

Morrie Kantrowitz was seated at the far end of the bar, brooding over a drink. He looked very young and very small sitting hunched on his stool, not at all formidable. But Gallagher's long acquaintance with him sustained a far different impression, for in this city of no-holds-barred toughness, Kantrowitz's reputation as a hard, tireless skirmisher was second to none. And if he was perhaps a little too glib, too sharp-tongued and overly ambitious for the tastes of Washington's more conservative elements, even those people did not hesitate to make full use of his talents.

He turned and saw Gallagher. "You're late," he snapped, glancing at his watch. "You're seventeen minutes late."

Gallagher ignored him and ordered a drink.

Kantrowitz said, "When I make an appointment for eight o'clock, I'm there at eight o'clock."

"Good for you," Gallagher said easily, then to the barman, "Make it a double. I expect to be working uphill tonight."

"You call me up after a murderous day," Kantrowitz complained, "drag me out of the office when I've got a thousand more important things to do, and you then keep me hanging around like a bar fly waiting for you."

Gallagher tossed off a handful of salted peanuts. "Stop worrying so damned much about your precious time and reputation. There hasn't been an acceptable Jewish alcoholic around for two thousand years." He peered consideringly at the dark-haired lawyer. "That's probably the basic cause of anti-Semitism. You people work too damned much and drink too little. It makes us poor *goyem* feel guilty and inferior. So we throw stones. It's our only weapon. We'd never be able to compete otherwise."

"Brilliant," Kantrowitz said flatly. He glanced again at his watch. It was an automatic gesture. "If that's all you brought me down here to say, I think I'll go back to my office."

The barman brought a double Scotch on the rocks and Gallagher lifted the glass, regarding it tenderly. "Take it easy," he said, smiling in the insolent, good-natured way that he knew disarmed people into thinking him refreshingly frank. "You're not doing me any favors. If you didn't want to be here, you wouldn't be here. You came because you want something out of me, just as I want something out of you."

Kantrowitz took a long sip of his drink. "If you think you're going to get the committee's position on Pilgrim's press conference this morning—to which none of us was invited—you can go whistle in the wind."

"Don't give me that," Gallagher snorted. "The committee *has* no position. You're hoping to get enough out of me to *give* you a position."

Kantrowitz did not say anything. Two men came in laughing and talking loudly and Gallagher said, "Let's move."

They picked up their drinks and carried them to a corner table behind a pillar.

"You know you're right," Kantrowitz said slowly.

"About what?"

"About what you just said regarding the committee. We have no position." Kantrowitz stared darkly across the stained wood table.

"And I'll tell you something else. At this moment I'd be the wrong man to state that position if we had one."

"What do you mean?" Gallagher said guardedly, automatically suspicious of any statement he had not anticipated, especially with a man as tricky as Kantrowitz.

"I mean," Kantrowitz said, "that it's always been a point of pride with me to disavow myself personally from the work I do." He smiled ruefully. "I know this may be difficult for you and some of your buddies to believe, but it happens to be so. Up to this point I haven't felt it was worth my while to stop and apologize and make it clear to you guys that every time I begin to question a witness, it isn't necessarily *me* talking. It's the counsel for the committee."

Kantrowitz paused. "The counsel for the committee," he repeated bleakly. He took a drink of his whiskey, making a sour face as it went down. "Anyway," he said belligerently, "why the hell should I apologize? I've come farther in the past three years in this job than I would have in fifteen years doing something else. So long as you people want to keep me on the front pages of the papers, I'm delighted. Absolutely delighted. It couldn't be better for me *or* my career."

He waited for Gallagher to attack, but the newsman remained silent, so Kantrowitz went on, his voice low. "But to be frank," he said, "this time I'm rocked. I *do* want to find out what you know. The word is out that you were the one who *took* Pilgrim to Blaine in the first place." He looked hard at Gallagher. "What's going on with you and Pilgrim? Has he hired you as his personal press relations man, or what?"

"I'm not for hire," Gallagher said. "And never mind about Pilgrim and me. That doesn't concern you. What concerns you is what actual evidence Justin Blaine has. Isn't that it?"

Kantrowitz frowned. "You know damned well it is. But you're not one to hand out presents. What are you going to want from me in return?"

"Nothing terrible," Gallagher said easily. "As a matter of fact, practically nothing at all."

"I'll bet."

Gallagher smiled. "A man as suspicious as you, Morrie, must have had an extremely troubled childhood."

"We'll discuss my childhood some other time," Kantrowitz said impatiently. "Right now, all I want to know is what you're asking for your lousy information."

Gallagher finished his drink and signaled a waitress for another round. "Well," he said, "I see an opportunity for myself here, just like the one you found for yourself. This case is going to shake the country to the roots before it's through, and I want to ride on top of it all the way."

"So?"

"So when your committee does decide on its position, I want to be the first to know. I also want to be the first to know about any future decisions on the case."

Kantrowitz seemed pleasantly surprised. "That's all?"

"What did you expect?" Gallagher said flatly. "The classic pound of flesh?"

"It would have been more in character."

"Thanks," Gallagher grunted. "Well? Do you accept my terms?"

Kantrowitz nodded slowly. "I accept."

The waitress brought the fresh drinks and Gallagher looked at Kantrowitz. "Did my ears deceive me," he said, "or were you launching yourself into a bit of honest soul-searching a few minutes ago?"

The lawyer shrugged. "Call it soul-searching if you wish," he said. "But I do admire Webster Evers. I admire anyone, I suppose, who doesn't at least *appear* to have the same base motives as I have." He gazed down reflectively, accusingly, at the yellow-gold liquid in his glass, as though the liquor were a symbol of his frailty. "I suppose, if you came right down to it, I don't want my idea of him shattered, because when they shatter men like Webster Evers, something in each one of us is also smashed." He glanced quizzically at Gallagher. "Do you have any idea at all of what I'm trying to say?"

Gallagher nodded, not wanting to interrupt. Morrie Kantrowitz was not given to random comment. "This too may be hard for you to believe," Kantrowitz said, "but I wasn't especially delighted when Blaine's testimony broke. As counsel for the committee I was, of course, pleased. I was happy to see the committee hit the headlines. Wouldn't I be crazy if I weren't? Listen . . ." He leaned forward across the small, whiskey-stained table, his voice gentle, confiding. "My father was an immigrant pants cutter in a Seventh Avenue sweatshop. His little boy, Morrie, has come a long way, against a lot of competition, and it wasn't easy. But I'm a human being. I *want* to see a man around who can counterbalance some of the idiots and opportunists we have in the government. I wasn't part of the decision to drop the investigation, but I wholeheartedly approved. I was glad, regardless of their reasons. I didn't like to see a man like Webster Evers damaged, perhaps permanently, by the testimony of a man who *might* even be insane. And remember that we've got a lot of opposition to face. You know why the President called that quick press conference today, just so he could call the whole thing a politically inspired smoke screen. He was mad as a hornet."

Gallagher twisted his glass in slow circles on the table. "Justin Blaine," he said quietly, "is not insane. And the President is going to regret this statement when friend Evers turns out to be what Blaine says he is."

Kantrowitz sagged back in his chair with the weariness of a man about to give up a cherished dream. "All right," he sighed. "You can tell me now. What *has* Pilgrim got?"

"Enough. I think both Pilgrim and I came away from Blaine's place with the same general impression. We were convinced, without any remaining doubt, that Blaine and Evers did know one another."

"Facts," Kantrowitz said sharply. "I want to hear the facts that convinced you."

"Well, for one thing," Gallagher said, "I've been a friend of Blaine's for more than twenty years and I've never known the man to lie. You can take that for what it's worth, this committee thing notwithstanding. Also, he reeled off incident after incident, describing a thousand details of Evers' life—where he lived, people he knew, things he was interested in and did. He was even able to go into the fine points of an ancient Greek coin Evers bought in 1935. I don't see how he could possibly have learned all these things if—"

"All right, all right," Kantrowitz cut in impatiently. "So he knew him, or knew people who knew him. But show me some solid evidence to make a charge of treason stick."

The juke box broke into a mournful rendition of "Good Night, Irene." Gallagher looked at him. "Pilgrim has that too, a film of a top-secret signed memorandum from Evers to the Secretary of State."

"It could be a forgery," Kantrowitz said. "Who can be sure it's not a forgery?"

"That's already been checked," Gallagher replied, "and it's very unlikely." He remembered the elation in Pilgrim's voice when he had phoned with news that the manufacturer made the film with that emulsion number in the summer of 1937. This was over two years before Blaine left the party, and it put the burden of proof on Evers to come up with a motive to explain why Blaine would have implicated him. Gallagher smiled over the rim of his glass. "My, you *are* impressed with our Mr. Evers, aren't you?"

Kantrowitz shook his head. "That's got nothing to do with my reaction. I'm looking at this coldly now. An insane man can pull some pretty cute tricks." He lit a cigarette and squinted narrowly through the smoke, his dark, intelligent face frowning in thought. "I'm sold that they knew one another. I'm even sold that Evers is deliberately lying, for some reason, about not knowing Blaine. But that's all I'm sold on. There's too much there that we don't know, that doesn't make sense. A big piece is missing from this puzzle. I don't know what. It could be that Blaine is nursing a grudge. He may hate Evers, for some reason, enough even to destroy Evers and himself. Maybe they even once had a thing for one another."

Gallagher dimly heard the juke box lament, "sometimes I take a great nooo-shunn to jump in the river and drow-unnn." The lawyer's reaction to the evidence had been pretty much as he had expected. But with someone as clever and complex as Kantrowitz, it was impossible to be sure of anything.

Kantrowitz was watching him curiously. "Well?" he said. "What do *you* think?"

"I think you've got to make them confront one another," Gallagher said with finality. "What other choice do you have? A face-to-face meeting will bring it all out. I don't see any other way to handle it."

Chapter Seventeen

1952: Washington, D.C.

A drizzle was falling and the air had grown colder as Webster started around the dark, tree-lined block for the third time. He walked slowly, his hands deep in his coat pockets, his eyes holding to the glistening pavement. When he reached the converted town house where Francine Moore lived, he looked up to the top floor and saw lights still on in her apartment. She had probably been expecting him for the past six hours, he thought, and here he was, circling the house, trying to put off for a few additional moments what could no longer be put off.

At the entrance he glanced at his watch. It was almost midnight. One more cigarette, he told himself, just one more and he'd go up and get it over with. He lit up, cupping the flame against the wind. She didn't deserve this deviousness, he thought. The least he should have offered her was the truth. He had wanted to, had indeed intended to tell her a dozen times since the mess had broken, but somehow it was always the same. Somehow, the words were twisted by a perverse alchemy of emotion that had always fiendishly transformed what he truly felt into the false gibberish behind which he had been hiding for over thirty years, so that he would say nothing instead.

Thirty years. Ending in a crowded committee room with carefully documented evidence nailing down the few final, and perhaps least important, lies. Ending in disgrace on five million television screens, with righteous legislators clucking in happy horror at this infamy. Investigation would finally brand him a liar and a betrayer of trust, but this did not hit him nearly so hard as he had expected. After nearly a lifetime of lies, this ultimate revelation now came almost as a relief.

The wind bit at his face and he leaned into the narrow shelter of the building entrance. He took brief, miserly puffs at the cigarette, trying to preserve it for another few seconds. In his mind, the familiar apartment on the fourth floor and the woman in it began to seem remote and impossible to reach. Word of Francine's outburst at the press conference had reached him late that afternoon, and he had felt sick inside ever since. She was willing to expose, perhaps even destroy, herself for him, while he, in his usual gallant fashion, allowed her to stake everything on a lie. Well, he thought numbly, at least he would be able to keep her from getting in any deeper. It was too little and too late, but at least he would be able to give her that much now. He flicked away the remains of his cigarette, pushed open the door leading to the small, dimly lighted vestibule and climbed the steps.

At Francine's door, he stood waiting a moment to catch his breath after the four-story climb. He refused to have her see him panting. Even in this he had to maintain the illusion of perfection. When he knocked, there was no answer. He knocked again. This time Francine's voice called from a long way off. "Yes?"

"It's Webster," he said.

"Oh, Christ! Wait a minute."

There was a sound of frantic activity, then the door opened. Francine stood struggling to belt on a flannel robe with one hand, while the other stabbed a Kleenex at her partially cold-creamed face. She had washed her hair earlier and a towel was still wrapped, turban fashion, about her head.

"You're lovely." He bent to kiss her, but she stepped angrily back and away, and he saw, with shock, her swollen lids and the dark places beneath her eyes.

Francine regarded him coldly. "I hadn't expected you any more." She went on trying to wipe the cold cream from her face, but only succeeded in smearing lipstick onto her chin, creating a clownlike impression.

Webster closed the door behind him, took off his coat and dropped it onto a chair. "With just a little more effort," he said, gravely studying her, "there's no telling what you might do with yourself." Even as he was saying it, he knew painfully that it was the worst possible thing at this time.

Francine glared at him for a moment, then turned away and picked up a half-smoked cigarette from a crowded ashtray. "I've been trying to reach you since eleven o'clock this morning," she said. "I must have made fifty calls." She started to work with the Kleenex once more, gave up in disgust and crumpled the tissue into a ball. "Do you have any idea what it's like to make fifty calls to someone and not get through?"

"Secret conferences," Webster said. "My boss is very big on secret conferences. He thinks they lend stature and tone to the Department." At the liquor cabinet he poured himself half a tumbler of bourbon. "We were all over town today and the rules are very explicit on incoming calls."

"What about outgoing calls?" she said harshly. "Do the rules cover those too?" She was in constant motion about the room, as though utterly unable to contain herself. "It's almost midnight. Considering what happened this morning, don't you think you might have made at least *one* attempt in the past twelve hours to call me?"

Webster sipped his bourbon. He had not wanted to talk with her on the phone. It was bad enough being here with her. It would have been impossible on the phone. He watched her move about the room, among the candy-striped drapes at the tall windows and the abstract paintings and the wallful of books. There were many ashtrays in the room, with cigarette butts in all of them. A half-filled pink medicine bottle stood ominously on an end table. Webster looked at these things, then at Francine's eyes and saw with bitter clarity the kind of day she'd had. Exactly, he thought. Instead of offering her what she needed and deserved—comfort, gratitude, reassurance, apology—he offered wry humor and misplaced urbanity. Forty-six years old, and still incapable of behaving like a human being.

Webster watched in silence from his chair, as Francine began once more to remove the cold cream and lipstick from her face. He sensed the emotion in her movements and knew that at any moment she might lose control. If he was going to do anything to prevent it, he had to do it now. Yet he continued to sit there nursing his drink, gripped by a not unpleasant feeling of lassitude. He sighed almost euphorically and let his gaze wander about the warm living room, into the darkened, familiar bedroom and into the bathroom with its shining pink tile.

Francine turned abruptly. Her hands were clenched at her sides and her lips drawn into a thin, tight line. "You egocentric louse!" she said. "You miserable, egocentric louse!"

Even expecting it, Webster was still surprised at the violence in her voice.

Shaking her head in bitter wonder, she said, "You haven't any idea of how to be decent to a woman, do you?"

Webster replied with a wan smile, knowing that what she said was true, but aware, too, that the smile had always enabled him to get away with it.

"Well?" she said, speaking more calmly. "What about it? How are you going to help yourself get out of this mess?"

Webster went over to the liquor cabinet and carefully poured himself another drink. He still felt tight and cold inside.

"Did you hear me?" Francine said.

"I heard you." Webster lifted his drink to the light and absorbedly squinted through it. "I don't need any help."

"Are you crazy? You know what's going on out there. You've seen the papers. The committee obviously has something solid on you. Are you going to tell me what it is?"

Well, there it was, Webster thought, the perfect opening. She had given him the chance, finally and without further hedging, to recite his confession. He looked at her, tall and slender in the ankle-length robe, the soft flannel clinging to her in subtle lines. He turned toward her and opened his mouth to speak, but no sound came out. He licked his lips, suddenly finding all knowledge of what he was going to say gone, as if he were an actor on opening night, abruptly struck dumb by the enormity of what he was at last to do.

"Are you going to tell me," Francine said again, frowning as she waited, "or have you conveniently lost the power of speech?"

Webster flushed. With welcome relief, he felt a sense of outrage spread through him. This, at least, was something he knew how to handle.

"There's nothing to tell," he said with genuine anger, weirdly capable, at that instant, of feeling falsely accused. "How many times do you want me to repeat it? Are you so naïve that you swallow whole everything that's handed out in a stinking press release?" He strode briskly across the room and turned, letting the fury build, yet watching his own performance with a mixture of amazement and disgust. My God, what sort of sickness was this? "Isn't it enough," he heard himself bitterly rush on, "that I have to put up with suspicious, snide looks at the Department, without coming here now and getting it from you?"

Francine poured herself a drink and shuddered as she drank it. She breathed deeply and her expression, as she looked at Webster, was one of confusion and exasperation. "Don't you realize," she said, "that you've got to start building a case for yourself? You can't just keep saying everything's a lie. You've got an entire nation to convince." She shook her head. "Damn it! You've got to convince *me!*"

"I *won't* convince you. I won't convince anybody." That was it, Webster thought, that was exactly right—lofty and stubborn. Place yourself above the battle and they can't touch you. Now we climb up on our dignity and refuse even to discuss it. "If you don't mind," he said, "isn't there something else we could talk about?"

Francine made a small, helpless gesture with her hand, put down her glass and went to him. "Oh, Webster!" Her head pressed against his chest and her arms circled him tightly. "What kind of animal is it that doesn't even know when it needs help? I love you. I want to help you. If you're in trouble, share it with me."

Webster stood breathing in the fresh aroma of her hair, but did not allow his arms to hold her. "I can't seem to make it clear to you," he said, "that I'm not in trouble." The things, he thought in wonder, that it was possible for a man to say.

Francine stepped back from him. "You're like a silly, stubborn child. I can't understand you at all. You refuse even to admit you need help. Well, I'm going to help you anyway. I'm going to *force* my help on you, and this is what I'm going to do. First, I'm going to resign my job. I'll need all the time there is in the day and I don't want any other allegiance or obligations. I want to be able to concentrate all my thought and effort exclusively on you."

"You can't do that," Webster said in alarm. "You can't just walk out on your job."

"Of course I can. I can get along well enough on my alimony. And after the show I put on this morning at Pilgrim's picnic, they'll probably be relieved to be rid of me." There was excitement and anticipation in her voice as she went on. "Then I'm going to start reaching into Blaine's background. I'm going to dig up everything I can find. There's *got* to be a reason for what he's doing to you. Maybe he has an imagined grudge. Maybe he's mistaken you for someone else. Maybe he—"

"That's not for you to do," Webster tried weakly. "There are investigating agencies that . . ." His voice died as he saw that she wasn't even paying attention to him, but was continuing with her plans. He walked to the window and looked out at the dark, empty street. Listen to her, he thought, listen to her and learn what it means to give of yourself, you tongue-tied ass.

"—was once in some kind of mental institution," Francine hurried on, looking somewhere over Webster's head. "He could very well be some kind of schizophrenic. That happens, you know.

With this kind of disorder, a man could suffer from a delusion, yet conduct himself with intelligence and control in other activities."

Webster watched a clot of rain form on the outside of the window and break into tiny rivulets. He had an unpleasant feeling that his own symptoms were being described.

"I'll operate out of my apartment," Francine was saying. "I have lots of friends. Most of the papers are on your side anyway. I'll see that public opinion isn't shaped by lice like Pilgrim and Gallagher. We'll hold our own press conferences. We'll—"

"Stop it," he whispered thickly. "There's no point to it. Stop it."

"—get sworn affidavits," Francine continued with fervor, "from people high in government, people with unimpeachable reputations who know you and can testify to—"

"Everything Blaine said is true," Webster murmured numbly. "I've been a spy. Everything he said is true."

"—your integrity, patriotism and honor," Francine soared on. "By the time we're through with Justin Blaine he'll—"

"Stop it!" Webster shouted, turning from the window, his face twisted. "For God's sake, stop it and listen to me. I'm trying to tell you something!"

Francine broke off in mid-sentence, her eyes puzzled at the violence of his outburst.

Webster was sweating, and when he swallowed, it was as if a rock were jammed in his throat. Not again, he thought, you're not getting away with it again. For once in your life, act like a man. "Everything Blaine said is true."

"What?" she said dumbly.

Webster nodded. "True," he said. "I *was* an agent for the Communist party."

He watched her face, seeing in awful detail what was happening to her, but determined not to spare himself by looking away. If he was going to have to start making back payments, he might as well begin here and now with the biggest of them. "I knew Blaine under another name—William Baker. We were close friends. We were also agents for the Soviet Union." He grimaced. "I had the notion that I could fight Fascism more effectively that way. Blaine quit right after the Hitler-Stalin Pact was signed in August of 1939. I hung on for a while longer out of pure stubbornness—admitting mistakes has never been easy for me—but even that was a token gesture. Once Blaine quit I was never contacted by the apparatus again. I was soon promoted and began to look forward to big things in the State Department, and I wasn't going to be so idiotic as to jeopardize something like that."

Webster swallowed once more, finding it easier this time. "Well, now you have it all. Neat and concise."

Francine shook her head slightly, as if to clear it, her face appearing collapsed and passionless. Then, moving quickly, as though not wanting to give herself time to think about it and perhaps reconsider, she got his coat from the chair and handed it to him. "Get out," she said quietly.

Webster held his coat. "Just like that?"

"Just like that."

He tried the wan, rueful smile, but it failed. "Do you really find it so obnoxious," he said, "being in the same room with an ex-spy?"

"Ex-spy?" Francine shook her head wearily. "You never understand, do you?"

They stood there, not quite looking at each other, suddenly with nothing more to say.

"Well," Webster said, vaguely conscious that he was still trying the smile and still failing, "good-bye, Fran."

She did not say anything, and he turned and went out the door, being careful to close it quietly behind him. He worked into his coat and listened for some movement through the thin partition. Hearing nothing, he started slowly down the stairs, feeling weak and empty. The second drink seemed to have gone to his head, because there was also a slight dizziness. The first payment, he thought, and where was he? And this from someone professing love and devotion not ten minutes before. Well, he'd get the rest of it over tomorrow, fast and clean. There was no point in waiting for a subpoena. He'd call the committee in the morning and give them the whole story. This is Webster Evers, he would say, I'm forty-five years old and I'm tired. My life has been empty, futile and one long lie, and I want to pay for it now though it never gave me joy or satisfaction. In your eyes I have committed a serious crime, though that was never really my intention. If I deserve to be punished for anything at all, it should be for the far more terrible sins of self-pity and despair. Of these, I am guilty.

Webster held to the banister with the excessive caution of the very old or the very abstracted. He came out into the cold drizzle, blinking his eyes, turned right along the empty street and then, realizing he would never find a taxi in that direction, started back the way he'd come.

He walked slowly through the darkness, feeling the dizziness begin to wear off and not wanting it to. Just down the street he saw a bar and headed for it, wanting semidarkness and the comforts of a drink.

He ordered a double brandy, downed it quickly and ordered another. Settled into the corner of the booth, he sipped the second drink, feeling for the first time in days a draining of the tension within him.

Tomorrow he would confess and that would simplify things. At last he would be able to strip off the mask. And gone, too, would be Francine and being needed by her. No one would need him, not Francine, not his colleagues, not his country. Any more than, when the chips were down, his country had needed Arthur.

1923: En Route to Harrisburg, Pa.

Is it the same train? Webster wondered, as he sat stiffly beside the window, feeling encased in his gray uniform, watching the tree-crowded Pennsylvania countryside flow past. It seemed the same—the old seats, the muted, aged colors, the swaying of the car—except for the emptiness around him. Is it the same car in which he had tried to swallow that terrible ham sandwich and had tried somehow to inject himself into the crowded, distant world of his brother? He remembered the panic of that day, the violence that was hidden behind small talk and careful considerations until the moment of the spider—that sudden explosion of himself—after which his hysteria had been again encased within him, as the spectacle of Arthur's return to the academy eclipsed him.

But now that spectacle was far in the past—and Arthur was in the past, with only the funeral left to recall something of the splendor before the void set in.

But the void was already with Webster. The unanswered question was a vacuum that could not be filled by the understanding of his fellow students or the sympathetic platitudes of Colonel Kearny.

In answer to Webster's simple question of what had happened, there had only been things like "Your brother was a fine man and I mourn him as I would a son"; "You've made a fine record here, like your brother, and his example has, I'm sure, lighted your way"; "I hope you won't let this tragedy affect you too much."

Tragedy. Yes, Arthur's death was a tragedy, but why the slight halt in the Colonel's voice, the tiniest catch, the looking away as he said it?

"Harrisburg! Harrisburg!"

Webster was jolted by the call of the conductor and the sight of the station platform beside him.

Aunt Laura answered the door, her face drawn and her eyes red.

"Webbie!" She tearfully clutched him hard and he could feel her body tremble.

He set his jaw as he embraced her, disliking the sensation of her hot cheek against his. At last she released him and stepped back to look at him, at his neat, austere uniform, his lean face, his straight bearing. He could tell how much she admired what she saw, but he also noticed the quick change in her eyes as they met his, a look of questioning.

"How are you, Aunt Laura?" he said as they stepped into the house. It was a greeting, not a question. He set his bag to one side of the doorway.

Part of the coffin was visible from the dining room, but he turned away and walked into the parlor. Walter Schaefer, Laura's husband, thick, sweating, leaning forward in his chair as if he were a tired football player just come out and waiting to go back in, seemed to be silently choking on something.

"Hello, Uncle Walter."

"Good to see you, boy." Schaefer gripped Webster's hand hard and shook it vigorously, as if the motion were a relief. "How was your trip down?"

"About as usual," Webster said with a slight smile. He walked to a straight-backed chair and sat down. His uniform bent easily with his body, as creaseless and immaculate as Walter's suit was rumpled and dull.

Laura had followed him into the room. She wiped her eyes and struggled to regain her composure.

"I must say you look just like Arthur," Walter Schaefer said, to make conversation, and at once his face seemed to break up as he realized what he had said.

"Thank you," Webster answered, feeling an irrepressible impulse to laugh at the chaos before him.

There was silence for a moment as both Laura and her husband drew forth handkerchiefs, Laura to wipe her eyes, Walter to wipe every part of his face but his eyes.

Webster leaned forward slightly as his mind worked and settled on something. "How are things at the store?"

Gratefully Walter Schaefer answered. "We're getting killed. Murdered by—" Again he seemed jolted, this time by his wife's look. "I mean the rains have really hurt the business." Suddenly there was a defiant sound to his voice as he glanced back at Laura. "And you don't get that kind of business back again!" As if encouraged by Webster's puzzled frown, he went on, "I mean once the news gets around, people don't forget easily. Of course, I have a lot of trouble making your aunt understand that."

In his confusion, all Webster could manage to say was "Well, Aunt Laura is an emotional woman."

He looked at her again and saw her look of reproach. "Aren't you even going to look at your brother?" she asked.

"Why should he?" Schaefer said. "He knows there's no point in looking at a pine box."

But Webster had immediately stood up. "Of course, I'm sorry."

He straightened his tunic, although it did not need straightening, and walked into the dining room, with Laura just behind him. He stood before the plain box, noticing the grain of it, the stark edges and corners, the incongruous flowers nearby, and knowing that he should be feeling more than this sense of ceremonial duty. But that wasn't Arthur, and grief had never been present.

Laura went to a mahogany sideboard and took out a sealed envelope, which she handed to Webster. "Arthur left this for you," she said. "The French police sent it along with the body."

Holding the thin, bluish paper in his hand, Webster felt something cold and weighty within him. As he said, "Thank you, Aunt Laura," his eyes caught the scattered, official-looking stamps signifying several openings and closings by Paris officials.

"Why don't you go into the study and read it in private?" Laura said.

"Yes, thank you."

He walked stiffly to hide a dazed feeling that was coming over him, into a large book-lined room off the foyer. It had originally been intended as his father's study, but was never used by Angus Evers, who kept to his office. For a second, Webster thought about his father—was he in his office now?—but he knew he could not go to him or ask about him. He closed the door behind him and stood in comforting darkness. Its outlines dulled by the gloom, the room was its own memory to him, a wonderful place where he and Mim had played, where he had once hidden for hours, ecstatic over the family's frantic search through the house and woods for him.

Switching on a lamp, he sat down to read the letter. Across the front of the envelope was scribbled "Webster Dilman Evers." On the back, along with the police stamps, was the printed address of the Hotel Gaspard, 5 rue Dominique, Paris. As he stared at the envelope, Webster began to feel resentment at this reintrusion of Arthur's death. He would be expected to react, and there would not even be the charade of normality that his fellow students had begun to play once the period of shock had passed. Here, in Arthur's house, in the presence of Arthur's people, grief was to be expressed, and where was he to find the source of expression?

He took out three sheets of hotel stationery, which were covered with downhill lines of Arthur's small, badly formed scrawl. The peaks and valleys weirdly resembled a seismographic record.

"Dear Webbie," he read, and suddenly had to tighten his elbows against his sides to stop the paper from shaking.

When the news of what I've done reaches home, it's going to come as a terrible shock to you. You're going to think I let you down—which I suppose is true. Also, you're going to think how unhappy I was to do a thing like this.

Well, don't think that. I've discovered that although I'm about to kill myself, I'm not miserable at all. Far from it. I'm relieved to be getting out from under. Not that I'm recommending this to anyone as a way out. I'm weak . . . flawed. There's something lacking in me. I feel it isn't lacking in you. I've had reports on how you're doing at school and I know you're making out beautifully. I'm sure you've finally gotten over the feeling that it was impossible to do what the *great* Arthur Evers had done. Don't think I didn't sense how scared you were the day I brought you up to school. But look how you've overcome it. So far as I can see, everything is great with you.

Webster had reached the bottom of the first page, but did not turn it. He sat holding the letter, waiting to feel something, waiting for a reaction. He'd been waiting for almost two weeks, ever since the Colonel had summoned him to his office and broken the news of Arthur's death. The Colonel—everyone—had thought he'd done a fine job of covering his emotion—stiff upper lip, good soldier and all the rest. Fine. Except that there'd *been* no real emotion to cover. Why? He *wanted* to feel something. He *should*. This was *his* Arthur, the only man ever to care, ever to show real interest in him. Why hadn't he, why *wasn't* he collapsing in tears? Wasn't this what people were supposed to do at moments like this? Wasn't this what was expected of them?

Hell! He wouldn't play a role. He was always thinking of *roles* to play. That was the trouble with him. Why didn't he just do things? The reason people expected certain reactions was because that was the way real, honest-to-God human beings *did* react.

Except that he wasn't a real, honest-to-God human being. *He was like his father.* He hated the thought, which frightened and sickened him, that he had become all the things he most despised in someone else.

Webster slowly lifted the scrawled sheets once more.

I think there was something good between us, even though we were ten years apart. It isn't easy for a man in his mid-twenties to be really close to a boy in his teens. I think if I had lived, we might, as we grew older, have become better friends. That, of course, won't be now, and I'm sorry. I'm sorry, too, about the mess last year and how it must have shamed you. You deserve some sort of reasonable explanation and I wish I could give it to you, but I can't. There's a weakness in me that I don't understand. I wish I did. I tried to understand it. If you knew how often and hard I tried to figure out why I was different from other men, what made me different. Are people right? Am I filthy and dirty? Should I be spat upon, kept apart from decent society, deprived of a way to earn a living? I haven't been able to get a job anywhere in the government since the story broke. For the past seven weeks I've been working in an American bookshop as a clerk, but that ended a few days ago too. The owner made a crack about fairies and I hit him.

All these things—everything—the whole stinking mess has really been getting me down lately. To the point where I don't much care any more. I don't know enough to understand myself, and right now I honestly don't much care. When I finally made the decision to do what I'm going to do in a few minutes, it was like having a tremendous load lifted off me. I think, if I can describe the feeling accurately, I'm about as happy now as I've ever been."

There was another page, but Webster had stopped reading. He closed his eyes and felt his brother's name lodged in his throat, hard and choking. "Arthur . . ." Why couldn't he cry? Trying to force tears, he swayed back and forth on the chair like an ancient Hebrew before the ruins of his temple. His brother had written to *him*. A single man deserted and alone in a hotel room three thousand miles from home. A man, any man, had a right to expect at least a tear from his only brother. In his loneliest moment, his brother had chosen *him* of all the people in the world to write to. And where was the pain he should be feeling now? What *was* he?

Desperate for feeling, Webster drove himself to think of Arthur. How far his brother had gone, until he reached that final lonely room in a corner of Paris. Out of the familiar streets of Harrisburg, across rivers and states, across the Atlantic Ocean, into war-torn Europe. With his eyes still closed, Webster tried to picture him, quick and brilliant, with handsome brow and well-formed nose and jaw, impressively walking into nobility-crowded rooms, his eyes lively and searching, a smile for everyone—Arthur, unafraid and confident in whatever he did. And then the heart-tearing disgrace as the scandal broke. Arthur's career exploding and jobs becoming harder to find, charm and confidence fading, the whole world grim-lipped and organized against him . . .

Webster opened his eyes and read on.

A wholly sane man wouldn't, I suppose, be about to blow his brains out. I've told you I'm happy to be killing myself. That's true. I am experiencing enormous relief. But that's hardly a sane reason to write you a letter. You're the one member of this family I'm proud of.

Oh, hell . . . I don't really know why I'm writing this damn thing at all, except that I had to talk to someone and you're the only one I have. We never did get to talk very much. I know you wanted to, many times. I did too. I realize I should have. But it's too late now.

There's just one other thing, about Dad. He thinks I don't understand about him. I didn't, but I think I do now. It wasn't that he didn't have any interest in me. It wasn't that he didn't appreciate me. I've got something I can't cope with. For seventeen years, he's been living with something he couldn't cope with. If he ever knew how many newspaper articles about me, how many pictures of myself in glory I clipped out to send to him, but never sent. How often I waited for him to show that he recognized, was even the least bit aware of, anything I had done. I guess, more than anything else, I just wanted him to show, in some way, that he cared. Now I know that he is incapable of caring.

That was all. No signature. Webster stared dully at the last words: "incapable of caring." Angus and Webster Evers. Two pieces of Pennsylvania shale. Like father, like son. His legacy. A heritage of stone.

He thrust the letter back into its envelope and left the study. But instead of returning to the living room, he walked down the hall toward his father's office.

The door was closed and there were voices behind it, but Webster walked in without knocking. His father and an elderly patient, a man he did not know, looked at him with surprise.

"Webster, hello." Angus Evers removed his pipe from between worn teeth. "When did you arrive?"

Webster dropped the envelope on his father's desk. "Here," he said, white-faced. "Read this."

Evers frowned at the envelope, then at his son. He had aged a great deal during the past few years; his eyes, behind their lenses, were faded and flat, and the flesh beneath his chin sagged. "I will," he said quietly, "in a moment. In the meantime, as you can see, I have someone with me."

Webster flushed. "Excuse me." He turned, almost making a military about-face of it, and walked out. He did not close the door behind him.

In the gloomy light of the hall, he listened to his father's pen scratching out a prescription and to his voice offering a last few cautioning words of advice and to the sound of the patient's departure through the waiting room. Then there was silence.

Webster remained to one side of the open door. He heard the rattling of paper as his father removed the letter from its envelope. Silence. A moment later a page was turned. Silence. Another page whispered in turning. Webster stood stiffly against the wall. He had thrust the letter at his father in a moment of unthinking anger, unconsciously trying to salve the guilt of his own void by sharing it with another, but he expected nothing.

Webster started to retreat down the hall, but stopped after only a few steps, hearing the sound. It was a snuffling whisper such as might have come from a small dog rooting the ground. He returned to the open door and peered into his father's office.

Angus Evers still sat at his desk, his back toward Webster. He was bent over, his huge body heaving convulsively in the chair. Webster stared disbelievingly. The small, snuffling sounds seemed unrelated to their source.

Webster stood there, unmoving. He should go in, he thought. He should go in to his father and speak to him, tell him everything was all right, that it wasn't all his fault, that there were too many other things involved. No one could say whose fault it was. This man was still his father. Damn it! *Go in to him!*

The weeping began to infuriate him. His father could, after all, *feel* . . . even *cry*. Why couldn't *he*? He felt himself sweating. *Now*, he thought, trying to will it, force it. *Now* the tears would come. *Now* he would feel something. *Now* he was going to be like a real human being.

His father turned and saw him. It did not look like his father's face at all. It seemed all in pieces. In the gloomy office light, each line showed, sharp and deep.

"Web . . ." It wasn't his father's voice.

They looked at one another. Now, Webster thought, now was his chance to go in to him, to tell him. His father was waiting.

Webster's body was rigid, his arms stiff at his sides. He tried to speak, but his lips were dry and no words came to tell this solitary, aging man what he most wanted to hear. Then able neither to soothe nor to face the suddenly exposed need in his father's eyes, Webster turned and walked back down the hall.

As he passed the dining room, he paused briefly, turned and walked over to the coffin. He looked down intently at the end where he thought the head would be. Almost tenderly, he reached forward with his left arm and stroked the raw wooden box. He leaned over and whispered, "He cried." Then he straightened, took his coat off the hall rack, picked up his bag and left the house.

Webster followed the dark, graveled edge of the road as it curved steeply uphill. He walked facing the traffic, but at this hour the highway was empty except for an occasional flash of lights. Not one word, he thought, he hadn't been able to offer his father even a single word. And he had wanted to. *What was he?* Not a tear for his brother, not a word for his father. Oh, he was something, all right, but *what?* And how many times had he felt the same thing at school this past year? Had he ever offered any sign of gratitude for the way they'd all been after the embarrassment of his brother's unexplained dismissal, no one mentioning it, no questions? They'd all made believe they didn't even know. And he'd been grateful. Had he ever let them know, in any way, how he felt? He had more acquaintances than anyone on campus, but not one real friend. It was always the same. He could let himself go up to a point with people, and then a gate dropped and he was alone behind it.

He was sweating beneath his uniform and breathing heavily. The lights of a car appeared, grew larger and passed in a rush of air. A long walk, what he needed was a good, long walk. Just keep putting one foot in front of the other, but don't really get anywhere. What was the point? Wherever he ended up, he'd still be alone, carrying his own damned shell with him. He wished he could dump the whole load there on the road and start from scratch. Maybe next time he could feel, *act* more like a human being. Maybe next time . . .

What next time? Only one chance to buy and no returns. What you buy you're stuck with. All sales final. Only one place to go for complaints and not many had the guts to go there. Of course, Arthur had made the trip, but there weren't many who could. *He* certainly couldn't. Not Webster Dilman Evers, the walking, talking mechanical boy, fake extraordinary. That would be too solid, too real . . . not his specialty.

Webster laughed aloud as his mind toyed with the idea. Not too hard at that. He watched the lights of a truck approach and roar past. Two steps to the right and it was done. Excitement tingled along his spine. How long, he wondered, could a person go on making believe, pretending things he didn't feel? Sweet self-pity flowed over him. He was seventeen years old and he felt like a hundred. He was tired. Everyone finally went away. Everyone finally left you . . . his mother . . . Mim . . . Arthur. . . . So how could you even *let* yourself feel? How could you take the chance? Whom could you trust?

Webster edged in on the road. But what a god-awful thing to do to his aunt and poor Uncle Walter. He smiled as he pictured Walter Schaefer's sulking, bad-business face. This would throw his figures off for at least another six months. And his father? Well, if his father had managed to cry for Arthur, he guessed he'd have a few tears left for him too. Of course, it was just an idea, and a crazy one at that, but beautiful, utterly beautiful and exciting. And what, after all, would he be missing? A lifetime of nothing, of lies? Finally, of course, he would be found out. And where would he go to hide then?

The next lights, he thought, enjoying the shudder that passed through him, perhaps the next lights. Arthur had been right. There *was* a good feeling to it. The road stretched darkly to nothing. He was walking very slowly now, almost reluctantly, an imagined hand hard against his back. Now fear weakened his knees and numbed his brain. What the hell was he trying to get himself into?

How could he even think like that? Was he crazy? But the hand, gathering strength, pushed him farther into the road.

A streak of yellow broke the blackness. It disappeared as the road curved distantly behind a hill, then broke out once more. Webster stared at it fixedly, as if entranced. It became brighter, moving fast. Webster's feet barely moved. He remembered, with sickening clarity, a dog he had once seen dead in the road, its insides spilled beside it. Unaccountably, he started to hum a little melody. His voice faltered and died. Arthur had known. Arthur had known, all right. He could hear the roar of the car's motor. The lights blinded him. A horn honked wildly. Webster stopped walking. The lights waved back and forth and tires screamed. Webster stepped to one side. The car swept past in a rush of curses and wailing brakes. It finally stopped a hundred yards away and a man's voice shouted angrily, but Webster did not hear him. He was walking numbly in the opposite direction. The brief glow faded. Even in this, he was thinking, a lousy fake even in this.

1952: Washington, D.C.

And in all things, a fake, he thought. He looked up to signal the waitress for another brandy and saw Francine sitting nearby regarding him sadly. She came to the booth, sat down next to him and said gently, "Let's go home."

And then the brandy hit him.

Not with stupor or loss of faculties, but with release, with something like joy.

He opened his mouth to speak but she said, "Shut up. Just shut up and come home. God, how I hate talky men."

When they reached the apartment he realized that he felt cold and weak. He shivered in his coat. She kissed him wildly about the face and eyes, while he stood there, stiff and cold.

"I'll make some coffee," she said. "You look terrible."

She hurried into the kitchen, while Webster sagged onto the

couch. "What makes you think that coffee's going to make me look any better?" He closed his eyes and gave himself up to the pleasure of defeat.

When he heard her come back into the room, he opened his eyes. "I wanted to tell you before. I tried. It's a little late now, but I did try."

Francine pushed a lock of rain-dampened hair from his forehead. "I don't care. I don't care about any of it."

"I want to explain. I want to tell you how it was, I want you to know how—"

Francine kissed him. "To hell with it. That was thirteen years ago."

"I *want* to tell you."

"Not now." Her hands searched his face, neck, hair. "Maybe tomorrow, but not now."

"Tomorrow I'm telling the committee."

"No!" Francine stiffened. "You're not telling them anything. I won't let you." She clutched him hard. "I won't let you just throw everything away like that."

Webster smiled thinly. "I'm afraid I'm not going to have much choice. Christ only knows what evidence Blaine's given Pilgrim."

"I don't care *what* it is," Francine insisted, "We'll wait and we'll fight it. We won't just give up. There are ways—"

"I'm tired of fighting." Still huddled in his coat, Webster was warming to a relaxed glow. Years ago, he thought, years ago he should have learned about the happy potential of complete surrender. He took off his coat and drew Francine to him. It was almost idyllic. After a lifetime of struggling, what sheer delight, finally, to let go and drift.

"Tomorrow," Francine sighed into his ear, "you'll feel differently."

Webster did not want to argue. He moved his hand under Francine's head, feeling the soft hair and the warm, firm skin on the back of her neck. He kissed her hard, beginning to want her. She softened against him.

"The coffee," she whispered. "The coffee must be ready."

Webster's hand searched inside her dress. "What is it with you and coffee?"

She jumped as his cold hand made contact with her warm flesh. "My God, you're an icicle." She squirmed closer and frowned, although Webster could not see it. There was a need, an urgency about him that she had never known before. For almost a year she had found him a willing and capable, but hardly an overpowering lover. There was, in his love-making, the same sense of control and lack of emotion that seemed to characterize him in everything else. Skillful but uninspired, was the way she had once teasingly described it.

"Darling," she said softly, "you're making me feel as shy as a bride."

Webster's eyes were lost somewhere. "Why?" he said.

Francine pulled back with an effort. "You're . . . different tonight. Wait, give me a minute."

When she called to him from the bedroom, he groped his way through the semidarkness. Watching, Francine saw him drop his clothes in a careless heap on the floor.

She laughed. "You're not hanging them up?" His fastidiousness, even before love-making, had often amused and sometimes irritated her. It fell into the same category as his stubborn insistence on wearing his wristwatch to bed. Francine called him a sexual clock-watcher, and yet she realized how much a part of him this eccentricity was, as if he regarded sex as something awkward and ignoble which nature had forced upon him and which he must do his best to accomplish with a minimum loss of dignity.

He came to her now without a word, and Francine gave herself to him as always, fully and without reservation, but knowing, too, that even in this he was still not entirely hers.

And yet now, as she clung to his hard, smooth back, it was different. He was not the same man, not from the instant she had reached him in the rain and dragged him back into the apartment, not in his face, or voice, or manner, not in need or wanting, not in anything. The change had come at that first agonized moment of confession, but she'd been too absorbed with her own selfish anger to care. She had seen the naked hurt and despair when she'd handed him his coat, but all she'd cared about, all she'd wanted to do, was punish him for the lies. What kind of twisted love was it that she felt? What sort of woman was she to beg for his need for her, and then drive him out when, finally, he gave it?

She stared up at the dark outlines of the face she loved. "I'm sorry, darling," she whispered, although she knew he did not then hear or care. Her own desire had faded with her thoughts, allowing her a clearer, a more grateful awareness of what was happening. His love-making seemed to have exploded into a frenzy. For a desperate moment, as in the old way, she felt him try to curb the rising excitement, but fight as he would, he was suddenly without a way of retreat. Francine held him, hearing him call her name as he had never before, feeling his wildness drain off into small, whimpering sobs. She did not let go, but rocked softly, gently, happy to relinquish all claims.

"I'm sorry," he whispered hoarsely.

She rubbed her cheek against his shoulder. "Shhhh."

"It was no good for you," he mourned. "I went off and left you."

"Idiot." She kissed his chin, his neck. "It was the first time you ever *really* loved me."

He started to say more, but her lips stopped him.

Later she stirred. "Darling?"

"Mmmmm?" He was on the edge of dozing.

"Would you like to make everything perfect for me?"

"I thought it *was* perfect."

"There's just one more little thing."

"Mmmmm?"

"Would you please, just this once, take off that damned watch?"

Chapter Eighteen

1952: New York City

Justin Blaine's office looked the same as it had six days before, when he had last seen it. The spare furnishings still had the functional quality that made them interchangeable with the furnishings of a dozen other CBN executive offices. The tenth-floor view of colorless buildings was as monotonous as ever. Yet Justin had the feeling of never having been there before, a weird, dreamlike sensation of moving among foreign landscapes peopled with familiar yet ghostlike figures.

The feeling had begun the moment he'd walked into the CBN lobby, had grown sharper in the elevator, and had become a dizziness as Justin walked along the corridors and into his office. He had sensed strangeness in the self-conscious, overly warm greetings of the doorman, the elevator operator, the office personnel, who met him with carefully averted eyes and with salutations uniformly rushed and eager. It was as though he had died, and had been properly eulogized, and then had vulgarly insisted on continuing to walk the earth. He had entered his office with eyes averted in order to spare as many people as possible from the chore of these awkward performances. He had rushed almost rudely past his secretary, a sweet young woman with dark, mournful eyes and gentle manner, so as not to force her to look sympathetically solemn or encouragingly cheerful.

Justin hung up his coat and went to his desk. The morning papers were arranged in their customary positions, but the pile of mail was heaped to several times its normal size and Justin saw that two additional baskets had been stored in a corner. He made no move to open any of the letters, for he could imagine the vituperation that would be in most of them, and he was past caring about the others. In the forty-eight hours since he and Alice had returned to their apartment there had been several abusive phone calls, as well as others—newsmen after more copy, well-wishers refusing to believe his confession, curiosity-seekers after the sound of his voice—forcing him to leave the receiver off the hook.

He looked at the headlines and felt his usual surprise at seeing his name in print. "BLAINE-EVERS CONFRONTATION SET FOR FRIDAY," read the *Times*. "BLAINE TO MEET EVERS AT END OF WEEK," the *Herald Tribune* declared. "FRIDAY IS C-DAY," screamed the *Journal-American*. There were more, but Justin could not look at them.

Without emotion, he considered the events of the past few days, the charges and countercharges, the accusations and denials all blending into a mélange of distortions and lies. Webster had, as was expected, continued to cling to his pose of offended innocence, but Pilgrim had done his work well and the committee had been forced to take action. A public meeting between the two principals —a confrontation, as the papers dramatically were calling it—had been arranged to take place in four days. Already, he knew, passes to the hearing were being pursued and sold at high prices. The major networks were scheduling extensive television and radio coverage. The mass marketing of living history was moving into high gear.

The UN's new push in Korea had taken on secondary importance. The terrible casualty cost of fighting for a place called Pork Chop Hill was hardly being noticed.

Primary campaigns were becoming colored by guarded Republican references to the affair as part of the Soft-on-Communism theme. Democratic candidates and incumbents were erecting walls of vagueness about it.

Justin walked into the outer office to ask for the evening's broadcast briefs, but his secretary had stepped out. He was scanning her desk for the missing sheets when a copy boy came in.

"Hi, Mr. Blaine." He was tall and gangling, with bad skin. A carefully cultivated greased forelock in the Tony Curtis style was like a great comma against his forehead.

"Hello, Mike."

The boy dropped a pack of mail onto the desk. "We sure missed you last week." He smiled too eagerly.

"Thanks."

"Mr. Allgood filled in, but it wasn't the same."

Justin lighted a cigarette and offered one to Mike, who put it behind his ear. Shifting his weight from one foot to the other, Mike concentrated on his next words. "You know, Mr. Blaine, I don't believe this guy Evers. My mom doesn't either. We hope you show him up good."

Justin's smile was polite. "We'll see."

Mike's weight shifted again; his concentration deepened. "It was a surprise to hear—well—that you'd been—well, you know—"

"It's all right to say it. A spy."

"Well, yeah. I mean, I guess everybody was . . . surprised."

"I'm sure they were."

The phone rang, and Justin, glancing into his office, saw the red light on his desk flashing on and off. As he went inside to take the call, Mike called after him, "Thanks for the cig, Mr. Blaine."

Justin picked up the receiver. "Hello?"

"Mr. Blaine?" It was a woman's voice.

"Yes."

"My name is Francine Moore. Does that mean anything to you?"

Justin frowned, letting his eyes rest on a bronze paperweight on his desk, which was inscribed with his name and a national magazine's Newscaster of the Year Award for 1950. "Yes, I know about you. You work out of Washington, don't you?"

"That's right, I—"

"And would you also be one of the people who, I hear, have been writing nice little lies about me?"

"Mr. Blaine, I'm a very close friend of someone in Washington whom you once called a friend. . . . Do you know whom I mean?"

Justin now sat down behind his desk. "Yes, Miss Moore, I know whom you mean. And that probably accounts for all that misinformation about me."

"Please, Mr. Blaine, I didn't call to talk to you about the press. I've—"

"Why not? Are you ashamed? Do you realize what my wife and I have been going through? Our phone rings at all hours, with all sorts of lunatics letting us know what they think about the things you newspaper people have been saying about me. Do you know what it's like to be called bastard, liar, fairy and worse? I've had to disconnect my phone. Since you people are capable of such things, I don't see why I should give an interview to any of you, and if you're calling in behalf of your 'friend,' I have nothing to say to him and certainly nothing to offer him."

"Please," Francine broke in, "you've got to listen to me. I know everything. *Everything*. The whole truth."

Seeing his secretary come into the outer office, Justin spoke quietly. "He told you?"

"Yes. That's why you have to see me."

"Miss Moore, I don't *have* to do anything."

"Can't you understand how important this is? It's the last chance we'll have to save something out of this mess. You owe it to all of us to try."

"No. There's no reason to talk. It's too late for talk."

"Please!" Her voice rose for the first time. "Are you so much of a fool that you think he's going to stand up there and admit all this? If he goes down, you'll go down with him. You *must* talk to us. A deal, some kind of face-saving deal, is still possible."

Justin watched an ash from his cigarette drop onto his sleeve.

"That's what I thought you had in mind. Well, as I said, I'm not interested in any deals."

"Why are you doing this?" Francine said fiercely.

Justin did not say anything. At least they are worried, he thought, at least they're not going through this untouched.

"Why are you doing this?" she repeated, the anguish remote and mechanized over the wire. "There must be a reason. No one sets out deliberately to destroy a man without a reason. Look into your heart. I hope you don't think it's sheer patriotism. *He* doesn't understand why you're doing it and neither do I. I hope to Christ you do."

The wire stretched silently to Washington, and for a moment Justin thought she had hung up. "Is that all, Miss Moore?"

"Just take down my number," she said wearily, "in case you change your mind. And I hope to God you do before Friday."

Justin noted her number and then heard a click. There was a tray of pencils on his desk, but he made no move to write down the number. He thought about what the woman had said and wondered about her relationship with Webster Evers. She was probably the latest, he guessed, in the long line of women swearing one-sided fealty to that remote man-god. He felt a stir of pity for her. Love was not only blind; it was apparently amoral.

There was a sudden pounding in his temples and Justin reached into a pocket for the pill he had forgotten to take earlier. He swallowed it without water and then spoke to his secretary through the open door. "Betty, where's the material for this evening's broadcast?"

The girl came into the office, her thin face flushing. "It wasn't sent down, Mr. Blaine." She hesitated. "Didn't you read the memo from Mr. Mannheim?"

Justin shook his head. "What memo? What are you talking about?" The words came out louder and sounded more impatient than he had intended.

Betty came to his desk and began to search through the clutter. "I put it here myself early this morning." She finally dug a pale blue sheet from under the newspapers and handed it to Justin, her fingers causing it to shake slightly. "Here it is." She turned and hurriedly walked from the office.

Justin scanned the interoffice memo. It was headed, "From the desk of Phillip Mannheim." The message, in the CBN President's scrawling hand, read: "For obvious reasons, your broadcasts have been discontinued indefinitely. Phil Allgood will take over the time slot." It was initialed, "P.M."

Justin stood holding the paper for a moment, breathing the faint smell of his secretary's cologne. He was less surprised by the contents of the note than he was irritated at its summary manner and delivery. Dear, sentimental Phillip, he thought. When the time came to swing an ax, he handled it with the same ease he would a golf club. Justin glanced around his office and found it still looking, astonishingly, as though nothing had happened to it or to him, as though success and fame and high income were permanent and irrevocable.

"Betty," he said quietly, "get my lawyer on the phone, will you, please."

When the red light flashed on his phone, he went behind his desk and picked up the receiver. "Hello, Henry," he said. "Yes. I'm fine." He listened while the lawyer assured him much too enthusiastically of his faith and confidence in Justin's ultimate vindication. Then Justin said, "Henry, would you please look at my contract with CBN. I'd like to hear the exact wording of the non-termination clause. I'll hold on."

Justin put down the receiver and lighted a fresh cigarette, noting with satisfaction that his hands were steady. He heard Henry begin to speak and picked up the phone. The lawyer's dry voice recited a long list of whereases and many-syllabled modifying clauses and cautious legal phrases. When he was through, Justin said, "In your opinion, after reading this, does Mannheim have the right to pull me off the air because of what's going on?"

Henry did not answer immediately and Justin could picture the pudgy lawyer's pursed mouth as he sat thinking.

"No," Henry said at last, and the single carefully considered word carried the portentous weight of legal certainty. "He can't touch you. You're protected."

"I thought so," Justin said. "Call Mannheim right now and tell him that."

"Trouble?"

"Trouble," Justin said. He ended the conversation as quickly as possible, got up and nervously paced the office, past the baskets of unopened mail and the headlines and the slip of blue paper. He looked at his watch. It wasn't eleven o'clock yet. He wondered how long it would take before he heard from Mannheim.

It took less than ten minutes for the CBN President to come into Justin's office, slamming the door behind him.

"Since when," he said harshly, "are you telling me how to run my network?"

The executive's sunburned face was darker than usual and his blue eyes were cold and angry. Good old Henry, Justin thought, feeling a flicker of affection for the lawyer, he must have really laid it on. "Not your network, Phillip," he said gently, "just me." He sat down behind his desk, pleased at Mannheim's anger, judging himself to have an advantage because of it. "It's a funny thing. I've a peculiar aversion to being callously discarded."

Mannheim strode over to Justin and stood menacingly over him. "I'll discard you, all right." His lips were pale and thin. "There isn't a court in the country that wouldn't back up the network on this. There isn't a court in the country that would make us put a confessed spy on a coast-to-coast soapbox. No snotnose of a lawyer is going to call me up and tell me what to do about something like this. Who the hell do you think you're dealing with, some cruddy little local outfit?"

"You're wrong," Justin said. "You can't deprive me of the right to be heard. I don't care how big you and the network think you are. I have a binding contract. And for another thing, there's something in this country called freedom of expression, and nothing, even so august and godlike as CBN, can tamper with that."

Mannheim snorted. "Don't give me that crap," he shouted, his voice surprisingly strong and malevolent. "Freedom of expression! That's typical, you sanctimonious bastard. You Commies always come up with that line. You do your damnedest to get rid of freedom of speech, but are always the first to come crying when it's taken away. You try to hide behind . . ." He stopped and glared at Justin. "What the hell's so funny? What are you smiling about?"

Justin hadn't realized he was smiling. "I guess," he said, "because it hits me as weird that everyone seems to take a perverse kind of pleasure in forgetting that I'm *not* a Communist, that I stopped being a Communist, of my own volition, more than twelve years ago. In fact, if I'm to be accused of anything right now, it should be for being overly patriotic in confessing the truth. I've found that people are embarrassed by confessions. They'd rather not know about unpleasant, disturbing things. And they'd especially rather not know that those they've placed in positions of power and trust have made gullible fools of them."

Mannheim's initial anger seemed to have lost its edge. He dropped wearily into a leather chair beside Justin's desk, his expression reflective and somewhat puzzled. Justin watched him light the cigarette in his long white holder. He looked aristocratic sitting in the big chair. Dying would come especially hard for such a man, Justin thought; there was so much he'd have to leave behind.

"I don't understand you, Justin," Mannheim said, speaking through the smoke, his tone abruptly warm, almost fatherly. "Christ! If you'd have only told me in advance what you were going to say to that committee, if you'd have only asked my advice, I might have been able to help you, I might have been able to tell you how to use what you had in the right way." He extended his pink hands, palms up, in a gesture of regretful helplessness. "As a major contributor to the Republican Party, I might have been in an excellent position to help you use this stuff against Webster Evers so it would do the most good for all of us. But you had to go off like a horse's ass and blow everything wide open." Mannheim shook his head. "If only you'd told me."

"I tried to," Justin said grudgingly. "I was in your office the night before with the subpoena. I tried to tell you all of it. But, if you remember, it was more important for you to run home to your wife's dinner party."

"Oh, no." Mannheim stared at him coldly. "You're not going to blame me and my wife's dinner party for this. If you wanted to tell me that night, you could have told me. How long does it take to say those four all-important little words: *I was a spy?* You were in my office for almost half an hour."

Justin did not say anything.

"You may have had your own reasons for not telling me," Mannheim went on. "You probably do. But they don't concern me. All that concerns me now is that you're through on this network." He stood up, straightening his suit jacket and, as though it were part of a ritual, he carefully smoothed the silvery hair above his ears and back of his neck. "If you want to fight this in court, go ahead. We have a firm of lawyers who get a quarter of a million dollars a year whether they do a damn thing or not. I'd be very happy to put them to work if that's what you want."

He started to go, then turned and looked at Justin sitting behind the desk. "Listen," he said, once more smiling. "Do you know I sent a telegram to that committee telling them to get off Evers' back? Why do you think I did it? Because I give a damn about him? Why the hell should I worry about Evers? On behalf of the Republican Party, I'd have ordinarily been delighted to see his Democratic ass dragged in public. I sent the telegram to disassociate myself and the network from the whole mess. I did it because you did something to me that nobody's done in twenty years and gotten away with. You lied to me."

"Lied?" Justin said. "When did I lie to you?"

Mannheim brushed the question aside. "You withheld vital facts and information," he said. "To me, it's the same thing."

"And what if I'm proved right on Friday? What if it's shown that Evers is guilty as charged?"

Mannheim laughed. It was an ugly, menacing sound. "I couldn't care less. I don't give a goddamn *what* happens at that great confrontation. I don't care if Evers is guilty or not. I'm only a mirror of what the public wants. Right now you're on the public's shit list. If the public mood changes—and it's got a long way to change— I'll give you back your show."

"Just like that?"

"Just like that. Tell your friend Henry to check the clause on extraordinary circumstances. I think you'll find I'm on firm ground."

Mannheim stood there for a moment without speaking. His puzzled frown returned. "I don't understand it," he said slowly. "You were a great commentator. The best in the business. You were earning a lot of money. All you had to do was keep your mouth shut and your future was assured. I don't understand it."

He looked once more at Justin, closely, searchingly, as if this final glance might yet reveal a reason for an apparently reasonless act. Then he opened the door and walked out. He did not close the door behind him.

Justin swiveled around in his chair and faced the window. The sun had broken through the smoke and early morning mist. The city's towers reared up into the blue haze. In the building across the avenue, men and women sat at desks, stood, or moved about with absorbed, productive urgency, talking, listening, writing, thinking, all with the hope of making next week's pay check a little larger, a little more secure. Well, he thought, as of a moment ago he was out of the race. He stood up abruptly, took his coat from the rack and went into the outer office. "I'm going out, Betty," he said. "I'm not sure when I'll be back."

The girl looked at him and Justin saw, with surprise, that she was crying. "I'm sorry, Mr. Blaine." Her dark eyes were moist and her lips were quivering. "I'm so very, very sorry."

Justin blinked through his lenses, finding himself touched by the girl's tears. She had been with him for more than a year, but he'd always had the vague idea that she disapproved of him. He reached out and touched her shoulder, which he found surprisingly frail under the cotton blouse. He did not know what to say.

"You're a fine man," she said thickly, "a *good* man. I don't care what anyone says. I know."

Maybe someday I will stop being surprised by people, he thought. "It's all right, Betty," he said, feeling helpless to comfort her, feeling that the better part of his lifetime had passed without profit or wisdom. "They haven't buried me yet."

He spoke to no one in the corridor. The elevator was full of secretaries on the way to their coffee break, and there was the familiar aroma of perfume and the music of their chatter. But again he felt the pain of being alien among them. He strode quickly through the lobby and turned north along Fifth Avenue. His pace outwardly was purposeful, but was really without destination, and after a while, with the sun warm on his face, Justin slowed to a stroll. He moved by habit, remotely aware of the crowds and windows, automatically stopping for lights at corners and going ahead with the flow of people. Suddenly he was struck by a sense of familiarity. What was it that now made him seem like someone else he had once known—or been? And then he realized that this pace, this purposeless stroll, was like those of the many jobless days of more than twenty years before, the days of bitter loneliness, the days of no future.

And, as then, his mind set itself to ask, Why have I done what I have done?

Now he had to answer it. Already within the day two others had pressed him, as if the reason were his identity, the thing to know him by. Perhaps that was it, perhaps, he thought, stopping in the midst of the moving crowd, I am my *reasons* and always have been. Perhaps I've always been a fool because I've fooled myself and I will die a fool unless I learn the truth. Why had he blown this thing wide open? Alice had warned him not to, but he'd refused to listen. The wise man chooses, the fool refuses. Why?

He tried to think clearly, but found himself going over the same worn argument again. The reason he'd done it, he thought, was the subpoena. He'd been sure it was going to come out, and he wanted to get it over with fast. But there was still no need to dive right in and do it that way. There were so many more careful, more sensible ways to handle it. He might have at least waited for them to give him a hint of what they had, to push him a bit. Then, *he'd set it up*. For some reason, *he'd wanted it that way*. He had wanted to be found out. He could no longer side-step it: consciously or unconsciously, he'd anticipated what was going to happen. He'd rigged his own trap. But *why* had he done it? What was he really after? *Whom* was he after? He couldn't claim any longer that it was just a crazy accident. You did things to *yourself*. Why had he done *this* to himself?

Because, he reasoned carefully, for all these years he must have felt some guilt. Just getting out of the apparatus may not have been enough. He'd left behind a dangerous man whom *he himself* had created. He'd walked out and left him there, still dangerous. Perhaps it was that he felt morally bound to go back and destroy what he'd created. Finally, then, was *that* it? Had he really waited all these years to leap back at the first excuse to destroy Webster Evers?

The noise of an automobile horn made him jump. The sun had become stronger and seemed to bake his face.

But he didn't even know, he thought, whether Webster was still active. What right had he, after an estrangement of nearly thirteen years, to pass judgment and take action blindly? He peered morosely at the faces of passers-by.

Why? Still, only the effects were clear—the damage, the error, the waste—but the cause remained veiled. And could the answer come from him alone?

Francine Moore's number had stayed in his mind, as if waiting for its inevitable use. Justin entered a drugstore, went to the phone booth and gave the operator the number. As he wiped his face in the closeness of the booth, he heard Francine's voice.

"Miss Moore," he said, "this is Justin Blaine."

"Yes?" He noted her surprise.

"I've . . ." He hesitated, wondering if again he were being the worst kind of fool. What if they were setting him up for something? "I've changed my mind," he said. "I've decided I'd like to meet with your friend."

There was a sigh at the other end. "I'm so glad."

"Please understand," he said quickly, "I'm not offering or promising anything. I just want to talk with him."

"Yes, of course, I understand." Francine tumbled it out in a rush, eager to pledge anything. "When and where would you like to get together?"

"As soon as we can," he said. "This evening, if possible. And I'd better come to Washington. I'm less well known there."

"All right," Francine agreed. "My apartment would be a good place. It's on an out-of-the-way street. No one's watching it, so there's little chance of being seen."

Justin thought briefly of concealed cameras and secret recording devices. "What's the address?" he said.

"Thirteen Elm Drive. It's the top-floor apartment. What time can we expect you?"

"Sometime around six or seven," Justin said. "I'm not sure of the flight schedules."

"Yes." Francine laughed nervously. "I'll see you this evening then."

Justin hung up and remained seated on the little curved bench. He still felt as though the decision he had made, as well as any others he would make, could not help but be wrong. This was a good time for a man to be confident, stupid and independently wealthy. All problems might not be eliminated, but they'd certainly be easier to ignore.

Chapter Nineteen

1952: Washington, D.C.

Nervously Francine again looked at her watch, rearranged the living room ashtrays into a new pattern, and again combed her hair in the bathroom. If one of them didn't arrive soon, she thought, she'd comb herself bald. She frowned into the mirror, lips pursed, comb poised for another stroke. This was probably the greatest absorption of the female sex, she decided, this combing.

Francine made a sour face and put down the comb in disgust. She did not like the way her mind was working, for now she was sure that nothing good would come of the evening. Her original hope had been quashed by Webster almost immediately. He had not only been certain that the meeting could serve no useful purpose, but had actually been angry when told of its arrangement. "Your apartment is a ridiculous place to meet. Anyway, it'll be an emotional disaster," he'd complained. "I know this man and I know you. There will be bitter sentiment and no results. If it wasn't too late to get out of it, I'd tell you to call the whole thing off." A lovely way, she thought, to be going into what she considered their last chance to escape the debacle of Friday's confrontation.

She went into the kitchenette for ice cubes. The refrigerator was in need of defrosting and the trays, as usual, were stuck. With growing anger she tugged at the unmoving tray. She stopped a moment, her hand wet and cold, and then she reached farther into the cabinet to push the tray off its icy cradle. Suddenly the tray let go, jamming her knuckle painfully. "Damn, damn, damn," she swore softly, looking down at the knuckle. A long, thin line showed pink, then turned red, then the blood began to seep out in tiny tendrils and run down the back of her hand. She watched it dumbly. She started toward the bathroom, but there was a knock at the door before she got there. Naturally, she thought.

Carrying the injured finger gingerly before her, she went to the door, opened it and looked at the round, solemn face of Justin Blaine.

"Miss Moore?" he said. "I'm sorry I'm late, but I . . ." He stopped as he saw the bleeding finger.

"Damn ice-cube tray," Francine said apologetically.

Justin came in and closed the door behind him. "Here," he said, hurriedly shrugging out of his coat and dropping it on a chair. "You'd better let me take care of that."

"It's nothing," she said, embarrassed, suddenly feeling ridiculous. "It's just a scratch." The blood was now running in a thin stream down her bare arm, making everything look much worse than it was.

"Where's the bathroom?" Justin glanced about, saw the door through the short hallway and led Francine toward it. "Do you have any iodine and bandages?"

She nodded.

He sat her down on the hamper, gently washed off the cut and stopped the bleeding. Francine winced as the iodine touched the open wounds.

"When I was a boy," Justin said, "my mother used to say it was a good sign when the iodine burned. She said it meant all the germs were being killed." He smiled. "My mother was a firm believer in the purifying powers of pain. She was sure that no real good could be accomplished in this world without a little nice, honest suffering to go along with it."

Francine watched as his firm, stubby fingers manipulated the Band-Aids out of their wrappers. Through his thick lenses his eyes looked watery, red-rimmed and tired and the hair drooping over his forehead was streaked with gray. She found him older-looking in person than she had in newspaper photographs, and not nearly as inscrutable and forbidding. Up close, she thought, even the face of calamity might be mistaken for a friend.

He put the Band-Aids on swiftly. "Now," he said, "keep away from all refrigerators for at least two months."

Francine smiled. "I would, but I hate warm Scotch."

As Justin looked at her steadily, his smile fading, she felt herself growing warm and uncomfortable. They went back into the living room and Francine busied herself for a moment hanging up his coat while Justin sat down stiffly in a straight-backed chair.

"I expected Webster more than half an hour ago," she said. "I don't know what could be delaying him." Now that the initial burst of action had passed, her original nervousness had returned. Maybe, she thought, it would help if she cut another finger.

Justin did not say anything. He, too, suddenly seemed tense and at a loss.

"Would you care for a drink?" Francine asked.

Justin shook his head. "Thank you, no."

Francine sat down opposite him on the couch. She had tried to prepare herself in advance with some sort of attitude toward this man, but had been unable to decide whether it should be friendly or hostile. She was grateful to him for having agreed to come this evening, yet despised him for all he had done. Also, the reporter in her was curious about what sort of man he was, about what had made him do this thing and—more than anything else—about what specifically he had against Webster.

"I'm sorry," she said, to break the heavy silence. "I'm sorry about those . . . those things I said to you on the phone and wrote. . . ." Her voice trailed off.

Justin's brows lifted. *"Are* you, Miss Moore?"

Francine looked at him. "When you feel about someone as I do about Webster, Mr. Blaine, you really have little choice in these things."

"Even knowing that what I've said is the absolute truth, that he's guilty of everything of which I've accused him?"

Francine leaned forward on the couch, shoulders hunched, hands pressed between her knees. "I'm afraid you don't understand, Mr. Blaine." She paused. She was finding it strangely difficult to speak. "Being innocent or guilty has nothing to do with it. If I thought it would help Webster, I'd swear under oath you were a murderer."

Justin nodded slowly and the light caught his cheek and lit up his hair, and for a moment Francine could see how he might have looked as a younger, less troubled man. "I believe you," Justin said dryly. He looked at her. "I've never heard mention of a Mrs. Evers. Was there ever one? There wasn't when I knew him. Was there in between?"

"No," she said. "There hasn't been. And, knowing Webster, there probably never will be." Francine had thought it often enough, but this was the first time she'd actually put it into words. It did not make her feel any better.

"That's too bad," Justin said, sounding, Francine thought curiously, as though he did feel genuine regret. "It doesn't take long for anyone with eyes to see what he'd have in you." He stared off somewhere. "I've always been thankful to have someone who's been with me, right or wrong. It's nice, no matter how this turns out, that Webster has someone too."

Francine looked surprised. "Those are funny words coming from the mouth of someone who is trying to ruin him."

"I hadn't looked at it exactly that way," Justin said.

"No?" Francine said, more loudly than she had intended. "Is there really some other way to look at it, to describe what you're doing to him?" She stared at Justin with a kind of harsh, religious anger lighting her face. "You're good at words. Tell me. How else would you put it?"

Justin did not say anything. The skin over his forehead seemed to be stretched too tautly and his eyes blinked.

Francine sighed. "I shouldn't talk like that," she said. "I didn't get you here to say things like that. I don't want to let myself become angry or be carried away. The reason for this meeting is to calm things down and find some way out for us." She recited it like a litany. "I'm sorry if—"

"No, no," Justin broke in. "That's all right. Please. I can't really blame you."

Francine felt her injured finger begin to throb. "Well, then, tell me," she said harshly. "Why did you do it?"

"I had to."

"That's no answer," she said wildly, appalled to find herself beginning to cry. "You *know* it's no answer."

"Maybe it isn't," he said, uncomfortably watching her lose control. "Maybe it isn't but—" The telephone rang and he broke off as Francine went to answer it.

"Hello," she said, then frowned abruptly. "Where *are* you? We've been sitting here and . . ."

The phone was across the room and Francine was turned away from Justin, so that he could not see her face. But her body stiffened noticeably as she listened.

"But he's *here!*" Her voice had risen. "He's been here for fifteen minutes. We've been—"

She stood there, frozen. Justin could faintly hear the voice, high, distant and unreal.

"But the man has come three hundred miles!" Francine shouted. "You can't just—I *know* it wasn't your idea, but I told him that—" She stood there, one hand opening and closing at her side. "God, you can be infuriating." She swung around and stared hopelessly, appealingly at Justin. Then she just stood listening, while the small voice at the other end rattled on. When it stopped at last, Francine hung up without saying good-bye. Seeming suddenly very tired, she returned to her seat.

Justin knew without asking, but said anyway, "What's wrong? The great man refuses to join us?"

"I'm sorry," she said, her voice small and defeated. "I'm truly, truly sorry." She peered mournfully at her bandaged finger. "I suppose it's more my fault than Webster's. I called you, made all the plans without even telling him. On my own. I knew he'd be against the idea of seeing you, but I figured that once I'd arranged the meeting he might scream a little but would come anyway."

"And," Justin said, not unkindly, "you figured wrong." Unaccountably he felt relieved that Webster was not going to show. Perhaps, he thought, he was going a little out of his mind. He'd come all this way, of his own free will, to see the man, to seek possible answers from the meeting. Then finding it called off, he was actually *grateful,* as if, in some way, he'd been afraid of what he might learn.

Francine sighed. "He was furious, all right, but when I spoke with him a few hours ago, he said he'd come. Now he's changed his mind. He's been thinking about it and just changed his mind. Sometimes that man . . ." Her shoulders hunched in mute despair.

"What did he say?" Justin asked, wondering if, for his own reasons, Webster too had feared the meeting.

"He said he distrusted your motives in coming here. He's angry and bitter, and he has good reason to feel that way."

They were silent for a moment. From somewhere in the building came a hint of orchestral music.

"So I guess this leaves us where we were, with the question of why you've done this—and why *now?* What have you gained from it? What can you gain? Your career must be wrecked, you've given up the world."

"I'm not gaining anything, Miss Moore. It's not a matter of that, believe me."

"Then *what* is it?"

Justin sighed. "I'm not sure. At first I thought I knew, but I'm not sure any more. I guess I want to make amends for past mistakes. I know *that.* And I guess that that was my reason for my testimony."

Francine shook her head in rejection. "That's no reason to destroy others."

"I'd hoped that I could talk to Webster today, that I could piece it all together with him. I suppose I was foolish to think so, but I really thought that Webster and I could bring back enough of our past feelings to see this to some good end."

"There couldn't have been much feeling if you are capable of what you've done."

He got up and walked to the window, shaking his head. Why did she have to be so obtuse? "You just don't understand!"

She leaned back in her chair, as if suddenly aware of having the top hand.

"I've wondered if there wasn't something strange between you—you know what I mean. Webster insists there wasn't, and I believe him, but maybe you secretly felt . . . *Did he reject your love? Was that it?*"

"For God's sake, *no!* Is that all the world's supposed to be made up of? We were *friends,* two people who were close and who shared beliefs and dangers and respect! Can't you understand something like that? I brought him into the apparatus. And when I left, I—oh, well, it doesn't matter. You just can't understand it."

"What about when you left?" she said in a voice of cunning. "I think I do see it. You're outraged because he didn't leave when you did. You said you'd brought him in, as if he were your creation. Of course, you thought you could control him. Sure! After all, what are *you* beside *him?*"

"No," he said, quietly and hesitantly.

"Yes, what are *you* beside *him?* It would make you feel damned good to know that a man like you could control Webster Evers. You're crazy for power. And if you can't control him, you'll wreck him. Isn't that it?"

"No."

"And you're hiding the whole thing behind repentance," she said sardonically.

"Am I?" He tried to make it sound sarcastic, but somehow what she said was hitting him.

"You're damned right you are! You said so yourself. And how long will it be before you'll start claiming to be a patriot? To do such a thing for such reasons! Think what a career Webster's had and where he could go. And for a man like you to come along and spoil it because of something that ended over twelve years ago—"

"Then it did end then."

"Of course, it ended then!"

"I should have realized that." Justin sat down on the sofa, feeling himself going dizzy.

"You didn't even bother to find out, did you?" she said with contempt. "Didn't you know that when you left, the chain was broken? Webster didn't leave the party—it left him. The apparatus dried up around him."

"But how could they let him live? If he would have talked—"

"Don't you see it? The apparatus dried up around him. You were his superior and you were gone; he didn't know your superior. What could he have told them, that there was a spy network? That was known already, but what details could he have given them outside of what he'd stolen? And why would he wreck his career? Oh, Mr. Blaine," she said ruefully, "you are a very dumb bunny. When you pulled out, you freed him from the whole thing. You both got away with it. And now you've blown it—for repentance." She turned from him and covered her face with her hand.

"I'd better tell you how it happened," he said. And he told her about the subpoena and his certainty about what they knew and his shock in the committee room. He could have stopped there, but he knew he must say more to make her understand.

"My wife was against the confession, even though she's always disliked Webster. That's strange, isn't it? I cared about Webster and I told. She . . . she hated him and tried to stop me."

"Why should she hate him?"

Justin shook his head at facing still another mystery. "I don't know. Even when Webster and I were close she—" He stopped abruptly.

Francine looked curiously at him. There was a new, cautious awareness in his face. He stood and turned to the window again. What about Alice Blaine? Francine thought. The obvious thing? Easily possible. And if so, couldn't Blaine see it?

She walked to where he stood. "You said that if Webster had come, you might have tried to piece things together. What did you mean?"

"It's unimportant now. He didn't show up."

"What did you mean?"

"Probably nothing. There's probably nothing that can be done. One of us is lying—it happens to be he. And he was under oath. I can't remedy that." He turned on her. "And why should I? What do I owe him that I should jeopardize myself any more?"

"Because he's a man with a lot to lose."

"Then perhaps he'd better lose it. Perhaps he's more of a danger now than he ever was."

"You're *crazy.*" With horror she saw a wildness come into his eyes. "I told you he's out of the party."

"Webster Evers is a coward. Everything he ever did while I knew him, even including his being afraid to come tonight—"

"He is bitter and angry!"

"He is *afraid,* because he would finally have to face me and I can see through his smoothness. Alice always saw that in him, his hypocrisy, his real contempt for people, his cowardice."

Francine went to the liquor cabinet, more to get away from Justin than to get a drink. "Stop that, it isn't so."

"What kind of a man is he then? Has he told the truth to his country? Did he tell you the truth right away?"

She could not answer at first. She gripped the table tightly. "He would be a fool to confess to the committee."

"But did he tell you? You love him, don't you? And I think

you'd be willing to risk everything for him. Well, did he tell you right away? How did you find out?"

She was silent.

"Oh, I remember his boastings about his little affairs when we knew him. Women were to be used, for one thing or another. And polite as he might be to them, he never respected them. I've never really understood before this how much of a predator Webster Evers was, how much he probably deserved Alice's contempt and—" the word died away as the realization hit him—"loathing."

The suspicion was real. Not just the act—the theft itself—but even the when and why. Vague but real now—Alice and Evers and he—as part of a sad pattern. His lip trembled and he felt a sharp pain in his heart. And then it all seemed to dissolve.

Francine stared at him as he sat down again, pale and sweating. "Are you all right?"

"Yes," he said softly. "It's past. But maybe you'd better think about what you're doing. He may not be worth your life."

"*Please,* stop that," she said, but she knew her doubt was growing.

"I'm sorry. It's just that you don't deserve all this pain."

Francine shook her head. "I don't want to talk about that. There must be something you can do to help him. On Friday Webster could agree that he knew you, but under a different name. He didn't recognize your picture, but after meeting you—"

"No."

"—after *meeting* you, he sees that he knew you. *Yes.* You met at parties during the period, you went to the same discussion groups and you assumed—you *assumed*—that Webster was a Communist." Her speech gained momentum. "But you never really had proof, you never in fact knew him to be a Communist. It was all a mistake."

Justin was still shaking his head no, amazed that she could go on like this. "It just is not possible."

"Why not?"

"Because I've already given Pilgrim written evidence of Webster's guilt."

Stunned, Francine asked, "What sort of evidence?"

"The film of a secret document," Justin said, half-regretting that he was divulging what his arsenal was, but feeling impelled to go on, "complete with his signature."

"Oh, God," she said, feeling her legs so weak. "And you're sure it's his signature?"

"His own and very unusual signature."

"We could claim it a forgery. For every expert you get, we'll get two. We'll just deny it."

"And add more perjury? He'd let you get in that deep too? Miss Moore, it won't succeed. Ultimately he's going to be found out. That's why your talk of a deal was so unrealistic."

"He didn't ask me to help him. It was—and is—my own idea."

"But he's letting you help him. He didn't tell you the truth right away, did he?" She said nothing. "Of course not. Well, I can see what he's doing. He kept you out of it, as he keeps everyone out of his real life, until he could use you, until he saw that he must have an instrument, and then he—well, I think you could fill that in much better than I. As for me, I see things more clearly now, present and past. I wish you could too."

She was weeping again, not even trying to cover her eyes, but standing before him, her hands at her sides, her face wet with tears.

"I'm sorry for what I'm going to do Friday—but sorry only for you."

He picked up his coat and left the apartment, closing the door gently behind him. He walked down the hall, trying to preserve the feeling of resolution and clarity he had felt in those last few minutes. But he could not sustain it. The old sadness returned, heavier than before, as he thought of Alice and of himself and of the qualities of repentance and revenge.

Francine stared at the closed door, her face collapsed and passionless. After a while she went to the couch and sat there. Where

was the answer to emptiness and what the replacement for love?
What was the true Webster and what the false? And at what point
did steadfastness and loyalty turn one into a fool?

Suddenly she went to the phone and dialed Webster's number
and Webster answered. "Tell me," she said immediately with a
firmness she had never shown him before, "tell me about you and
this delightful Alice Blaine! What in the dear . . . sweet . . . hell
. . . was there between her and you?"

Chapter Twenty

1952: Washington, D.C.

Justin had to walk five blocks from Francine Moore's apartment before he found a cab to take him out to the airport. The first two drivers he stopped claimed to be going off shift and the third just looked at him and drove away when he heard where he wanted to go. Finally, one took him, looking sullen and muttering under his breath. Everyone, Justin thought, had his own unique and personal brand of problem, his own reasons for saying no to his obligations to others.

The city's streets slid past darkly, looking empty and dangerous. Justin stared morosely out at the slum areas through which they were passing and smiled ruefully. That's it, he thought, when confronted with the need to place blame, look everywhere but at yourself. It was less painful that way; it was easier to accept and to live with. Here he was, in the middle of disaster, and so far he'd tried to place its blame everywhere but on himself. But how long could you live with self-delusion? How long could you go on accepting this panicky and disguised attempt at self-preservation as the truth? He did not know, except that for him that time had passed. In some way, the responsibility for what had happened was entirely and indisputably his, and he was still without a reason for having brought it about.

It was nearly eleven o'clock, but the airport terminal was bustling and crowded. Flight announcements echoed urgently over the public address system and streams of passengers flowed to and from departure gates. At the reservation counter, Justin learned that mechanical difficulties had caused a slight delay in his flight, and he walked restlessly about the huge, coldly lighted building, barely conscious of the activity about him.

He approached a souvenir stand and stared at the clutter of pennants, replicas of monuments, trick hats and plastic toys. His eyes focused on a toy pistol which he picked up and held curiously in both hands. It looked very real and deadly, with the grip authentically gnarled, and the metal of the barrel a smooth, steely blue. His palm slid over the grip and his finger inched past the trigger guard and pressed the trigger. The pistol fired with a sharp click and the hammer snapped back into position.

"May I help you, sir?"

Justin looked dully at the plump, pink-faced woman behind the counter.

"Would you like to buy the revolver?" she asked, smiling.

Justin put down the revolver. "It's not a revolver," he said.

"It isn't?" she said, without great interest.

"No," Justin said, "it's an automatic."

"Oh." The woman's expression had changed from pleasantness to caution. "That's very interesting."

Justin continued to stare consideringly at the toy automatic. Justin Blaine, expert on firearms. He smiled faintly to himself and walked away from the souvenir stand, wondering what had suddenly made him pick up the gun. It had been years since he'd even held one in his hand, yet the cold metal had felt familiar and right against his palm. Somehow it had all seemed of a piece, his thoughts of Webster, the day of their break and . . . the gun. He stopped in front of the baggage claim area, frowning. Of course, he thought, the gun. That, too, had been part of it, part of the same day, the same instant in time. How long ago? Thirteen years? No, not quite. September. September would be thirteen years. He remembered it clearly, because August of 1939 had been the month the Soviet Union made its deal with Nazi Germany by signing the nonaggression pact. September would be thirteen years.

William Baker had taken a taxi across the Potomac to Virginia, and changed to a trolley for the ride into Arlington. It was late afternoon, but still too early for the government workers to begin their exodus from Washington. He had sat almost alone in the swaying trolley, feeling the roll of film secure in his inside jacket pocket, automatically checking the faces of the few other passengers to make sure none of them was known to him. His mind had traced, with the clarity of solid discipline, the rest of the established procedure: the getting off the trolley at the busiest stop, the circuitous walk through downtown Arlington to insure his not being followed, the apparently casual choosing of a park bench for a moment's rest, the contact's sitting beside him a moment later, the barely noticeable transfer of the film, and then the return trip to Washington by a different route—all done with an air of careless detachment, each part clicking off with carefully planned and rigidly controlled accuracy.

Justin let himself sway loosely with the roll of the trolley. He glanced at his watch and noted that it was 4:16, which allowed him forty-four minutes to reach the rendezvous point on time. It would be more than enough. He hadn't been late for a drop-off in fourteen months and he wouldn't be late today. All would go well, he thought. Dependable Alex would take the package and deliver it to dependable Rosoff, who in turn would deliver it to a nameless but equally dependable courier for final transmission to double-dealing, not at all dependable Stalin and Company.

Justin stared bitterly at the empty straw seat across the aisle. The bastards, he thought, the miserable, cynical bastards. It had been only ten days since Stalin's sellout to Hitler had stunned and horrified a world already on the edge of disaster, but to Justin this had been merely the final stone cemented into a charnel house of dead illusions that had been building in anguish for many months.

The backtracking, the lies, the sweeping purges and blood baths that swallowed uncounted thousands with only the flimsiest, most transparent attempts at justification had all been increasingly difficult to excuse and accept. It had been the basis for painful soul-searching, alone, together with Alice and sometimes with Webster —yet only just now did Justin realize how vague Webster's reaction had been. Were they, after all, enlisted in as just and righteous a cause as they had supposed? How sure, he wondered, could you be of your virtue? How sure that you were right? The torturers of the Inquisition had probably also been sure that theirs was the just way. You did your work and you wondered.

You went along with it as far as you could, because you were committed and had been committed for a long time, and it was a hell of a lot harder to get out than in and you were still not that sure anyway. But you wondered, and watched, and talked, and waited, knowing you would have to do something soon, but putting it off because you were badly frightened.

Though you wouldn't admit that, and preferred to think it was only that you were "unsure." So the memory went.

The trolley clanged to a stop and Justin got off, pushing through those pushing to get on. The bank clock said 4:20 and he checked it against his watch and found it a minute fast.

The late sun was still warm as he started to walk north, and he kept to the shade of the store awnings. His hand automatically went to his coat pocket, found the roll and dropped to his side once more. He turned east on Shenandoah Avenue and narrowly missed being struck by a small boy on a bicycle. The men and women who walked past him on the avenue moved sluggishly and looked angry, as though they thought the humid weather was a personal attack.

He headed into an area of run-down stores and buildings. There were at least two bars to a block and the men who went in and out of the bars seemed dispirited and beaten. Justin stopped in front of a store window, pretending to study the display of merchandise, but actually scanning the street to make certain he wasn't being followed. The street was empty behind him, except for a woman carrying a shopping bag and two children playing ball.

He started to walk on, but had gone only a few steps when he stopped and went back to the store window. The store was a pawnshop, with the three gold balls hanging overhead and its windows crowded with a miscellany of guitars, violins, binoculars and guns. Justin looked at the guns: revolvers, automatics, rifles and shotguns, all polished and gleaming, all lethal and ready for use. If the revolution ever did come to America, he thought, the nation's hock shops might well be its major source of armament.

There was a protective iron-mesh grill in front of the window that made it difficult to see very clearly, and Justin had to stoop and angle his head to peer past it. A fat man in a blue, sweat-stained work shirt came up beside him, looked gloomily at the display for a moment, then walked on. Justin straightened. He was breathing heavily, as if he had just run a long distance, and he could feel his shirt collar suddenly moist and much too tight about his neck. Scared, he thought with disgust, scared half to death at just the idea.

Abruptly and without further thought, he went into the store.

Coming in out of the sun, the place seemed dark to him and was airless and musty. Justin blinked to accustom his eyes to the light. A wizened man stood behind a brass-barred cage writing in a notebook. He glanced up as Justin came in, but went on writing. Justin walked slowly down one of the narrow aisles, looking at the variety of goods displayed. He stopped in front of a hanging guitar and tentatively plucked one of the strings. It made a dull, unmusical sound, as if smothered by the heavy air.

"What do you want, a guitar?"

Justin almost jumped. The proprietor had come up silently behind him. He had apparently been standing on some sort of platform in the cage, because he was now nearly dwarflike, with his head appearing much too large for his stunted body.

He smiled with bloodless lips. "I've got some very beautiful guitars. Barely used. Better than new. Fine, Spanish guitars. Some of them made by hand." He picked one out of a pile and blew off the patina of dust. "Now here's a very nice one. I can let you have a good buy on it. It's a—"

"No, no," Justin said. "I'm not interested in a guitar." He moved down the aisle, anxious to get away from the rasping sales pitch and from an unpleasant odor of stale sweat and half-digested onions. He stopped in front of a case of watches. His collar was still choking him and he loosened his tie and opened the button.

"What do you want, a watch?" The man had followed close at his heels. "We have some nice watches. Every one of them guaranteed to work. Guaranteed accurate."

Justin shook his head and moved away once more, feeling pursued and trapped, his eyes searching among the jumbled masses of stock until he saw the display of guns. He stopped in front of them, feeling his shirt cling moistly to his back.

"Ah, of course." The man grinned knowingly. "You want a gun. Why didn't you say so? Everybody's the same." He wagged his head. "They come in for a gun and they look at everything but a gun. They tiptoe around them like they're afraid they'll explode." He went behind the display case and unlocked it. "What do you want, pistol or rifle?"

Justin swallowed dryly. "A pistol." Even the word, he thought, sounded deadly, frightening, more so than rifle or shotgun. Rifles and shotguns were for the hunting of animals. A pistol was for the hunting of men.

"Ah, of course," the man gasped again. "A pistol." He took three of them out and placed them on the counter casually. "There we are."

Justin stared at them.

"Pick one up," the man said. "Try it for size. Get the feel, the heft of it."

Justin stood as if paralyzed.

"This one's a Luger," the man said, holding the weapon up. "German. Very fine mechanism. Very accurate and dependable. One of our boys took it off a dead Kraut during the war."

He thrust it at Justin, who took the pistol and held it gingerly, awkwardly in both hands with the muzzle pointed straight at his stomach.

The proprietor laughed, his face splitting into tiny cracks. "No, no! Never towards yourself. It's not loaded, but never toward yourself. It's always the empty ones that go off."

Justin turned the pistol around and this time it was aimed across the counter at the man's head. The man reached over and patiently twisted it to one side. Justin smiled wryly. Here he was, a theoretically dangerous spy, an agent for a foreign power, who'd never actually held a gun in his hand before, who wouldn't have known what to do with it if he had.

The gun felt surprisingly huge and heavy. He'd somehow never thought of a pistol as being that heavy. He put it down with a feeling of relief.

"It's . . . it's a little large," he said. "Perhaps something a little smaller might be more what I need."

The man peered curiously up at Justin. "What are you going to do with the gun, Mister? What did you have in mind?"

Justin stared dumbly back at the proprietor. His mind, his body, everything about him had seemed almost trancelike in their behavior since he'd walked into the store. Right now his mind was a complete blank.

"Of course it's none of my business," the man said quickly, answering Justin's silence. "I only thought if I knew what you were going to use it for, I'd have a better idea what you need."

"Valuables," Justin said, coming to life. "I carry a lot of valuables in my work. There've been some hold-ups lately. I thought it might be smart if I—"

"Sure. Sure." The man picked up a smaller, sub-nosed, blued-steel pistol. "Now this here's a Beretta. Italian. Very fine construction. The Italians are lousy soldiers, but they make a fine gun. This here's just what you need." He put it into Justin's hand, this time making certain that the muzzle pointed safely to one side. "Six tiny inches in length, weighs a measly twenty-three ounces. You won't even know it's in your pocket."

Justin held the gun. It felt smooth, cold and solid. "I'll take it," he said, suddenly anxious to get it over with. "Do you have bullets for it too?"

"Sure thing." The man probed under the counter and came up with a small box of cartridges. "Nine millimeter. Good size. Makes a nice, neat clean hole." He laughed. "Here. Better let me show you how the thing works. Don't want you to blow your own head off."

He showed Justin how to remove the magazine from the hollowed-out handle, load it with seven cartridges, draw the slide to the rear and release it to place the first cartridge in firing position. "And this here is the safety," he said, indicating a small button directly above the trigger. "Push it back like this and the gun can't go off. Push it forward and you're loaded for bear."

The man had large hands that moved with astounding speed and dexterity as they manipulated the well-oiled mechanisms and his eyes were alight with a deep and private pleasure. Justin watched his skill with the admiration of the physically awkward and mechanically inept. Then the man made him go through all that he'd shown him and when he was convinced that he understood, nodded with satisfaction.

"All right," he chuckled hoarsely. "You're now a very dangerous type to fool with."

He extended the automatic, butt forward and fully loaded, to Justin. "Here."

Justin looked at it as if it were a snake. "Please put it in a bag," he said, "and you'd better unload it. I won't need it today."

The man appraised him pityingly, then shrugged and did as he was told. When Justin had paid him and was leaving, he called after him, "Good luck," making the two words sound, Justin thought, like a prayer for the dead.

Justin walked out into the sun. The air was still hot and humid, but he breathed it gratefully. Then reassured by the weight of the gun, he started briskly along the street.

It was only after he had reached the corner that he realized that he was walking away from the rendezvous point and not toward it. From the moment he had entered the pawnshop until the time he had left, he had been like a sleepwalker. Now he saw, with a wave of relief, that the long-delayed decision to leave the apparatus and everything connected with it had really been made and acted upon. After all the months of fearful brooding, of consideration and self-torment, suddenly he was on the run. He had the gun, the ammunition, the top-secret State Department documents. He was due at the rendezvous in five minutes and he was heading in the opposite direction. He knew that for him there could be no other choice now; he would not turn back. He knew and understood what this meant for him, just as he knew and clearly understood what would happen to him if he were caught. And he felt lighter, less anxious and burdened than he could remember feeling in a long time.

Well, he thought, they would have to find him first, and he had no intention of making it easy for them. And if they did find him? He smiled in grim amusement and shifted the package to his other arm. Like the man said, was he not a very dangerous type to fool with?

2

An announcement was blaring over Washington National Airport's public address system, but Justin did not hear it until it was given the second time. "Flight 217, nonstop to New York, is now ready for boarding at Gate No. 1. Passengers holding space on this flight will please proceed to the boarding area."

Justin scanned the terminal, located Gate No. 1 and shuffled slowly toward it. He removed his glasses and shook his head, trying to make the airport and the people in it more real than the reality of that lost day of his break, thirteen years before. He felt relieved at doing so, as if the day were a thing in time better left where it was, better left forgotten.

He followed the other passengers down the corridor to the

boarding area and waited in line for his ticket to be checked. He kept his hat low over his eyes to insure not being recognized, though he doubted if there was much chance of that happening. Despite all the recent publicity and newspaper magazine photographs, he had the kind of ordinary face that people did not notice. The built-in anonymity of the undistinguished, he thought, did have its moments of compensation. A majority of these same people would probably have been able to identify Webster Evers on sight.

On board the big DC-7, he found it increasingly difficult to keep his mind functioning in the present. His thoughts kept slipping backward as though an unacknowledged portion of himself were still involved in some half-forgotten piece of unfinished business. He moved automatically through the usual preflight routine of choosing a seat, handing his coat to the stewardess and fumbling with the baffling mechanics of his seat belt.

But even the simple click of the metal tongue slipping into place insisted on drawing him back to the hauntingly similar sound of the Beretta, as the automatic's slide was pulled to the rear and released for loading. Justin sighed and reluctantly gave himself up to the prodding of his remembrance of that other, that earlier day.

Thirteen years before. The small, deadly package was under his arm as he signaled the first cab he saw and urged the driver to speed back to Washington, back to where he would see the startled expression on Alice's face as he burst into the living room.

She looked at her watch. "What are you doing home so early? It's only ten after five. You're supposed to have left the contact point only a few . . ." She stopped, her face suddenly white. "Did something go wrong?"

"No," he said, surprised that his voice sounded calm. "Nothing went wrong. I just didn't go."

"You just didn't go?" she echoed.

Justin nodded. Without speaking he opened the package and placed the automatic, along with the small box of cartridges, on a table. This, he thought, should make everything clear enough. He hoped there would not be too many questions, because he felt incapable of answering them. What, after all, could he say? That he'd walked into a pawnshop on pure impulse, bought a pistol, and walked out with all problems resolved, with all the long-considered decisions instantly and irrevocably made?

But there was no need to worry about questions. Alice simply picked up the weapon, clicked out the magazine, neatly drew back the slide and peered into the chamber to make sure it was empty. Then she placed the pistol back on the table as Justin watched in awe. The things, he thought, that women somehow know about.

"I'm glad," she said. "I'm glad you've decided. I think you've done the right thing."

Justin looked gratefully at his wife. If ever he had loved her, he thought, it could never have been more than he did at this moment.

"How much time do we have?" Alice asked.

Justin dropped into a chair and lit a cigarette. "I don't know," he said. "I haven't stopped to figure anything out yet. It all happened so fast." He shook his head. "And I've always been so careful. Everything I've ever done, I've always planned for so well, so systematically. But this is one thing I didn't plan. This is one thing I did entirely without thought." Now he felt dazed. "How much time do you figure before they start looking?"

Alice picked up the empty clip and regarded it thoughtfully. "Well," she said slowly, trying to think it through aloud, "let's see what's going to happen: You're not going to be there, so Alex is going to wait only fifteen minutes—he's not allowed any more, right?"

Justin nodded. "And Alex is a stickler for discipline. He'll leave at 5:15 on the dot."

"All right," Alice went on. "He'll leave and report back to Rosoff that you didn't make the contact. That gives you another half-hour to an hour till he gets in touch with Rosoff." She opened the box of cartridges, took one out and carefully pressed it into the automatic's magazine. "Then Rosoff's going to try to figure out what happened to you. He'll try calling here. There won't be an answer here. At this point Rosoff still doesn't know you've defected."

"He'll probably check my office next, to see if I showed up for work today. He'll . . ." He stopped, finding it difficult to project his thoughts clearly and logically. He watched with fascination as Alice's hands fed another cartridge into the magazine. "He'll then have to get instructions from higher up. He won't dare to make another move without instructions."

Alice went on absorbedly pressing in the cartridges. "Not only that," she said, "but he's also going to have to wait to see if there was some sort of accident. It's going to kill him, but he's still going to have to wait. Because if there *was* an accident, you'd be found with the film on you. And if you were hit by a car, the *police* would find you *and* the film." She smiled grimly. "Rosoff will be just as worried and frightened as we are. This could blow up his whole apparatus. So he *has* to sit tight for about twelve hours to see if an accident was reported. He may use his contacts to check hospitals, morgues and police stations, but this will all take time. I figure it should take at least until tomorrow morning before he can be sure enough to report that there's been no accident, that this was a conscious act on your part and you've got to be crossed off the list. Then the OGPU starts operating. They're going to check every possible spot we might go. But we'll still have all night and into tomorrow morning to move ahead of them. And we'd better start right now and make the most of it."

She looked at Justin. "We're lucky we bought the cabin when we did. I'd hate to have to start groping for a place to hide with them after us."

Justin stood up and ground out his cigarette. They had bought the small country house in upper New York two months before for just such a contingency as this, but now he was not that certain of its effectiveness as a hideout. "Are you sure we might not be better off moving around for a while before we go directly there?"

"Definitely not." Alice pushed the loaded magazine into the receiver with a decisive click. "Moving around is the worst possible thing we can do. Sooner or later, we've got to stop moving, and the place we'll go to will be the cabin. Moving around will just make things harder for us. The cabin is perfect. We bought it under a different name. No one knows us in the area. And living there will be cheap enough to stretch our money for months, if necessary."

Justin did not say anything. He glanced about the tiny apartment in which they had lived for the past two years, seeing the undistinguished collection of secondhand furniture they'd picked up haphazardly at auctions and Salvation Army warehouses, but to which time and use had lent warmth and pleasant familiarity. No possessions, he thought; life was simpler, cleaner and infinitely better without possessions. They only tended to clutter things and choke you with sentiment. He turned abruptly away from the worn, leather chair in which he had sat reading for perhaps two thousand hours, and wished it might have been possible to take at least this.

"I'll go for the car," he said. "Pack whatever you can into the two suitcases. We'll have to leave the rest."

"Two suitcases?" Alice said, and, looking at her, Justin could see the pain in her eyes as she mentally crossed off dishes, lamps, books and lovingly accumulated but no longer to be possessed memorabilia.

"I'm sorry."

"Don't be sorry," she forced a smile. "As long as it doesn't bleed, never be sorry. I'll be ready by the time you get back."

When he was leaving, Alice stopped him at the door. "Wait," she said. "You'd better take this." She pulled back the automatic's slide and released it to chamber the first cartridge and cock the gun for firing. Then she set the thumb safety and handed the pistol to him.

Feeling uncomfortably melodramatic, Justin put the weapon into his inside jacket pocket. As he did so, his hand touched the roll of film. He took it out, undid the tape, peeled the film off the spool, walked to the window and held the long strip up to the light. Then he rolled it into a wad of useless paper and stuffed it into his side pocket with the empty spool.

As he walked out the door Alice spoke. "Get rid of it, Jussie. Even though you've exposed it, get rid of it."

The garage where Justin kept his ancient Chevrolet was half a dozen avenue blocks from the house. He walked there by a round-about route, watching passing cars, other pedestrians and occasional shadowed doorways with a cautious eye. He did not expect trouble this soon, but watched anyway, wondering when, if ever, he would be able to walk down a street again without feeling threatened. At the third corner he paused, one hand in his side pocket, and casually looked around. There was no one in sight. He removed the wad of film and the empty spool and quickly dropped them through the grates of the storm drain.

He reached the garage without incident and stood tensely waiting his turn. He lit a cigarette directly under a large "No Smoking" sign, then suddenly had to go to the men's room. He searched it out, but changed his mind when he saw a pay telephone on the wall close by. He picked up the receiver, inserted a nickel and gave the operator Webster's office number. Webster would still be there, Justin knew, because of the crisis. Germany had already invaded Poland and Britain had issued an ultimatum. The German desk at the State Department would be very busy—which meant, Justin suddenly realized, that Webster might not be able to get away at all.

When Webster answered, his voice showed no excitement.

"This is Bill."

"Oh? How are you?" The words were uttered guardedly but quietly. It was against apparatus discipline for a member to call another where he worked, except for a great emergency.

"I just called to invite you to a little get-together this evening. It's special and we'd love to see you."

Evers responded with his suave social voice. "I'm afraid it's impossible now. I guess you can imagine why."

"I hope you won't disappoint me. We won't expect you to stay long, but it is sort of special." Justin tried to make his voice match Webster's performance, but he knew the urgency was coming through.

There was a pause, as if they had been cut off, and then Webster was back. "As I said, I'm needed here. Business before pleasure at times like this."

He's right, Justin thought. If he leaves there will be questions—even suspicions. He closed his eyes tight as the decision faced him.

"Bill?" Was that a hint of fear Justin heard?

Justin swallowed hard. "If you refuse me another invitation, I'll just have to cross you off our list."

Again there was a pause. Dimly, Justin could hear Evers' voice. ". . . a friend . . . right with you, sorry." And louder, but more hurried and conspiratorial: "I'll see what I can do, but I can only make an appearance. Is it at your town place?

"No, at the other. It starts at seven."

"I'll do my best. Good-bye."

Justin's hand trembled as he replaced the receiver on the hook. Party discipline—unfailing as a savior, and perhaps as a weapon—what had it been just now? An urge came to call back to cancel the meeting. After all, he had called because he thought he owed Webster an explanation, but he had forgotten—how *could* he have forgotten?—what taking Webster away from his post would mean. Now it was all wrong. As usual, it was all wrong. Still, he thought, it need only be an hour's absence for Webster, and he must know and understand.

He was glad when the attendant honked the horn of his car to signal him, to relieve him—he told himself fervently—of the burden of this decision.

3

"Would you care for a pillow, sir?"

Justin glanced up at the smiling stewardess and shook his head. "Thank you, no." He adjusted his seat to a reclining position and settled back. The moon had broken through, silvering the clouds, and Justin wished that he might have been able to come out of himself and enjoy the beauty of such things more often. Too much of his life, he thought, had been spent looking inward.

He closed his eyes and pretended to himself that he was drowsy. There was no point in thinking about the past now. There was nothing to be gained by trying to relive a few hours that had died thirteen years before. He could use sleep far more than this post-humous searching.

After a while he did actually begin to drift off, but even though he tried hard to believe that his thoughts were simply dreams, he was aware of exactly where they were taking him.

Alice and he were in the car, with the two suitcases in the trunk, and they were driving north, toward Baltimore, along Route 1. Justin was driving, his hands, as always, clutching the wheel much too tightly, his thick body hunched tensely and gracelessly forward. They rode without speaking. Occasionally, Justin glanced at his wife's face as he drove, but Alice did not appear to notice and merely stared ahead through the dusty windshield. The soft evening light edged her blond hair, making her look wonderfully pretty and desirable. So many years, he thought, and he still felt a mixture of wonder and gratitude when he looked at her. How could a woman such as this have fallen in love with a type like himself? Surely it was one of life's more pleasant mysteries.

They came to an intersection and Justin slowed the car and turned onto a narrow unpaved road going off to the right.

Alice looked at him in surprise. "Where are you going?"

Justin did not answer. He appeared very absorbed in avoiding ruts in the road.

"Where are you going?" Alice repeated.

"We're meeting someone before we go."

Alice stiffened. "Who?" she asked sharply, clearly suspecting the answer, but asking anyway.

"Webster," Justin said. After thinking about it, he had decided to do it this way, without telling her in advance. He figured it would save a lot of time-wasting, pointless discussion.

"No!" The word was almost shouted. "You couldn't be that much of a fool!"

Alice had swung around on the seat to glare at him. Her face was white with anger. Justin glanced briefly at her, then looked once more at the road. He'd expected disapproval, not fury.

"At a time like this, you're going to announce that you're breaking? You can't trust him with something like this. What if he turns us in? Our very lives depend on getting a safe start that can't be traced. Now you're going to trust this—this—" she groped for a bad enough word—". . . this two-faced bastard, this hypocrite, to keep information like this to himself?"

Justin steered carefully around a deep hole in the road. His wife's antagonism toward Webster had puzzled him too long for him to seek a logical reason for it now. Over the past year it had grown so intense that Alice had absolutely refused to see him at all. Webster Evers, she claimed bitterly, was the worst kind of fraud, and she despised frauds. He gave her the creeps. He was obnoxiously ambitious, supercilious, smug, and he'd do anything to further his own precious career. It was fine that he served some purpose in the apparatus, and if Justin wanted a man like that for a friend he could have him, but she herself was bowing out of the entire relationship. She wanted no part, not even the sight, of him. And this was the way it had been for more than two years.

"Jussie, please!" The anger had changed to an almost desperate pleading. "You've *got* to listen to me."

Justin turned off onto another, even narrower dirt road. They had not passed a house since they had left Route 1, nor had they seen another car. The area was heavily wooded and the underbrush was high, so that it was impossible to see more than a few yards in any direction. Justin abruptly swung the car onto a grassy shoulder and stopped. He squinted through the trees ahead. Behind a stand of pine and almost hidden from view, a dark blue car was barely visible.

Justin cut the motor. "There's his car," he said. "He's waiting. Come on. I want to get this over with as fast as possible and move on." He opened the car door and put one leg out.

"I'm not going with you."

Justin brought his leg back in. "What are you talking about? What do you mean, you're not going with me?"

Alice's face was set. "Just what I said. Maybe I can't stop you from doing this idiotic thing. I don't have to sit there and watch it."

Justin frowned at the violence in her voice. "Now you're being completely unreasonable. This is going to be a very important discussion. I want you to be part of it. You have some of the responsibility for bringing Webster in too. You know why I'm here. I got him into this thing. Now I've got to at least let him know why I'm getting out."

"Would he do as much for you?" She didn't wait for an answer. "Like hell he would!"

"I can't see what—"

"This isn't the time to stop," Alice broke in. "You know how much time we've got. And letting one person know what we've done—even in which direction we're headed—there are twenty directions we might have gone. By knowing we're on Route 1, going north, they can almost rule out the others. Instead of sending them scurrying all over the place, you're narrowing it down."

Justin shook his head, brushing her arguments aside. "There are certain decisions that *I* have to make by myself, with or without your approval. This happens to be one of them. And I'm not going to let you sit here acting like a pouting child." He stared at her, genuinely puzzled. "My God, I've never heard of such a thing. I've never known you to act like this before. Just because you dislike the man is no reason to behave with such vengefulness and spite. Webster's still a man, a human being, and despite the way you feel, I consider him a friend."

"Friend!" Alice spat the word like something vile.

Justin looked at her for a moment in silence, then got out of the car, walked around to her side and opened the door. "You're coming over there with me," he said quietly. "If I have to drag you bodily, you're coming."

Alice studied the backs of her hands. She started to say something, then changed her mind.

"You're coming." Justin said.

She did not move. Justin put his hand on her arm, but she shook it off. "All right," she said with resignation, "all right."

They walked stiffly toward the clearing in which Webster was parked. When they reached the car, Justin opened the front door so that Alice could get in beside Webster. She hesitated and then climbed in. Justin took the back seat.

Webster's long face was serious, but he said cordially, "Hello, Alice, it's been a long time."

The answering look on her face stunned Justin. My God, how she *despises* him, he thought. Webster, seeming unmoved, turned back to Justin.

"This had better be important, Bill. I had to do some very fancy talking to get away. I should be there now—and you know why."

"All right," Justin said heavily, "what I called you for was . . ." He stopped, trying to figure how to best present it. "This probably won't come as too much of a surprise," he tried, "in view of some of the discussions we've been having, but I've decided to break. I'm getting out of the party, the apparatus, the whole mess. I've had it."

Webster looked at him for a long moment. Then he smiled faintly.

"Is something funny?" Justin said, annoyed at the reaction. He glanced at Alice, but she was staring off somewhere into the trees.

"No," Webster said, "not really funny at all. I was just thinking of something you once said. It was when you first were trying to get me in."

"What was that?" Justin said curtly.

"That the only way they let you out, once you were in, was if they want you out. And the implication was it would be with a bullet in the back of the head."

Justin nodded slowly. "That's still true. But they're going to have to find me first to do it."

Webster looked at him, then at Alice's frozen expression, then at Justin once more. "You mean you're all packed and on your way?"

"All packed," Justin said. "In fact, we shouldn't even be here now. Every minute of time we can get is precious." He glanced at Alice. "That's probably why my wife is sitting there looking as though she's ready to chew nails." Alice turned to glare at him, and Justin wondered why he *had* felt it necessary to explain her behavior to Webster.

Webster's face showed nothing as he lit a cigarette and tossed the match out the window. "Alice is right," he said. "If you've made the break, you *shouldn't* be here. You've told me yourself there's no room for sentiment in this business."

"Maybe not. But I did feel I should let you know. I did feel I owed it to you. And I think you understand why I'm doing this."

"Thanks," Webster said coldly. "But how do you figure that? I don't see where each of us owes the other anything. We were both working for something in which we believed. You were never my keeper."

Justin took off his glasses and polished them on his sleeve, puzzled and irritated by a reaction that seemed unreasonably close to belligerence. "Listen to me," he said with forced calm. "I've talked to you before about why I'm leaving. You're the only one I *have* talked to outside of Alice. I've been able to talk to you not only because you were a friend, but because you weren't a fanatic about Communism. It's almost impossible in the party to find someone you can talk to. You never know what the other man is thinking, whether or not he'll turn you in the next day as a revisionist. I've never had that feeling about you." He put on his glasses and squinted through them. "That is why it's possible for me to come to you now, when I've made a move from which there's no returning, and tell you about it. I brought you into this originally. I made you do much of what you've done. I feel I owe you the chance to get out with me now that I'm leaving."

"What do you mean you *made* me?" Webster said angrily. "I'm not a child. Nobody *makes* me do anything."

"Talk sense, Webster. *I've* made up my mind about getting out of this mess, and I'm here because I want to see you do the same."

"Oh, do you?" Webster nodded slowly. He looked off, past Alice, at a hawk circling a tall, dead tree. He watched the bird closely until it had landed on an upper branch, then turned to Justin. "You feel," he said, "that just because you've made up your mind, that just because things have suddenly become crystal-clear to you, the next step is to pass on the good word to me. You press the button and I jump. Is that it?"

"No, that's not it. All I wanted to—"

"Well, I don't jump that way," Webster went on. "I still think I can be useful—more so than ever now. I can see why you want out. Stalin's sold your ideals down the river. Well, don't forget I never shared those ideals of the perfect Communist state." Webster smiled wryly. "You disappoint me, Bill. I thought you had a stronger stomach for reality than to be queasy over the demands of what must be done. Perhaps I'm more experienced—or more sophisticated—in these matters than you, but I still believe that Russia is the last hope against Hitler. Oh, yes, Britain and France will go to war against him, and the Commonwealth and so on, but they're weak. And what could Stalin have done to protect Poland? Don't you see? This pact buys time! Now he can get ready so that Hitler won't dare attack him, so that he might even attack Germany. Sure they may parcel out Poland between themselves. Rus-

sia needs a buffer for security's sake. Good God, Bill, wake up to
the facts of life. Stalin is a master at the game."

Justin frowned, feeling sick and hopeless. He could not look at
Alice.

Webster continued. "Don't waste any eloquent little arguments
on me. You may just as well save them. I've no intention of joining
you in exile." He smiled sardonically. "Maybe I can even talk you
out of taking this badly misguided step yourself. Think about
it."

What was he to do now? Justin wondered. He'd given Webster
what amounted to a gun pointed at their heads and had done
everything but invite him to pull the trigger.

No one said anything and overhead a flock of birds made a
metallic racket in the trees. Alice turned around in the front seat
and looked squarely at Justin and he knew, without any doubt,
what she was thinking.

"Who knows, so far, that you're breaking?" Webster said, unaware of the heightened tension in the car. "Has anyone had time
to find out yet?"

Justin shook his head. "Not for sure. We've figured they won't
know for about another twelve hours." That's right, he thought,
with disgust, tell him everything. The only thing he didn't know
was exactly where they were going, but now he had an idea of the
direction. His hand slipped into his jacket pocket and touched the
smooth, cold surface of the Beretta. His stomach tightened and a
pulse in his temple began to beat insistently. But he forced his
hand to remain on the gun and his finger groped past the trigger
guard onto the trigger.

"I still think it's crazy," Webster said stubbornly. "I still think
you should turn around and go back. You'll have to be in hiding for
God only knows how long, and in the end they'll probably find you
anyway."

"How will they find us," Alice said, almost in a whisper, "unless
you put them on our trail?" She did not look at Webster as she
spoke. Her eyes were still staring, as if transfixed, at Justin's face,
clearly waiting.

Webster looked as though she had struck him. "I hope for all our sakes," he said quietly, "that you're joking."

Her face swung harshly, accusingly toward him. "I've sat here listening to you speak for the last ten minutes and you sounded like an editorial from the *Daily Worker*. I told Justin he was making a mistake in meeting you, but he wouldn't listen to me. Now he'll have to judge for himself just how far you can be trusted."

Webster stared at her. "Alice, do you really . . ." He broke off as he saw the gun in Justin's hand. With the careful deliberateness of a drunk an instant from passing out, Justin held it awkwardly, away from his body, his stubby fingers clutching the receiver and trigger guard with stiff intensity. The muzzle was pointed downward, but as Webster watched, it slowly rose until it was aimed directly at his head. He looked mutely into the small dark hole, unable to speak or move. But his brain, somehow, coldly recorded the fact that he was about to die. There was no doubt that this was so and, considering the facts, it should not have been surprising. He waited for the impact of the bullet, wondering, with an odd apathy, what the sensation would be.

A crow glided down from a branch overhead, circled the car curiously and landed without sound on the path ahead. Justin barely noticed it. He was staring at the gun in his hand. It was steady, he thought, it was absolutely steady. This fact, the fact that his hand was not trembling, amazed him. He felt no other emotion, but was sharply aware of the pulse pounding in his temple. He looked at Webster over the pistol barrel, seeing tiny beads of sweat edging his upper lip.

Alice stirred on the front seat as she moved farther away from Webster. The small action drew Justin's attention; he looked at her face and suddenly, crazily, did not know her. He squinted behind his lenses, as if to clear his vision, but there was no change in what he saw. The strange, awful distortion of her features remained, her eyes wide and shining as they stared at the pistol, her lips pulled to a taut, expectant line, her nostrils flared with some secret, unacknowledged passion, her entire expression one of explosive, barely contained eagerness. My God, he thought, she *wants* to see him killed. She's *waiting* for him to be killed. The gun began to tremble in his hand, but he could not stop looking at her face.

4

"Would you please fasten your seat belt, sir?" the stewardess said. "We're about to come in for our landing."

Justin glanced up at the girl with a start and then groped for the two halves of his belt and fumbled them together. He turned toward the window where, far below, the lights of New York were beginning to show, but he saw only the terrible outlines of his wife's face as it had been in the car. Why, he wondered, had she so wanted Webster to die? Her intense desire for it, the look on her face as she waited for it!

The plane shuddered as the landing gear was lowered. Then the "No Smoking" sign flashed on. Those passengers who had been talking gradually allowed their conversation to die, as though without their full attention the descent might be jeopardized.

Moments later the wheels touched the ground and the plane taxied toward the sprawling terminal. The stewardess brought Justin his coat and he took it without thanks or acknowledgment. When the plane finally rolled to a stop, he followed the other passengers down the aisle to the rear. He stumbled heavily down the steps, missing the one at the bottom and almost falling, and walked slowly toward the terminal. Some passengers rushed past him, jostling him in their excitement, but he did not notice. Why had she wanted Webster killed? Why hadn't he ever wondered about it before? And the wondering now brought back the dark, saddening suspicion that had stolen upon him in Francine's apartment. He started down a long corridor lined with telephone booths that led to the main terminal area. And Webster? Thirteen years ago in that car . . . what about Webster then?

Justin felt the gun trembling in his hand and the sickness rising to his throat. He knew he could never pull the trigger. How could he have even thought of killing him, of killing *anyone?* Would this have been any way to begin a new life, to erase the errors of the wasted years?

Outside, on the path, the crow took off and flew back toward its tree. Justin slowly lowered the automatic.

Without warning, Alice suddenly reached back and snatched the pistol from his hand. She pointed it at Webster's head and tried to squeeze the trigger. Nothing happened. Her finger pulled at the trigger again, and again the pistol did not fire.

The safety, Justin thought, he'd never released the safety. He grabbed the gun from his wife's hand just as she too remembered the safety and was frantically reaching for the button.

Webster had remained motionless. Now he sagged limply against the car door. His face was white, and his hands seemed palsied. He stared at Alice with horror and disbelief. "You would have killed me," he whispered. "You actually would have killed me."

Alice was shaken by deep, convulsive sobs. "I'd never have believed it," Webster breathed softly, as if to himself. "I'd never have believed you cared that much."

Justin groped for the door handle and got out of the car. He pulled Alice out, and they walked back to where the Chevrolet was parked.

5

The sound of the telephone dial seemed to intrude. Justin shuddered, looking around him. What was he doing in a telephone booth? He was holding the receiver to his ear and could hear the dull buzzing of the phone at the other end. Then the buzzing was interrupted and he heard his wife's voice say, "Hello?"

"Hello?" Alice said again. "Hello? Who's there?"

Justin stared at the phone. "Why?" he asked hoarsely, his voice sounding deep as if lost in his throat. "Why did Webster say that?

Why did he say he'd never have believed you cared that much?"

"Justin? Is that you?" She began to sound frantic. "Where are you? What are you talking about?"

Justin took off his glasses and wiped his face with the back of his hand. It was not that hot in the phone booth, but he was dripping sweat. "When we were in the car that day, when we—"

"What car?" Alice asked wildly. "What day? Justin, what's wrong with you? Are you all right?"

"All right?" Justin leaned against the wall of the booth. He felt dizzy. "Of course I'm all right."

"What about the meeting with Webster and Francine Moore?" she asked.

"Don't talk about the meeting," he said angrily. "I'm not interested in the meeting."

"Justin? Did something happen there?"

"No! No!" He was shouting into the phone and did not know it. "Nothing happened at the meeting. Webster didn't even show up."

"Well, then, what's the matter?" she pleaded. "What happened to you? What's gotten you so . . . so excited? Why don't you come home? Tell me about it when you come home. You'll be home in half an hour. Do you want me to come down and pick you up?" She was speaking quickly, soothingly, as though trying to calm an hysterical child. "I'll drive out to the airport and pick you up. I'll get a cab and meet you there. You *are* at the airport, aren't you? Tell me exactly where to meet you."

"No. That's ridiculous." Justin closed his eyes as the walls of the booth began to waver, but it was worse that way and he opened them once more. "I've got to talk about this now. I can't spend even another half-hour with it." He put his glasses back on and tried to focus on the blur of people hurrying past the booth. "I've been living with this for thirteen years. But I've been too thick and stupid to understand what was in my mind. What was I listening to that day in the car? How could I have shut off my senses that way?"

"What are you talking about?" Alice said, a new note of caution suddenly shading her voice. She was silent for a moment and the muffled sound of a flight announcement filled the gap. "Are you sure Webster wasn't there? What did he tell you?" she asked anxiously. "What lies did he tell you?"

"He didn't have to tell me," Justin mumbled thickly. It was hard to form the words. "Suddenly it was all there for me. That you had turned to *him!*"

"You don't understand!" Alice broke in fiercely. "You couldn't possibly understand. Why are we going on like this on the phone? It's insane. You've got to come home right now and let me talk to you. I won't talk to you over the phone this way. I'm going to hang up right now."

"Don't you hang up!" Justin shouted. His mouth was less than an inch from the receiver and he was breathing heavily, with a harsh, rasping sound. "Don't you *dare* hang up!"

Alice started to cry at the other end of the wire. "You've got this thing all wrong. It's something I can't explain to you this way." Alice's words were hard to understand through her sobs. "I'm not going to talk or listen to any more. Not like this."

Then there was a click and silence.

"No!" Justin yelled. "Don't you . . ." He jiggled the hook savagely. "Hello! Hello!" His voice echoed, lost and hollow, in his ears. His face was twisted and sweating and he suddenly could not breathe. His vision went dark, and he slipped slowly from the seat onto the floor.

Only the top of Justin's head could be seen from outside the booth. His hat had fallen off and a few inches of rumpled, graying hair were visible through the glassed, upper half of the folding door. The wooden bottom half shielded his body from sight. Three of four minutes later, an elderly man approached the apparently empty booth to use it, tried to push open the doors and found they were stuck. He glanced down and saw the top of Justin's head.

"Jesus," he said softly and tried again to push open the door, but Justin lay crumpled against the hinges of the door so that it could not budge. The old man tapped nervously on the glass. When Justin refused to respond, the old man looked about anxiously for help. But the corridor was deserted, except for a woman who had just come out of a nearby booth.

The old man beckoned to her and she came toward him, frowning suspiciously. "A man," he said, pointing, "a man is unconscious in there."

The woman glanced into the booth and sniffed. "Probably drunk," she said, and walked away. The old man looked after her with faded eyes. A tall cashmere-coated man carrying a tan leather attaché case strode briskly out of another booth and the old man called him over. "A man is unconscious in here," he said. "Please. I can't open the door."

The tall man looked through the glass at the top of Justin's head. He pushed tentatively at the door and shrugged when it would not open. "Don't get involved, Pop. Life is complicated enough. He'll probably come out of it himself." He hurried off down the corridor.

The old man stood worriedly peering into the booth. He tapped once more on the glass, and then stood there, maintaining a solitary vigil.

Justin stirred. His head was pounding, but he heard strange noises that did not seem to have anything to do with his head. He forced open his eyes and looked up at the walls and ceiling of the phone booth. The sounds seemed to be coming from somewhere to his right and behind him, where he could dimly see a blur of faces staring in at him. There were voices, but he could not understand what they were saying. Then he felt the pressure of the door jiggling against his back and side, and it came to him that it could not be opened.

He tried to shift his weight and straighten, but the walls of the booth started to turn.

"He's moving," a muffled voice said through the door. "I swear, I just saw him move."

"No," someone disagreed. "It was just the door jiggling him. The guy's probably dead. He sure looks dead."

"Where the hell's the fire department?" a third voice asked. "Why don't someone call the fire department?"

"They're getting an ax. I heard they're getting an ax to chop him out."

Justin stirred and heard an encouraging response from the other side of the door. He lifted a hand and the voices grew louder. He squirmed slightly to one side, so that his hand might reach the pills in the side pocket of his jacket. The effort exhausted and dizzied him and he needed to rest twice before his fingers finally closed about the small, plastic bottle. Prying loose the cap with his thumbnail proved to be another weirdly difficult problem, but he managed this also, spilling the pills into his pocket and at last getting two of them into his mouth. He swallowed hard and gagged before they went down.

Moments later he had moved himself enough to allow outside hands to snake inside the booth and help him out. With some surprise, he found he was able to stand almost unaided. Someone got a chair and put him into it and someone else gave him a paper cup of water. A small cluster of people gathered curiously about him, but when it became apparent that he was going to be all right, they drifted away, looking vaguely cheated.

Justin sat sipping the water. He was very thirsty, but found it hard to swallow.

"Here are your glasses," someone said quietly. "They're not even cracked."

Justin took them and looked up at an old man with faded eyes and very wrinkled skin. The old man smiled, seeming greatly pleased at his recovery.

"You'll be all right," the old man assured Justin. "You'll see. You'll be just fine."

Justin looked at him. He was a nice old man, he thought, with compassionate eyes and a gentle voice. He'd lived a long time and knew about many things. But this was one thing he knew nothing about at all.

Chapter Twenty-One

1952: New York City

Alice had wandered tensely through every room in the apartment and had finally settled in the living room with all but one of the lamps darkened. She sat before the fireplace in the gloom, stabbing a poker at the remnants of a fire. The antique clock in the foyer had just tolled four times, the usually pleasant musical chimes suddenly sounding tragic and foreboding.

Justin had called at twelve-thirty. Where could he be? What could he be doing? It took only forty-five minutes to get home from the airport in a taxi. Her mind had already churned through most of the disastrous possibilities, starting with the ever-threatening blood-pressure attack and ending in the morgue. She expected the phone to ring and to hear an impersonal, official voice informing her that her husband would not be home on this or any other night. She kept trying to prepare herself to receive the news. There would be no point to screaming and tearing her hair. She had accepted and lived with other disasters; she would accept and learn to live with this.

She tried to imagine what it would be like to live without Justin. She'd never stay on here in the apartment, of course. Even if she could afford it, which she knew she couldn't, she wouldn't want to stay on, drifting through all these rooms, obsessed with thoughts of the way it had once been. She would probably take two rooms and a kitchenette someplace and eat in restaurants most of the time because there was no pleasure in cooking for one and she hated to eat alone. She'd try to get a job in an office or department store, for which she had neither training nor desire, and after a respectable interval, friends would try to fix her up with dates, assuring her of her youth and attractiveness and the need for life to be lived. She'd look for things to do at night to keep from having to go home, and she'd remember Justin when he was twenty-four and hopeful and full of beautiful illusions about people and things, and she'd brood about the night she lost the baby and the way Justin had held her and comforted her, and how he always looked at her as though she were someone special. And after a while, of course, whatever bad there had been between them would be forgotten and all the good would seem far better than it actually had been.

"He's coming home," she said aloud. "He's all right. I've got to stop thinking like this. Any minute now, he'll be coming home."

She got up and walked to the window and looked out at the deserted street. And what if he did come home, she thought, what then? From the way he'd sounded on the phone, wild, accusing, fiercely irrational, anything was possible. She still wasn't sure of exactly what he knew, but from what he had said she assumed it could be only one thing.

She stared out at the silent street, feeling empty and frightened. Why would Webster have told? What could he possibly have hoped to gain by it? How would this help him to fight the other, the far more important thing? Unless it had simply been the bitter vengefulness of desperation, the need to strike back *some* way, *any* way, to hit where it would hurt most. Maybe you'll get me on Friday, you bastard, but I got your wife fifteen years ago! Could this have been it? Somehow, she did not think so. It didn't sound like Webster. And Justin had said on the phone that he hadn't seen Webster. Although she couldn't really put too much faith in that. From the way Justin had sounded, he might just as well have said anything. Then how?

Alice left the window and went back to the fire. What difference, she thought tiredly, did that really make? Who cared about how? All she cared about was what would happen, what might have already happened, because of it. And the damned frustration of having to just sit and wait and do nothing. There was no one she could call up and speak to about it. There were no close relatives or friends to confide in now and she couldn't call the police. With the confrontation in four days, she was afraid to chance the unfavorable publicity. If the papers had even a hint of irrational speech or behavior from Justin Blaine, the credibility of his position before the committee would be jeopardized.

She picked up the poker and probed among the embers. She felt shaky and weak, as though she hadn't slept for nights.

Almost half an hour later she thought she heard a sound at the front door. She straightened in her chair and listened, but heard nothing. Then she heard it again and knew it was a key groping for the lock. She stood up and hurried toward the foyer.

The door opened slowly and Justin stood there, looking at her, hatless, his clothing and hair rumpled. He seemed uncertain as to whether or not he was expected to come in. "It's late," he mumbled apologetically. "I'm sorry. I know it must be very late."

Seeing how his face and eyes were, Alice looked away to keep from breaking into tears. "Your hat," she said, "you've lost your hat."

Justin touched his head. "I guess I have." He shuffled past Alice into the foyer, forgetting about closing the door.

Alice went to close it. When she turned around, he was no longer in the foyer. She walked quickly into the living room, and he was there, still in his coat, staring blankly at what remained of the fire. "I've been sitting here going out of my head," she said, watching him closely, trying to gauge his state of mind, what he was feeling, what he might do. "I've been sitting here for three and a half hours. Where on earth have you been?"

"Walking."

"That's all?"

Justin did not answer. He slumped into a chair facing the fireplace, and seemed to melt into the upholstery. Alice sat down a few feet away, almost wishing for the accusations, wanting the anger he'd shown on the phone. She had never seen him like this. His face was a pasty color and without expression; his eyes were watery and focused on nothing.

"I didn't know what to think," Alice said, needing to talk. "I thought maybe you'd had an attack somewhere. The way you sounded before, I didn't know what to do, whom to call. With the committee meeting on Friday, I was afraid to call the police. I was afraid . . ." She stopped as she saw that he wasn't listening. "Justin," she said. "Justin, are you all right?"

He nodded from a long way off.

Then, looking at him, she was unable to hold it in any longer. "What is it?" She wept. "Tell me. At least tell me what it is."

"Forget it," Justin said. "It's not worth talking about. Just forget it." He looked at her and saw that she was crying. "You don't have to cry. There's nothing for you to cry about. There's nothing that's your fault. I don't blame you. I want you to know that. I don't blame you at all."

Alice brushed at her eyes with a sodden handkerchief. "But you said," she began, puzzled. "On the phone you said that I . . ." She stopped, unable to remember the wording of the accusations and afraid of what she might reveal by saying the wrong thing.

"Forget what I said on the phone," Justin said dully. "I was crazy on the phone. I talked without thinking." He stared into the fire. "I've had time to think since then. I've had plenty of time to think. Whatever happened between you and Webster—whatever it was, I can't really blame you." His face twisted convulsively. "I don't know why you ever married a fat, stupid-looking slob like me anyway. I guess I've never known why. I've never really believed it was possible for someone like you to love me. I accepted it. I was grateful for it. But I suppose I never believed it. Of course I tried to fool myself with the idea that I—"

"No! No! That's not true. You mustn't—"

"Look at me!" he shouted, standing up and throwing his arms wide. "Look at me! A clumsy, half-blind slob!" he yelled hoarsely. "A flatfooted, meat-faced, apoplectic slob! Don't you think I know what I am? Don't you think I've always known?" He laughed harshly. "I've known, all right. I was taught. I had good teachers. The world is lousy with good teachers. I had the best, starting with my father. Look at me! I'm living proof of his judgment." Justin's face was contorted with pain. "I *am* nothing. I never *have* done anything right. My God! If anyone should know that, it's you."

"Don't . . ." Alice pleaded. "Please, Jussie, don't . . ."

"Wrong," Justin went on inexorably, "everything I've ever done, every important decision—wrong. You've lived half a lifetime with me. You've seen. At every crucial moment in our lives you're the one who always knew what to do." His voice turned into a flat, lifeless singsong. "When you told me not to go to the committee and confess, you were right and I was wrong. Right down the line . . . everything. You said I should never have gotten involved with Webster Evers—I went and *got* involved with Webster Evers. If I'd followed your advice and *not* stopped to see Webster that day thirteen years ago when we left Washington, I might never have realized what I did tonight. I'd be a much happier man. Right down the line, you were right, always right, and I was wrong."

"No," Alice wept. "Jussie, no. Don't do this to yourself." She tried to go to him, to comfort him, but he moved away, determined not to be comforted.

He removed his coat and jacket. In his rumpled shirt and creased trousers, his body seemed flaccid, as though there were nothing beneath the flesh holding it together.

"I don't blame you for what you've done," he went on. "I don't blame you. I don't blame . . ." His voice drifted off, broken and hoarse and unrecognizable. "And on Friday," he whispered, "I'll make a fool of myself again. You'll see. Everything will come crashing down on our heads. Be smart and get out now. You should have gotten out years ago, but at least get out now. There's no future with me. I'll give you a divorce. Go marry someone else. Go marry a *man*. You're still young and good-looking. Marry someone who might be able to touch something and not have it turn to shit every time."

"Stop it!" Alice yelled. "Stop it! Stop it! Stop it!" She was on her feet, her hands formed into fists. "I can't listen to any more of that. I *won't* listen." Her cheeks still wet with tears, she forced anger to blot out everything else. She was no longer frightened or worried about herself. She knew now what it was that she had to face. "I've got to make it clear to you. I've got to tell you how it *really* was with Webster."

"No. No. I don't have to hear about it. I don't want to hear about it." Justin spoke very quickly, running the words together in little breathless spasms. He went over to the fireplace and leaned weakly against the mantel, his back to Alice. "Why go through all that? It's bad enough as it is. I can understand how you needed someone like him. You needed a man and you only had me. How could I blame you?"

Alice strode over to him and glared at the back of his head. "I know you don't want to hear about it," she said grimly. "You'd rather let yourself wallow in self-pity. You'd rather just stand there and torture yourself." She was genuinely angry now. "Well, you're going to listen to what I have to tell you anyway. You're the one who brought it up. All right, so you've found out now, fifteen years later. What did you find out? What was so awful about it? Do you know what the whole idiotic thing, the whole stupid, disgusting thing amounted to?"

Justin stood facing the wall above the mantel. "I don't care," he said flatly. "I don't want to hear about it."

"It amounted to nothing. That afternoon when he came to have the memo shot—I was miserable then, half-crazy. You know how

I was. I'm still not sure how it happened. I was wretched and confused and—it happened. And I hated him for it. That's why I kept the film! I never turned to him, Jussie, I couldn't have. It was just that I had no defenses, I didn't know what I wanted or what was right or wrong. There's only been one man in my life I've ever loved, and that's you. How could I ever have loved that weakling? How could I have compared him to you?"

Justin stared back at her. He shook his head, but this time did not say anything.

"I was ready to clutch at anything. I felt so lost, so helpless."

Justin had been standing, but sat down now, looking anguished and lost. "I was there," he whispered. "I was there." He stared at his wife's face as if trying to discover something that had been there for a long time, but which, for some reason, he had never been able to see. "Why didn't you clutch at *me?*"

"It's not really the same thing," Alice said. "It sounds crazy now, but when you're like that . . ." She shrugged. "In a way, I suppose, I was a little insane." She suddenly shuddered and walked to the window and looked out. Against the glow of the single lamp she looked youthful and slender. "I suppose Webster was vulnerable too, but I'm not blaming him. It was me. These things don't happen if the woman . . ." She turned and looked at Justin. "Did he say anything tonight? What did he tell you?"

"I told you, he wasn't even there. I just spoke with the Moore woman," Justin said listlessly. His thoughts were on their life of fifteen years before. "She tried to get him to come, but he refused to see me."

"You mean that woman got you down there on a fool's errand? For nothing?"

"It wasn't her fault. She thought he was coming. He just changed his mind." Justin's eyes were sorrowful. "And the trip wasn't for nothing," he said harshly. "Look at all the lovely, heart-warming things it brought into proper focus for me." His mouth twisted in a bitter parody of a smile. "Just think. Perhaps, if I hadn't gone to Washington last night, I might have gone to my grave never realizing that you and Webster—"

"Insanity!" Alice shouted, "an instant's insanity and you want to destroy a lifetime over it." There was a large mirror in a baroque frame opposite the fireplace, and she stared broodingly at her shadowed image in it. "I despised him. It wasn't all his fault, but, God, how I loathed him."

"I know," Justin said grimly. "Enough to want to kill him in the car that day. And enough to keep the film so you could use it against him."

Alice moved away from the sight of her reflection. She nodded slowly. "That's right."

"You cared that much," Justin said, echoing the remembered words, suffering even now as he spoke them.

"No," Alice said. "I felt exposed, naked, dirty in his sight. That's the only true feeling I got out of it."

Justin tried to light a cigarette, but the match went out. It was his last one and he sat staring at the empty match cover, his hand shaking.

They were silent for several minutes.

"Are you hungry?" Alice finally said. "Would you like something to eat?"

Justin started to shake his head, but stopped as he discovered that even this slight movement tended to bring on dizziness.

"Are you sure? There's some nice cold chicken in the refrigerator. You probably haven't eaten since God knows when."

"No," he said. "I couldn't eat anything right now."

Again they sat in heavy, strained silence. Upstairs, a faint sound of footsteps drifted over them.

Alice sighed. "It's after five," she said. "You look half dead."

"I'm all right."

"You ought to go to bed."

"I wouldn't sleep."

"You ought to at least try."

There was more silence, as they sat, not quite able to look at one another.

"Do you have your pills? I'm afraid for your heart."

"Yes, I've got them. Besides, my heart's all right. Just a little high blood pressure."

"All this excitement is bad for you. You have to take care of yourself."

"Sure," he said.

After a while Alice stood up. "I'm going to bed," she said and then added uncertainly, "Are you coming?"

"Not right now."

Alice hesitated, as though to say something more, but changed her mind and left the room.

The apartment became very quiet. Outside, a few early morning city sounds—trucks moving by, a siren, a boat whistle on the river—hinted at the coming day. Justin sat still.

How could he not have understood her better? How could she have lived with this all these years with him on the outside? In spite of everything, they had, after all, been two very separate—isolated—people. This, it turned out, was what it really was to be alone. It was worse than he had thought it could be, this knowing that a good part of a lifetime had passed partly obscured. It was much worse than that other time he had for so long thought was the worst that could be.

1940: Upstate New York

This was the worst time, Justin was thinking, late in the afternoon. It was bad all day and all night, but late in the afternoon was the worst. He stood looking out from the small, north window set high in the cabin wall. From here he could see the narrow, dirt trail leading down to the road, but not the road itself. A screen of trees and tangled brush cut it from sight, making it seem as though the trail wound on and on through the grim, thickening woods, when actually it ended less than a hundred yards away. The cabin was situated close to a lake, but only the far shore was visible, beside a thin strip of still-frozen water. Ice at the end of March. You looked out and everything was dead, bare or frozen. Inside, after six months of self-imprisonment, it was not much better.

It was dark enough to light a kerosene lantern, even at 4:30, but no lights! There was supposed to be no one here during the day. He'd have to wait almost another hour for lights, when Alice came back from work. The invisible man of the mountain. Six months and not a soul but his wife had seen him, or even knew he was there. It was remarkable that Alice had managed to get away with it this long. A woman with her looks, waiting tables in a roadside diner, living up here on the mountain alone. Fortunately, people in these parts minded their own business. She had told them she was a writer and they probably had decided she was an eccentric as well. Without her working, they'd have starved a couple of months before when the last of the money had run out. But he still nervously awaited the day when some truck jockey would follow her home and discover the little man who wasn't there.

Justin recited aloud:

> Yesterday, upon the stair,
> I saw a man who wasn't there.

He turned away from the window. He'd been talking to himself for several months now and was no longer self-conscious about it. They couldn't have a radio because there was no electricity to run one, and he needed to break the stillness.

With distaste, his eyes brushed over the room and hardly noticed the few peeling sticks of furniture, the scrap of carpeting. Salvation Army Renaissance, he called it.

A mirror on the far wall offered his image across the room to him. He advanced toward it. Ugly! Three days' growth of beard darkened his face. Why bother to shave at all, except for Alice? His eyes were red and lined with black. The night was for listening, not for sleep. He had been careful and lucky so far; but he still lay there, the sweat cold in his armpits, listening. There was always the rifle within easy reach; but he knew how the executioners operated, and the gun would probably not be enough. Still he liked to hold it, to feel the stock cradled against his hand. And he listened, as if for something familiar, expected. Perhaps no more than the snap of a twig . . . a dead leaf scraping across the porch . . . the wind, always the wind, moving branches, a shutter, the loose shingle. These were all whispers heard every night, yet every night he listened for them, unblinking and staring. Only when the first dull light had chased darkness and ghosts, did he sometimes, finally, let go and sleep.

If only the waiting were not so indefinite. It was the not knowing, not knowing if they'd been traced, that gnawed the most. Not knowing how much, if anything, Webster had told. Not knowing how long they'd have to go on like this. You could put up with anything if only you knew it would end. But when, if ever, would *this* end?

Enough of that ghastly, accusing face. Damn the *mirror!* Did he need *this* too? With fierce pleasure, he swept it from the wall. Even the sound of it smashing was good. One of the simple enjoyments still left him. And what would there be to break tomorrow?

Justin prowled the darkening room. The remains of a fire still glowed on the rough, stone hearth and he stopped as if to gather in the faint heat still in the embers. He couldn't remember the last time he'd felt *really* warm. At first he had tried to get through the days without a fire, because the chimney smoke was too dangerous. But the cold had been unbearable. His joints began to ache and he rose with a groan. After a while he sat down at the manuscript table, picked up a pencil and whittled the point with his penknife, put the pencil down and carefully started on another. There were a dozen more pencils scattered about the table. If he worked slowly, the project would be good for at least fifteen minutes.

Inevitably, the pencils were done. Justin pocketed his knife and stared resentfully at the great pile of yellow sheets that littered the chipped enamel table. Justin Blaine's folly. It was all there, scrawled in a tortuous longhand over more than four hundred scraps of paper. A bitter and confused *nothing*. As some men tried to drink away the anguish of a hopeless situation, he had sought some answer to his own calamity by writing. *Nothing.* He had hoped that by sitting and writing and writing, all day, every day, week after week, month after month, he might draw some faint hint of order and reason from the chaos of the years. How he could have been so wrong? How could so many people have been deceived? He'd searched his mind for the meaning of what he'd read on Communism—hopes, ideals, theories, the entire labyrinth of dialectics—seeking logic and explanations where they did not seem to exist. *How could he have been so wrong?* What could lead an intelligent man to make the kind of mistakes *he'd* made? Spying for the Reds. For what? And how did you live with yourself afterward? Well, he'd find out that much anyway. He was finding it out now.

A pencil snapped between his fingers with a small explosion.

Four hundred and thirty-seven pages of nothing gleaned out of the seven months of writing. Where did he go next? Maybe there *was* no place to go. Maybe it would just be simpler to put a bullet in his head now, and save his former comrades the trouble.

Justin rose from the table in disgust, chilled as much by his thoughts as the cold. Returning to the fireplace, he threw in some newspapers to rekindle the fire. It wasn't enough. The half-burned remnants of the logs refused to catch. He looked for more paper, but couldn't find any.

"Goddamn it! Not even a stinking scrap of paper for a fire!"

The final frustration. His furiously searching glance was caught by the manuscript.

Why not? *Why in hell not?* With grim pleasure, he grabbed a handful of the laboriously scribbled pages and threw them onto the smoldering logs. When the flames caught, he began, slowly and deliberately, to crumple more of the pages and drop them, one at a time, into the fire.

A painfully slow writer, Justin had once estimated his production rate at something more than two hours per page. Now, with perverse, bitter joy, he began to add the hours of labor going up in smoke. ". . . Fourteen . . . sixteen . . . eighteen . . . twenty-two . . . thirty . . . thirty-six . . ." His strained voice mixed with the dull crackle of flames.

He suddenly froze at ninety-eight, his hand extended, ready to drop the one-hundredth hour. Was it a car door closing down at the road? He glanced at his watch . . . 5:10. Twenty minutes too early for Alice. She tried to arrive home the same time every day, to spare him unnecessary worry. Had he imagined it?

Again. His pulse quickened, but he was otherwise calm. Two doors closing meant two people, possibly more. They couldn't be that sure, or they'd have stopped farther down the road. Had they found Alice at the diner and taken her along? *Fool! Stop guessing. Get the gun. Move!*

He rushed for the bedroom, took the Beretta from its drawer and slid a cartridge into the chamber. He looked at his hand. It was steady. Good. He almost welcomed the threat, the action needed to meet it. Whatever it was, whatever happened, it was better than having to stay holed up here for another six months. He went back into the front room, to the high, north window, where a Winchester 30.06 lay loaded and ready. In the last of the fading light, the steep dirt trail showed empty. It would take a few minutes to climb from the road. Justin waited.

He *wanted* it to be them. Four hundred and thirty-seven pages of looking for reasons, and the final, most logical answer still lay before the barrel of a rifle. He released the safety.

The sound of branches, twigs snapping. They weren't being very cautious. Probably didn't consider him that much of a threat. Well, they'd find out. He lifted the Winchester to the window ledge and sighted along the barrel. The front sight cut the trail where it disappeared into the brush. Twenty yards. He'd wait for ten, maybe even five. He couldn't miss at that range. The front sight wavered. He braced the barrel on the ledge and the wavering stopped.

Twigs cracked nearer now. *More doubts.* What if they had Alice
. . . and used her as a hostage or a shield? He began to sweat. Why
fool himself? He wasn't any good at this. Not at all. Let it be
nothing, he hoped, let it be a false alarm.

A tall, stout man appeared on the trail. A smaller figure followed close behind him. No Alice. At least she'd be out of it. The
two men stopped when they saw the cabin. Justin squinted hard,
but he could not make out their faces. They wouldn't be anyone
he'd recognize anyway. The OGPU never were. They seemed to be
catching their breath after the steep climb. They wore city clothes,
long dark coats and snap-brimmed fedoras. They couldn't be sure
he was there, Justin thought, or they wouldn't be coming straight
up the trail. Their hands were deep in their coat pockets and Justin
could almost see the outlines of pistols against the fabric.

They were very close now. The front sight wavered on the big
man's chest. Justin scanned their faces: soft, close-shaven, nondescript. No one he knew.

"Looks empty," the big man said. "Son of a bitch!" He was
gasping a little from the climb. "After all this, probably no one
even home."

"Chimney's smoking," the other observed. "Try knocking on
the door."

"Try it yourself," the big man grumbled. "I'm not moving my
ass another inch without a damned good reason."

The voices were muffled by the closed window. The men's open
advance on the cabin and their lack of caution had eased Justin's
sense of danger, but the front sight remained on the big man's
chest.

All at once the rifle seemed wrong—too large, unwieldy—and
Justin set it down and picked up the pistol. The short man had
climbed the front steps and crossed the porch. The man was out of
Justin's sight now, but his feet echoed on the planking. There was
a knock on the door. "Anyone home?"

"Come on," the big man called. "We're only wasting time here.
Can't you see the place is dark?"

His companion moved along the porch and peered into a window. Justin flattened himself out of sight behind the hearth.

"There's a fire going."

"So what? It might have been left that way two hours ago."

The footsteps retreated down the stairs. Justin returned to his post at the window. The men were going back along the trail. Justin watched until they disappeared, then listened for the sound of their car starting. When it did, he remained at the window, taking no chances. The departure could have been a trick.

He was still there moments later, staring rigidly through the dark, when he heard another car door slam. Alice. It was time for her. He waited until he saw the familiar silhouette coming toward the cabin, then hurried to open the door.

He kissed and held her longer, more intensely than usual. He was lucky. With it all, he was still damned lucky. Alice pulled back, staring at the pale blur of his face. "Are you all right? You're shaking."

Justin wondered if he should tell her. He'd better. They might be back. "Two men were here." He tried to keep his voice matter of fact. "They just snooped around a bit and went away. It probably didn't mean anything."

"How long ago?"

"Not long. A few minutes. Why?"

"Two men stopped me on the road," she said. "They were looking for Route 9, claimed they made a wrong turn back near Poughkeepsie. I just wondered if they could have been the same ones."

"What did they look like?"

Alice put down the newspaper and bundles she was holding. She started to light one of the oil lamps. "City types. Both fat-ish, clean-shaven. One big, the other kind of small."

"The same ones." Justin felt himself go slack. "Guess they were just looking for directions."

Alice looked at the automatic still in his hand, then at his haggard face. "That must have been lovely for you." Her eyes suffered through the fright, the whole of the experience, with him. In the flickering, sorrowful lamplight, Alice too showed the effects of the past months. But despite the hollows, the drawn, chapped cheeks, she was still, unmistakably, a pretty woman.

"At least it was *something*," he said. "There was a moment when I was actually *hoping* for a chance to squeeze that trigger."

Alice took off her coat and hung it over a wall peg. She had on a black waitress' uniform that fitted much too snugly across the chest. She turned and saw the crumpled manuscript pages scattered near the fireplace. She began to gather them up and put them back into some sort of order.

Justin saw her. "Leave them."

Alice went on gathering up the scattered pages.

"Leave them!" Justin shouted. "Just leave them for the fire! They're good for nothing else." It was good to have someone to witness, to react to his despair.

"You may change your mind. You're upset now. You may want them tomorrow."

"For what?" he said tiredly, the false anger abruptly gone. "They don't mean anything. They don't give any answers. They prove nothing but stupidity. And I don't need any written record of that. It's not something I'm likely to forget."

Alice had finished picking up the manuscript. Without further comment, she stacked the pages with those still on the table and then brought her packages into the kitchen. Justin followed, unwilling to be separated from her by even the space of a room. Like a small boy clinging to his mother's side, he stood watching from the doorway. Alice opened the parcels of food, some of which were bought groceries, others containing edible scraps taken from the diner. The money she earned was barely enough to cover their needs, and she had begun to supplement their food supply with leftovers from her customers' plates. Part of a pork chop and a half-eaten piece of layer cake were unwrapped. Justin turned away in anger and disgust at this ultimate affront. The first time he'd furiously hurled it into the garbage. Alice had stared at him. "It's still food. Do you know a better way?" Pride had died in his throat. It was she who worked, who fed them. He had not mentioned it again. And even his revulsion was fading.

Sometimes Justin wished Alice would scream at him for getting them into this mess, or at least complain. She never did. Yet all that her quiet acceptance and understanding achieved was the further compounding of his own sense of guilt.

"Would you like a roll and butter before dinner?" Alice said. "I've brought some of those seeded ones you like so much."

"No, thanks." His stomach still felt twisted. He doubted he'd be able to eat dinner.

Conversation died. As time passed, there seemed less and less for them to say to one another. With their lives suspended, what was there to talk about? Justin drifted back into the living room and rekindled the fire, and picked up the newspaper Alice had left on the table, a day-old copy of the *New York Times,* regularly brought to the diner by a friendly truck driver who made the run to the city four times a week. It was Justin's sole contact with the outside world, and he always read it through, from first page to last, without skipping a word. But he hoarded this pleasure for later in the evening. Now, as merely an appetizer, he allowed himself to scan the front page.

Russia had signed a peace treaty with Finland, the French were sitting confidently behind their Maginot Line, the Mayor had come out against corruption in the city government, the United States was still determined not to enter the phony European war, Mussolini had made another inflammatory speech in Rome, the FBI had identified a dismembered body dug up in a woods near Washington, D.C., President Roosevelt was reported in good health after his latest examination. . . .

Justin's eyes returned to the article on the FBI. After a single paragraph, the print began to blur. He had seen the name Leon Rosoff. His hands shook. "Alice!" It came out a hoarse, half-choked cry. "Alice!"

His wife came running from the kitchen, face white, a knife and half-peeled potato clutched in her hands. "What's wrong? *What is it?*"

"The paper . . . !" He stared dumbly at it, unable to read, yet unwilling to remove his eyes from the general area. Was this really how it happened? You went along and went along, then one night you just picked up the paper and . . . "Haven't you read it? Haven't you even *looked* at it?"

"What's *wrong* with you? You frightened me half to death. Do you think they pay me down there to read the damned newspaper? Now what's so important that you—"

"Read it!" He thrust the newspaper at her, pointing to the FBI article. "Just shut up a minute and read right here."

Reluctantly, she dropped the knife and potato into her apron pocket and took the newspaper. She began to read the article.

"Aloud," Justin said. "Read it aloud." He was pacing the room. His eyes blinked furiously behind their lenses and tiny drops of moisture spotted his forehead. "My eyes blurred. I couldn't even finish it."

She began to read. " 'The FBI announced today that it had positively identified the dismembered body of a man, dug up last week in a heavily wooded area near Arlington Cemetery, as a member of the Russian Embassy staff here. A fingerprint check revealed the man to be Leon Rosoff, an interpreter who . . .' " Alice stopped reading, but her mouth remained open. "Rosoff!" She stared at Justin.

"Read it!"

" '. . . an interpreter who," she read on more quickly now, "has been in Washington for more than six years. Russian officials admitted that the man had been absent from his office for three days, but had not reported it to police in the belief his absence may have been involved in some way with his normal work. The FBI also revealed that they had been keeping Rosoff and three other members of the Russian Embassy staff under surveillance, because of suspected espionage activities. The men named were Boris Tomischev, Dmitri Roskalnin and Alexander Shukhov.' " Alice looked up once more. "Alex. Did you know the other two?"

"*Of* them," Justin said. "We'd never met, though I did know they worked with Rosoff." He was still pacing, his steps small, quick, nervous. "Go on. Read the rest of it."

" 'Tomischev, Roskalnin and Shukhov returned to the Soviet Union last month for new assignments, a Soviet Embassy spokesman said. The embassy also issued a protest over the surveillance and demanded more competent police protection for their officials.' "

As if in a trance, Alice lowered the newspaper and sat down.

"That's all?" Justin said.

"No. There's some more stuff about when Rosoff was found and when he came to this country. What does it mean?"

"What does it mean?" Justin was growing still more excited. "It means that it may be over, that we can start to live again."

"But how can we be sure?"

He had sat down in a tattered armchair and now leaned forward.

"Listen. With those three back in Russia and Rosoff dead, it means the ring is dead. Besides, only Shukhov and Rosoff knew me. Rosoff was Alex's superior too—the leader of our chain." He paused, working it out. "In fact," he said meditatively, "they may have killed Rosoff to put an end to the chain. The dismemberment could have been a blind."

"Why couldn't they have sent him back?"

"Because that would have looked too suspicious. Besides, Rosoff may have suspected that he had been too badly compromised by my defection and might have been thinking of defecting too. They couldn't take that chance. This means they've neutralized the damage I could have done. I wasn't even a regular party member, and no one knows my real name. Also, as you know, we've never met any of our former friends since we started the apparatus. I think we're in the clear."

Alice listened, her face showing her worry.

Justin looked at her in surprise. "What's wrong? Aren't you happy?"

"Of course I'm happy."

"You don't look it."

"I'm sorry. I'm too tired. I guess it all happened a little too fast for me."

"Too fast?" Justin was in motion once more. He purposely chose to misunderstand. "Six months of being cooped up in this hole and you call it too fast? I'm getting out of here as soon as my flat feet can take me."

Alice stood up, alarmed. "You can't just walk out like that. You've got to think this through. There may be something . . . someone you've overlooked. At least take a few days to think about it."

"No, no, no. I've got to—*we've* got to make a move, *some* kind of move." He glared at the hateful walls of the cabin. "After news like this, do you think I can just go on sitting here? This is what I've been hoping, been . . ." He shook his head as though to clear it, as though this wondrous thing were intoxicating him. "Look, I know as well as you do that there are no guarantees of safety for us. Sure we have to be careful. But we can't stay cooped up here forever, can we?" He seemed to be almost pleading with her to agree.

"But where can we *go*? What can we *do*?"

"Well, first . . ." Justin rubbed his brow and fumbled with his glasses. "First," he said, "we've got to climb out of this tomb. We've got to find someone—contact someone we can trust. Someone who can help us."

Alice felt lost and unable to think. "Yes, but whom? We've no money, no decent clothing. We've been out of things for so long. Whom do we know that we can just call?" She stared down at herself, at the still strange sight of her body in the waitress' uniform, a costume for a masquerade. Yet even this suddenly seemed more real, more natural, than the thought of venturing out into the unknown. "Whom can we call?" she asked again, but without hope of an answer. Even before their break, there had been the years of confinement behind false identities. And before that? Any other life or associations seemed so distant, so strange, they might never have existed at all. They'd never had any really close friends. Neither opportunity nor need had existed to share with anyone but each other. From the beginning, almost from the first night Tom Gallagher had inadvertently brought them together, they'd never had . . . *"Tom!"*

Justin looked at her. "What?" Lost in his own thoughts, he hadn't heard.

"Tom," she repeated, "Tom Gallagher. We can call Tom Gallagher. We can trust him. I'm *sure* we can trust him." For the first time, she began to feel some of her husband's excitement. "With all the people he knows, with all his contacts, he should be able to get you some kind of job."

Justin beamed. "Wonderful! Tom Gallagher. Great idea." He laughed loudly. "Tom!" The name suddenly conjured forth warmth, affection, hope. "Will he be surprised! I'm going out to call him right now."

"No, don't." Alice's fears flooded back. "You can't leave the house. Not yet. Not till we're sure."

"I'm sure." He was putting on his coat. It was a small ceremony of liberation. "It'll take me ten minutes to get to the phone. I'll call him and you can have dinner ready when I get back. I'm sure I can locate him."

She saw he couldn't be stopped. He had the door open. "You haven't the car keys." She got them from her coat, gave them to him, and he went out.

"Money!" Alice called after him. "You haven't any money."

Justin returned, took the bills she handed him and grinned. "Looks like you'll have to cut the umbilical cord all over again." He went down the trail toward the place where the car was parked. He looked back once. Alice still stood in the lighted doorway, watching. He knew she could no longer see him in the darkness, but he waved anyway. Then he hurried down the path.

2

It had turned warmer during the night and a heavy fog rose from the lake in the early morning and hung low over the trees. But by eleven o'clock the sun had burned through and Alice and Justin left the cabin and walked down the road to meet Tom Gallagher. They stood waiting where the two-lane road met the state highway, knowing it wasn't time, but watching for his car anyway.

After a while they sat down on a fallen tree. They said little. They had talked through most of the night about what to tell Tom, and now they just watched the highway. Only a few cars passed and these went by very fast, in a rush of sound.

Justin lifted his head and felt the sun, warm on his freshly shaven face. A mangy, gray rabbit hopped by out of the brush. Justin watched, with conscious pleasure, until it disappeared. The woods were full of them, yet this was the first he'd noticed in months. He breathed the pine-scented air deeply. One man dies, he thought, and another is let back among the living. If there was anyone to keep a record of such things, it was a fair enough exchange.

It was close to noon when the car finally came. At first small and dark in the distance, it appeared like all the others. But instead of speeding past, this long, black Buick slowed, turned off onto the narrower road and stopped.

"You two waiting for a goddamned streetcar?" The familiar red hair followed the brash, insolent voice through the window. Alice and Justin rushed toward it. Gallagher got out, his hair aflame in the sun, looking to Justin ten feet tall. A Messiah.

"Tom." Justin's voice was strange, thick. He pumped his friend's hand. Alice embraced and kissed him. No one said anything. They stood there, touching, looking at one another.

"Listen . . ." For once, Gallagher was inarticulate. "I mean . . . I thought you were both *dead*. How . . .? People just don't *disappear* like that. They just *don't!* Not if they're alive."

Justin took off his glasses, wiped them on his sleeve and put them back on. He'd told Tom nothing on the phone, only where they were and how to come out the next day if he could.

Gallagher looked at first one and then the other. His pale eyes were reproachful. "How the hell could you *do* a thing like that? How could you even——"

"Wait. Wait." Justin cut him off. "It's a long story. Let's get up to the cabin and we'll tell you everything." He felt soft with gratitude. He'd asked the man to come, and without question or hesitation he'd come. He knew of no one else who would have done it. "Thanks for coming."

"Crap!" Gallagher fled the unaccustomed emotion. "Come on." He grasped each of them by an arm and pulled them toward the patiently idling Buick. "Let's get these damn troops out of the sun."

They were sitting in front of the fire. Gallagher listened quietly as Justin talked, so quietly that Justin wondered if Gallagher believed him. The story he and Alice had concocted came out in a remarkably easy, flowing stream, without hesitation, as though it had really happened that way. Justin told him how the party had ordered them to the Washington headquarters, assigning them to the publication division. He had traveled some of the time through the Middle Atlantic States as part of his job, but he also had had a part-time job at the Library of Congress. They had left the party out of disillusionment, and he had been trying to write a book to clear his own mind. At the finish of it, Justin poured himself a cup of coffee and waited for the reaction.

After several more seconds, Gallagher said, "Well, well, well. So the two of you became real comrades—I should have guessed it." He grinned at them. "Alice, I don't wonder Justin could not resist your party line. But, Justin, just what did you do?"

"Nothing important. I wrote some pamphlets, did research, attended meetings, did some minor agitation work. I'm afraid most of my time was spent debating with my fellow members."

"Didn't you spy on one government official?" Tom asked, half-facetiously. "I mean, didn't you cloak-and-dagger it, just a little bit?"

"Do I look like the spy type? You must be kidding."

Gallagher laughed. "You're right."

"Everyone thinks that if a man is a member of the party, he's a spy. The Communist Party is a political party. I don't agree with the party any more, but at least I know that it isn't the sinister web of espionage the public thinks it."

"Then why all this agony? Why'd you have to pull into yourself that way? I never even heard from you."

Alice had remained silent while the two men talked, but now she spoke. "Tom, when you get involved in the party, even when you do the innocuous things Justin was doing, you begin to live a different kind of life. The Cause becomes all-important. You don't avoid your old friends, you just . . . well, you just neglect them."

"And then, when I saw the way the party was heading, supporting Hitler and that pact with Stalin," Justin went on, "and especially turning around and advocating that we stay out of the war, well, my doubts became greater and greater and I had to think them out. I had to get away to make time for myself to think and to understand. I had committed myself to a belief, to a way of life, to a cause, and all of a sudden that belief was all wrong."

"And have you figured it out yet?"

"Not entirely. Ask me in ten years or so. Maybe I will have then."

As they had talked, Gallagher had taken swift inventory of the cabin and its contents. Now he said, "So, what you really need now is a job, right? I don't suppose there's a chance of going back to the Library of Congress."

"I wouldn't want to. Talk about 'nonsensitive jobs.' It was so nonsensitive it hardly existed. No, Tom, I want to put my life to use. I learned a lot, and I want to make something of it."

"Do you want to expose the party?"

"There's nothing to expose—at least, nothing that I know about.

I mean that I've done a lot of thinking and reading—a lot of learning. I want to use that."

"Okay. Let's see about a job."

Justin shook his head. Suddenly too much seemed to depend on his friend, and he didn't like this new feeling of dependency. "Listen, Tom, don't think we expect you to . . ." His voice died, along with the leap of pride. This was no time for games. They *did* expect. "Of course, we'd be grateful if . . ."

Gallagher was too busy thinking to hear him. He stood up and walked slowly to the window and back. "I may be able to find you something at the network. In fact, I'm almost sure I can." He grinned at Justin. "While you've been nonspying, your old buddy's been moving up in the news department. You know, radio news is becoming a big thing, expecially what with the war. There's still room on the ground floor. Interested?"

Justin nodded vigorously. "Of course."

Gallagher paced to the window again. "We'll work out a good story for you. Did many people know about you and the party?"

"I kept it quiet," Justin said.

"Well, that's good. No one need know about it. We'll just say that you worked at the Library of Congress and left because you wanted to write a book. That's always a respectable reason for cutting out. Say, where is the manuscript?"

Justin indicated the remains of the manuscript on the table. "That's what's left of it. I threw the rest into the fire yesterday."

"You what?"

"I burned it."

Gallagher went to the table and leafed through the yellow pages of the manuscript. He stared at Justin. *"Why?"*

"It didn't say anything. I was looking for answers, and it didn't give me any. Everything I wrote was just different ways of asking the questions. It was just a record of naïveté."

"So what about all that you say you learned?"

"I learned about innocence. It's been the biggest lesson of my life. Maybe someday I'll be able to straighten out the rest of what these years have been about. But at least my mind's clearer about itself than it has ever been."

"Justin, you carry that conscience of yours around like a two-ton hump. But destroying months of work—that isn't like you."

Justin's shoulders shrugged and then drooped. He looked older, more confused. "I'm not really that sure any more what *is* or *isn't* like me. If I could have believed . . . could have done some of the . . ." His voice drifted off, mournful and defeated.

Gallagher's eyes clouded. Then he smiled, the nurse cheering the patient. "Too bad you burned it. True confessions are big this year. The screen rights alone would have been good for a hundred thousand."

Justin did not seem to have heard him. Gallagher glanced at Alice, and she shook her head. Wrong treatment, he thought, too soon for the light touch.

"All right!" he barked, and Justin blinked. "Now that we've got you fixed up with a respectable past and a job, how about getting some decent food into your gut? You two look as if you've been living on crickets and grass."

Alice stood up. "If you're hungry," she said quickly, "I have some things in the kitchen that I can . . ." She stopped as she saw his face.

"You don't have to play games with me. Don't you think I can see how things are?" He pulled Justin to his feet. "Come on. We'll ride down to the store. I'll pick up some groceries and we'll celebrate your resurrection with a Gallagher Special."

Alice had to restrain herself from hugging him. This was a man, she decided, whom she'd always sold terribly short. She wouldn't again. "What's that? Scotch with a whiskey chaser?"

Gallagher looked offended. "Spaghetti and meatballs," he said primly. "A secret, Neapolitan recipe, revealed to me by a dying Italian whore on Mulberry Street. Gratitude. I was absolutely the only man, she said, who'd ever been able to turn her work into pleasure." He threw Justin his coat.

Alice watched them go down the trail together, her husband's head barely reaching the tall man's shoulder. She heard Justin laugh at something and it drifted back, a very special and wonderful kind of sound. There was no memory of trouble in it, no fear of the dark. Instead, it seemed both gay and serene, as if, hidden somewhere deep at its source, lay a peaceful, contented man who went to bed at ten o'clock and slept through the whole of the night without waking.

1952: Atlantic City

The clock sounded the half-hour. Justin slowly rose and turned out the light. They had come far since that dark period twelve years ago—and now, was it over? He walked through the foyer into the bedroom.

In the darkness he could see Alice's hair against the pillow and the dim outline of her body beneath the covers. She stirred heavily, as if to show she was awake, but did not say anything. Justin undressed in the bathroom and took another pill because he still did not feel right. He did not really expect it to help, but took it anyway. Then he went back into the bedroom and climbed into bed beside Alice.

He lay there, stiff and relaxed, taking care not to let any part of his body touch his wife. It seemed very important that he not touch her. She smelled warm and soapy and clean beside him and her breathing was relaxed and deep and regular.

But later he felt her body shake the bed beside him and her breathing was no longer regular. She cried without sound, her face buried in the pillow, while Justin stared hot-eyed in the direction of the ceiling.

"You're right," she wept softly. "You're right not to touch me. You're right. I deserve whatever's happened to me, everything in my life." Her voice was muffled by the pillow. "Everything deserved," she whispered, "a judgment. Even the baby. You pay for everything. There's always a reason." Her voice drifted off.

Suddenly Alice sat up in bed.

"Of *course!*" Her voice rose in startled, yet cautious discovery. She nodded as the affirmation grew. "Not only am I being paid back, but I'm being paid back by my own *husband.*" She turned to look at Justin, who was tense beside her in the darkness. *"That's* the reason you've done this. *That's* the reason you started this whole mess, spilled everything to the committee to begin with. It was your way of finally striking back at us—at both Webster *and* me."

Justin frowned. "You're crazy. That had nothing to do with it. Where do you get these ideas?"

"Am I?" The joy of revelation, of the final uncovering of something after long search, had almost driven the pain from her voice. "You must have unconsciously suspected, maybe even *known* about us, all these years. A time bomb, lying there ticking away inside you. Then when the committee subpoenaed you—"

"Crazy!" Justin did not even want to hear it. "Absolutely crazy!" Yet even as he swept the possibility aside, the germ of it infected him. Was it *really* that crazy? He had been turning himself inside out to find reasons. Had he come up with any that were *more* logical? Maybe that had been the trouble. Maybe he'd been looking for too damned much logic. Maybe logic had nothing at all to do with it.

"Then when the committee subpoenaed you," Alice repeated, feeling herself onto something now and refusing to let go, "they finally set off the explosion. They finally gave you your chance, your long-awaited chance to get even," she said bitterly, as though to herself. "Your chance to get even. Oh, Lord." She fell back onto the pillow. "To get even, to get even with Webster and me . . . and yourself." She began to cry once more. "How could you?" she wept. "How could you want to destroy us all over something that was never anything to begin with?"

About to brush this aside as nonsense, Justin changed his mind and said nothing. What would be the point of more denials? he thought wearily. There was no arguing with this emotionalism. Or

was he simply afraid? What if there were actually some truth to it?
What if he had *actually* started this whole god-awful thing for no
better reason, no better motive than a petty, dirty little hangover of
vindictiveness? Would he—*could* he—have allowed something as
small, mean and malevolent as this to happen? At any other
moment of his life he would have quickly dismissed the idea as
incredible. But now, suddenly, he was no longer that sure. If, for
thirteen years, he had somehow managed to keep from himself an
awareness that something had existed between his wife and another man, if he had not allowed himself to face this fact until just
a few hours ago, then was it not also possible to have shielded
himself from this other unpleasant fact as well?

Justin's throat ached as he swallowed. He had always considered himself a decent, moral man. Whatever he had done, whatever mistakes he had made, were, he believed, made with good
intent. Then how this? Was it *really* possible to perform an act of
which you were ashamed, an act which you would normally abhor,
without being conscious of it? Probably, he thought with the
anguish of growing certainty, it *was* most certainly possible. Justin
shuddered beneath the blankets. And was there a new moral defense based on the concept of unconscious acts of evil? He hoped
to God there was. Because he had an awful, a frightening feeling
that he was going to need it badly in just a very few days.

Chapter Twenty-Two

1952: Washington, D.C.

The dark-haired girl, once desired but never had five years before, beckoned teasingly in Henry Pilgrim's final dream before she disappeared. The Congressman awoke, feeling frustrated and deprived.

He opened his eyes in the soft, early light and looked at his wife, still asleep beside him. And what secret dreams, he wondered, did *she* live through and keep hidden from *him?* For a moment, his desire was transferred to her and he turned toward this more real, more readily available warmth. Then he remembered what day it was and a different kind of excitement took over.

The clock on the night table said 7:25. Pilgrim stretched, hearing the dull hum of the city of Washington coming awake. Even this seemed to have a triumphant note to it this morning, and he got out of bed, walked barefoot to the window and lifted the shade expectantly.

The sun angled into the back gardens with the promise of a clear, bright day. It hit the brick of the Georgetown houses and touched the pleasantly faded walls, flagstone terraces and dusty winter ivy.

Pilgrim smiled, delighted that the day was sunny and that he

425

lived in such a pleasant place. He breathed deeply and then padded across the carpeted bedroom floor into the bathroom. He showered under stingingly cold water, shuddering with the shock. Drying himself afterward, he studied his body in a full-length mirror, first from the front, then more critically in profile, sucking in the incipient thickness about his middle, resolving again, as he did at least once each month, to work out more often at the gym. But generally he thought he had little cause for complaint about his shape. He looked good, felt good and could still do twenty-five push-ups without breathing hard. What other member of Congress could do that?

Pilgrim lathered his face for shaving, absently humming "Hail to the Chief." Then, realizing the tune, he laughed aloud. Easy, boy, he thought, let's not be carried away. You're not nearly *that* far—not yet anyway. But he did not stop humming, nor did he bother to change the tune.

"If there's one thing I can't stand," his wife's voice grumbled sleepily from the bedroom, "it's a happy, early riser. Darling, please shut up."

Lather brush in hand, Pilgrim scowled darkly at his wife from the bathroom doorway. "Is that any way to talk," he said, "to your next Vice President?"

Elizabeth Pilgrim tentatively opened one eye. "My next what?" she murmured.

"Vice President," Pilgrim said, delighted that his wife was awake at last. "And how can you lie there so calmly on this of *all* mornings? Sometimes I think you've got more of your father's ice water in your veins than blood."

Still not wholly awake, Elizabeth yawned and buried her face in a rumpled pillow.

"You don't even care?" he said reproachfully. "You're not the least bit excited about the fact that Aldous Breisen's office called me yesterday?"

"Oh, yes." Elizabeth's voice came muffled and indistinct, from the pillow. "You said something about that last night when you came in."

"Yes," Pilgrim said sarcastically, "I said something about that." He turned and went back to his lathering before the mirror. Elizabeth had been asleep when he'd come in from what she thought had been a late conference, and had only half-wakened when he'd told her the news. Then she'd mumbled something about saving it till morning and had rolled over and gone back to sleep. The next time around, he thought, he'd make sure he married a devout insomniac. "Well," he declared, wanting to hold out, but bursting with it, "it wasn't just Breisen's office that called. It was Aldous D. Breisen *himself* who called. He invited me to his place to talk."

There was no response from the bedroom.

Pilgrim peered at his lathered face in the mirror. "I said," he repeated more loudly, "that it was Aldous Breisen himself who called. I was at his place last night."

This time there was a somnolent answer. "What did *that* old saber rattler want?"

"That old saber rattler," Pilgrim said pettishly, "is going to be our next Republican President."

"All right," Elizabeth yawned. "Let it be your way. Then what did our next Republican President want?"

Pilgrim returned to the doorway. He wanted to be able to see his wife's face when she heard. "It really wasn't anything very much. He just wanted to know if I would be open to a nomination for Vice President."

"Of the United States?"

Pilgrim grinned beneath the heavy lather. His wife was finally and truly awake, with just the proper amount of awed disbelief in both voice and expression. "Of the United States," he echoed grandly.

Elizabeth sat up in bed. "Oh, darling!" With her shoulders bare and her dark hair tied loosely with a pink ribbon, Pilgrim thought she looked absurdly young and almost beautiful.

"Well, don't just stand there!" she said excitedly. "Tell me all about it."

Pilgrim savored the moment. "I don't know," he teased, going back to his shaving. "I might not tell you anything at all. A few seconds ago you seemed to treat the whole thing very casually."

"Henry!" Elizabeth said. "Stop that this minute and tell me. I'm overwhelmed. Honestly!"

"All right." He laughed and washed the remains of the lather from his face.

"To tell the truth," he said, entering the bedroom carrying an oversized bath towel, "I was overwhelmed myself. It's still early for thinking about Vice Presidential candidates, but then Breisen needs me." He nodded firmly, as though still trying to convince himself a little. "It wasn't a definite, firm offer to be talked about, but he's still fifty votes short of a first-ballot nomination, and it would do him a lot of good to be able to rumor it that I might be his running mate. And it would wrap up Illinois for him, at least."

"Then it isn't certain," she said, pouting.

"For this time of the campaign, it looks damn certain. He as much as said so. If this Blaine thing comes off right—that's up to me—and if he can work those delegates right, I'd be the logical man for the spot. It's beginning to pull together."

"But what did he *say?*"

"It was really something." Pilgrim sat down on the bed beside her and stared into her eyes. "He looked me in the eye like this— we were sitting in his library—and he said, 'Hank, you're doing a great job on that committee, a *great* job. It took courage to do what you did, real courage. Well, I like that.' And then he sat back and poured himself another drink and sipped it real slow. I was nearly dying. And then he set his glass down very casually and said, 'As you know, things are looking very good for me convention-wise.' Charlie Glick, his campaign manager, was sitting there and he said that was right. And Breisen said, 'I'm looking over running-mate possibilities. As you know, I can't make any promises now—for obvious reasons—but I do want to know: would you be open to a nomination for Vice President if it was offered to you?' Well, I said yes and he said, 'Fine. You just keep it up on that committee. Give 'em hell, because I'm going to make this Commies-in-Government thing the center of my campaign, only I might want you to carry the ball on that while I talk about the war and being soft on Communism abroad.' And then he told me that the effectiveness of the issue may hinge on how well I can pull this thing off."

Elizabeth clapped her hands delightedly. "Vice President Pilgrim!" she chorted. "Just wait till Daddy hears. Everything's working out just as he said it would."

The moment she said it, she knew it was the wrong thing, but the words were already out. Pilgrim regarded her coldly. "Jesus Christ," he said. "I know your father deserves some credit, but please try to remember this isn't just another William Garland enterprise. *I'm* the one who's doing this. *I'm* the one whose neck would have been sliced if it had failed. *I'm* the one who's run the show from beginning to end." He turned away and took his trousers from the valet stand beside the window, the pleasure of the moment spoiled. "Can't you forget your goddamned father even at a time like this?"

Elizabeth flushed. "I'm sorry," she said. "I didn't mean it that way. You should know that. Of *course* you've done this on your own. All I meant was that Daddy would be so delighted to hear how wonderfully everything's turning out."

She watched him as he stepped into his trousers, trying to see if the quick apology had helped soothe him. But Pilgrim's face was averted and Elizabeth silently cursed her own stupidity in even mentioning her father. "Why don't you call Daddy in Rome," she said, "and tell him about Breisen? I'm sure he'll be as proud of you as I am."

Pilgrim grunted as he reached into a bureau drawer for a clean shirt. "Maybe tonight," he said, his mood too bright to stay subdued for long. "Maybe tonight when the big show's over, I'll call him." He considered the idea in silence for a moment and it seemed to appeal to him. "By tonight I should have a hell of a lot more news to tell."

Elizabeth shivered with a sudden chill and slid back under the covers. "What time does the committee meet?"

"At eleven o'clock. Will you be there?" Pilgrim spoke with forced casualness, unwilling to admit, even to himself, how important her presence would be to him. The grand illusion of indifference, he thought, wondering why it was so damned necessary for him to maintain it.

"What do you mean, will I be there?" she said indignantly. "Do you really think I'd miss the biggest thing that ever happened to you?" Elizabeth shook her head on the pillow. "Sometimes I honestly believe half the things that come out of your mouth are said for pure effect and nothing more."

Pilgrim smiled as he buttoned his shirt. "Who can tell with you? I thought you might have had an appointment at the hairdresser's this morning, or something equally monumental."

Elizabeth made a face. "You don't know how lucky you *are* to have a nice, unconceited, unself-absorbed wife like me. You should see some of the narcissistic women in this town. I don't spend any time at all on my looks."

Pilgrim regarded her thoughtfully. "I was just thinking," he said, "maybe you should."

She picked up a slipper and threw it at his head. Pilgrim ducked and it struck the wall behind him. He grinned. "You'll have to be more careful of my profile, darling. In a little more than three hours, fifteen million television viewers across the nation will be staring at its finely chiseled lines."

"Fifteen million?" she said, awed.

"At least. This is the biggest political sensation since the Hiss-Chambers affair."

He studied a crowded rack of ties, finally choosing a plain, black knit. He held it up for Elizabeth's inspection and she nodded approval. "Today," he declared, "I'll project a public image of flamboyant conservatism, worthy of even the great William Garland."

Elizabeth frowned, wishing he weren't nearly so preoccupied with her father. Yet she supposed she couldn't really blame him. She herself had been obsessed with William Garland all her life. It was logical enough for her husband to fall under the same spell.

Pilgrim studied the knot he'd just made in his tie, then pulled it apart and started all over again. He grinned. "I'll tell you something," he said gloatingly, "I don't think I've ever done a more thorough job in my life than I've done on this case. I don't know *how* many hours I've spent this past week with Gallagher and Kantrowitz, drilling on things we've probably gone over fifty times before, but going over them once again, point by point, just to make sure. In fact, we were still hard at it last night until after midnight. Blaine need only answer the questions, and there's no doubt about the outcome. We've *really* got Webster Evers nailed."

Finished with his tie, Pilgrim faced his wife, suddenly looking grave. "I'm glad this is working out, Liz," he said softly. "Because I'll tell you this much, I was pretty damned scared at first. I took one hell of a gamble here. If this went wrong, I'd be through. I did an unforgivable thing for a junior Congressman. I practically forced the committee into this. Everyone in the Republican Party would turn on me if this ever went sour. I'd be on every shit list in the city of Washington." He laughed coldly. "And worst of all, I'd be *driven* into working for your father."

Elizabeth beckoned with a finger, and he sat beside her on the bed while she undid his tie, adjusted the two lengths and started to knot them again for the third time. "Would it really be that awful for you?" she said quietly. "I mean, having to work for Daddy?"

"Your father overwhelms me," he said. "Even in my best moments, I feel like a fraud, like less than nothing, when I'm around him. No matter what I did, no matter how good it seemed, I'd always feel he could probably have done it better." He smiled and lifted his chin like an obedient child as his wife carefully worked on the tie knot. "Now would that be any way for a grown man to go through life?"

Elizabeth shook her head. She finished the tie and hugged him tightly, impulsively. "I love you," she whispered. "To me there's no one in the world who could do anything better than you."

She released him and he laughed, strangely embarrassed by the moment. "Hey, what's going on here? I haven't lost. I've *won!* There's not a thing that can possibly go wrong now." He went for his suit jacket and put it on. "When Justin Blaine begins to talk, there'll be no question of whether or not he knows Evers. He *has* to know him. Just *listening* to this man is believing him. This is what I'm counting on, fifteen million people watching Blaine, as I've watched him, recite what is unquestionably the truth."

Elizabeth got out of bed in her nightgown, took a small whisk broom from a drawer and began to brush some lint from her husband's suit. "This will go down in history as the Pilgrim Committee," he went on, his face glowing. "You'll see. From now on they won't speak about the Subversive Activities Committee. It'll be the *Pilgrim* Committee. And this will be the moment when Henry Pilgrim started on his way."

Elizabeth went to him and kissed him, delighted and grateful to see him in such a mood.

"Darling," she purred, snuggling against him, "I don't know whether or not you're going to be the *best* President this country ever had, but you're sure as hell going to be the *sexiest*."

2

Francine Moore sat alone in her car, a 1947 Plymouth, parked among a string of 1951 Cadillac limousines near the west portico of the White House. A scattering of Secret Service men mixed with the uniformed guards in the area, checking the credentials of the occasional dignitary entering the closely restricted driveway. Sometimes some of the men glanced toward the place where Francine was waiting and spoke among themselves and she knew that they were talking about the case.

A tall, wide-shouldered Secret Service man walked past the car and smiled politely and Francine forced a smile in return. Everyone seemed to have been treating her with special consideration in the past few days. Friends, newsmen, people whom she met in the course of her work and who knew of her association with Webster, all seemed to speak in low, understanding voices, carefully avoiding mention of *the* subject. It was as though in moving nearer to the climax she had moved beyond the belligerence, the nervous mistrust, the general surliness and bad manners with which she had always felt surrounded. It was also, she thought dryly, very much like the deference with which the newly bereaved were treated. Webster had also felt a difference. At the State Department he had quickly been assured of their trust—and had been suddenly put onto a minor, "nonsensitive" assignment.

She glanced nervously at the dashboard clock for the fourth time in ten minutes. It said 9:17. Webster had been closeted with the President since 9:00. She had driven him to the White House for the early, hastily called conference, with the first hope she'd felt all week. Until last night, she had resigned herself to the certain debacle. Then Webster had come up with the idea. It wasn't really that monumental a plan, nor was there even a guarantee it would work at all. But at least, she thought, it was *something*. At least it offered the possibility of an orderly retreat, rather than complete annihilation. And he had managed to change the President's mind and obtained this meeting.

They had gone over the new story Webster planned to tell at the confrontation—and which he was at this moment outlining to the President—twice the night before and once on the way to the meeting. The logic seemed to hold up each time. Now, as she sat waiting, Francine found herself compulsively reviewing it still another time.

After minutely searching his past, Webster intended to say, he had finally remembered a man whom he'd once known under the name of William Baker, who might conceivably have been Justin Blaine. This, of course, was judging purely from the photographs of Blaine that had been shown him. He remembered having met this William Baker along with Mrs. Baker, at Henrietta Crowley's house one night in 1934. Mrs. Baker's baby had arrived ahead of schedule. Webster had volunteered to drive them to the hospital himself. He had done this, had sat there for a while keeping Baker company, and then had left the hospital with him afterward. That had been eighteen years ago and he had not seen the man since. It hadn't occurred to him until late last night that Baker was possibly Blaine. The photographs he'd seen of Blaine were all recent ones, and the man had aged considerably since he'd seen him last. That single meeting and incident had comprised his total association and knowledge of William Baker, alias Justin Blaine. And why the man had chosen this moment, eighteen years later, to bring forth his irresponsible accusations was as much of a riddle to Webster as it was to everyone else.

Francine stretched tiredly behind the wheel. It wasn't too bad a story, she thought, needing to reassure herself once more. Against the detailed evidence Blaine would undoubtedly present to prove that he'd known Webster, it would have been suicidal for Webster to go on claiming he'd never seen him. Particularly since they'd be meeting face to face, without even the comparative refuge of fuzzy photographs for Webster to hide behind. As for the details, they could be accounted for as they came up. This way, Webster would be absolved of a possible perjury charge on at least one important count. She didn't dare think about what would happen with the rest of the charges. She was resigned to Webster's career in the State Department being ended. All she asked for now was that he be kept out of Leavenworth.

A long, black limousine pulled up under the portico and three top-hatted officials emerged and went into the White House. Francine looked at the clock. It was 9:25. The President of the United States, with his crowded schedule piling up, had already given

Webster twenty-five minutes of his time. If further proof were needed of the importance of the case to the administration, this last-minute conference surely provided it. There was little doubt that when Webster Evers went down, the entire Democratic ship of state might sink with him in November's election. Guilt by association was too popular a political weapon not to be used by the Republicans. They were already having a field day with it in their newspapers. The administration's decision to keep out of the affair was clearly not doing any good.

There was a sudden stir among the Secret Service men and a moment later Webster came out of the White House. He stood bareheaded in the sun for a moment, then he turned and came toward Francine.

Anxiously watching his face, Francine could, as usual, tell nothing from his expression. He opened the door and slid in beside her. They drove out of the White House grounds.

"Well?" she said. "How did it go? How did he take the story?"

Webster took an exasperating moment to settle into the seat, adjust his coat beneath him and pull the door shut. Then he looked at Francine. "I didn't tell them that story."

Francine felt the too familiar sinking inside. "I don't understand," she said, working to remain calm and not finding it easy. "We'd decided. Why didn't you tell them?"

"It didn't seem right," he said quietly. "At the last minute, when I was in there with him, it just didn't seem right. I could see no point to the story. Why do I have to admit *anything?* I never met Justin Blaine. That's all. Period. I just never met him."

Francine's gloved hands tightened on the wheel. "But we'd been all over that," she said frustratedly. "I don't understand you. We give all that thought to something, come to a logical conclusion, then you walk in there and in two seconds throw it all away on some kind of—of crazy hunch."

"It wasn't a hunch. It wasn't something I—"

"What was it then?" she cut in, feeling weak. "What other kind of name can you come up with for it?"

Webster stared straight ahead through the windshield. He shrugged. "A feeling. Maybe I can't put it more specifically than that, but I do know the other story would have been dead wrong, an obvious phony."

"But Blaine must have so *much* on you," Francine said helplessly. "We went all over it. Why, even that one document that he told me about, the one with your signature, even this alone—"

"A forgery," he said. "I'll swear it's a forgery."

"He'll name names and dates and places, all sorts of details about your life and habits during those years, things he couldn't possibly have made up. How are you going to stand up to those? How *can* you?"

Webster lit a cigarette and fastidiously placed the match in the dashboard ashtray, not seeming at all disturbed. "Blaine could have obtained that sort of information from any one of a dozen sources. I was well known in Washington. Many people might have known these same things. There's nothing absolutely conclusive there. Besides, we would have faced that problem with the other story." He looked at the way Francine's hands gripped the wheel, taut and unmoving. "Listen to me," he said softly. "I've come along this far denying everything. I can carry it off the rest of the way. I know myself. You've got to trust me. Let me handle this my own way. I think that to give even a little ground at this point—to admit I knew Blaine at all—is to give everything. Once I admit I'd even met him at a party, I'm dead. That's all they're waiting for. Just let them see one loose thread, and they'll be able to unravel the whole fabric."

Francine did not say anything and Webster studied the tip of his cigarette. "No," he said. "I watched the face of the President, and he still believes me. He is still convinced I'm innocent." He smiled coldly. "Evidently there's something about me that makes people believe me. That's my big ace in the hole, a clear and abiding air of integrity. And as long as I've got that in my favor, I'd be a fool to let even one chink show in the armor. It might be enough to crumble the whole thing."

Francine breathed deeply, far from convinced, but aware of the pointlessness of further argument. She glanced at the dashboard clock and saw it was 9:45. "We still have an hour before you're due at the hearing," she said flatly. "Is there anything you want to do in the meantime?"

Webster shook his head. "Nothing." He looked out at the sun, burning the dew from lawns. "It seems like a nice enough day. Why not just drive along the river for a while?"

They rode without speaking. The avenues were crowded with taxis, buses and cars. Cruising slowly, they passed the Jefferson and Lincoln memorials, graceful and shining in the sun. The Washington Monument stood gaunt and bright nearby. Crossing Memorial Bridge over the Potomac, they headed toward Arlington. Ranks of white stones rested in their setting of green. Above these, the Lee Mansion majestically crested a gracefully sloping hill. Webster let his eyes rest on the mansion, appreciating the serene balance of its columns. Lee, another man who was once reviled, he thought, another man of great position and equally great principles, who confronted his own agonizing decision of conscience before turning from his country for the sake of a cause. Lee, so much more a man than Webster Evers as to be a different order of man, but still not unlike him in facing a grim paradox of choice and consequence. Except that when the time for confrontation came, Lee stood in the open, to do honest battle, ready to accept openly what defeat might bring. Open, honest, prepared with the best that was in him to face the worst that destiny would force upon him. A different order of man from Webster Evers, whom the President of the United States still believed honest.

Webster stretched, seeming relaxed. The Lee Mansion disappeared behind them as they drove along the river. He looked at Francine, at the tight anxious line of her mouth, the dark beneath her eyes. He touched her arm. "Cheer up. Things aren't *that* bad."

"They are," Francine said, fighting to keep her voice steady. "How can you do this foolish thing? How can you believe that this air of bravado will keep them believing you? It's illogical! It's . . ." She groped for the word, but did not want to find it.

"All right," Webster said wearily. "My approach is illogical, but as I see it, it's the only approach I've got. It's the only *chance* I've got, because logically I *have* no chance. Logically, the odds are stacked so heavily against me that it's not even a contest. Don't you think I know that? Don't you think I know, *really,* the exact position I'm in?"

Webster looked away, out the window, the sound of the Plymouth's engine metallic and sure in his ears, the tree-lined road stretching ahead into the green-smelling air of Virginia. How nice, he thought regretfully, how nice to be able sometimes just to see and breathe. But why wasn't he aware of it more often?

"Let me tell you something," he said gently. "At least one good, decent thing's come out of this mess for me. At least, for the first time in my life, I've been able to let myself get close to another human being. Maybe that's nothing very special to other people, but I think you know what it means to me." Webster looked at the rigid profile of the slender woman beside him. "Do you have any idea of just how much I love you?"

Francine stared hard through the windshield at the road stretching before her. The car swerved very slightly and then straightened.

"I know," he said, "that you've had one pretty miserable experience, and I'd be a bad enough risk under the best of conditions, but if you'd be willing to chance it—well, I'd try." He looked away. "I *would* love you. I *would* do the best I could for you." He finished weakly, uncertainly. "That is, if you'd chance it."

Francine did not say anything. A horn honked behind them and she let a red MG streak past.

"I meant," he added lamely, fearing she hadn't understood, "that maybe it's not too late for either of us. Maybe if we got married we . . ." He stopped as he saw she was crying. "I'm sorry," he said quietly. "I didn't mean it that way. I didn't mean it to upset you. I've done enough to upset you this past week."

Francine shook her head and brushed impatiently at her eyes. Webster sat waiting tensely beside her.

"Well?" he said at last, "will you or won't you?"

"Yes," she whispered. "Yes. I will."

"Are you pleased?" he asked, thinking it an absolutely idiotic question to ask at such a time.

Francine nodded.

"Well, why don't you say or *do* something?" he said a little desperately.

"I'm . . . I'm driving."

Webster frowned at her. "You certainly look strange for someone who's supposed to be pleased. You look as though you've just lost your last friend."

"No," she said quickly. "No, that's not the way I feel. I'm happy. I'm very happy." She forced a smile to show exactly how happy she was. "It's just that I've waited so long to hear you say it. I guess I never thought I *would* hear it."

"Is that all?"

Francine nodded, keeping her eyes firmly on the road as it curved to the right with the river.

Webster hesitated and then said, "And you do understand about Alice Blaine?"

"We went all over that the other night," she said. "I understand. I'm not going to drive you away because of one crazy moment like that."

"It didn't mean anything to me. You know that."

"I know it. I'd rather forget about it."

Again they rode for some distance in silence. Webster moved closer until he was touching her. Francine smiled.

"Feel better now?" he said.

She nodded. "Much better."

"Good," Webster said. He took one of her hands from the wheel, peeled off the glove and pressed his palm to hers. "We'd better consider what can happen. Even if I come off well, there's still a very good chance the powers will come to me nicely and say, 'Webster, we'd never force you to resign, but we'd consider it best for the Department and the country if, in a few months from now, quietly and for personal business reasons, you decide it's best to leave the government service.' " He gazed thoughtfully at a row of fair, green hills rippling off against the sky. "But if this happens," he went on, "I'm sure they'll do the best they can to get me a fine position somewhere. With a university, or some kind of foundation, or . . ." He shrugged. "I'm sure there are many places where my talents can earn an excellent living, where I can lead a constructive life. I'm sure there are many organizations that can use my experience, knowledge and contacts."

"Of course there are," Francine assured him. "With your mind you can do anything you *want* to do!"

Webster's eyes seemed to be off somewhere. "And who knows?" he said. "Maybe I *will* be able to carry it off all the way. I react well under pressure. Crowds, cameras, all the excitement of a public spectacle—these things have never bothered me. Ever since I went away to school, I've been at my best on some kind of platform, with people watching me. I don't see why it should change today. Maybe the country *will* accept me. Maybe they *will* believe me. Who knows?"

"I'm afraid," Francine said, "that may be dreaming just a little *too* far."

"Who knows," Webster soared on, "how I might come out of this thing? Crazy things happen. Odds can swing very quickly from one side to the other."

She glanced at Webster's face, which was suddenly alight with fresh hope. "You know," she said, "I almost think you're beginning to enjoy this. I almost think you're looking forward to it."

"In an odd sort of way, maybe I am. I'm *doing* something. Whatever is involved here this morning is *my* decision. Nobody's doing this for me. Whatever Blaine and Pilgrim may have planned, there's still an element of control that *must* remain with me. I may still be able to surprise them."

Francine drove for a while in silence, her eyes reflective and puzzled. Then she slowed the car and prepared to turn. "I think we'd better start back," she said. "It's getting late. I hadn't realized we'd come this far."

Webster remained silent and Francine saw that he hadn't even heard her.

3

In the large committee hearing room, Morris Kantrowitz was looking over his notes one last time. His hair was already rumpled—its usual condition—and his intense, dark face was beginning to glisten with perspiration. Not only was the excitement which he was trying to conceal a cause for this, but the heat of the camera lights and the closeness of the rapidly filling room did their share. The room was a maze of cables punctuated by batteries of lights and a dais in the center of the room on which were mounted television and newsreel cameras. More chairs had been moved into the room for the press and for spectators, and these were now filled. Other spectators lined the walls, while still others tried to squeeze themselves into untaken positions. Technicians moved about hurriedly; photographers roamed about looking for possible subjects. Kantrowitz had never heard so much noise in the room. Only the raised platform of leather-covered seats for the committee members and counsel, the magnificent desk behind which they sat, the regular tables and chairs for witnesses and secretaries and the paneled walls of the room still suggested legislative dignity and continuity, but as the room continued to fill and the noise to grow, even this disappeared.

The director, J. Aaron Simmons, who would handle the television coverage, was a veteran of many hearings. Investigations of rackets, political heresies and other sins had become his specialty. He knew who the stars of this show would be, he knew the ritual of this drama in all its complexity, and he wished fervently that he could know the outcome. Blaine and Evers would be, of course, the most important figures. The committee was more of a problem.

Chairman Kelly had his due of coverage because he was, after all, Chairman, and the other members had to be served, but at one end of the table would be Morris Kantrowitz, the counsel who would ask the key questions, and beside him, in what should have been a place of obscurity, would be Henry Pilgrim, whose show this really was, and who would occupy more and more of the political stage in the future because of it. Fortunately, he was good-looking.

Simmons gave his orders, made his checks, went through his crises and felt very important. When these things had occurred, the stage could be considered set.

4

Justin Blaine was staring at the three framed prints on his hotel room wall when the telephone rang. He waited a moment, without much hope, for his wife to come out of the bathroom and answer it. On the fourth ring he reluctantly picked it up himself. "Hello," he said.

"Hello, Justin?"

The voice was deep and resonant, and belonged unmistakably to the CBN President. Oh, Christ, Justin thought, Mannheim himself. "Yes?" he said.

"This is Phillip. Phillip Mannheim."

"Yes," Justin said, coldly, making no effort to conceal what he felt for the man. "I know."

Mannheim's laugh was forced. "Good old ebullient Justin," he said. "How have you been?"

"Great." One more question like that, Justin thought, and he'd hang up.

"Listen," Mannheim said. "I'm sending a car over to pick you up and bring you to the Capitol. It should be at your hotel in twenty minutes."

Justin felt the small, telltale pulse begin to pound in his temple. "I don't need any car to pick me up. I can get a cab without any trouble."

"No, no," Mannheim said quickly. "It's all right. Please, Justin. I insist."

The line was silent and Justin could picture the network President preparing himself for the conciliatory remarks he knew, without any doubt, would be coming. He just wished he were in more of a mood to enjoy the crow-eating.

"Listen, Justin," Mannheim said, as though they both had the same script and he was right on cue. "I've given a lot of thought to that last time we talked. You know, I did act rather hastily." He laughed. "That's one of my problems. I go off the deep end at times; I blow my top. But I've had time to think, to see things in their proper perspective. In many ways what you've done is a heroic thing, a very heroic thing. We're all emotional. I know I was that day. But I think it took a lot of guts to do what you did."

Justin stared without expression at the ugly, modern, hotel bureau. "What's the matter, Phillip?" he said dryly. "Has Pilgrim's father-in-law been putting on the pressure?"

There was a pause at the other end of the line. "Look," Mannheim said. "We'll talk about it later. I'm in rather a rush to get over to the hearing myself. I'll have the car pick you up. It'll be there in about twenty minutes. Will that be all right?"

Justin was about to suggest to Mannheim what he could do with his car, but then he thought, Why not? Why the hell not? "That will be all right," he said.

"Fine." There was relief in Mannheim's voice. I'll see you later. Good luck today. You know we're all behind you over here."

"Yes," Justin said. "I know."

He hung up the phone and settled back into his chair with a sigh, smiling a little, knowing what it must have taken for Mannheim to make that call. How sad, he thought, that moments like this came so few and far between. They almost made the rest of it seem worthwhile.

He heard Alice come out of the bathroom behind him, but did not turn around.

"Who was on the phone?" she asked.

"Mannheim."

"Mannheim? What did *he* want?"

"He just called to say he was sending around a car to take us to the hearing."

Alice snorted. "How sweet," she said. "Webster must *really* be sinking when rats like Mannheim start deserting him. I hope you didn't accept."

"I almost didn't," Justin admitted. "Then I figured we might as well take advantage of the convenience. Besides, I'll probably be back working for CBN next week. But don't worry. I didn't make it that easy for him." He turned then and looked at his wife. Alice was putting on final touches of makeup before a dresser mirror, absorbed for the moment with the line of her upper lip. The dress she was wearing was one he didn't remember seeing on her before. It was of a pale blue material that tended to cling to every curve of her figure. As Justin watched her bending toward the mirror, his initial response was one of pleasure at how attractive she looked. Ordinarily he would have complimented her, but they had become overly polite and self-conscious since earlier that week, with both of them avoiding all mention of things personal. So he made no comment.

Alice glanced over and saw him watching her, his face solemn. She peered anxiously down at herself, taking a brief, uncertain inventory. "What's wrong?" she said. "Is there anything wrong with the way I look?"

Justin flushed in resentment at finding himself on the defensive. "What are you so dressed up for?" he said stiffly. "This isn't a party we're going to, you know."

"Dressed up?" Alice's face showed hurt and surprise. "I didn't think I was dressed up." She stared at herself in the mirrow. "You saw me pack the clothes. I just took along a few old dresses."

"That's no old dress," he said accusingly, surprised to discover he was actually growing angry, and somehow helpless to stop it. "I've never seen that dress before."

"Of course you have." Alice laughed. "I've had this thing almost two years. As a matter of fact, you once commented on how much you liked it. That's why I wore it."

"I'll just bet you did." His anger now real and growing, Justin groped for some way to justify it. Here he was, he thought, going to one of the most decisive events in his life, and his wife looked as though she were about to attend a garden party. Then it all clicked into place. Of course. Webster Evers would be there. Naturally she wanted to look her best. But even as he thought it, he was ashamed and so he said nothing.

Alice was still worriedly studying the dress, trying to find some justification for the criticism where there actually was none. Ordinarily, she would have been confident enough not to let it disturb her, but she too was still struggling to recover from Monday night's debacle and at this stage wanted only to please. "But what's wrong with it?" she pleaded. "Just tell me one thing that's wrong with it."

Justin stood up, feeling queasy in the stomach. All he'd had for breakfast was coffee, and he wondered if he should have taken something solid. He walked to the window.

"What's wrong with it?" Alice insisted.

Justin turned, regretting having started the whole thing. He gestured uncertainly at her bosom. "Don't you think it's a little tight on top?"

Alice plucked at her bodice, trying, hopelessly, to loosen the clinging fabric, but there was no denying the curves beneath. "It's all there, darling," she sighed, "and I'm afraid there's not too much I can do to hide it."

Justin did not say anything.

"If the dress bothers you that much," Alice said, "I'll take it off. I'll put on something else."

"No," Justin said sullenly. "Leave it alone. It doesn't really matter anyway." He walked over to the night table, took one of his pills from the small bottle there and washed it down with a quick drink of water. "The car will be here to pick us up in a few minutes. It's silly to start getting undressed and dressed all over again."

Alice frowned, certain he was being martyred in his acquiescence. "I'll change it in a second," she said, her decision made. "I've got another—"

"Leave it alone!" Justin shouted, feeling idiotic about the whole thing now and knowing he'd only feel worse if she actually did change the dress. "This is becoming nonsensical."

About to say she wasn't the one who had started it, Alice changed her mind and said nothing. It was very unlike Justin to be this unreasonable, although today he had good enough reason. She buttoned the two buttons she had already undone and busied herself putting some things into her purse.

Justin put on his suit jacket. His face and hands were moist with perspiration, but he felt cold inside. And how, he wondered, was Webster Evers feeling at this moment? Worse than he or better? By all that was logical, Webster should be feeling a hell of a lot worse. But then logic had played a very small part in this thing from the beginning. Had there been more good, clear logic involved, neither of them would be in his present position. Neither of them would come out of this entirely whole. It was like a double funeral, he thought grimly, with the two corpses waiting in separate parts of the city before being brought together for the final joint ceremony. Thinking this, Justin felt a fleeting kinship for his former friend.

And of what clichés and fulminations would the eulogies consist? In what terms of conflicting ideologies would the departed be described? Peace and freedom, of course, would be mentioned often, as though they were private property. The "warmongers and totalitarianists" would also come in for their full share of attention, with "the lying and bloodthirsty press" being given a few light slaps in passing.

And what of the truth? Would nothing of the truth be able to break through? Would none of those sober-faced witnesses to the event hear anything at all of what had *actually* taken place? Would no one rise to say that it had all been a terrible mistake, that none of it need truly have happened? Would no one interrupt the rhetoric to declare that Justin Blaine had been a misguided, vengeful fool, hiding behind the façade of patriotism? Of course not. Even if the truth were spoken, it wouldn't be accepted. It was too small and contemptible and pathetically human. It wasn't imposing enough. You had to have properly imposing motivations placed behind imposing events. The Blaine-Evers controversy had swollen to huge and far-reaching importance. Who would now be satisfied with so picayune an explanation as the truth?

"Don't forget to take your pills," Alice cautioned routinely behind him. She had put on a small, simple hat with a bit of veil which she considered beyond reproach. But she said, "Does this hat meet with your approval?" She hadn't meant it to come out that way, but there was a sardonic edge to the question.

"I'm sure it's fine," Justin said without turning from the window.

"Don't you think you ought to at least look at it?"

Justin turned and looked at it. "Very nice," he said, regretful over his earlier outburst and overly cautious about its happening again.

Alice nervously looked at herself once more in the mirror, now certain that everything about her was wrong. "Do you think we ought to wait downstairs in the lobby for the car?" she said, anxious to get out of the room.

"No. They'll call us when it arrives."

Alice forced herself away from the mirror. She found a *Guide to the Nation's Capital, Its Monuments and History,* provided by the hotel, and settled into a chair with it. Justin turned back to the window and stared absently at the building across the street. The truth about Justin Blaine's life, he thought; or, rather, the truth *in* Justin Blaine's life. Justin felt an instant of gratitude for areas of his life. God knows he'd made enough mistakes, but whatever he'd done or tried to do, at least it was for something in which he believed. At least he hadn't been afraid to commit himself, to take a chance, to challenge, to fight. And if in the process he was finally being forced to do something of which he was not proud, this blunder too had at least been an honest one; he could still take his chances on the hard way.

A moment later the phone rang and he answered it. "Your car is here, Mr. Blaine," a deferential voice informed him.

"Thank you," Justin said. "We'll be right down."

Alice put aside her guide to Washington and rose. "Well, at least," she said, "we'll be going in style." She bustled through a last-minute flurry of female activity, while Justin waited impatiently. She stopped for a final, doubtful glance at herself in the mirror.

"It's all right," Justin assured her. "Stop worrying about the way you look. You look fine."

Alice sighed and preceded him through the door.

Downstairs, a long, black limousine was waiting at the curb, its paint and chrome glistening in the sun. A uniformed chauffeur stood beside it. Justin felt a touch of amusement as he recalled his earlier analogy of the funeral. This part was certainly in perfect keeping with the mood. The Republic's basic theme of Democracy, he thought, carried stubbornly through to the end, with each citizen entitled to at least this final ride in a chauffeured Cadillac.

The ride through the sunlit streets of downtown Washington was not long, but seemed that way to Justin. He sat stiffly apart from his wife on the wide rear seat, making no effort at conversation, yet reasonlessly resenting the fact that Alice had nothing to say either. He needed her approval this morning. She should know this, he thought resentfully, without his having to tell her. She should do everything possible to make things easier for him. But what if she really didn't *want* to help him? What if she were deliberately trying, by her brooding silence, to upset him? What if somehow, through the years, some barely acknowledged remnant of her feeling for Webster Evers had survived and was breaking through at this moment to alienate her sympathies? The thought itself, wild though it seemed, was enough to make Justin's stomach churn.

He glanced carefully at his wife's pretty and composed face and at the smooth, clinging lines of the dress. She still looked, he thought bitterly, as though she were going to some sort of occasion. She looked *too* good. If she felt anything at all for him, if she were concerned as she *should* be for him, she *couldn't* look this good. And it wasn't only the dress. If she were wearing sackcloth and ashes, she would have still looked too good. Face, hair, makeup, expression, all added to the festive, glossy illusion. The reporters for the women's pages would have a field day. The surprisingly youthful and attractive Mrs. Blaine, the wire services would gush, wore a seductively revealing blue dress. If only, he thought, she would turn and look at him, smile, touch his hand. If only she would give some sign, say something, *anything* to let him know she understood how he felt, that she forgave his nervous stupidities, that regardless of what happened she . . .

Idiot, he told himself, don't you know by now that she understands? Don't you know by now the way she feels? You've lived half a lifetime with the woman. Isn't that enough?

It wasn't enough. Justin still waited for the sign that did not come, his stomach still churned fiercely, and by the time the limousine pulled up in front of the House Office Building he was more tense and uncertain than ever.

A committee staff member met them at the entrance. He extended a limp, cold hand in greeting. "Good morning, Mr. Blaine," he said and offered a brief bow to Alice. "Mrs. Blaine."

Noting the tall, somber-faced man in the dark suit, Justin thought, Of course, the custodian of the chapel. Which way to the Blaine-Evers services?

"My name is Conklin," the man said briskly. "A private anteroom has been set aside for your use. If you'll follow me, please?"

He turned without waiting for an answer and led the way to a room at the far end of the corridor. It was dark and drably furnished in leather and oak. Looking out of place, a large television set stood in a corner, its screen blank but portentously expectant.

"And this," Justin breathed softly to himself, "must be the embalming room."

Alice looked at him. "What?"

Justin shook his head. "Nothing."

"If there's anything you want," Conklin said, indicating a phone, "please call." He risked a smile. "Good luck, Mr. Blaine."

The man left and Justin stood broodingly for a moment. Then he looked across the room, where Alice was staring out the window at the Capitol dome looming above them. "And what about you?" he said. "Do you also think I'll need luck?"

"You know how I feel," Alice said distantly, without turning, half lost for the moment in some vagrant thought of her own.

"I don't know anything of the sort," Justin said, still wanting reassurance. "What am I supposed to be, some sort of mind reader? How am I supposed to know what's going on in your mind if you don't say it?"

"You should know," she said quietly. "After twenty-two years you should know."

He leaped fiercely, almost elatedly at the opening. "Until a few days ago," he said, "I thought I did. But now . . ." He shook his head. "Now I don't know anything about what you're thinking. If you could fool me about something like that. If you could—"

"Jussie, Jussie," she said wearily. "Why do you torment yourself like this? We went all over it the other night. I explained it was nothing. I told you I—"

"You told me a lot of things the other night," he broke in. "I know what you told me." Groping for something on which to hang his anxiety, his frustration, his collection of injustices, past and present, Justin's eyes fastened, inevitably, on the hapless blue dress. "That's why the first time you're going to see the bastard in thirteen years, you doll yourself up. Do you think I'm an utter fool? I knew why you were dressed like that the moment I saw you this morning. I didn't say anything about it before, but I knew all right."

Alice stared at him, shocked and hurt that he could say such a thing even in anger. Yet for an instant the accusation touched her. Could there not be, after all, a hair's-breadth of truth to it? Could she not, unconsciously, have wanted to look her absolute best for that reason? She almost seemed to recall a moment, while dressing, when she *had* considered how she would look to Webster after so many years. And if she had, would it really have been that awful and unnatural a thing? She was still a woman. She was still human enough to want to be admired. She told herself these things, yet did not believe any of them. She suddenly felt weak and vulnerable.

"Do you really believe that?" she said.

"Do you deny it's true?" Justin countered wildly.

Alice wrapped her feeling of guilt in anger. "All right!" she said. "If that's the way you feel, I won't even go out there and see him. I'll stay right here in this room the whole time. Will that make you feel any better?"

"Much. You don't *know* how much better it'll make me feel."

"I'll even turn away from the screen when his face is shown. I won't even look at him. All right?"

"All right," Justin breathed, beginning to sweat heavily.

"Would you like me to leave? If it'll help, I'll leave right now so you won't have to look at me and be reminded of what a faithless whore of a wife you've got." She was on the verge of tears, but somehow managed not to cry and was grateful, at least, for this. "I'll go out and walk around the streets while it's going on. Do you want me to do that?"

"I don't care what you do," Justin said miserably, wishing he had never started this thing. "Do whatever you want. Only for God's sake, give me a moment's peace before I go out there."

Alice's anger crumpled into hurt. "That's unfair," she said. "You know I didn't start this. Why are you doing this to me? What is it you want from me?"

Justin began to pace. It was all him and he knew it, but he couldn't tell her. It had nothing to do with her. He just couldn't live with himself. He hadn't been able to live with himself all week, and the one person in the world he cared anything at all about had to be the scapegoat. He despised himself for what he was going to have to do, as well as the reason for doing it, yet there was no escape. It had to be either Webster or he, and the desire for self-preservation was still a hell of a lot stronger than even the pangs of one's conscience, awful as they might be. He was as trapped as Webster.

Justin felt a touch of dizziness and sat down, closing his eyes in sudden panic. He was all right in a moment, but the brief spell made him realize just how close to the edge of something he was. He'd better watch himself, he thought, really worried now at the way he was behaving. If he could work himself up as easily as he was doing, he wasn't in proper control. He wasn't going to handle things at all well if he was still like this half an hour from now. Success or failure hung on his being able to remember dates, places and details coolly and accurately.

Feverishly, he tried to test himself by going over several important points in his mind, but he found it utterly impossible to concentrate. His brain refused to function. Great, he thought, his panic growing. What was wrong with him? He had nothing to be upset about. The man who should be in this condition was Webster Evers. Webster should be the one in a blind sweat, edgy, unable to remember. Webster was the one who had to face the lethal committee and the cameras. All right. Then why was he, Justin Blaine, falling to pieces at the very time when he had to be calm and able to convey confidence?

There was a knock on the door and Pilgrim came in, followed by Kantrowitz. There was an exchange of greetings, the Congressman and the lawyer seeming to exude, Justin thought, a forced and unconvincing cheeriness.

"Well, you look fine," Pilgrim said, but somehow managing to assure Justin of exactly the opposite. The Congressman glanced nervously at his watch. "We've got about twenty minutes yet, but I just want to make sure we've got everything straight." He frowned, suddenly remembering something, and turned to Kantrowitz. "Where are you going to be during Kelly's opening remarks?"

"At my usual place beside the committee. Why?"

"I was just wondering if it might not be more effective, more dramatic, to have you sitting apart from us—slightly to the front, to emphasize your special identity as counsel."

"I don't think it really matters that much one way or the other. And since it's already set up this way, why not leave it?"

Justin listened to the discussion of this point, as well as several others, concerning procedure. There they were, he thought, ironically, the producer and director planning their big extravaganza, while he, merely an actor, stood by, to be given his cue to appear when the proper time came. Finally, his part was reached.

"Don't forget," Pilgrim said, turning to him, "to keep everything straight in your mind as we've gone over it. At the beginning, you're to let Evers do all the talking. The cameras are going to be on him every second. They won't miss *anything,* not the slightest change of expression. Be sure you don't interrupt to force material on him. Let *us* do the questioning. Let the committee handle that part of it." He frowned, sifting the thoughts as they crowded his mind. "The big thing," he continued, "is that Evers will be on first. He'll be out there waiting when you come onto the stage. There'll really be nothing for you to do at the beginning. Someone will be sent in here to get you and you'll come out in front of the committee and sit down. We'll start asking you questions when we think the time is right. But first we want to give Evers a chance to react. We just want the two of you to sit there in front of the cameras, the committee, the press and fifteen million viewers."

Kantrowitz smiled. "Hey, wait a minute, Hank. *I'm* the one who's going to be asking the questions. *I'm* the committee counsel, remember?"

Pilgrim nodded apologetically. "You're right, Morrie. I didn't mean to take over like that. I get carried away sometimes. Was there anything else you wanted to tell Justin?"

"I don't think so," Kantrowitz said slowly. "I'm sure everything will go smoothly enough." He looked closely at Justin, seeing the light patina of perspiration that dotted his forehead and chin. "How do you feel?"

"Awful," Justin said. "Like an actor on opening night."

Kantrowitz and Pilgrim laughed.

"Do you really think this is funny?" Alice said, resenting everything about the meeting and making no effort to conceal the way she felt.

"No, I don't think it's funny," Pilgrim said, sobering immediately. "You should know I don't. Look, Mrs. Blaine," he said quietly. "I want you to know I understand how you feel. And you're right. I *am* treating your husband like an actor. But this is very important. Even though he's speaking only the truth, it must come off exactly right to be accepted as the truth. This doesn't apply only to your husband. It applies to me as well. Maybe I am carrying on a bit strangely with all this, but you'll just have to understand and forgive me. I've got a lot at stake too. When this is over, I'll apologize to you more fully." He grinned. "Let's all have dinner together tonight. We'll have champagne and debate the whole thing in detail."

Pilgrim looked at his watch once more. "We'd better get back out there," he said to Kantrowitz. "It's getting close to eleven." He walked over to Justin and shook his hand. "Good luck. And for God's sake, relax." He smiled once more. "I'm nervous enough for both of us."

He went out the door with Kantrowitz close behind him. They walked quickly down the corridor, but Pilgrim stopped as they neared the meeting room and touched the lawyer's arm confidingly. "Before we go out there, Morrie," he said, "I want you to know how much I appreciate all you're doing. I realize what a tough position you're in. As counsel for the committee, you were sort of caught in the middle when I put the squeeze on them to push this case. But I think you've handled yourself like a gentleman."

Kantrowitz offered a small, mock bow of gratitude. "Gee . . . thanks, boss."

"I'm not kidding," Pilgrim said gravely. "I've given a lot of serious thought to this. I don't know what you have in mind for your future, but things seem to be breaking pretty well for me and I'm going to need someone around that I can rely on. You're a man with values and ethics and you've got a good mind. I'd like you to consider perhaps working with me."

Kantrowitz stood there, his face impassive.

"You know what I've got my eye on, Morrie," Pilgrim continued. "I'm not thinking small. And I can take you all the way with me." He squeezed the lawyer's arm for additional persuasion. "Well?" he said. "What do you say?"

"A week ago," Kantrowitz said slowly, "I'd have probably said you were crazy and laughed in your face."

"And now?"

"Now?" Kantrowitz said. "Now I'm not laughing, Hank. I'm listening. I think you're right. You're definitely on your way."

"Then you'll help me?"

Kantrowitz nodded. "From what I've seen lately, I'd say the thing you probably need least in this world is help. But I'd be happy to join you in whatever capacity you might consider most valuable." He grinned. "And if it ever becomes a question of urgent and drastic need, I'll even vote Republican."

Pilgrim laughed loudly and they started along the corridor once more.

Much of the earlier confusion had disappeared from the hearing room, although a few sound technicians and cameramen were still fussing over their equipment. Pilgrim noted that three committee members, Kelly, Norton and Quennell, were already seated at their assigned places, talking. Kirby stood off to one side, trying, inevitably, to placate his ulcerated stomach with a hastily sent for glass of milk. The deep, steady hum of a great many voices, broken by scattered bursts of subdued laughter, came from the area reserved for the press. Several hundred reporters and correspondents had crowded into every available seat, with an overflow standing at the rear. Pilgrim recognized representatives of *Pravda,* Reuter's and *Paris-Match,* as well as writers from every wire service and news syndicate in the United States. The last event with coverage like this, he thought with satisfaction, must have been V-J Day.

Chapter Twenty-Three

1952: Washington, D.C.

At two minutes before the hour, Alice and Justin Blaine were alone together in the dressing room, while a television set played a commercial about a king-sized cigarette, and the mellow-voiced announcer declared, over and over, that the enjoyment was in the taste. Justin sat, his back to the screen, in an overstuffed leather chair that he had swung around to face the window. He had put on a crisp, freshly laundered shirt not two hours before, but a thin line of perspiration was already beginning to break through and darken the edge of the collar.

There was a station break, and then the solemn-faced image of a slender, distinguished-looking man came on. The man was seated at a wide desk, staring blankly into the camera. He suddenly burst into life at some invisible signal, and said in hushed tones, "Ladies and gentlemen, this is Patrick Shawn speaking to you from the main hearing room of the Subversive Activities Committee in Washington, D.C. In just a few moments we will be privileged to witness what could be a significant and dramatic meeting. We here at . . ."

Justin pushed himself out of his chair and began to prowl the room.

"Justin," Alice said, "why don't you sit down and try to—"

Justin impatiently waved her quiet as he stopped to stare, with vacant eyes, at the screen. The announcer's face had disappeared and was replaced an instant later by a panoramic view of the hearing room. "As you can see," the announcer's voice went on, "the Subversive Activities Committee is seated at the long table facing the cameras. In the center is chairman Eustace B. Kelly, Democrat, of Iowa, with Representative Henry Pilgrim, Republican, of Illinois, directly to his right. Mr. Kantrowitz, the committee counsel, is at the moment standing at the far end of the table. It is he who will do most of the questioning of the two witnesses. And now you can see the table and chairs where the witnesses will testify."

Justin glanced, almost reluctantly, at his wife to see what, if any, reaction she displayed, but Alice's face, as she watched the screen, showed nothing.

"Mr. Evers will evidently be the first to testify," the announcer continued, "and it is to him that—"

A loud, rapping noise intruded on his commentary and the camera picked up the committee chairman tapping with his gavel. The sound had not been turned on, and although Kelly's lips began to move, his words could not be heard. The announcer's voice returned and said hurriedly, "We see that Chairman Kelly is already calling the committee to order, so we're going to switch you over to the hearing room."

For a moment there was no sound, and then Kelly's voice broke through in mid-sentence. " . . . that, considering these circumstances, Mr. Evers will be the first witness. Would you please call Mr. Evers."

The camera moved to the door where Webster Evers appeared, at first largely hidden by the standing spectators and then clearly seen making his way through them and to the witness table. He moved easily, as if he were an official at the hearing, almost as if he were the accuser and not the accused. The white streaks in his hair caught the bright camera lights as he passed beneath them.

At the table, he sat down gracefully and placed his hands on his lap.

Chairman Kelly moved his hand over his gray hair and peered across the table to where Webster sat amid the flashes of news cameras. He waited until the photographers were done and then said slowly, "Before Mr. Kantrowitz has you sworn in, Mr. Evers, I would like to offer a few remarks to serve as what I consider a necessary explanation."

Webster nodded, as if it were his choice whether Kelly would be able to speak or not.

"Because of the nature of this meeting, we will not go through the usual question-and-answer period. We all know why we're here. Testimony has been given before this committee, by yourself and Mr. Blaine, which is contradictory. We're here to determine the truth." The chairman leaned across the table and frowned. "One of you two gentlemen is lying. I hate to use that word, but I'm afraid there's no other I can substitute . . . such as exaggerating, or distorting, or misrepresenting."

Justin felt his fingers trembling at his sides and thrust them into his pockets. How conveniently oversimplified, he thought. One man is lying and the other is telling the truth, therefore the liar must be guilty, and the liar must be punished. Yet in this case it was the one who spoke the truth who was guilty, who *really* deserved to be punished.

"Mr. Blaine claims," Kelly pressed on, "that he knew you intimately, Mr. Evers, during the period from 1934 to 1939. In addition, he claims that you worked as part of a Communist spy apparatus under his direction during that time, and were responsible for handing over to the Russian Government many secret documents of great importance to this country. Needless to say, Mr. Evers, it's vital to the people of this nation, as well as people all over the world, that we find out the truth of this matter. Since you are a respected and honored member of our government, I want to repeat that this committee has taken no position in this case. However, certain documents and information brought to our attention by one of our members simply must be examined and discussed. That's the reason we are here today. For that, and to give both you and Mr. Blaine an opportunity to face one another in person, and once and for all either to confirm or deny under oath whether or not you knew one another during the period in question."

There was a short silence, then Kelly's voice said, "Mr. Kantrowitz."

Justin closed his ears against the dull drone of the swearing in. When it was finished, Kantrowitz said to Evers, "When Mr. Blaine comes to the witness table, you will please look at him and study him as long and as closely as you wish. Then you will declare, under oath, whether or not you have, at any time in your life, known him. Is that clear, Mr. Evers?"

"Perfectly," Webster said.

Kantrowitz looked off to the right. "Mr. Conklin, please call Justin Blaine."

Alice turned away from the screen. "All right," she said nervously. "They're coming to get you now."

Justin tried to smile reassuringly for his wife, but it did not come off very well. Still a lousy actor, he thought, dreading all that was to come and knowing it showed.

"Good luck," she said.

He nodded and went into the corridor to meet Conklin and to follow him into the hearing room. The glare of the lights was blinding, but he could see the empty witness chair reserved for him and headed directly for it. He sat down and automatically raised his right hand and was sworn in.

Justin stared across the less than ten feet that separated him from Webster Evers. The two chairs had been placed to face each other, and once again Justin felt himself part of a weirdly contrived stage setting. Webster, he thought grudgingly, looked damned good, even better than his news pictures. He didn't seem to have aged in the thirteen years. Although they were close to the same age, Justin was sure he looked old enough to be Webster's father.

"All right, Mr. Evers," Kantrowitz was saying, "now I repeat. Examine Mr. Blaine carefully. Take as much time as you need. Ask him questions if you wish." Kantrowitz cleared his throat. He appeared more tense than the two witnesses.

"May I leave the witness chair?" Webster asked.

"If you wish. Yes."

Webster stood and approached Justin's chair. Calmly, he peered into his face. The room was silent. At the committee table, the Congressmen leaned tensely forward on their elbows. Webster walked in a slow circle about the chair. Justin sat staring directly ahead, growing increasingly uncomfortable under the deliberate scrutiny. He felt his face beginning to sweat and resisted an impulse to pull out a handkerchief to wipe it.

Webster came around and stared into the watery eyes of this man so intent on destroying him. If there was any malice, any bitterness in Justin's face, it did not show. If anything, the aging, troubled face seemed blurred with despair. Then *why?* Again, the same nagging, frustrating question. Justin was so close, two feet away, Webster could reach out and touch him. And where was the answer? In this last desperate instant, his mind groped for a reason, something, anything he might use for his own defense. Alice? Had Justin in some way found out? Not likely. But even if true, it was obviously nothing that could be used.

Webster circled Justin's chair once more, stalling, unwilling, now that the moment had arrived, to commit himself irretrievably to denial, this course that would be so damned final, without chance for retreat. But what else? What motive, real or imagined, for Justin's wanting to hurt him could he possibly uncover and use in his own defense? It seemed a forlorn prospect. He peered coldly at a bead of perspiration running down the side of Justin's face. Perhaps Fran had been right. Perhaps he'd made a fatal mistake in not using the story he'd prepared for the President. It might have at least saved *something* from the wreckage.

He moved around, to go through the further farce of studying Justin from the front. Of course, he thought, he might still be able to use that story. It wasn't too illogical for a face-to-face meeting to make *true* identification possible. Wasn't that the major reason for the confrontation? He might labor through the remembrance of that single night, the night of their meeting . . . the snowstorm . . . the drive to the hospital . . . the accident with the car . . . the— *Oh, Christ!* His mind skidded to a stop. *The accident!* Good God, *of course! The accident!* It was all suddenly so clear, so obvious, so *perfect,* that he could only wonder at not having thought of it before. A shiver of excitement ran through him. Christ! He might just carry it off.

Something must have shown in his face, because Justin was gazing at him rather curiously. Webster moistened his lips. The first thing, he thought, covering his excitement, the first thing was to prepare to identify him; slowly, carefully, convincingly. He *had* to make it convincing. He asked, "Would you say something for me, please, Mr. Blaine?"

"What do you want me to say?" Justin asked. "How about the weather? Would you like me to discuss the weather?"

"Well," Webster said quietly, "why don't you try saying a few things like 'Communist conspiracy'? Or 'I accuse you, Mr. Evers, of being a spy'? You know. The same sort of thing we've been hearing from you these past days."

"I'm afraid I can't oblige with that. I'd be happy to count for you." Justin tried to settle himself more comfortably in the chair. "One . . . two . . . three . . . four . . . five . . . six . . . seven . . . eight . . . nine . . . ten . . . Isn't it a lovely day today? I wonder how the weather will be tomorrow." He looked at Webster. "How long would you like me to go on with this?"

"Mr. Blaine!" Kelly broke in from the committee table. "Whether you're aware of it or not, this is a very serious business and we can do without your sarcasm. It is Mr. Evers' privilege to ask to hear your voice."

"Thank you, Mr. Chairman," Webster said. Clearly, he at least had Kelly with him from the start. "I appreciate the consideration of the committee." He turned toward Justin once more, stared at him long and consideringly. "I believe," he said slowly, "after seeing this man close up, in the flesh and not merely in photographs, after hearing and listening carefully to his speech, I believe there *is* something familiar about this man." He nodded with decision. "Yes. I believe he *does* look familiar to me."

The reaction from the assembled audience was immediate and audible. The words had scarcely left Webster Evers' lips when the buzz and stir began in the room. Kelly banged for order with his gavel. "Quiet!" he demanded. The gavel hammered again. "I want quiet in this room." The buzz died. The cameras were trained on Justin now, waiting for his response.

He sat looking at Evers, a faint, rueful smile softening his mouth. He was surprised by the admission, but took little satisfaction in it. It had come too easily. Clearly, Webster intended to use the admission for a purpose. "Do I, Webster?" he said. "Do I *really* look familiar? Do you *really* think you may have seen me at one time?" His voice was weary, weighted with irony. "Well, then I'm not a total imbecile, not a total liar?"

"Of course," Webster went on, as though there had been no reaction, no interruption, no comment at all, "the man I'm thinking of—if this *is* indeed the man—was someone I met only once many years ago. The name he claims he used at that time, the name I read in his testimony as reported in the newspapers, meant nothing to me. Baker, wasn't it?"

Justin nodded sardonically. "Bill Baker, Webster. Is it all coming back now?"

Webster's expression did not change. He paced slowly in front of the witness chair—once, twice, then stopped. "Of course," he said, "the newspaper photographs were of little help. The man I knew as William Baker was much thinner than Mr. Blaine. There's a puffiness about the cheeks that I don't remember and the years have taken a toll. Yet I think unquestionably that this is the man I have in mind."

"Unquestionably?" Kantrowitz said. "You *unquestionably* identify Justin Blaine, then, as the man you once knew as Bill Baker?"

"Yes. I do."

"Thank you, Mr. Evers. Now would you please return to the

witness chair." Kantrowitz's early nervousness seemed to have disappeared. Obviously pleased with the way things were going, he faced the committee. "Mr. Chairman, since we have now established the fact that Mr. Evers *did,* at some point in the past, know Justin Blaine, I would like, before going into the details of that relationship, to take a moment to question Mr. Evers concerning a document that, if genuine, would substantiate Mr. Blaine's claim that our Under Secretary of State was indeed an active member of a Communist spy apparatus."

"You may proceed," Kelly said.

The committee lawyer took something from his briefcase and had it passed to the witness chair.

"This is a photographic print of a memorandum to the Secretary of State. It is stamped 'Top Secret' and dated August 4, 1937. It is signed by Webster Evers." The paper was within Webster's sight, but he only glanced at it and passed it back to the lawyer. Kantrowitz asked, "Were you with the State Department at that time, Mr. Evers?"

"At what time?"

"August, 1937."

Webster frowned in thought, then nodded slowly. "I was."

Kantrowitz nodded. With a dramatic flourish, he held the photograph aloft. "This memorandum outlines the latest intelligence information on German rearmament, and recommends a course of action for the United States in meeting the growing German threat. It is still listed as classified material and cannot be publicly revealed. It was delivered into the hands of this committee several days ago by Mr. Blaine, who has testified that it was *you* who gave it to him in August of 1937, when he was your immediate superior in a Communist spy apparatus."

Kantrowitz paused for a moment and just stood there staring at Evers, as if to make him admit his guilt by the dark intensity of his gaze alone. Directly behind the lawyer, Justin shifted restlessly in his chair. But Webster sat quite still, his eyes steady and unblinking.

Kantrowitz held the photograph toward Webster. "Would you care to study it, Mr. Evers, before I ask you to testify as to whether or not you consider Mr. Blaine's statement to be the truth?"

Webster's hands remained folded in his lap. "There's no need for me to study it. Since I've never given any document whatsoever to Mr. Blaine, it would be rather pointless for me to examine a specific one in order to deny having given it to him."

"Then you *do* deny it?" Kantrowitz asked.

"I do. Most certainly."

"Mr. Evers. I must insist that you at least look at this signature, and testify as to whether or not it is yours."

Webster took the photograph and stared at it. Yes, there it was. The report on the new German fighter plane along with the dreadful figures of secret aircraft production and his recommendation for sanctions on critical materials. And there was his signature too. His mind ranged back over the years and focused with startling clarity on that day so many years ago, seeing again Alice as she had been, remembering how she had locked the door, how it had angered him—and what it had led to.

"Mr. Evers? . . . Mr. Evers?"

Startled, Webster looked up.

"Do you recognize that signature as your own?"

Alice Baker's face as it had appeared in passion faded. "Just a moment, please," Webster said, trying to refocus his thoughts. "Well, it does look a great deal like my handwriting. . . ."

Kantrowitz smiled faintly. "Mr. Evers, the committee has had this signature examined by a handwriting expert. He has positively identified it as your handwriting and will so testify later."

"Mr. Kantrowitz," Webster replied pleasantly, matching the lawyer's smile, "I have not claimed the signature is a forgery. I could have written that memorandum—its information was certainly in my area of responsibility and the signature looks like mine. I am puzzled, however, that you have not produced the original memorandum."

Kantrowitz hesitated a moment. "Unfortunately, some documents of this period are missing, perhaps because of overzealous housekeeping. We do not have the original of this one. But in this case it—"

"Just a minute, Mr. Kantrowitz," Webster broke in, his tone a shade sharper than before. "I don't know what you mean by 'overzealous housekeeping.' We're not in the habit of tossing out important documents as if they were cigarette butts. I don't remember having written this memorandum. I could have written it, of course, but it just as easily could never have existed. It just as easily could be the case that this film is of a forged document, a forgery made to support Mr. Blaine's accusations."

There was a stir among the spectators. Kantrowitz waited for it to die down. Kelly raised his gavel, but the noise subsided as quickly as it began.

"I won't go into the matter of State Department housekeeping now, Mr. Evers, except to say that in other investigations we have found several cases of incomplete files. As for this matter of a possible forgery, we have learned from the manufacturer of the film from which these prints were made that according to the emulsion code number on the film itself, this batch of film was produced only in the summer of 1937. If this is a forgery, Mr. Blaine would have had to have decided to accuse you more than two years before he left the Communist Party, that is, at a time when, according to his testimony, you were still working with him, supplying secret information to the Soviet Union. Are you prepared to say for the record that this is a forgery?"

Webster smiled. It was an expression of reasonableness and self-confidence. Justin's stomach tightened as he watched Webster's performance.

"No, I'm not. I don't know what this thing is. I do know that I have not done the terrible things you say I've done."

Kantrowitz tapped a pencil on the table. "All right, Mr. Evers, let's start from the beginning. You admit that the information in this document was available to you. Is that correct?"

"That is correct."

"And this information, being highly secret, was available only to a very few people. Is that correct?"

"Yes."

"Who was allowed access to this information? Or rather, who would have been allowed access to such a memorandum as this?"

Webster paused and then said slowly, as if to be as precise as possible, "Assuming that this memorandum actually existed, it probably would have been for the eyes of the Secretary of State and the Under Secretary."

"What about other people working on the German desk?"

"Probably not."

"Why?"

Webster paused again. What was Kantrowitz getting at?

"This was a memorandum recommending an alteration of policy. It was a working memorandum to the Secretary. I would not be in the habit of showing it around to subordinates."

"Not even for comments? Not even to make sure the information was correct?"

"That's right. I might even have typed it myself."

"Then you simply drew up the document and passed it on to the Secretary?"

"That's right."

"Then the document did exist!"

Webster paused again.

"That is what *you* are saying, Mr. Kantrowitz. As I've said—"

"I'm sorry," Kantrowitz broke in harshly, "that's what you have been saying. You've just told us how you drew up the memorandum and passed it on. You suddenly seem to remember just what the circumstances were. The memorandum did exist, didn't it?"

Again a slight pause. The room was completely silent.

"No. I cannot say with certainty that it did. I am describing a procedure that I have followed throughout my career with the State Department. I know my working habits. If I wrote this memorandum, I would have followed that procedure, as I have with many other memoranda I have written."

"You would have shown it to no subordinates."

"Not usually."

"Not *usually?* Then sometimes you would."

"It isn't impossible. It would be unusual in a case of this kind. Bear with me. I'm trying to be precise."

"Then we can say that no one beneath you saw this memorandum—if you wrote it. Therefore, if you wrote it, no one beneath you would have been able to transmit it to the Communist Party apparatus."

"I'm not prepared to say that. Documents have a way of getting out of the proper hands. The incident we are discussing is supposed to have happened nearly fifteen years ago. Lines of security change. Procedures change. I can't be expected to remember this matter with *exact* precision, even if—"

"Of course not, Mr. Evers." Kantrowitz's tone was suddenly soft. "However, we have checked the files for this period. The procedure for a memorandum like this would have been for it to be transmitted in a sealed envelope which could be opened by only three men—the Secretary of State, the Under Secretary and the chief of the department concerned—in this case, the German desk. Mr. Blaine says that the document was delivered to him. Unless it was the Secretary or the Under Secretary, it would have had to be you. Unless you wish to suggest that it was one of these two gentlemen."

"No, Mr. Kantrowitz, I wish to suggest no such thing. Nor could I suggest how Mr. Blaine got the paper—if indeed he got it."

Suddenly Kelly broke in. "I would like to ascertain something. If the film used in this case was manufactured only in 1937, does that prove that whatever was photographed had to have been photographed at the time or shortly thereafter?"

Kantrowitz frowned. "Yes, sir, it would. The film would have been good for only a limited time thereafter."

"Then the probability is," Kelly went on, puffing on a large pipe, "that the document was what the photograph purports it to be—a memorandum to the Secretary of State, written and signed by Mr. Evers."

"That is right, Mr. Chairman."

"Then I see no reason, unless there is further evidence, to pursue that point further," Kelly said.

Kantrowitz nodded and turned to Webster. "Now, Mr. Evers," he said, leaning forward and pointing his pencil at him, "you have agreed that only you, besides the Secretary and Under Secretary, would have had access to that document. And you cannot account for its coming into the possession of Mr. Blaine. . . . Now, this document was delivered to the Secretary."

Webster started to speak.

"All right," Kantrowitz said hurriedly, "let us *say* it was delivered to the Secretary. It would have been transmitted directly to him. These papers are kept closely guarded at all times, aren't they? In fact, in the Department even the messengers are checked and rechecked for security, isn't that right?"

Suddenly Webster sat straighter. He paused a beat and then said, "Exactly."

Kantrowitz looked at him quizzically. "Exactly what?"

"Only the most highly trusted messengers are used in the Department, but it is not impossible—and perhaps it has not been unknown—that a messenger could turn out to be a security risk."

"But we are not talking about a messenger, Mr. Evers."

"Why aren't we? Since we are talking about possibilities and things imperfectly remembered *and* Department procedures, we should consider the possibility that a messenger was entrusted with delivering the document."

"Are you saying that a messenger gave this paper to the Communist apparatus?"

"I don't know anything about this paper," Webster answered, sounding annoyed. "I'm merely saying that if any secret document was turned over to the Russians, the guilty party could have been a messenger."

Kantrowitz' face was flushed now. He leaned back in his chair and regarded Webster dourly. "Mr. Evers, can you name one messenger who to your definite knowledge has been known to have done such a thing? More important, can you name a messenger who would be likely to have turned the document in question over to Mr. Blaine—or Mr. Baker, as he was then called?"

Webster stared gravely back at Kantrowitz, his mind now beginning to shape a past that he could use.

"Yes, there was one such man that I definitely know of, and he was a messenger with us during the time in question. . . . Bellows, I believe his name was—Charles? No, *Paul* Bellows—that's right, Paul Bellows. He was dismissed for security reasons about—oh, eight years ago. I think it was because he was a compulsive gambler, a definite risk. As I recall he was suspected of violations of security."

"Just a moment." Kantrowitz leaned back to whisper to an assistant. The room grew noisy as the spectators talked among themselves. After a minute, the assistant handed Kantrowitz a paper, which the lawyer read and then placed before him. He turned again to the assistant, who was blushing.

Kantrowitz turned back to face Webster. "Mr. Evers, in this case, at least, your memory is remarkable. I wish it were always this cooperative. There *was* a Paul Bellows; he died in 1950. Our records show he was dismissed in 1945 as a risk. The specific offense or reason isn't given."

The committee members looked from Kantrowitz to Evers and back again. Pilgrim sent a note down the table to Kantrowitz, which Kantrowitz glanced at and set down before him.

"Very well, Mr. Evers, let's get on—" Kantrowitz began, but suddenly Pilgrim leaned forward to his microphone.

"Excuse me, Mr. Kantrowitz, but I'd like to say something at this point."

Kantrowitz looked at him, puzzled, and said, "Of course, Congressman."

"Isn't it true, Mr. Evers," Pilgrim said, his voice hard with anger, "that there have been an unfortunate number of State Department dismissals for security reasons. In fact, that seems to be a special problem for the State Department, doesn't it?"

Webster bristled. "Just what is that question supposed to mean, Congressman?"

"I think the question is clear."

"I really have no idea of how the State Department compares with other government departments in matters of this kind. There have been, of course, many accusations of late, accusations which have been unfounded. In fact, the charges made against me seem to be part of that same pattern of attack on the State Department, and they, too, as I hope you're beginning to realize, haven't a grain of truth to them."

Pilgrim's anger had increased. "On the contrary, Mr. Evers, it is well known that the State Department has had more than the usual number of security risks. People of questionable character and reliability have been turned up by other investigations. My point is that you could point to any number of people, some in highly responsible positions, as being capable of giving secret information to the enemy. If not Paul Bellows, then someone else. Is that what you intend to do, keep throwing the blame to more and more people? Or are you prepared to say here and now that this Paul Bellows—who is dead and therefore unable to contradict your statements—actually did carry that document in 1937 and may have passed it on to William Baker."

Kantrowitz barely suppressed a groan over Pilgrim's blunder. Evers didn't have to name anyone else; Pilgrim had done it for him. In one stroke, Pilgrim had undone the isolation of Evers that Kantrowitz had so carefully worked to create.

Smoothly, almost gently, Webster was saying, "I'm not going to accuse anyone, Mr. Pilgrim. As you say, there have been other security risks in the State Department. There certainly have not been the great numbers of them that you and people like you have pretended to find, but it is inevitable that there would be a few. We do our best to keep risks out, but no department or government agency can be completely successful in trying. All we can do is try to keep them from getting into the Department and to find them and weed them out if they do get in. Mr. Kantrowitz asked me for an opinion about how the document could have reached the Russians. I have merely offered a possible explanation. I do know that *I* did not pass any documents of any kind to any unauthorized persons. And as a member of the Department, who wants the best for my country, I'm just as eager to find any breach of security as you are."

Kantrowitz stared at his papers. This had become ridiculous. Not only had Webster Evers produced a tangible scapegoat who could not be questioned, but he had also been able to suggest any number of other scapegoats and had even put himself in the light of being on the side of the committee in trying to ferret out breaches of security. He would, of course, have to investigate Bellows, but unless they could pin something on Evers now, something on which they could continue to base the investigation, he wouldn't get the chance. He glanced at Kelly and saw that the chairman's face was grim. If Pilgrim would just not grab the ball again.

The note Pilgrim had passed to him still lay before him. "Drop it. Get to knowing Blaine."

Justin caught himself slumping in his chair and tried to sit straighter. His throat was beginning to tighten. He reached into his jacket and took out his bottle of pills. As he removed a pill and put it into his mouth, he noticed an uneasiness among the committee members.

Kantrowitz cleared his throat and started to speak. "Now, Mr. Evers, would you please tell us exactly when you knew William Baker. How did you meet him?"

"Well," Webster replied slowly, "I'm afraid it's difficult for me to remember the exact time . . . the exact year. It was, as I say, a long time ago."

"Yes, we know it was a very long time ago," Kantrowitz said with exaggerated patience, "but would you please try very hard to remember? If you must, take a guess."

Webster stared thoughtfully at a point on the far wall, as if seeking his answer there. "Roughly, I'd judge it to be sometime in the mid-thirties. I think it may have been during the holiday season

—a party and . . . there was snow. Yes. There was quite a blizzard. I seem to recall a party."

"Go on."

"I think I can help you," Webster said smiling. "It is coming back a little. There were quite a few people there—Crowley—it was a party given by Mrs. Crowley, a prominent hostess; you may remember her. I began to talk to this gentleman. I remember that his wife was also there. I can't describe her except that—oh, my God! How could I have forgotten?"

Justin watched entranced as he saw Webster's face register complete surprise and dismay. Suddenly he felt a sharp pain in his chest. The pill wasn't working. Quickly he took another.

"She was pregnant. In point of fact, she began to feel labor pains, and I volunteered—it was a terrible night; there must have been four or five inches of snow on the ground by then—I volunteered to drive Baker and his wife to the hospital, which I did. Except that, as I did, there was some trouble. I was going fast—I didn't want the poor woman to have the baby in the back of the car—and while we were on the way the car skidded and crashed into a hydrant or a light pole or something. At any rate, we were all pretty badly shaken up. I was afraid that Baker's wife—I don't remember her name—" Webster looked at Justin, who at first seemed not to be listening.

"Alice," Justin said finally. "Baker's wife's name was Alice, Webster. It still is. Surely you remember Alice."

"You're out of order, Mr. Blaine," Kelly said. "Go on, Mr. Evers."

"Alice. Yes. Well, I was afraid that something might have happened to her," Webster said, as if groping through a terrible dream. As it turned out, she did lose her child that night at the hospital. It was a terrible thing. Terrible. Mr. Baker was quite understandably upset—*very* upset. I remember that he broke down in the car on the way home. I must admit I felt a deep responsibility for what happened." He sat there as if brooding, a man recalling a painful burden, silent, surrounded by silence.

Then he looked up.

His eyebrows were formed into a frown, and his jaw jutted forward. His elbows rested on the arms of the chair, his arms converging until the hands met at the fingertips, behind which the lean, almost skeletal face bespoke meditation.

Justin felt an onsurge of terror, for he had caught the predatory gleam in Webster's eyes. The pain in his chest was growing, and every breath hurt.

The mellow voice began slowly. "Now that I think of it . . . now, in searching back, in re-examining events, in trying to remember *all* I can about this man, in trying to discover why he chose *me*—because, believe me, I've been as puzzled as *any* American and—" a slight, self-indulgent smile—"of course, much more intimately concerned—I've been puzzled as to why Justin Blaine or Bill Baker or whatever he'll choose to call himself next, why he selected *me* for defamation, for *ruin*."

The head bowed slightly behind the pointed tower of well-sleeved arms and well-manicured hands. The voice fell quiet, briefly.

Behind the great table, the committee seemed transfixed, as if painted on a backdrop. Even the smoke from Kelly's pipe seemed motionless, suspended above the chairman's head. Throughout the great room, spectators leaned forward, expectantly.

This is going to be bad, thought Justin, this is going to be very bad.

The voice resumed its dirge.

"Now I begin to wonder. Could *this* have been the why of it? Could this sorrow . . . this lamentable, deeply sorrowful tragedy . . . could this be the reason why I was chosen?"

Justin looked up to find himself dolefully regarded by Webster's eyes.

"Is it not true, Mr. . . . Blaine—and I gather this from what I have read in newspapers—that you and Mrs. Blaine—forgive me—have never had a child?"

Justin felt the small nerve in his eyelid begin to pulsate rapidly.

Behind him he could hear a gushing of talk from the spectators. Before him, the faces of the committee members reflected pity and, as they regarded him, suspicion. Suddenly the faces blurred. Breaking into a cold sweat, Justin tried to refocus his eyes. Was the second pill going to fail too? What would he do then?

He licked his lips before he said, "That's right. We've had no children."

And now added to the mournful ring of the voice were bewilderment and just the right touch of righteous anger.

"Then have you—all these years—have you and your wife held me *responsible* for that unfortunate night . . . and for your childlessness?"

The last word was like a menacing caress.

"No, of course not. That's ridiculous," Justin said quickly, angrily. It was becoming hard for him to breathe. His chest ached. "That is an . . . absolutely ridiculous thing to say."

As Justin shivered and tried to keep his composure, Webster's voice came to him like a distant chorus. "I cannot help but wonder—indeed, I cannot help but believe—that this has been the reason." Suddenly Webster leaned forward and pointed his finger at Justin. "And if it is ridiculous for me to say, how much more ridiculous, how . . . *insane* it would *have* to be if it were *indeed the cause!*"

Chairman Kelly made no move to halt the growing roar of talk among the spectators. Around him the members of the committee were also talking excitedly, keeping their hands over their microphones as they did. At last, Kelly began a regular beating with his gavel. As the noise subsided slightly, Pilgrim's voice became audible.

"Mr. Chairman, I would like to ask a few questions of the witness."

Kelly looked at Kantrowitz, who shook his head no. Kelly looked back to Pilgrim, who seemed determined to take over the questioning.

"No one is going to question the witness, Congressman, until there is order in this room." He banged the gavel again, hard. "I will have *order* here," he said loudly. "I will have order or I will clear the room and take this hearing into executive session."

The noise died.

"Mr. Chairman," Pilgrim said again, "I would like to ask the witness a few questions."

As unobtrusively as possible, Kantrowitz shook his head no again.

Kelly noticed it and smiled slightly. "Is that all right with you, Mr. Kantrowitz?"

Kantrowitz took a deep breath. "Well, I have a few more—yes, it's quite all right." He slumped back in his chair.

Henry Pilgrim began a steady tapping of his pencil against the table. He shifted in his chair, squared his shoulders and cleared his throat.

"Now, then, Mr. Evers, you have said quite a lot here and it's made quite an impression. But it is all irrelevant." He noticed Webster raise his eyebrows quizzically. "Yes, irrelevant! We are here to establish certain things as being true, namely that you knew Justin Blaine well and that during the five-year period when you were his friend you *knowingly* gave him secret documents which you *knew* he would turn over to the Soviet espionage ring in Washington. We are not here to investigate motives, however heart-rending they may be. We are here to establish facts."

Evers smiled. "I am not aware that you *have* established either of these facts, Mr. Pilgrim. You have established that I have met Mr. Blaine before on one occasion and that is all. I deny categorically that I ever saw this man again after that night or that I ever gave any unauthorized person any documents."

"We will establish beyond any doubt that your denial is false, that you did know William Baker for five years."

"Just a moment," Kelly broke in. "The day is getting on. Unless I am mistaken, Mr. Pilgrim, Justin Blaine is the only witness you plan to call. Am I correct?"

Pilgrim looked over to Kantrowitz, but the attorney's face was averted. He could feel his hands begin to tremble. "It won't be necessary to call corroborating witnesses, Mr. Chairman. Mr. Blaine's testimony will establish beyond—"

"Just a minute." Webster was leaning into his microphone now. His voice suddenly boomed. "Do you mean to say that you are making these charges only on the basis of what Mr. Blaine says? On the word of a self-confessed spy and liar? This is an insult to me and to the American people. And if this is what you intend to base your case on, then the question of Blaine's motive is of the utmost importance, and *I* intend to press the issue until Blaine is shown to be a vindictive—perhaps psychotically vindictive—perjurer."

Webster's outburst triggered a new roar of talk from the crowd, but Kelly's gavel silenced them again.

"Then you intend to call no witnesses?" Kelly said to Pilgrim.

Pilgrim's voice was barely audible. "That's right, Mr. Chairman."

"Then I would like to speak privately with the members of the committee and with Mr. Kantrowitz." The six men gathered in a little knot at a corner of the room.

Justin did not see them. His eyes were shut tight against the sudden pain that seemed to fill his body. His chest was like a furnace, and breath came only with great efforts to capture it. He gripped the arms of his chair, unable to speak and knowing himself too weak even to stand. When a sudden new pulsation began about his heart, it occurred to him that there, in that room, *then,* he might die.

He looked toward Webster and saw him through a film of tears. Webster sat across from him, observing him gravely. Did Webster know what was happening?

That he might die, with so much unsettled, so much unknown! It couldn't end without an answer. He couldn't just fall away without an inkling of why he had brought all this about.

The baby? Could it have been the baby and Alice's misery that long, long time after? And had Alice felt the same way? But then why did she—oh, God!

Get up. Get up and get out of here, he ordered himself. Get to Alice, to a doctor. Get out. But he could not move his arms. His legs seemed wooden. He remained in the chair, while Webster, with quick glances toward the corner where the Congressmen stood talking, continued to sit motionless, watching him.

It couldn't have been because of that night. *It couldn't have been that night!* And yet such a sudden, terrible loss. He saw again the snow, the flakes swooping at the car, and he felt the sickening sliding of the car on the white, fragile carpet that was the street, the sickening slide to the crash. It couldn't have been that—his mind felt numb with pain—it wasn't Webster's fault . . . and yet what else—Alice and Webster? But he hadn't known about that. . . . Oh, God! He'd never know.

The fire was blazing in his head now, and no one seemed to notice. He hung on desperately, staring straight ahead through half-closed eyes, and dimly he became aware of Webster staring at him. Suddenly he realized that of all the people in the room only Webster knew he was ill. . . . Of course, you cold-blooded bastard. No heart, no real feeling for *anyone,* not even yourself. Never. Maybe *that's* why I did it, to stop you. Where would a bloodless robot lead us, into what final disaster? Maybe *that's* why. No heart. And with it all, I've failed. They won't even believe the truth against your lies. And now you sit there, watching me die and feeling nothing . . . nothing . . . a *machine.* Alice was right. Alice was *always* right.

In the corner of the room, three of the committee members, the chairman and the committee counsel looked at each other uncomfortably while Pilgrim tried to convince them that the investigation must continue, his voice rising and falling in an insistent whisper.

Finally, Kelly raised his hand for silence and turned to Kantrowitz.

"This is getting out of hand," he said. "Morrie, do you actually think you're going to get anywhere without witnesses? What can you establish without them?"

"We have a solid case," Pilgrim said.

"I was talking to Counsel. I'll get to you in a minute. I ask again, what can you establish that would make a more solid case than you've got now? And what makes you think you can do it without witnesses?"

Kantrowitz rubbed his mouth with his hand thoughtfully but made no reply. Kelly waited for a moment and then went on, his voice now like that of a kind schoolmaster. "You're beginning to look bad up there, Henry, and if you and Morrie don't have something a lot more incriminating—hell, a lot more *convincing* —than what you've shown, you're going to look a lot worse— which means we're all going to look a lot worse. *And I won't have it.* As it is, this little affair today has been a real lesson for me. Now you just tell me right now, have you got any more of a case than this, and I don't mean going on further with the fidaddle we've had so far."

Pilgrim looked at Kantrowitz sourly, but could not catch the lawyer's eyes. "No. Evers is guilty as hell, but we don't have anything more that can prove that Blaine knew him well. We can prove Evers is a liar; once we do—"

"It's Blaine's word against Evers', and that's not enough," Kelly said. "It isn't even going to matter if Evers did know him. You're talking about espionage, Henry, and you're not only accusing a high-ranking official with a brilliant record, but you're beginning to drag in the whole State Department. If you can't *prove* that Evers was guilty of aiding the espionage ring, I'm going to order this thing into executive session right now."

"And let it die again," Pilgrim said resentfully.

Kelly put his hand on Pilgrim's arm. "Henry, when you've been around for a while—if you are, after November—and when you've learned a little more about politics, you'll realize what a favor I'm doing you. A favor you don't deserve. Now I think you'd better let us pros handle it from here on."

Pilgrim yanked his arm away.

"Now, Henry, don't be petulant." Kelly's voice was gentle but contained unmistakable warning. "All right. Let's get back and put this thing where it should have been left all this time."

I'm going to die, Justin thought, as a new wave of pain hit him. He could barely make out the table in front of him. He could not move. He saw blurred shapes moving, their colors mingling, flowing. Webster, can't you see me . . . the pain . . . oh, God, Alice . . .

The colors swirled far off, growing dimmer, and then, right before his eyes, there was the face of Webster Evers blotting out the light.

As the committee members returned to their seats, Webster had risen from his chair and crossed over to Justin. "Mr. Blaine is ill, he needs a doctor," Webster announced anxiously. Ignoring the stunned reaction of the Congressmen, Webster bent over Justin, loosened his tie and peered into the half-closed eyes. Justin sat still, one hand clutching his heart, the other gripping the arm of the chair. Then his supporting arm went limp, and Justin slumped sideways.

The chairman was the first to recover. Half-rising from his chair, he boomed into his microphone, "We need a doctor. Is there a doctor in the room?"

There was a moment of shocked silence, and then bedlam. Spectators rose from their seats. Some photographers pushed forward to get a shot of Justin and Webster, and a young man walked quickly to the front of the room calling out that he was a doctor. Kelly banged his gavel, but the sound could barely be heard above the babble of excited voices and the scurrying of reporters as they rushed to the nearest phones. Only Pilgrim heard the chairman say for the record, "This hearing is adjourned until further notice."

As Kelly rose to join the growing knot of people surrounding Justin Blaine, Pilgrim intercepted him. "I'm not going to let this thing be swept away," Pilgrim said furiously.

Kelly grasped him roughly by the arm and spoke into Pilgrim's ear. "Henry, you don't know how to keep your mouth shut or your soul saved. I'm through being gentle with you. You tried to run away with this thing. You tried to bulldoze me, and I'm not going to forget it, nor will the right people in your party. You'd better start replanning your future."

Pushing Pilgrim aside, Kelly forced his way through the crowd toward Justin's chair. Pilgrim stared after him, too stunned to move. He recognized Gallagher looking over someone's shoulder at Justin. Gallagher turned, saw Pilgrim and then walked away in the opposite direction.

Suddenly, unexpectedly loud and resonant, the voice of Webster Evers broke through the din around Justin's chair. "Step back and give the doctor room. Step back. Mr. Blaine needs air."

The noise subsided for a moment, and a space was cleared around the chair, leaving only the doctor bent over the slumped figure. He straightened up and without turning said, "Give me a hand here. I want to get him into a more comfortable position." Webster and another man stepped forward, and with the doctor they lifted the limp, heavy form of Justin Blaine from his chair and stretched it out on the floor. Someone found a chair cushion and slipped it under Justin's head, and someone else produced an overcoat and placed it carefully over the motionless body.

"Did anyone call an ambulance?" Webster asked.

"It's on its way," called a voice from the back of the crowd.

The sound of popping flashbulbs, excited voices, the commands of television crewmen echoed through the hearing room. Only the people in the packed circle surrounding the kneeling doctor and the still form of Justin Blaine bothered to speak in hushed tones.

The doctor stood up and stepped over to Webster. "I can't do anything more for him here," he said. "They may not be able to do much more for him at the hospital. How long did you notice something wrong with him?"

"Only a few seconds," Webster said. "I hadn't really been looking at him, but I glanced over and all of a sudden saw something was wrong."

"The attack must have come on awfully fast then," the doctor said. "I noticed there was a bottle of pills in his pocket. I don't know if they would have made any difference, but I guess he never got a chance to use them."

"I didn't notice," Webster said.

There was a jostling in the crowd and the sound of a woman's voice.

"Please, please let me through. I'm his wife."

There was an opening in the wall of people and Webster saw Alice Blaine push through. She knelt quickly beside Justin and fumbled for his hand under the overcoat. Then she leaned forward and looked into his face.

"Jussie," she whispered. "Jussie, it's me. Everything's going to be all right."

But there was no response, and she looked up desperately, questioningly, at the circle of faces. Her eyes fell on Webster, and for a moment he thought she was going to speak. Then she turned back to Justin, and Webster realized with a mixture of sadness and relief that her eyes had stopped at him just enough to show recognition and dismissal, as if to undo the fact that they had ever met.

Chapter Twenty-Four

1952: Washington, D.C.

As Webster was dressing for dinner, his doorbell rang. He answered through the speaking tube.

"Mr. Shargut to see you, Mr. Evers," the doorman's voice said.

Shargut was a special assistant to the President, highly trusted, a handler of "sensitive" tasks. Webster took a deep breath. "Yes, send him up."

He finished tying his tie, trying to shake off the depression that had settled on him. He had successfully punctured Justin's testimony. He had regained the confidence of the committee and the press. He had reduced Pilgrim's sensational evidence to a shambles. And the man who had threatened to ruin his life lay comatose on a hospital bed, possibly dying. Yet the mood would not go.

He sprayed cologne on his shirt and ran a comb once more through his hair. The phone call half an hour earlier from Shargut's secretary had puzzled him. Shargut had never exchanged more than a few words with him at White House meetings; they almost never met socially.

When the buzzer sounded, Webster slipped on his jacket and went to open the door. Shargut's moon face, with its pursed lips and long straight nose, smiled at him boyishly. A forelock of black hair hung over his forehead, adding to the youthful, straightforward, eager look.

"Webster." He held out his hand. "How nice of you to see me on such short notice. I hope I'm not disrupting your evening."

"Not at all. I'm early for my dinner engagement," Webster said. "Let me fix you a drink, Barrett. I'm making a martini for myself. Would you care for one?"

Shargut remained standing in the center of the room, looking about him. He seemed preoccupied and didn't answer.

Webster waited a moment. "Or would you prefer something else?"

"Oh, no, I'm sorry. A martini would be fine. Whatever you're having."

Webster searched the voice for hints. He could find nothing but impersonal cordiality. "Dry?" he asked.

"Yes . . . fine."

As Webster made the drinks, neither man said a word. Shargut had settled down on the edge of an upholstered chair and leaned forward, elbows on knees, staring at the carpet. He accepted his drink, lifted it an inch in silent salutation and took the barest sip. Webster raised his drink in return and to his own surprise emptied almost half the glass.

"I imagine you're very tired after what happened today," Shargut said casually.

"Yes, I am," Webster said, "but it appears the strain was too much for Blaine. I can't pretend to be overly concerned after what he put me through, but I'm disappointed that there wasn't more opportunity to cross-examine him."

"Yes," Shargut said, showing no real interest. Then he was silent, as if expecting Webster to finish something he had to say. He sipped his drink and continued to stare down at the carpet.

Webster felt that a beat in the conversation had been lost, but this was obviously supposed to be Shargut's show; let him keep it running. Webster unbuttoned his jacket and sat down on the sofa. He lit a cigarette.

Shargut finally looked at him from across the room. "As you probably guessed, I'm here at the President's suggestion."

"Really?"

"I was impressed by the skill with which you handled the charges this morning and especially by how well you handled what happened afterward—and I'm not speaking only for myself."

Webster nodded slightly. "Thank you. I'm glad to hear that. The meeting brought out, basically, what I had already told the President, except, of course, that when I saw Blaine I did remember having known him—briefly—many years ago when he went by a different name. I'm glad that I was able to pinpoint the reason for Blaine's picking me as his target. In any event, it's good to hear that the President was satisfied."

"Yes." Shargut took another sip. The level of his drink had not perceptibly changed. "The President is gratified that you have rendered Blaine's charges ineffective. I think we can be sure the committee will leave you alone now. Congratulations."

Webster tensed as he listened to the guarded words. He finished his drink and rose to pour himself another. "Barrett, that sounds more like an official statement than a true expression of confidence. Or am I being too sensitive?"

Showing no expression, Shargut sipped his drink.

Webster couldn't allow the point to be ignored. "I am prepared to have the committee continue its investigation until the last shred of doubt is removed. I—"

"No. Let it die." The words came crisply. Shargut's manner had changed, causing Webster to sit down warily.

"Barrett, suppose you tell me exactly what's on your mind. I have to pick up my dinner companion shortly."

Seeming relieved to be able to shift the tone of the conversation, Shargut placed his drink on a table and looked straight at Webster for the first time.

"The President has selected you for a fact-finding tour. You will leave next month."

Webster nodded. "I see. Where am I being sent?"

"Around the world."

Again Webster nodded, his mind now beginning to race. "I can see the advantages of my being out of the country for a while. How long will I be away? Precisely where am I going?"

"That's State's decision. The Secretary will probably fill you in on the details. Personally, I can think of a lot of underdeveloped countries that need study. The trip will be rather taxing, so it would be wise to grab a vacation while you can."

"I hadn't thought of taking a vacation. I've a lot of unfinished work that's piled up since this thing started."

"Your accommodations on Barbados have been arranged. You arrive there Monday."

Webster rose. His face felt flushed. "Have the President and the Secretary really considered the ramifications of this . . . decision? It's bound to be seen as a lack of confidence in me. It will do just what Pilgrim and Blaine wanted to do."

"Everything has been taken into account. There will be no shocks, no sensations. After all, there's no disgrace in being a special Presidential envoy, is there? And who would doubt that after this trying affair you deserve a vacation? It will be handled smoothly."

"As long as I cooperate. Look, Barrett, you started by congratulating me, but I can hardly interpret what you have said since as a vote of confidence. Am I still trusted? I've given most of my life to the service of my country and now, because of the unproved accusations of a sick man, suddenly my whole career seems to be in jeopardy. If there are still doubts about my innocence, I deserve a chance to clear myself. Suppose I decided to fight this thing through to the end?"

"I wouldn't advise it."

"If you still don't believe me, what would I have to lose?"

"A great deal." Shargut's voice had an edge of steel, but his eyes were wide with innocence. He watched Webster pass a hand over his cheek and try to gain control of himself, and then he began to speak quietly, measuring his words. "If you cooperate, no one will be embarrassed. Not you, not the Department, not the administration. It's to your advantage to cooperate, and you know it. You won't fight Blaine's charges, because you know you got off on the strength of a cool performance, some quick thinking—and a sick man's heart attack. How much would this Paul Bellows story bear checking? How long would this motive you concocted for Blaine stick? I don't suppose you'd know this, but the records show that Bellows was on sick leave—a two-month sick leave—at the time the memo was written. You can sell Pilgrim and Kelly and Blaine short, but don't sell the Secretary short—or the President. If you try to carry this matter any further, the President will authorize the release of all necessary information to ream you."

"Then you all think I'm guilty. I didn't say that Bellows *did* handle the memo. I still don't remember that there even was a memo." Webster stepped toward Shargut; he stared intently at Shargut's face. "For God sake, Barrett, I have a right to be considered innocent unless I'm proved guilty. What can I do to prove to the President that these charges are false?"

"You had your chance. One half-hour, uninterrupted, of the President's time this morning."

Webster's face was ashen as he pleaded. "Look, can I see the President? Can I just talk to him once more?"

Shargut stood up, set his glass on a table and went to the door. "You don't want to see him, Webster. Believe me, not now."

"What do you mean?"

Shargut smiled in contempt at how badly Webster was playing the game. "When the President sent me here, he called you a lying bastard who had sold out his country. Those were his exact words. You're not going to get a chance to lie to him again. Cooperate, Evers. Cooperate and be grateful that more important things in the national interest prevent us from really reaming you."

He opened the door and walked down the hall.

After a few moments, Webster closed the door and poured himself another drink. Then he deliberately removed his coat and his tie and started to dial Francine's number to call off their dinner. She would understand, he thought. Of course she would understand.

2

There had been a great deal of activity earlier, but by ten o'clock that night there was only a single nurse left with Justin in the white-walled hospital room. She sat beneath a lamp, a heavy, middle-aged straw-colored blonde, doing a crossword puzzle. Another lighted lamp was over the bed, glaring harshly upon the intravenous rig and the suction machine that kept Justin from drowning in saliva he was no longer able to swallow. The machine hummed softly, with a steady, soothing monotony that contrasted sharply with Justin's labored breathing. Occasionally the nurse would glance over at the bed, but she did it without great interest and most of the time just worked at the puzzle.

At ten-thirty, a tall, dark-haired man with a gaunt face came in. The nurse Miss Hanley, put down her newspaper and rose quickly. Dr. Mizener was Chief of Neurology at the hospital.

"No change," Miss Hanley said briskly. "There's been no change at all."

The doctor did not look at her, but picked up the chart from the foot of the bed, studied it for a moment, then put it down.

He walked to the head of the bed and flashed a small light into Justin's staring eyes. The pupils contracted slightly, but otherwise there was no change. Mizener put away his light and stood there for a moment listening to his patient's labored breathing. "Has there been any break at all in the Cheyne-Stokes respiration?"

"None," the nurse said. "Not since I came on shift anyway." Once they started this rasping prelude to the death rattle, she thought, only a miracle could pull them out of it. And she could recall but few of these. Finally, there would be a total circulatory collapse, and that would be the end of it. From the steady falling blood-pressure count on the chart, this wasn't very far off.

The doctor's face did not change expression as he turned away from the bed. "Shut off the suction machine for a moment."

Miss Hanley did as she was told and an instant later the steady hum of the pump had stopped. Mizener studied the slow accumulation of saliva. "All right," he said after a moment. "You may as well turn it back on." He sat down with sudden weariness and looked at the headline in Miss Hanley's evening newspaper. "BLAINE SINKING," read the bold, black type.

Dr. Mizener shook his head. "I'm afraid we've fallen heir," he said flatly, "to quite a bit of excitement."

"Lord, haven't we though!" Miss Hanley agreed. She raised her dark eyes heavenward. "You should have seen what was going on when I came in on shift before. I had all I could do to fight my way through the door downstairs. My God! Those reporters are swarming all over the place."

The doctor nodded slowly. "I noticed they set up a whole section of the out-patient admitting room for the press."

"I've never seen such excitement, such activity. We've had celebrities here before, but never anything like this." Miss Hanley's arms waved in a mute attempt to describe the turmoil. "And all those cameras and different types of equipment! It was a good thing the hospital didn't allow any reporters up here on the floor, or we'd never be able to get *anything* done."

Dr. Mizener frowned. "What about this man, this Representative Pilgrim? Has he been bothering you at all? Has he tried to come in here?"

"No," Miss Hanley said. "Not since I've been on duty."

"That guy has been driving me crazy," the doctor complained. "Would you believe it? I got a call from the President of the Board of Trustees a few hours ago. He wanted permission for Pilgrim to bring a tape recorder into the room, along with some damned reporter he's got with him. What do you think of that?"

Miss Hanley clucked in sympathetic disbelief. "What did you tell him?"

"I refused, of course. I'm sure I'll have trouble about it from the Executive Director, but I'll be damned if I'll be pushed around on something like this. I've already warned Pilgrim twice to stay out of my hair. I don't care if he's a Congressman, or who the hell he is. He's not coming in this room." Dr. Mizener stood up, growing angrier as he thought about it. "Understand this, Miss Hanley. He's not to be admitted under any circumstances. *Any circumstances!* Did you ever see a man like that? Were you watching that spectacle on television this morning?"

"Yes. Yes I saw it."

"I've never see anything like it. An utterly incredible thing."

"Wasn't Evers wonderful?" Miss Hanley said. "I'm so glad he wasn't guilty after all."

The doctor did not say anything. He seemed to be listening to his patient's breathing. He had a small, bald spot at the back of his head and he kept fingering it as if still needing to confirm the bad news, by touch, at regular intervals. "I haven't seen Mrs. Blaine for a few hours," he said. "Has she been in recently?"

"Well, I let her come in about forty minutes ago. She stayed at the bedside a short while. I must say, she's been very self-contained and quiet, not at all hysterical." Miss Hanley had intended the words as something of a compliment, but they somehow did not sound that way.

Dr. Mizener considered this carefully. If Miss Hanley had said it was raining outside, he would probably have considered that statement just as carefully. "She does seem to be rather a strong, well-controlled woman. You can let her in every now and then. You don't have to worry about her upsetting the patient."

"Incidentally, she's been wanting to speak with you. I put her off. Would you like to talk to her now, or shall I keep stalling her?"

"I may as well talk to her," Dr. Mizener said. "You can't put these things off forever. Where is she?"

"In 842," Miss Hanley said. "It was empty, so she's been staying there. At least it keeps her out of the hands of those wolves downstairs."

Dr. Mizener nodded, tossed a final, brooding glance toward his patient and went out. He knocked softly at a door down the corridor and opened it on hearing Alice's answer. Alice Blaine was sitting in a chair facing the room's single window, but stood up as the doctor entered. She simply stood there, watching Dr. Mizener's face and waiting for him to speak.

"Well," he said, glancing about, "they seem to have made you comfortable enough here."

Alice did not take her eyes from his face. "Yes. The hospital has been very considerate. I'm grateful." She waited.

"The nurse said you wanted to talk with me." Dr. Mizener sat down on the edge of the bed, feeling the dull ache go out of his lower back. "I'm afraid there's no change to report in your husband's condition," he said more brusquely than he had intended, but still finding it easier this way. One break of softness in the protective veneer and you were dead. This woman, he was pleased to see, had evidently learned the same lesson. It would make it less painful for them both.

Alice remained standing, her face composed. "Exactly what does that mean?"

"It means that the paralysis is still total and that he's comatose and responsive only to painful stimuli."

"Has he been conscious at all?"

"Not so far as speech or movement are concerned," the doctor said. "His pupils are reactive to extreme light, but that's about all we can see."

Alice looked hard and with increased intensity at the doctor. "Is it possible," she said, "that my husband could be conscious, could hear and understand voices, yet not be able to give any sign?"

Dr. Mizener shrugged. "It's difficult to say for sure, but in extreme cases such as your husband's, it's not likely. Not likely at all."

"But possible?" Alice insisted.

The doctor shrugged. Alice did not say anything for a moment. When she did speak, her voice was hard and cold. "You don't expect my husband to live, do you?"

About to take automatic refuge in medical ambiguity, Dr. Mizener hesitated. He had respect for this woman. If he could do nothing else, he might at least offer her the truth. "No," he said. "I don't."

Alice's eyes fluttered briefly, and she paled. But this was purely reflex reaction over which she had no control, and she showed nothing else. "How long?" she said. "How much time do you think he'll have?"

"One doesn't know these things."

"How much time?"

"A few hours," the doctor said grudgingly. "Maybe a bit more, maybe a lot less. It depends on several things. It's a question of respiration. When there's a circulatory collapse—"

"Don't tell me!" Alice cut in sharply. "I don't have to hear that. I don't want to hear it."

Dr. Mizener looked at her.

"May I go in to see my husband now?" she said, her voice once more calm.

Dr. Mizener stood up wearily. He'd been at the hospital since before eight that morning and it was now less than an hour until midnight.

"Yes," he said. "You may go in."

"I want to stay with him a while," she said. "I want to stay with him alone."

"Just the nurse will be there."

"I don't want the nurse there. I want to be *alone* with my husband."

Dr. Mizener sighed. "I'm afraid that's not possible. Regulations require that—"

"I don't care about the regulations," Alice hissed softly. "Do you really think I give a damn about the regulations?"

The doctor stared at her. "I'm afraid, Mrs. Blaine," he said feeling idiotically prim, "that there are certain things we—"

"Look!" Alice broke in. "My husband's going to be dead in a few hours. You told me yourself. What difference can it possibly make?"

Dr. Mizener stood rubbing his bald spot, wondering why he even bothered to argue. He opened the door for Alice and escorted her into Justin's room. "Allow Mrs. Blaine ten minutes alone with her husband," he told Miss Hanley.

The nurse nodded but, apparently not understanding, made no move to leave.

"Alone," Dr. Mizener said defeatedly. "Mrs. Blaine would like to be alone. Please wait outside."

Miss Hanley looked doubtfully at the doctor, then shrugged and left the room.

"Ten minutes, Mrs. Blaine," Dr. Mizener said and followed the nurse out.

Alice walked over to where Justin lay. The lower part of his face was covered by the suction apparatus, but his eyes, strangely naked and vulnerable without the glasses that had shielded them for so many years, stared at the ceiling. Alice sank to the edge of the bed and touched his hand, which was mottled and cold on the sheet beside her. "Jussie?" she whispered. "Jussie?" She looked at what could be seen of his face and it appeared strangely young, childish and exhausted. "Jussie, can you hear me?"

Alice waited, not knowing what sort of sign, if any, of her husband's awareness she was expecting. Her mind had recorded everything the doctor had told her, but had not been able wholly to accept it. She listened to the hum of the suction machine and the heavy breathing.

"Jussie, can you hear me?"

No sign. For an instant she felt a helpless, irrational anger, as if Justin were deliberately thwarting her by not responding. She pressed his hand hard and shook it, hoping for some slight answering pressure. No sign. "Jussie?" The anger dissolved in tears and she began to weep. "Listen to me," she pleaded softly. "You never listened to me before, but, darling, please listen to me now. Please, please hear me now." She dropped the cold, unanswering hand and clutched his body, feeling the familiar, thickly solid, form beneath the sheets and blankets. "Jussie, help me," she wept, her voice sounding young and faint. "Don't do this to me. They think I'm fine and taking it well and that's what I want them to think, but, Jussie, don't do this to me. I'm not fine. I'm not taking it well. I'm taking it terribly. I'm in pieces inside. I think it stinks. Please, please don't do this to me. Her words were barely audible and muffled against the blanket, yet still held desperate urgency. "Show me," she whispered, raising her head and peering once more into Justin's eyes. "Show me you can hear." No sign.

She kissed his eyes. "I'm sorry about the dress," she wept into his ear. "It was my fault. It was my fault about everything. My fault . . . my fault . . . my fault . . ." Alice's voice throbbed with old hopeless sorrows, and the tears and anguish pulled at her face. "Listen to me. My fault . . . my fault . . . Jussie, it was my fault." She clutched Justin's shoulders, rocking him back and forth.

But when the nurse came into the room moments later, Alice was sitting, composed and dry-eyed, beside the bed, while Justin stared, as before, at the ceiling.

"I'm sorry," Miss Hanley said. "But I'm afraid you'll have to leave now. Perhaps you can come in again for a while."

Alice stood up. "Yes," she said quietly. "Perhaps later." She looked at what she could see of Justin's face. A drop of moisture beneath one eye caught the light and glinted like a tear. Her own, she thought, it was probably one of her own that had fallen. She walked out into the corridor.

When she returned to the room in which she had been waiting earlier, the lights were still on and she sat down in a straight-backed chair and stared, half-blindly, at the photo-cover of an outdated copy of a magazine that someone had left there. Then she stared at the neatly made, empty hospital bed and tried not to think at all. But there was always a thought there, and it was unfailingly bad.

She shook her head angrily. Never mind the bad, she thought, forget the bad. Think of the good. There was plenty of good and she'd had it for a long time, which was more than most people were ever given. She'd been lucky. She'd had the best and there'd been no compromise, or just settling and having to drag it along. Yes, but when you lost the best, it was that much harder. It hurt that much more.

She tried to swallow, but her throat was suddenly swollen hard and shut and she could not do it. Maybe he won't die, she thought wildly. Maybe the doctor was wrong. Doctors didn't know everything. There was a hell of a lot they didn't know. They weren't God. People died when their will wasn't strong enough, didn't they? It was like falling asleep. You could stay up for days and days if you willed it strongly enough. And Jussie was stubborn. Lord, was he stubborn. She should know. She'd lived with him long enough to know. If Jussie didn't want to die, he *wouldn't* die. Yes, but what if he *wanted* to die? Don't be an idiot. No one wants to die. Yes, but what if *he* does? He doesn't. He couldn't. Why not? Other people have wanted to. You've wanted to yourself. Yes, but they don't. But what if *he* does? What if he'd rather die than have to go back there and do something that's even harder for him? Nothing's harder than dying.

All right, she thought. And she sat very quietly and tried to hold onto herself, although she felt certain that things were slipping away from her as surely as you felt a car with locked, useless brakes slipping down an icy hill.

Dr. Mizener did not knock this time, but merely opened the door softly and came into the room. Alice was still sitting, unmoving, in the chair. She looked at the doctor. "He's dead," she said, "isn't he?"

"Yes." Dr. Mizener wearily stroked the barren spot on his head. He looked tired and old. "I'm sorry."

Alice did not say anything. She had expected it, she had known, yet there was still no softening of this final, uncancelable word.

"Would you like to go in to see him?" Dr. Mizener asked.

Alice shook her head. "No," she said slowly. "He's not there any more. There's no point in looking at what's left."

The doctor stood there for a moment. "I know there's nothing to say," he began. "I can't—"

"No. There's nothing to say." Even if there were, Alice thought, she did not want to hear it. Not now, anyway. She had only a very fine edge of control. She did not want to take any chances with it. "Is there anything I must do tonight?" she asked.

"No. It can wait until morning." He hesitated. "Is there anyone you'd like to have called?"

"No one. I'm alone." She stood up carefully, not quite certain her legs would behave as expected. They were fine. "I think I'd like to go to my hotel now."

"If you wish, you may spend the night here." The doctor was watching her closely. "Sometimes the shock of these things . . ."

"Thank you, no," Alice said.

Dr. Mizener frowned. "All right. But I'm afraid it's going to be very difficult for you to leave the building. Those news people are still waiting downstairs. It might be wiser to let me take you out one of the back entrances."

Alice was gathering her things. "I'd rather not sneak out," she said. "I'll go out through the front."

"If you insist." Dr. Mizener looked at her curiously. "But I'd better go with you. I think you're going to need some help getting through."

They went out into the empty corridor and Alice did not look at the door to Justin's room as they passed it. They reached the elevator and Dr. Mizener pressed the button. Alice stared silently at the white elevator door. Far below, in the shaft, there was an iron clanking. She guessed it would have been smarter to have gone out the back, as the doctor suggested, but she did not feel like being smart. She did not especially know *how* she felt like being, but she did know she didn't want to let them make her run away from anything. If they expected a show, she would give them a show, even though it wasn't going to be the kind they wanted.

There was going to be no collapse, no tears, no widow's wailing.

They rode the elevator down the eight floors without speaking. Then the door slid open and for an instant, as Alice saw them all there, jamming the huge lobby, cameras and equipment poised and ready, she was afraid she'd be unable to go through with it. But the moment passed and, with Dr. Mizener's hand firm and sure at her elbow, she walked out to face them.

"Here they are! Here's Mrs. Blaine and the doctor!"

Flashbulbs exploded, singly and in barrage. Questions flew in loud, confused bunches, and as Dr. Mizener raised his hands and tried to call for order, another squad of newsmen dashed for a string of phone booths at the far side of the lobby.

When comparative quiet had been achieved, Dr. Mizener said in a cold, flat voice, "I regret to announce that Justin Blaine is dead. He died at exactly—"

The rest of the announcement was lost in the shouting that followed.

"He's dead! Blaine is dead!" The words were flung across the lobby at those waiting in the phone booths. "Hold those lines open! We're going to try to get his wife to say something!"

Half a dozen microphones were thrust at Alice's face. She stumbled backward and would have fallen if Dr. Mizener had not been holding her arm. She stood there, cheeks white and drawn, lips set in a tight, hard line.

"For God's sake, Mrs. Blaine!" a photographer yelled. "How about giving us some reaction?"

Alice was staring at the microphones as if at a nest of snakes.

"Say something for the American people, Mrs. Blaine!"

"Do you blame Webster Evers for your husband's death?"

"What are your plans now?"

Dr. Mizener looked at Alice. "Are you all right?" he said anxiously. "Do you want me to get you out of here?"

"No, no," she said quickly. "I'm fine." But her eyes still stared at the microphones, frightened, hopeless.

"Say *something*, Mrs. Blaine!"

"Yes," she said softly. "I'll say something!"

"Louder, Mrs. Blaine! We can't hear you!"

Alice nodded. "As Dr. Mizener just told you," she said more loudly, hearing, with some surprise, the calm, level sound of her voice as she addressed the microphones, the reporters, the steadily whirring cameras, "my husband is gone. I see nothing to be gained by discussing what led up to this. It won't bring my husband back. And I have no desire to hurt anyone else." She paused.

"Not even Webster Evers?"

Alice did not say anything.

"What are you thoughts about Evers right now, Mrs. Blaine? What are your thoughts?"

Alice stared blindly at the microphones.

"Are you going to pick up the case against Evers? Are you going to try to make your husband's charges against him stick?"

Alice shook her head slowly, wearily. "I really have no interest in the case at this point. I know nothing about the pertinent details. It was my husband's personal experience that was involved. I'm afraid I can be of no further use in this case."

"How do you feel about your husband dying now?" a reporter called from the rear.

Another newsman, standing in front, turned angrily on him. "What do you mean, how does she feel about her husband dying?" he yelled back. "How the hell do you think she feels, you imbecile?"

"Oh, come on," the first man said defensively. "You know what we're trying to get here. We've got a job to do on this thing."

"Well, that's a hell of a way to do it. I've got my living to earn too, but you don't have to ask a woman how she feels about her husband dying. We all know how she feels."

No one said anything and the whirring cameras suddenly sounded very loud. Alice looked gratefully at the reporter in the front row.

"All right," Dr. Mizener said. "I think that's about enough of this. I don't think there's any reason for Mrs. Blaine to have to answer any more questions right now."

He led Alice through the crowd of reporters and outside. "My car is here," he said. "I'll drive you to your hotel."

"Thank you. But that's not necessary. I can take a taxi."

"I know you can take a taxi." He looked at her. "And for God's sake, stop being so damned sturdy. There's no need to put on any performances with *me*."

But she managed to hold on all during the ride to the hotel and up in the elevator and even alone in the room itself. But then she went into the bathroom and saw some of his toilet articles, where he had left them on the washstand. "Oh, Christ!" She wept. "Look at his goddamned toothbrush."

Hours later she lay staring into the darkness through swollen, burning eyes. What about the nights? She was thinking. She'd take the days one at a time and get started doing something and maybe, after a while, it wouldn't be too bad and she'd manage to get through them. But what about the nights? How would she get through each night? Would she never sleep again? She'd sleep, she assured herself. Finally, everyone sleeps. Yes, but what kind of sleep? She'd find out soon enough. She guessed she'd find out about a lot of things soon enough. She was finding out about some of them right now. She guessed you found out about everything in this life before it was over. Yes, but what was she going to do about the nights?